Miriam Wakerly

Secrets in Appley Green

A 1960s Village Novel

ISBN 978-0-9558432-7-3

Published in November 2015
by Strongman Publishing
Printed by CreateSpace

PART ONE

1
1960

As the family sat round the tea-table, Molly felt a deep sense of frustration welling up. She should be on her way to the pictures by now and all she had to look at was a set of glum faces whose stony expressions made her want to run away, and damn the consequences.

'Once we get the letter from the school, then we'll know how things stand,' said Bill, her father.

'I'm going back to school tomorrow, anyway,' said Molly, feeling brave and unable to contemplate the idea of being kept home prisoner.

'Excuse me, young lady. I don't think that's for you to say!' said her mother.

'Well, I think it is!' she cried out, overcome by anger.

Bill glared at her while Dorothy sat with pursed lips as if her daughter had just announced she was going to take her chances living on the streets. Why could they not just discuss things, like normal people, thought Molly? Like some of the teachers. For all their faults, the good ones did at least usually talk to you if you opened up with a problem. Their earlier attempt to talk over their mid-day dinner had left a pea-souper of an atmosphere.

Molly took a steadying breath. 'Mummy, who did you speak to at the school? What did they say?'

She watched her parents exchange glances. 'They said they were looking into what happened to get to the truth of the matter and would send a letter. Meanwhile, please would you keep your daughter at home! Those were the headmaster's words, if you must know.'

Molly pushed back her chair and stood up, bursting into tears. 'This is just crazy! I did nothing wrong. I'm going out. I'm going to see Alison, or Nicola, and you can't stop me!'

'Sit down and shut it!' bellowed her father. 'This minute.'

'Molly, do as you're told. If you behave like this, it's perfectly obvious to me that you've done something wrong. This is a guilty conscience if ever I saw one.'

Her brother, David, walked out and her ten-year old sister, Susan, looked close to tears.

'It would be nice – really nice, if for once in your life, you could believe in me, stick up for me. A bit of support would be really … really, well, quite a surprise, as a matter of fact. I *am* going out and, unless you strap me up in chains and padlock me to my bed, you can't stop me.'

Her father stood up and blocked her way. He then grabbed hold of her shoulders and shook her. Feeling the pressure of his large, rough hands Molly looked at them as if they were vermin.

He spoke with menacing calm. 'Go to your room. Now. Or you'll have no pocket money for six weeks.' That would be the entire summer holidays, thought Molly, aghast at the prospect. 'And,' he added, 'you're not too old for me to …'

She looked him in the eye. 'What?' Her father had never raised a finger to her. 'Put me across your knee and give me a good hiding? Like you used to with David when he was much smaller than you?'

'Don't push me,' he growled, giving her arm a tight squeeze and then a light shove in the direction of the hallway.

Her whole body shaking, she stormed out of the house, with no raincoat, no money and no clean hanky.

As she strode off to meet her friend for their trip to the Odeon in Bloomstock, she thought back to mid-day after she had come home from school for dinner, when trouble really began to brew.

It was the complete lack of support from her family that infuriated her more than the incident at the school.

Typically, without a jot of sympathy, her mother had said, 'But surely the teacher couldn't have got it wrong?' As she spoke she divided up a shepherd's pie between Bill, David, Molly, Susan and herself. Lameness due to childhood polio, combined with rheumatoid arthritis that set in at an early age meant she was largely wheelchair bound; so serving up at the table was one of the few things she could do for her family. Molly sometimes had to remind herself to be sympathetic.

Her father leaned forward in his chair, with knife and fork held ready to attack his dinner, 'Hmm. No smoke without fire, I reckon, Dorothy.'

'The school haven't been in touch. I don't understand that. Do you need a bit more, David?' she asked Molly's brother, who passed back his plate for another spoonful. Now David was a 'working man', their mother seemed to think his helpings should double in size, to give him muscles like Charles Atlas.

'You were ordered to go home in the middle of the morning. Just like that. Is that right?' asked her father.

'Yes. The teacher told Nicola Bates, Alison Marshall and me to leave the school and go home.'

'The headmaster did? Or, the teacher who was teaching you?' said Bill, like a terrier digging for a bone.

Molly decided to keep explanations short. 'The art teacher, Mr Finchley, said we should get out so Nicola and I went home. He was het up.'

David was smirking as Bill shook his head, perplexed. 'You must've done something very wrong. I never heard of anything like that before. What if nobody had been at home and we'd locked up? It's only by chance that it's half-day closing at the shop.' Her father worked at a furniture shop with a workshop out the back where he did repairs and re-upholstery.

Molly made no comment on that. Since getting home around half-past eleven, she had become bored of the whole storm in a teacup thing and she just wanted to get on with her homework, pot-roast a piece of brisket for tomorrow's dinner and bake a Victoria sandwich-cake for tea, so she could go out in the evening. Her friend's father had agreed to take them to the pictures in his car. It was all arranged two weeks ago and, having saved her pocket money for this, she was not going to let a stupid fuss at the school spoil a rare trip out that might promise some fun.

'I expect we'll get a letter or something,' said her mother, after a pause. 'It all began in a painting class, you say, Molly?'

Molly sighed. 'Art. There was an ... accident ...' Her parents looked at each other again, as if they believed the truth would now come pouring out. 'Some tins of powder paint toppled over and the stuff spread all over the place and the art teacher, Mr Finchley, was hopping mad. He shouted at us to get out.'

'What, all three of you?'

'Yes. Alison stuck up for us, but she was still sent out. He wouldn't listen.'

'Ah! So you and this Nicola – you were ones who *caused* this ... accident.' Her father raised his eyebrows, head inclined, fork held mid-air, as he absorbed his assumption.

'We didn't actually do it. Someone else did, but ...' Her voice tailed off and, out of the corner of her eye, she caught sight of David still grinning, as if he were enjoying this – his younger sister getting into trouble; she didn't want to snitch on anyone, not even the boy who had deliberately committed the prank. People were always playing tricks and Edward Phillips probably had no idea it would then cause such total chaos, the entire form running out of the classroom in support of her, Nicola and Alison. Without any discussion, the whole of the fifth form felt an unspoken sense of injustice and collectively concluded that Mr Finchley was an idiot. Taking advantage of his weak discipline, they surged out, given a strength that comes from being lost in a crowd. 'The headmaster then found the whole class ... it was like a ...' Molly faltered, searching for the right word, '... a sort of stampede, you might say, I suppose.' She shrugged. 'Then other teachers came out to see what was going on and their pupils trailed after them ...'

'What is happening to discipline with young people these days?' muttered her mother, who, from hours spent alone at home, was prone to asking rhetorical questions. Nobody around the table was likely to answer that, although it prompted Molly to wonder what was happening to *teachers*

4

these days, if it was beyond them to even keep control of a Grammar School class not known for misbehaviour.

As the mealtime scene replayed over in her head, she could see her friend waiting for her on the village green and she waved, then pointed to her wrist-watch and flapped her hands by way of an apology for being late. They were going to see *Pure Hell at St Trinian's*, a comedy about schoolgirls who burned their school to the ground. Joyce Grenfell would make them laugh for sure and she secretly imagined having a Dad like that smooth-talking charmer, John le Mesurier ...

But her thoughts were sliding again, this time into the wider story. Had Mr Finchley managed to spin a tale and plead his case, she wondered? When she walked out of the school that morning, Molly caught sight of him trying desperately to speak to the headmaster, Mr Bird, as he and his robes swept past him in the opposite direction.

Her father's hostile glare earlier on even now made her eyes sting. He had finished his plateful, taking care to scrape all traces of gravy from his plate. He always ate fast, to give him more time to get on with projects around the house, so many unfinished or not yet started, but this time he folded his arms and looked down his nose at Molly, as if with distaste.

'You know, when a criminal has done some act whatever it may be, the first thing that often comes to mind, when it all goes badly wrong, as it seems to have done in this case, not that we're talking criminals here,' he said, with all of them wondering if he was ever going to reach the end of his sentence and get to the point, 'then that person, well, more often than not, he, or she, will blame someone else.' She still quivered at the memory of his steely eyes.

'No, I did nothing wrong. Honest, Dad.'

'Hmm.' He gave her mother a look.

'I'll telephone the school,' her mother replied.

'Good idea. David, take your mother to the phone-box, will you?'

'He can't be late for clocking in,' said Dorothy. 'Molly can do it. After all, she's not at school, is she? It needs to be done now, this afternoon, before school closes. Do you know when you'll be allowed back? Oh, you silly, silly girl. What will people think? Our daughter expelled? I've never heard of such a thing, really I haven't.'

Susan piped up, 'What does expelled mean?'

Dorothy did her best to explain and the child was left wide-eyed with envy.

Molly cleared up the plates, her mother following her to the kitchen in her wheelchair. As a do-it-yourself project, her Dad had removed the door and part of the wall dividing the lounge and the kitchen, replacing it with an archway large enough to give her access.

'I made an apple pie, you know,' said Dorothy. 'I managed to roll out the pastry, lovely, buttery shortcrust – actually Doris helped me.' Doris was a salt-of-the-earth, gossipy neighbour who came in most mornings to see if she could do anything useful. 'She is a real treasure, that woman. When you're like me,' Molly froze momentarily, horrified, wondering what she meant, 'you find out who your true friends are … anyway, all this seems to have spoilt our meal, doesn't it?'

'I am sorry, but … really, it wasn't my fault, Mum.'

Dorothy glanced at her disparagingly. 'I don't know whether to believe you. Your father's right. You don't want to get into trouble, so you probably wouldn't admit it anyway.' She looked away, quietly speaking her thoughts, as if her daughter wasn't actually standing six inches from her, feeling hurt and upset that her parents were not taking her side. In their eyes, she was guilty until proven innocent, and suddenly felt very alone. Maybe this was not going to simply blow over as she thought it would.

She ventured to confirm, 'I did nothing wrong.'

'Don't answer back!' snapped her mother suddenly, irritated, Molly surmised, at the prospect of facing village tittle-tattle and shame. 'And what is more, don't you have anything to do with those other two girls, now. Is that understood?'

Her mother could be frightening. Because of her disability, people rarely contradicted her and bouts of ill-temper were excused out of pity. Molly had been conditioned from an early age never to argue with her, but to give way, and have only sympathy for the pain and suffering she endured.

6

Molly didn't talk much about pupils in her class so her mother was probably unaware of who they were, Alison the brainy one with even brainier parents and Nicola the sexy scatterbrain with funny parents. 'But Alison was the one who stood up for …' she added, softly.

'Molly!' Increasingly agitated in the confined space, her mother carelessly bumped the wheel of her chair into the kitchen table. 'Leave those dirty dishes. You can do them later. I'm going to telephone the headmaster right now and get to the bottom of this.' Molly's heart sank. 'Molly! Can you fetch my bag? I'll need some coppers for the telephone. Should come out of your pocket money really.' Her mother pursed her lips, squinting at her reproachfully.

'Where is it?'

'Where it normally is.'

So that would be where she left it, perhaps by the divan in her mother's downstairs bedroom that in every other house in their road was the dining-room; hanging on a peg in the under-stairs cupboard; or … It was pointless to ask, so Molly did a quick scout around the house, eventually finding it inside the sideboard. Her father had a habit of tidying things away, which was not always helpful. As her feet pounded upstairs to make a quick visit to the bathroom, dust puffed up reminding her that the carpet needed vacuum cleaning. Her parents often reminded her how lucky she was to be one of her generation with all the so-called 'labour-saving' devices. 'When we were young there was just a stiff brush and pan!' She was such a lucky girl.

'What are you up to, Molly? I've found the number. We need to go,' her mother was calling to her, impatient to be off. 'Is it still raining?'

She came downstairs as fast as she could.

'Child! Don't thump your feet like that. You'll wear out the carpet.'

Molly passed her mother the cardigan she guessed she might need to put round her shoulders. Dragging her foot with the built-up shoe, her mother limped to the front door, with the aid of a stick, and Molly took care to coax the wheelchair down the step outside; it was a tight fit and she knew what her mother would say next, since she had heard it a thousand times before.

Dorothy eased herself into the chair. 'I'll be glad when your father has replaced this door-step and made a ramp. I don't know what takes him so long,' she grumbled.

The phone box was on the west side of the village green, no more than a hundred yards away. Molly pushed and Dorothy sat. 'Oh, Molly … you know how much your education matters. You might have spoiled your chances now. I hope we don't see anyone … I mean, what do we say? You've been expelled from school?'

There were Grammar School and Secondary Modern pupils everywhere making their way back for afternoon lessons after dinner. She knew what her mother meant by 'anyone'; her Women's Institute and Mothers' Union friends and respectable churchgoers.

'You don't need to say anything,' said Molly. 'I don't think I've been *expelled*.'

'You can say you're feeling badly, or something … we better be quick, any rate. This drizzle is soaking my cardigan. Get my brolly out can you?'

'We're nearly there now, Mum. I'll put the waterproof over your chair.'

Her mother then managed to ease herself inside the phone box and close the door. Leaning against the window on one side, she lifted the receiver. Molly could make out her blurry profile through the grime on the window-panes; she watched her put in some coins then press Button A and, with some pennies lined up ready in case they were needed, she began talking and occasionally pausing to listen. It would be hard for her to stand, even for a few minutes.

Although burning with curiosity, she knew better than to quiz her mother then on how the conversation went, once they were making their way back home; she knew that to ask would be 'none of her business', even though it very much *was*.

But now, as revealed by her mother less than an hour ago, she did know. They were sending a letter and meanwhile she was to 'stay at home' – but no, she had escaped!

2

Nicola spent some time flicking through magazines in the newsagents before making her way home from school that strange morning. Later she bounced in through the backdoor of her family's beige, pebble-dashed council-house, glad to get indoors, out of the grey summer drizzle. As her stomach growled with hunger, she pulled off her damp duffel coat and hooked it onto a peg on the wall in what the family referred to as the 'back-place', that others called a scullery, housing a poss-tub, mangle and tin bath, the smell of washing soap always hanging in the air. Her blonde hair-do was sadly flattened by her hood, but she didn't care just at the moment. Their black, 'Heinz 57' mongrel, shiny as a slug, came rushing to see her, barking with wild excitement, sliding on the kitchen lino, claws clattering.

She ruffled his ears playfully. 'Hello, Boot! You a good dog?' She bent down so he could lick her ears. He was the only living creature in the house allowed within an inch of her beehive.

Roy Orbison was belting out *Pretty Woman* and a tantalising smell of sizzling sausages and fried onions filled the kitchen.

'Mu-um! I'm here! Your washin's gettin' wet. It's piddling down.'

Granny Allsop came through to the kitchen, her silver hair in rollers covered neatly in a mauve chiffon scarf. 'I thought I heard the lid rattling on the spuds – it's my job to make the mash today. Hello then, my lovely, what you doing here so early? I'll just go and get them sheets in ..'

'You'll never guess what. Where's Mum?'

'Dinner ain't ready yet, my love ...' her Granny added, over her shoulder as she rushed out the back door.

'Mu-um!' yelled Nicola. 'Mum!'

9

Her mother, Lily, wearing a purple and green flowery crossover apron, came bustling through from the dark hallway with a dustpan and brush in her hand.

'Mum, you'll never guess what!'

'Oh, what *now*? Let me just get the ironing put away. Call your Grandad, will you, I need him to stoke the boiler, the hot water's run out. He's with his veg, pinchin' his tomato plants, I think he said. Some hope of growin' tomatoes in this British summer! You'll have to holler – he might be in the lavvy. And your dear dog got out this mornin', got another one of Mr Simmonds's hens. Feathers flying! I had to buy it off him, you can pluck it tonight.' Whenever Boot did something wrong, he suddenly became 'her dog', *her* responsibility.

'But Mum – I've got summat to tell you.'

Resting one hand on her hip, Lily gaped and opened her eyes wide. 'No!' She stared questioningly at Nicola, then looked her up and down.

'No – not that.'

'You had me goin' there for a minute. Not at your age, my girl. Remember that little talk we 'ad? About keeping your legs crossed?'

'Mu-um, don't be daft.'

Once her Mum had removed the pile of clean laundry, Nicola wiped over the orange and green trellis-pattern, plastic tablecloth, took dinner plates and cutlery out of the kitchen cabinet and set the table for four. Her Grandad entered with a tall scuttle of coke in one hand, holding a Daily Express over his head. 'Cor blimey! Flamin' weather ..'

'Excitin', this is, Mum. You'll never guess what. I been sent home from school – for the day, or maybe longer, I dunno.' She shrugged her shoulders.

Her mother was now tending the frying pan but said she was 'all ears'. 'What's 'appened then?'

'Three of us got sent out the classroom, then the whole class rushed out as well and our teacher told us to go home!'

'Now, that don't really make a lot of sense, my darlin'.'

'The teacher thought that another girl, Molly and me had knocked down a whole load of paint tins, on purpose, makin' a heck of a mess. We didn't. A boy did. And this girl, Alison, she saw what happened, but the teacher didn't believe any of us.'

'What teacher is this then?'

'The art teacher. Mr Finchley. He's as useful as a glass hammer.'

'So he just told you to scarper?'

Nicola nodded and shrugged. 'He got in a right tiz.'

'Nutcase. I mean, over such a daft little thing like that. Any rate, you're finished with school at the end of the week, so it makes no odds really. Here, open the beans, can you, my love? I forgot about 'em.' She pulled a saucepan off a hook and lit a gas-ring with a match, while Nicola expertly stabbed the tin with a tin-opener and began hacking into the lid.

'Your tomato plants not doin' so well, then George?' Lily asked her father-in-law. Turning to Nicola, she added, 'I've a mind to get your Dad to complain, though, official like. It don't sound right to me.'

It was hard to explain to her Mum, it was all so silly, now she thought back. Her mother would just laugh, but then she hadn't been there to see the livid expression on Alison's face when she found her and Molly in the girls' outside lavatory block that reeked of Jeyes fluid, slumped on the cold concrete floor, bemoaning their mistreatment.

'He dismissed me for telling him it wasn't you,' Alison said, bristling with resentment.

What a drip! thought Nicola. They had only been whispering about his hair, the way it hangs over his collar but he'd obviously held a grudge.

She had tried to lighten the mood. 'He's got no sense of humour …' she pointed out, adding with a chuckle. 'Perhaps he heard what we said. Serve him right. Ooh!' she said, as a distraction. 'You've got a ladder, Molly …'

Molly glanced down at the offending leg self-consciously, but then jumped to her feet. She always seemed rather shy and quiet to Nicola, but appeared to be unfazed by her comment. 'Too bad. Not much I can do about that here, is there?'

'You could try a smudge of carbolic to stop it,' suggested Nicola, then staring pointedly at Alison's regulation white ankle socks, wondering whether to tease her about being such a toady, but Alison was in enough of a bad mood already so she bit her tongue.

Alison sighed. 'Look, you two! What shall we do?'

'You tell us. You're the clever clogs,' replied Nicola, who pulled a comb from her skirt pocket and began back-combing her bee-hive to give it extra height. Molly's parents would probably be horrified that she was even talking to her; her council-house family was thought of as 'common', she knew that. 'What a pig. I hate him,' she muttered. 'And cobalt and crimson are not good for my peroxide. Blimey, everyone on that side of the class got smothered in the stuff.' Nicola giggled, then pulled a pack of Wrigley's chewing-gum from her cardigan pocket and offered it to Alison and Molly, who both shook their heads.

Alison paced about. 'I tell you what,' she said, her lips pinched and jaw tight. 'My parents say that human rights and social injustice are things you should defend. So, I say we stick together. We must. Whatever happens.'

Nicola replied, 'Like the three musketeers?'

'My parents will go mad!' said Molly, on the verge of tears.

'I'll stick up for you,' Alison assured her. 'It was that goof, Edward Phillips – he was the one who did it, you know.'

Nicola grabbed her arm. 'Really? You actually saw him?'

'Was it by accident?' asked Molly.

'Oh, no! On purpose!'

'The twit!' cried Nicola.

'His right arm shot out suddenly; he pulled a tray, then just to be sure, gave one of the legs an almighty shake so the whole lot came tumbling down like a tower of dominoes.'

'He's a worse scumbag than the hairy Finch then.'

'I told him I was going to see Beaky.'

'No!'

'You dared?'

Alison shrugged. 'I don't know – I just said the truth. I thought our headmaster should know what happened.'

'Really? You think we should?' said Nicola, feeling rather excited.

'Beaky won't believe us though,' Molly pointed out, frowning.

'He'll believe Alison. She's won prizes every year since she was born.'

'Remember – at all costs, we stick together,' Alison reminded them, assuming the role of leader, with which was Molly seemed particularly happy. 'United we stand, divided we fall.'

'Through thick and thin … for better or for worse … for richer for poorer …' sang Nicola, exhilarated by this dreamlike break from school routine. 'What a lark!' She couldn't wait to tell her Mum and Dad about this.

Giggling, they linked arms and strode outside, down the path bordered by lilac bushes hung with spent spring blooms, into the girls' playground, heading for the headmaster's office on the far side of the red-brick Grammar School building.

Ahead of them was a sea of schoolchildren, squirming, pushing and shouting. Nicola thought it likely that never before nor since, in the history of the school, had there ever been anything like it.

'So, Finchley. Please sit. What the deuce happened?'

An earlier brief befuddled exchange that same afternoon when the school ran amok was cut short by an urgent need for the headmaster to attempt to restore some order. Children were squealing with excitement, boys had removed their ties, whirring them round above their heads like helicopter rotor blades; rows of girls linked arms and, in this formation, were sweeping round the playground. There seemed to be some theme of destruction here based on a circular motion which the headmaster could not fathom.

Now, the classes had more or less re-formed and afternoon lessons were under way; so it was just past two o'clock before he called Finchley in, as he had gathered from various murmurings that this teacher in particular might be able to throw some light on the situation. A member of staff who had a free period was taking care of his class.

Peter Finchley sat down in a plain, armless chair opposite the headmaster, George Bird, who was seated in his studded leather chair on the other side of an imposing mahogany desk, adorned with blotters, framed pictures and a black telephone. Behind him was a glass fronted cabinet filled with silver sports cups. George Bird, who liked status, order and neatness, with everything in its place, always dressed at school professionally in the black robes of academia, mortar-board at the ready.

He wondered how much, or how little, he should say about the classroom incident. After morning break he had split up two fifth form girls for talking and placed them near the front of the class, on the end of the first two rows, where he could keep the troublemakers under his watchful eye.

Two tall piles of bun-tins loaded with bright powder paint were on a table to their right, ready for Class 2G. Suddenly, with a heart-stopping clatter, the twin tower of trays apparently imploded, collapsing like a demolished chimneystack. Sprays of colour then scattered and settled, puffy clouds of dust coating hair, drawing paper, desks, lining the nostrils of pupils nearby and even reaching the queue of lopsided grey pots and vases on the window-sill waiting their turn to be fired.

Failing to contain his anger, he yelled, 'Nicola Bates, Molly Watson! Get out, please – now! Now! Out of my sight.'

'But sir …'

'We didn't …'

'It wasn't …'

They were obviously guilty, so he thought.

Then a female voice called out with unusual confidence as the two girls left the room.

'Sir, Molly and Nicola were not responsible.' Alison Marshall, who had spoken up, was a reserved but clever pupil, her studious nature respected by the teachers.

He had tried to keep calm by striding about, feeling his brow exude tell-tale beads of sweat he could not mop away with his handkerchief as this would draw attention to his anxiety. He was worried about his reputation as a raw, new teacher. Damn it, he could smell the paint hanging in the air. Why had he not noticed the trays piled high like a house of cards, just waiting to topple? Who had *done* that? Should he wait until the end of the lesson to clear up this carnage? Get the perpetrators to clean up? Heaven knows, they would make a dog's dinner of that, for sure. Anyway, he had sent them out and they had fled and who knows *where*?

His heart pounded like a sledgehammer against his ribs. Panic.

'Alison Marshall – I am surprised to hear you side with such, such … miscreants.' He had struggled to find the right words, knowing he sounded pompous in his attempt to assert himself.

Alison stood up and confronted him, looking him in the eye with such candour and conviction, he felt weak at the knees. The collar of her neat, white blouse was smudged with vermilion fingerprints.

'It was someone else who pulled out two trays from the bottom of the pile and … shook the table.' Alison had been sitting right behind a boy called Edward, son of a school governor, whose face, hair and shirt were by then brightly hued. 'Where I was sitting I could see clearly – probably no-one else could.' That smile she gave him, it was unnerving, as if she were trying to be understanding and this felt somehow terribly out of place.

He pulled himself up to his full height, still at eye level with this well-spoken, well formed, fifteen year old girl with glasses, long chestnut hair and impeccable manners. His other pupils, waking up from the catatonic state into which this unprecedented drama had thrown them, were now stirring and murmuring.

'I don't know what your game is, young lady, but it's perfectly obvious that those two sulky girls, whom I'd already reprimanded three times, have stupidly – very stupidly,' he added with due gravitas, 'decided to cause trouble, wasting lesson time. Now, please leave the room. I will not have this … this argument about what is so obviously clear cut.' Even then, he realised deep-down that sticking to his guns was his big mistake.

'But I have done nothing wrong. Why should *I* leave the class?' She gave him a look of what seemed to him like feigned bewilderment.

'Insolence,' he hissed, digging himself into an ever deeper hole, vaguely aware of tiny globules of his own spit spraying the air between them. 'Do as I say.'

'I shall go to the headmaster on my way home,' was her confident, parting shot, stated simply and expecting no rebuttal. She turned and walked away from him to the classroom door, through which Molly and Nicola had now fled, and a short-lived hush fell, as if a feather cushion had briefly smothered a wireless.

'There was an … accident, sir.'

George clasped his hands across his chest, raised his chin and sat back, expectantly, waiting to hear more. 'I think it may have partly set things off, but why …? I don't really know.' Finchley scratched his head to denote bewilderment in a manner that was rather deliberate, it seemed to George.

'Please. Details. If you would?'

'Fifth form. Suddenly a pile of paint tins – you know, loose powder, not yet mixed with water – toppled over and the stuff flew everywhere.'

'So – who did this?' George now prepared his fountain pen to write down something useful.

'Headmaster, I was sure it was Nicola Bates and Molly Watson – I had already reprimanded them for talking so they were clearly wanting to get their own back.' The headmaster winced; this was not his language. 'However, Alison Marshall claims otherwise.'

The headmaster looked up from his jottings with interest. 'Alison Marshall?'

'Yes, sir.'

'Ah, yes, my secretary said she was asking to see me. I think she's an entirely trustworthy pupil. What did *she* say?'

'She says it was another pupil who caused the tins to fall – I think she meant Edward Phillips, sir.'

There was a long pause as the implications of this registered.

'Hmm. Sir Matthew Phillips' boy? Hah! The papers would have a field day with that!'

'Really? Why?'

'Not the trifling incident *per se*, of course, but the rumpus that followed. It hardly went unnoticed in the village, you know. And who was to blame for that?'

Peter Finchley sat forward in his chair. 'You cannot hold me responsible for that, sir. No, no. I mean, with respect, who would've guessed that it could have turned into total mayhem?'

'Now that's just the kind of language we want to avoid. A mild disturbance, I think, should anyone ask you, quickly brought under control. Then who *is* responsible? *Who* is accountable for this? Such a brouhaha has never, in the long history of this Grammar School, occurred before. Nothing remotely like it.' George now stared reprovingly at the young teacher, who clearly felt his glare intimidating and said nothing. 'There will be reporters sniffing about. I just know it. They'll be asking questions, scouring Appley Green for tittle-tattle. So when they come here we must have our story clear. Vital we are all singing from the same hymn sheet. Get my drift? It's the kind of nonsense and stupidity the popular press short of proper news will seize upon.'

'So what do we say?'

George rolled his eyes, as if dealing with a child. 'Well, as you rightly said at the start, there was an accident, the pupils got excited, but everything is quite calm now and nobody was hurt, and no lasting damage was done to property either.'

'So, we should play it down, then? Make light of it.'

The headmaster sighed. 'It's really a very small event on a global scale, wouldn't you agree? Riots and a massacre of blacks in South Africa, the Congo claiming independence … more important things going on, eh? Ghastly state of affairs. Look, Finchley, I can't say I am very pleased with what took place. It shows poor discipline and there will be closer investigations. It should never have happened on your watch … but I have a phone call to make. Come back here at close of play this afternoon. Quarter to four sharp.'

George Bird drummed his fingers on the desk as the art teacher left his study, then got up to make sure the door was firmly closed after him.

He asked the operator for a number that he thought might reach Sir Matthew, though trying to reach him by phone would be like hitting a moving target. He had his home telephone number and two London office numbers in a card index system kept in his desk drawer. Within two minutes, he tried the first business number and got through to a secretary.

'Sir Matthew Phillips is in a meeting at present. Who may I say is calling?'

Lucky bullseye! At least he was on the premises.

'Bird, headmaster of Appley Green Grammar School. Would you please tell him I need to speak to him *urgently* about a matter concerning his *son*.'

That should shake him up. It certainly got the attention of his secretary, who was now all of a flutter. 'Oh, my goodness. Is he all right? That would be Edward, would it?'

'Correct, my dear. Now just pass on the message, if you please.'

'I will. In fact, I can interrupt his meeting. I'm sure he'd want me to.'

The line went quiet as he was duly fetched. Pleasantries were bypassed since the message had been fully conveyed and Sir Matthew was just anxious to know more. George explained what had happened in the classroom.

'Good grief! Why are you bothering me with this? I'm a busy man. You could've called my wife perhaps, at home?'

'I'm thinking of possible repercussions if it got out, which it surely will. Village gossip is the most efficient way of spreading unwelcome news. Although the teacher says others are to blame, I think your son did this silly thing …'

'Oh, for pity's sake. Just knock it on the head, man.' There was a pause. 'I … I don't want Eddie in the papers, if that's what you're suggesting might happen. He would be picked on, only because of me, of course – political barbs, business rivals, and all that. He deserves better. See to it, George. It'd reflect badly on the school too.'

As general benefactor to the school, and backbone, though not Chairman, of the Board, the word of Sir Matthew Phillips was heard and heeded. If Sir Matthew's feathers were ruffled and he pulled out as governor, generous donations would be cast to oblivion. It would be the kiss of death on future plans; no PT room, stage or swimming pool without his personal involvement, support and, above all, money. The questions from parents would never cease, and broken promises would mean a shattered career for one headmaster.

The conversation closed after precisely two minutes. There was a timid knock on his door, which he recognised to be that of Marjorie Collins, his secretary.

'Come!' he boomed.

'Mr Bird, sir, there is a gentleman here from the Bloomstock Gazette. I told him you wouldn't want to speak to him, but he seems to think you would.' She clutched her spiral shorthand notebook with trembling fingers.

Blast. He would have to see him. No escape. Fill in Finchley later and the rest of the staff before assembly tomorrow, then an extraordinary Governors' Meeting. The press would have to hear their, or rather his, side of things; now rather than later perhaps the best strategy, or they'd just make something up.

He forced a smile. 'Thank you Miss Collins. Please show him in, would you?'

3

Alison let herself in. Like her twin brother, Julian, she had owned a door-key for almost four years, since their twelfth birthday.

'Coo-ee!' she called. Sometimes Mrs O'Reilly, a young Irish woman who came in to clean the rather draughty, musty family home, was there, but Alison had no idea what hours she worked, since she was usually at school when their char did her round of polishing, sweeping, re-arranging the ornaments and generally hiding things, which her mother said was Mrs O'Reilly's way of keeping their house neat and tidy. Alison knew she was there on Friday mornings, when Jan the Polish vegetable man called, but other than that her working hours were unclear. Today, the house was empty and silent as the proverbial tomb.

On the way home, she had called in at the small village library, no bigger than her father's study, to pick up some books she requested a couple of weeks ago: *The Country Girls* by Edna O'Brien and *Gigi* in the original French. It had taken a while to find copies, they said, but they had finally come in from a larger library in Guildford. She browsed the fiction shelves while she was in there and was also pleased to spot the newly published book A *Kind of Loving* by Stan Barstow. She had her two library tickets, as well as one of her mother's, in the side-pocket of her satchel, which was lucky as she had not actually planned on visiting the library today. The librarian silently took out the small cards from the inside front book covers, slotted them into Alison's reader tickets and, thus married together, slotted them into her indexed filing system. She ignored the librarian's cursory glance first at the wall-clock, then a more pointed, puzzled look over rimmed glasses at her school uniform, as if checking that, oh dear yes, this was a schoolchild during lesson time, out of school. However, Alison felt secure in the knowledge that Miss Fisher, gatekeeper of books, knew her parents well and would assume there was a valid reason for this. She would also choose to tacitly assume that they would know what their not-quite-adult daughter was borrowing; so the books were duly date stamped and handed to her with a polite smile which Alison returned with an equally courteous 'Thank you.'

Now she had a few extra hours or so of free time when she could settle down to read and listen to Neil Sedaka singing *Stairway to Heaven*, a single her favourite aunt had given her for her fifteenth birthday, not something her parents would ever have chosen. The beaten-up, ancient gramophone she and Julian were allowed to use needed a new needle but she could bear the odd crackle. It would do until Christmas when they hoped to get a record-player. There was something about Neil Sedaka's voice that made her tingle inside.

She scanned the shelves and cold-counter in the pantry, and then the new fridge purring away in the kitchen, to see what might offer possibilities as to lunch. There was a round tin on the table that often held some kind of bought cake, a cut-and-come-again fruit-cake from the village baker or a Battenberg from Willetts, the grocer; and a biscuit barrel usually filled with an assortment. Her mother was not brilliant at planning or cooking meals. She was, after all a dedicated career woman, and how on earth she and Julian had ever been a part of her plan for life would be forever a mystery.

There were some leftovers from the Sunday roast, the best part of a leg of lamb. Alison quite liked cold meat; she was used to it. Roast beef, hot, cold, rarely minced as in 'normal' households; for special occasions, roast chicken, hot, cold then soup if Mrs O'Reilly was around to make it; pork chops; sliced ham off the bone; and lamb in various forms were pretty much the staples, the basis of the family evening meal, with potatoes in some form and two boiled vegetables. 'It makes life simple, so why tamper with tradition?' This was her mother's light-hearted view to which she sometimes added that, 'after all, during the war, we had to do without you know.' Alison's suggestions that they have a rabbit casserole; a tinned steak and kidney pie; or even sausages with a fried egg fell on deaf ears. Her mother sometimes skipped dinner and Alison suspected she had been out to lunch but she never talked about it. Fish and chips were heavenly, Alison ventured to suggest one Saturday evening three years ago, when she sensed no hint of food preparation whatsoever. Sudden converts, her parents enthused at the radical idea of their little girl popping out to the Fish and Chip shop the other side of the village green and coming back post-haste with a warm meal. Even though it meant a sprint if there was any hope of their supper keeping hot, it had pleased Alison no end; to influence her very clever parents in any way was a major achievement and happened rarely. Next time she was allowed to use her bike.

Alison smiled a secret smile as she remembered this. She could have easily picked up four penn'orth of chips today and she was annoyed now she had not thought of it. Before the end of morning school, she could have sat on a village-green bench eating chips, straight from the newspaper, just how they tasted best, hot, greasy and salty with the tang of vinegar, and her parents would never know, not that they would care tuppence anyway about something so trivial. The mundane was something they seriously despised. Alison could never talk to her mother about split-ends or the fact that her bra did not fit well and made her look deformed, or anything that did not open up a proper debate. Her mother did once have some kind of dutiful and embarrassing talk with her about sanitary towels, what sexual intercourse was, its legal restrictions, moral conventions and, above all, unwanted consequences. Mealtime conversation was founded on current affairs, politics, the economy, history – especially 'lessons to be learned from the past' - and, occasionally, music and theatre. Just recently, issues relating to Cuba, the 'Cold War' and communism were discussed, her parents both wearing frowns and sounding grave. Jean-Paul Sartre and existentialism were raised as a more cerebral topic to be dissected; it could all get very abstract and conceptual and Alison and Julian struggled sometimes.

Now, as she sliced some lamb for a sandwich, picking out the fatty bits, Alison briefly thought about the morning and how ridiculous it all was. She would quite like to see Nicola and Molly even though the nonsense was not her problem; maybe she would ride her bike over to Molly's house. She wasn't entirely sure where Nicola lived; somewhere on the pretty rough council estate beyond the green, she suspected. Molly, she knew, lived in a terraced row of cottages and she would soon find out which was hers, if she knocked on someone's door. When Julian was thirteen he had posted secret Valentine cards to the four prettiest girls in their class and Alison could remember the trouble he took to find out where each of them lived. None guessed it was him and nothing happened as a result, much to his disappointment.

She felt huffy, despite the triviality of it all. Why had she been sent home? It confirmed her suspicions that the Grammar School teaching staff were not on the same intellectual level as her father, the professor, or indeed her mother who did something in the Civil Service that was so clever it was beyond description, apparently. These teachers were dunces, to put it mildly. Images of some of them popped up in her head; wearing pointy hats and being made to sit in the corner of the school hall. She laughed out loud as she munched her sandwich.

For once in her life, she really was eager for Julian to get home from school. As a first-hand witness, he was well placed to report to her on subsequent events and, knowing him, he would have taken the initiative to enquire about her whereabouts. In fact, she would not put it past him to challenge the headmaster. As siblings, they did not always get on in their teenage years, as their gender difference naturally led to a certain social divide, but they were twins and had a special loyalty to each other. He had always defended her fiercely against possible playground bullies and that sort of thing.

She settled herself down in a hard brown leather armchair, with Neil Sedaka working his magic on her; afternoon sunshine was now streaming in through the sash window and she had decided that a ride round to Molly's would be a good idea. First, she unbuckled her old leather satchel, releasing a familiar smell of ink and rubber, pulled out an exercise book and turned to an essay plan she had prepared during the History lesson that morning. It seemed like a long time ago, with Mr Whittle holding forth on Corn Laws; she had thought

23

how stupid it was to stop cheaper corn imports when people were hungry and could not afford home-grown wheat for their daily bread. 'You ask too many questions, Alison,' the teacher had said. 'For now, just learn the facts if you want to pass your exams.' Could he not see that this was what made his lessons so stultifyingly dull? She sighed again at the stupidity of teachers.

The Stan Barstow book slipped out on to her lap and as she flicked through its pages, her eyes caught a few words she had not come across before. It felt strangely exciting as she read about what a boy might do to a girl on a date. Her faltering steps into an altogether new world were suddenly halted by a sharp rap on the front door. The knocker was made of cast-iron, designed to resonate its sound to the rooms furthest away upstairs. Close to the lounge where Alison was, it was enough to make her heart stop, especially in her current dreamlike state.

Perhaps it was Molly or Nicola, she thought.

She opened the door to find a stranger, a rakish-looking young man, on the doorstep, with a camera around his neck. With dark wavy hair in need of Brylcreem, yet shining in the light of a shimmering sunbeam, and twinkly sky-blue eyes, he was so good-looking she hardly knew where to look, yet vaguely aware that her gaze had, without permission, meandered down to just below his waist. His brown, worsted trousers gave no hint of what they might contain.

'Hello, dear. Could I have a word with your mother?'

'She's not here. What do you want?'

'Are you on your own? So you must be one of the girls sent home from the school today.'

'Yes. I am, but it was all so ridiculous, you know. I did nothing wrong. I suppose I shall just go back tomorrow, but it was all left very unclear ...'

'So you're not actually expelled. What happened?'

Dazzled by his smile, Alison began to tell the full story then, seeing a rather over-zealous glint in the man's eyes, she stopped. 'Excuse me for not asking you in, but I think I shouldn't ask strangers into the house when I am on my own.' Warnings of how valuable her father's collection of first editions were had been drummed in like the eleventh commandment. Other people always seemed much more easy-going and trusting, but it was one of the few rules that prevailed in their home: never invite unsavoury looking tradespeople into the house, although this one looked savoury enough.

He gave a friendly chuckle and nodded. 'Quite right. It was your parents I was planning on speaking to but, of course, I expect your Dad is at work. What does he do?'

'He's a University Professor,' she replied, proudly. 'And my mother is a professional person too, you see. But who are you? Why are you so interested?'

'Would you like your photo taken, love? I can let you have a copy and you could make a little frame for it out of passe-partout. Nice surprise present for your parents.'

Alison felt herself blush. 'Oh, all right.' He adjusted his camera to the light and she heard the shutter make a clickety sound a couple of times as he drew it up to his eyes to focus it. Her brain was beginning to spring to life. 'But, how did you know I was here? Did you hear about it from the school?' At least the rush of blood to her cheeks would not show in the photograph, she thought.

'Seems like they've neglected their duties to keep you youngsters safe.' It seemed to Alison that he was capable only of asking direct questions, not answering them. 'One way to look at it, anyway. I'm from the *Bloomstock Gazette*. Thought I'd get the full story by asking around the village. Very curious to hear all sides!' He rubbed his hands and gave her a conspiratorial grin, as if they were in this together, partners colluding in crime. 'I mean, it's only fair, isn't it?'

Alison approved of this, in the circumstances. 'You'll need to speak to the others then. Molly Watson and Nicola Bates.'

'You're a little love, you are,' he said, scribbling in a small note-pad with a shiny red cover with times tables on the back, just like the one she used for French vocabulary. She avoided eye contact, feeling acutely embarrassed by his compliments.

They had been standing on the doorstep for a while and she looked at her wristwatch.

'I'll be off now then,' said the reporter, but as he turned to walk back down the garden path, Alison saw Julian come bursting through the front gate, in more of a hurry than usual.

He brushed past the man, probably thinking he was an insurance salesman or selling household bits and bobs from a catalogue, thought Alison. Now she would find out a bit more.

'Julian! What's happened at the school?'

The reporter turned back, like a bloodhound picking up a new scent. 'Is this your brother?'

'I am,' replied Julian quickly, as if quick to prove that he did not need his twin sister to vouch for his identity, on his behalf.

'We're twins,' added Alison, used to explaining that they were in the same year at school. 'Not identical, obviously.'

The reporter's pupils dilated as he raised his eyebrows. 'I see that. I think you're prettier.' Alison could feel her cheeks burning. 'So you were in the class …?'

'Yes, I was. This afternoon there were a lot of people coming and going. Some other pupils, I mean from other forms at the school, ran off as well … it was all …very … odd.'

Once the reporter had gone, Alison and Julian sat at the kitchen table with tea and a slice of fruit cake, mulling over events together. Her brother asked, 'Have you seen Nicola and Molly since, then?'

Alison shook her head. 'No. I thought I might go round to Molly, but then that newspaper chappy came.'

'So you're going to be famous now. In the local rag!' She knew he meant this ironically; this would not be something to be proud of.

'I'm sure he won't be mentioning me!'

Her brother gave her a puzzled look. 'Are you bonkers? Of course he will!'

'Oh! Oh Lord. He just took my picture, you know, before I really had time to think.'

There came a light knock on the front door, someone who had decided to use their knuckles. Alison looked over the rim of her cup. 'You go.' Her brother hesitated. 'Go on, it might be one of the girls.'

Her brother blushed! 'All right.'

Too inquisitive to stay put, she followed him to the front door. Of all people it was the loathsome Edward Phillips.

'What are you doing here, you little rat?' asked Julian. In fact, Edward was tall and lean, but Julian was standing two steps above him.

He stood quietly for a moment, nervously folding and unfolding his school cap. Through the open garden gate, she could see his shiny new racer bike propped on the curb under the cherry tree. It was an enviable machine of gleaming metallic red and chrome. Lucky boy!

'I came to say sorry.'

'Oh. Well, you've said it now, so you can buzz off.'

Alison wanted to make him suffer a bit more. 'Come on in and have a biscuit or something.'

Now the three of them were sitting round the table. 'I'd like some squash please. Orange if you have it.'

'No, we don't.' She had never heard anything so cheeky; she hadn't even asked him.

'Please, please, don't tell on me,' he suddenly squeaked, looking from one to the other. 'I shall be in the most terrible trouble. My father will ... quite possibly ... *kill* me. Honestly, if he knew that ...'

'Why did you do it? What possessed you?' asked Julian, using a phrase his father had used against him when he once climbed up to the top of the elm tree at the foot of their long garden and was too scared to make the descent.

He paused, as if working out how to reply. 'I don't know. It was stupid, but I never imagined, even for a single second, that it would cause such fuss and bother and lead to all this trouble. It was just a little prank – meant to be. Not that I'd planned it or anything; just on the spur of the moment.'

'Your father is a school governor,' said Alison, feeling it only right to rub his nose in it for a bit longer.

Edward nodded miserably. 'If people know that I was the cause ... I mean, imagine if this got out to people who know my father. He's a big wheel, you know, not just with the school, but he has important business and government connections in the City and Westminster and the thing is, we

… we just fell out anyway over … something else.' Tears welled up in Edward's soft grey eyes. 'And any scandal over that would probably ruin him.' It sounded to Alison as if he were repeating phrases he did not fully understand.

'What?' asked Alison and Julian in unison.

'I can't tell you.'

'Why not? Is it secret? Has he said not to tell?'

Edward nodded again, sniffing loudly.

'Have you got a handkerchief?' asked Alison, wincing at the sight of his runny nose. Boys don't cry! What was going on with this dunderhead? The world is full of complete drips today, she thought, despairingly.

He hastily pulled one, probably Irish linen, perfectly laundered, from his blazer pocket. 'Sorry.'

Alison exchanged glances with her brother, still feeling angry with Edward for both causing her own personal humiliation and for his cowardly behaviour towards Nicola and Molly.

'So we have to keep what you did a secret, even though some others probably saw anyway,' said Julian.

'I don't think they did,' he replied, quickly, hopefully. 'I think Alison was the only one who actually saw, as she was right behind me. It all happened so fast …'

'Others must've worked it out. No-one else could've reached …' began Alison, but her brother raised his hand to cut her off.

'Perhaps, if you tell us your secret about the row with your father, then we won't tell on you. That sounds fair,' suggested Julian with a hint of malice that Alison felt was on the right side of justice. She was aflame with curiosity. What could be so bad that he couldn't tell? Had a crime been committed?

Edward then broke down, burying his face in both hands. 'No! No, you can't do that. That's … well, it's blackmail. Isn't it?' He sounded unsure.

His anguish only fanned the flames of their desire to extract the truth, its secrecy making it so very appealing. 'It's just a simple deal, I think,' said Julian, patiently. 'Fair exchange.'

'But if I tell you then you'll be in possession of two secrets and you mustn't tell anyone, *ever*, about the big one, about how I fell out with my father.'

'We won't tell a dicky-bird.'

'We promise.' They stared at Edward expectantly.

'I don't trust you.'

'Well, I think we ought to tell the headmaster about how Alison saw you clear as day,' said Julian. 'Mr Finchley must realise that she knows who did it.'

In fact, thought Alison, Mr Finchley must be perfectly aware of who did it! The school governor's son! He would plead ignorance to cover his own back, and persist with blaming the two girls. He was not likely to go back on his word now and lose face. I may be still a child in the eyes of the law, she thought, but I am not stupid.

Her animosity transferred to the teacher again. Teachers, pah!

'I absolutely promise, Edward, that if you tell us, then we won't tell on you – about those silly old paint tins, I mean,' cajoled Alison, now pulling her chair towards him, offering him a smile and another custard cream.

'It's really difficult, this is. You see, I have these …well, hard to describe … feelings for a … boy … a boy who is in another class. I'm not saying who he is, but …'

Alison and Julian froze, not even looking at each other. At that moment nothing could have shocked them more.

4

'What homework have you got tonight?' Molly asked her little sister, drying her hands on a rough kitchen towel after washing up baking tins.

'I have to make sure I know all my tables for a test next week,' replied Susan, 'but I don't have to do that tonight.' She felt her ribbon bows to check they were in place then shook her long plaits back over her shoulder. Molly really hoped that Susan would have more confidence than she'd ever had; that in her teenage years, she would stick up for herself and not be pushed around; but for now she was still like putty in her hands, desperate to please her older sister and be her friend.

'It's very important though, Susan. You don't want to fail your eleven plus, do you?' Expertly sandwiching together two sponge cakes with raspberry jam, she adopted a motherly role.

Susan frowned. Molly knew full well that this would fill her with fear and dread; their parents would never recover from the humiliation. It was bad enough that their one and only son had been a Secondary Modern kid.

'I could test you. Like a game. Come on, let's go up to our bedroom.'

Molly correctly predicted that Susan would take readily to this idea. The ten-year-old sadly watched the cake disappear inside a tin with carol-singers under a lantern on the lid, that once held Christmas chocolates and toffees. She bargained, 'If I get half of them right, I get a slice of cake.'

Molly playfully chased her up the stairs. 'If you get them *all* right you get cake, but after pilchards on toast.'

'Ugh!'

'Sorry – Mummy insisted. It's brain food, she says.'

They curled up together on the pink candlewick bedspread that protected the quilted satin eiderdown on the double bed they shared. The springs squeaked when they moved.

'We don't need any books for this test, do we?' said Molly.

'Don't you need to check?'

'Of course not. Are you sitting comfortably?'

Susan nodded eagerly.

'Twelve thirteens.'

'Oh, that's a really tricky one to start off with!'

'No, it's not. You know what twelve times twelve is …' she paused.

'A gross! A hundred and forty-four! Easy!'

'Correct. So add another twelve?' Molly wondered, when she practised on her sister, if she would really want to be a teacher as her parents had decided for her. Teaching seemed to them a big step up from a secretary, apparently the only other career choice even worth consideration.

'Um … A hundred and fifty six!'

'So twelve thirteens make …?

'Um … but that was thirteen twelves.' Susan looked aggrieved and Molly sighed.

'Did you hear anything on your way home about what happened at my school today?'

'I need to do this on paper, or go through the whole twelve or thirteen times table from the beginning.'

'In real life, Susan, you can't recite like a parrot each time you want to multiply one number by another.'

'Why not?' she asked, genuinely perplexed.

'There isn't always time! You just need to know, or work it out quickly. Are you any good at mental arithmetic?'

'Sometimes.' Susan's eyes lit up. 'I worked out a trick! To multiply by 11 you can add the two digits together, like this … say you times 11 by 25, so you put 7 there in the middle and wrap the 25 around it and that makes 275 …'

'That's really clever …' said Molly, genuinely impressed that her little sister was thinking for herself. 'And you just spotted this trick?'

Susan nodded. 'I like maths.'

'That is *really* good. Anyway, did you hear or see anything?'

Susan was now clearly glad to be distracted. 'Well, I did see lots of older boys and girls in groups on the green. They seemed a bit noisier than usual, when I came through them on the way home. And some of them looked – I don't know - dirty, as if they'd been rolling around in mud or something.'

That would be red paint mixed with green, thought Molly. 'Mm. Are you seeing any friends this evening? What about Sandra?' Molly knew that Sandra's brother was in the sixth form.

'No. I'm helping Mummy wind some hanks of wool for Auntie Margaret.'

'You would be better off learning your times tables.'

'But Mummy said I must.'

'Oh, I see, well if she said you must, there's absolutely nothing more to be said, is there?' Molly slid off the bed, bringing this sisterly chat to a sudden conclusion.

'Not really,' said Susan. 'It makes her arms ache to do it using chair legs.'

Alison was practising a study by Bach on her violin in the music room when she heard raised voices downstairs.

'Darling! Could you come down a moment please?' called her mother from the foot of the wide staircase.

It was unusual for her company to be requested at this time, when the parents were usually glad to be home at the end of the week, relaxing with a pre-dinner sherry, probably looking though the day's post. Already the strains of violin music were at work on their brand-new High Fidelity stereogram when the melodies of Bruch replaced Neil Sedaka.

Her father, Gordon, sitting at the kitchen table, had an especially amused expression playing around his benign, bearded face, as if he had just heard of a small windfall on the football pools, or seen a Giles cartoon that had caught his fancy. He was reading something in the Bloomstock Gazette, delivered weekly to the Marshalls' house, but not seen by Alison's parents until they both came home from work. Alison sometimes flicked through it but had not noticed it on the hall-stand where Mrs O'Reilly had put it underneath the morning's post. Now she remembered the reporter and felt herself blush.

'Got your picture in the paper, Alison. What's all this about? They say that your story is that Sir Matthew Phillips' son misbehaved in class. Ooh-hoo! Whereas the headmaster states that he was entirely innocent. What on earth is this doing in the Gazette? Have they run out of proper crimes to report?' Her parents laughed.

Alison told the story as it was, lightly, all the while her heart thudding as she thought about Edward Phillips. She had already filled in the reporter before Edward came round on Tuesday afternoon, when he pleaded with them to keep quiet; and now the paper had gone ahead and published it. In Edward's eyes, she had broken her word twice over, for not only had she spilled the beans to the reporter, but later the headmaster had collared her and forced the truth out of her, although he, *weirdly*, seemed unable to accept her word, as if he were trying to dismiss it as impossible to prove.

'I went back to school the next day and it was such a trifling matter, I didn't think you would be all that interested.'

Her father nodded. 'I smell a rat here, though. The Head is an inherently weak man and is clearly protecting himself – and Sir Matthew. What do you think, my dear?' her father said, turning to his wife.

She was reading the front-page article, with the picture of her daughter inset in the bottom right corner. 'Seems like pandemonium broke out! It's obvious what's happened. We should lodge a formal complaint with the Chairman of the Governors. No point in going to the Head. It could have been handled better by him.'

'I agree. Harriet, you happy to do it?'

'Yes. I'll find the parents of the other girls. See what they think.'

The matter soon forgotten as they ate dinner together, her parents began discussing the locally revered patrons of the village of Appley Green, who had deeply rooted historical connections. The Devonish family were planning a big party to celebrate the engagement of their son Ted to Geraldine, a banker's daughter who was said to be charming and beautiful. Apparently, a former wartime colleague of her mother, someone called Winifred, and her husband, had also been sent an invitation. Her mother was quite flushed with excitement, waving the letter she had found in the envelope with the invitation. Alison spotted gold, embossed, printed lettering; this was no ordinary Basildon Bond missive.

'*This* is from Mrs Devonish,' she announced, then raising her eyebrows, went on, 'She says that it came out in conversation … I find that extremely unlikely … mm, very surprising,' she muttered, as an aside, 'Anyway, Winifred mentioned in passing that she knew me from the old days,' she gave a furtive glance at her husband, 'and she was hoping we could rekindle our friendship at the party. Oh, how wonderful, darling! A coming together of the great and the good!'

This was deemed as quite 'important', not 'trivial', although some might have regarded hobnobbing with the gentry as no more than that. Her parents' definitions were flexible with a habit of coming and going to suit, but one thing was clear, the invitation proved to be a thorough distraction away from the matter of school. It did not seem to involve either her or Julian, however, and Alison's mind drifted off over a strawberry trifle that Mrs O'Reilly had kindly made for them 'without even being asked'. 'What a treasure she is', added her mother, as she offered second helpings around the table.

Alison was left wondering what she should do with the other big secret that poor Edward had left in her and Julian's possession. She was in no doubt that she, for one, would keep it to herself, closely guarded. She had heard about what could happen to homosexuals and it was best nipped in the bud or ignored. But, on the other hand, were they 'accessories after the fact' – after all, just being one was illegal, wasn't it?

By Monday the national press had got hold of the story. George Bird spluttered over his ten o'clock morning coffee and fig roll biscuits, unable to believe the headline on page five of his newspaper that jumped out of the page to greet him.

Finchley was summoned and his ignorance of how the coverage had escalated was immediately evident. Damn the man! You'd think he would be a little more concerned about his own part in this, and his doomed future. George felt thoroughly exasperated.

'Finchley, I saw a reporter last week, as I explained to you. He has, however, twisted things completely and gone with the tittle-tattle which has, I'm very sorry to say, spread to the broadsheets. It's an unmitigated disaster.' He passed the article across the desk and watched the blood drain from Finchley's face. 'Yes. Please clarify again what happened. I want to know, precisely, what you told the three girls to do.'

Finchley cleared his throat as beads of sweat broke out on his forehead.

'I'm not sure of my exact words.'

'Well, let me remind you of what Alison Marshall told me. She said, and I do believe this girl,' said George, feeling his palms sweat a little as he said this. 'She has always been an exemplary pupil of this school and her parents are distinguished academics, she said that you told them to get out. To leave! There were no instructions to see me or the deputy for disciplinary procedures to be followed; or even to wait outside the classroom door for a period of time until you called them in again. What were they to think?'

'I ... I ...' Now loosening his trendy, knitted tie the colour of French mustard, Finchley looked sickly, as if he might faint.

'I do feel some responsibility myself for what followed, Finchley, but pressure is on me for your dismissal. We'll see you off as generously as possible – and I shall see to that personally. It was one mistake, well a series of mistakes that should not have occurred. Imagine if something serious had happened to any or all of those girls. They just left the premises and went home, because they thought that was what you intended.'

'Yes, I see that now. Stupid. Stupid. It all happened so fast.'

'Things can move quickly when they get out of control, Finchley. I suggest that your lack of discipline, common-sense and respect from the pupils does not equip you well for the position of teacher here. I don't want your career to suffer irrevocably and am prepared to provide a fair reference.'

'This was my first teaching post, sir ...er .. as you know. Is there anything I can say to change your mind?'

George smiled. 'No. It will be put before the Board of Governors and your dismissal will be with immediate effect.

However, you've achieved a lot in your short time with us and will be sadly missed.'

He tried to make his tone warm, persuasive, sympathetic for one thing he could do without now was a denounced art teacher loose in the teaching community filled with hatred and armed with a vengeful tongue.

5

Alison returned to school as normal, head held high, innocent of all blame. Mild warnings from her parents not to collude with the other two girls involved, whoever they may be, meant she did not openly talk to Molly who returned, following receipt of the letter from the school sent to her parents, the day before the end of term. Her classmates seemed glad to see her and Molly looked relieved to have their support.

Scribbled notes were passed around, hand to hand, and finally all three girls got together on Saturday, after school had broken up for summer. Their meeting place, suggested by Nicola, was Jim's Snack Bar down a lane off the village green close to a repair garage and small filling station. As go-betweens sworn to secrecy, only Susan and Julian knew of the trio's unlikely rendezvous. It had a juke-box and was a steamy, smoky hidey-hole where older teenagers whiled away many an hour drinking Coca Cola, smoking cheap cigarettes; and lorry-drivers stopped by for a greasy breakfast or builders' tea and a rock-cake. It was that kind of a café and Alison, barely aware of its existence, felt strangely excited by what her parents would call a 'dive'.

Alison and Nicola both bought a milk-shake and a Wagon-Wheel and found three tall stools where they could sit in the window. Molly claimed she didn't need anything; she was still full from breakfast, she said.

Smears and finger-marks were more effective than expensive textured glass found in some bathrooms for obscuring a view through the window overlooking the lane, but even so there was a flowery cotton curtain strung half-way up for customers' added privacy. If they stretched up a bit and craned their necks, they could peep over this and see folks outside coming and going, but they soon tired of that. Anyway, they were in hiding. Molly said she had never ventured in there before either, but it soon became clear that the café was

Nicola's regular haunt, especially since she had officially left school.

'Golly ...' said Molly, her cheeks unusually pink, making her look innocently beguiling in her violet-print cotton dress with a sweetheart neckline. 'This is fun!' Nicola wanted to undo Molly's pony tail and fluff up her naturally blonde hair; she seemed to have no idea how gorgeous she looked, but, a little jealous, Nicola decided not to tell her to her face. It occurred to her that the pink lipstick she was wearing would suit Molly better than it suited herself; it was a generous thought.

'*Good Golly Miss Molly*!' sang Nicola, creased up with giggles. 'We can get that on the jukebox! Little Richard! Got any change?'

'Here!' said Alison. 'I have.' It amused Nicola to see Alison go off to work out how to use a jukebox.

'So you really have left school?' Molly asked Nicola, dressed in tartan trews and a yellow hand-knitted sweater with dolman sleeves. Clip-on pearly ear-rings brought out the whites of her eyes; lipstick echoed the rose-pink in her cheeks and, perched daintily with crossed legs, she felt sure she looked like a model out of the new Honey magazine.

'I put my school uniform in the dustbin. After that business with the Finch, I never want to be reminded ... Did you get a letter from school?'

'Well, my parents did,' said Molly. 'By hand on Wednesday, saying I should return to school right away. I managed to sneak a peek when my mother wasn't looking. The headmaster said the most ridiculous things, that it had all been a 'misunderstanding'. No explanations and not a word of apology, though.'

Alison returned. 'Cheerful Charlie over there is going to put the money in when it's finished.' She pointed to a young man who was serving, wearing drainpipe trousers, winkle-pickers and a tea-towel strung around his hips. He was well-known as coming from a large family of trouble-makers, but was generally pronounced to be the best of the bunch.

Nicola nodded without taking her eyes off Molly. 'They believed you, though didn't they? You told your parents who did it and everything?'

She shook her head and looked away. 'They wouldn't listen to me. They assume I was guilty and then even more guilty for lying. Nothing *I* say will change their minds.'

'Really?' Nicola looked at her, open-mouthed.

'They tell me I was very lucky that the school didn't make more of it and ruin my exams!'

'We need to get that Edward Phillips to own up. It was all in the Gazette, anyway.'

'Best to leave things as they are, I think,' said Alison.

'Why?' Molly and Nicola replied, in unison.

'Trouble is, the Gazette makes me look like a big fat fibber, even though they told the true story, as I told it to them. Readers are more likely to go with the headmaster's version of events, aren't they? My parents are not very happy about that, I can tell you.' Alison shrugged. 'We'll just have to wait and see how it works out.' Then she grinned, tapping her nose.

Alison was just a little bit too superior sometimes; not her normal kind of friend at all. 'But surely you want to defend yourself?' said Nicola, eyes wide with astonishment. 'To defend your … your honour?'

Alison pulled a face, saying nothing.

'You *know* something! Don't you?' Nicola launched herself at her, tickling her armpits in an attempt to get more information out of her. Over went Alison's chocolate milkshake, spilling all over the counter and dripping onto her pleated, plaid skirt.

'Oh Nicola, look what you did, you complete sp…!' Alison put her hand to her mouth.

Nicola gasped. 'What? What? Spiv? Spaz?' She was laughing, and grabbed some paper serviettes to absorb what now seemed like gallons of sticky milk. The young man who had helped Alison with the jukebox came along from behind the serving counter with a grey dish-cloth and a galvanised bucket of sudsy water.

'Clumsy clots!' he said, sourly, a cigarette hanging off an equally cheerless lip.

'My parents would be really cross if they knew I used a word like that, but it was your fault. You're always causing trouble, Nicola Bates,' she teased.

Nicola looked contrite. 'I'll buy you another one,' she agreed good-naturedly. 'After all you are my sister now - but I'm not washin' your stinky skirt.' Alison smiled. 'I can afford it, though, as from next Tuesday, I shall be earnin' money! A real wage. Got that? Aren't you flippin' envious?' She asked the curdle-faced youth to please bring another milkshake and she would pay. She fluttered her eyelashes, clogged with cheap mascara and managed to force a lopsided smile from him.

'What's the job?' asked Molly. 'I could do with a holiday job.'

'Hairdresser – right here in Appley Green. I'll just be learnin' and trainin' but it's a proper job, a real career. My ambition is to have my own salon within two years. What do you think of that then?'

Molly was very impressed, Alison more reserved. 'Well it's not something I'd want to do myself, but I wish you all the best with it. You're like a walking advertisement for hairspray and Amami lotion anyway, so it's a natural progression really.'

Nicola was not sure what this meant. Alison did speak oddly sometimes. 'Oh, well if you say so, brainbox. What're you gonna do?'

'What, today? Or with my life? Thanks for this.' Clutching the tall glass firmly with both hands she sucked through her paper straw.

'After school, of course. Your *life*!'

'Oh, Oxford or Cambridge, of course, then who knows? Too soon to say. Something fascinating and worthwhile, I'll make sure of that!'

'Oh, get you! How can you wait all that time, though? Takes years doesn't it? What about you, Moll?'

'Me? Oh, well, my parents think ...'

Nicola waved her hands about impatiently. 'No, no, no – what do *you* want to do?'

There was total silence as Molly considered this. 'I have absolutely no idea. My Mum and Dad say ...'

'Molly!' shouted Nicola and Alison, just as '*Good Golly Miss Molly*' blared out.

'Oh what a lark!' said Nicola and the three of them broke down in a fit of giggles.

'Listen! My parents will be going to a party in two weeks' time,' whispered Alison, much to Nicola's surprise. 'You could come round and we could ask a few others ...'

'Have a party of our own?'

Alison nodded.

'Wizard!'

'We could bring some cider and get chips or something ...' Nicola brought out a pack of Player's No 6 cigarettes and offered them to her two friends. Alison smoothly took one and leaned forward to reach Nicola's lighter. Molly looked around her nervously, then shook her head.

'Have you never smoked before, little Miss Molly?' asked Nicola, trying to sound worldly-wise.

'I think I may have ... but ...'

Nicola raised her chin, narrowed her eyes and expertly blew smoke out sideways. 'You haven't, have you?'

Molly chewed her bottom lip. 'No,' she confessed.

'So why say you did? Have you French-kissed?'

Molly blushed. 'No!'

Alison was looking on, regarding them both with cool interest. 'Have you read *A Kind of Loving*?' she asked them, blowing smoke up to the nicotine-stained ceiling. 'Either of you?'

Nicola grabbed her arm. 'Have *you*?'

'I have. Have *you*?'

'Is it mucky ... you know ... what d'they say?' asked Nicola, smirking. 'Near the knuckle?' This was an expression she had picked up from her Mum when she listened to *Beyond our Ken* on the wireless.

'It's everything they say - and more,' said Alison, mysteriously.

'Gosh!' Silence fell for a few seconds as Nicola and Molly looked at Alison in awe, probably thinking the same thing.

41

'So - can we borrow it?'

'Come round to my house on Monday, if you like. In the afternoon.'

Nicola shook her head. 'I'll be working, remember? My first day at the salon. I could do Wednesday, my half-day. Anyway, what about your parents?'

'OK, Wednesday then. They're never there. Out working.'

'What? Both of them?' asked Molly. 'Your mother too?'

'Oh yes. I think we should agree, by the way,' said Alison, 'that if we are proper sisters, we don't tell lies, and we don't have secrets, or ... there's no point. Agreed? Molly?'

Nicola nodded and Molly fell in.

6

Walter Finchley and his younger brother, Peter, came away from Bloomstock hospital, where they had spent a difficult visiting hour at the bedside of their sedated father who now claimed he could see seagulls flying in the room, swooping and wheeling, out of a calendar hanging on the wall opposite his bed. His eyesight was extraordinarily good for a man in his fifties, the kindly nurse in attendance pointed out, seeing that he could make out such small details at a distance of about three yards.

'Do you think they know everything? The odds and so on?' asked Walter, as the two brothers walked to where Walter had parked his flashy, open-top Sunbeam-Talbot. 'Probably not. But the doc said, by contrast with other similar cases, he was doing well. He's otherwise in good health!'

It was distressing. They had learned the week before the rumpus at the school, that he was suffering from an illness that did not give him long to live and that news was tragic enough in itself. Their father's illness was a newly diagnosed and partially understood condition said to be genetic so, naturally enough, Walter was equally terrified of his own health and the prospect of an early death. With his past constantly threatening to catch up with him, he had enough problems, without this.

Hereditary illness. The full implications were, of course, immense and it had knocked both brothers sideways.

Walter lit two Benson & Hedges and passed one to his brother; the smell of Dettol was in his nostrils and he inhaled deeply in a bid to refresh his airways. 'What a meaningless thing to say!' he said, referring back to the nurse, his voice tinged with anger as well as sadness. 'Like saying a dying man has a hearty colour in his cheeks. Pretty cold comfort.'

'I think the point she was making, Walter, was that in others the prognosis has been worse. That he is, in fact, lucky to have lived this long. He has always led a healthy life – fresh air and quite good food, apart from wartime rations, being short of sugar and butter and things we all take for granted now … in fact as a child there were nights he would go to bed starving hungry, he told me once about how …'

His brother was gabbling, nerves having got the better of him. Walter sucked in a deep breath. 'Of course, what's happening to the old bugger is terrible, bloody tragic, but what I'm thinking is that *we* could have this thing too and die at a younger age than him, couldn't we? Well, couldn't we?'

Peter looked at him, without saying anything. They both slipped into the first pub they came to, The Duke's Arms, without any need to consult each other.

A fug of smoke and stale air hit them as they entered the dark, oak-panelled saloon bar, but it was nothing out of the ordinary on busy market-day. Walter ordered two pints of mild and bitter and they both knew these would be the first of many.

There was nowhere to sit so they stood, 'propping up' the bar. 'Nice place this. Appley Green,' commented Walter, after swallowing half a tankard in one draft. 'Ah, that feels good.' He ordered a whisky chaser and raised a quizzical eyebrow to his brother, to check if he would like one.

'No thanks. I think I need to keep a clear head. A lot to think about. You think Appley Green village might be a good hideaway for you? Is that what's going through your mind?'

Walter considered this. Maybe this was going through his mind, but he just hadn't yet acknowledged it. 'Hmm. That would be a big change from London! I may stay on a few days; my financial director can run the business without me for a while, and well, I'm a free agent these days really … is that OK with you, old bean?' Peter hesitated, just long enough to intimate doubt. 'If you have other plans, then just say …'

'No. That's the problem, Walt. I have no plans, no plans at all, and by God, I need some. I can't promise to be very good company. That's all.' The fingers of his right hand were absently tapping the bar. It seemed to Walter that Peter had downed most of his pint, almost without realising it.

'So – you've left teaching.'

Peter shrugged and looked away. 'Well, hopefully not, but I have lost my job.' He gritted his teeth, shook his head and appeared to be seething deep-down. 'It was all so ludicrous, so unnecessary. One of those moments when you just want to turn back the clock – just five minutes – and make everything all right, back to normal.' He paused and Walter watched his brother's gaze turn to a middle-aged man who was lighting up his pipe with a match, puffing and puffing to get the thing going, smoke billowing into the room, just the way their father did. There were tears in his eyes. 'Whatever I did, I don't deserve this!'

'Are you going to appeal?'

'Certainly I am.' He looked up at the ceiling and sighed. 'I will have that whisky ... but I don't imagine it will do me any good at all.'

Compared with the worries he was shouldering, Peter's problems seemed pretty minor. Walter tried to help assemble his brother's case, scribbling notes on the back of an envelope, based on Peter's account, which at first he thought was hilariously funny. He was sympathetic regarding his situation, but the event itself! He appreciated the farcical, pantomime, slapstick humour and only began listening seriously when he began to appreciate the nature of school politics.

As it became quieter in the pub, they retreated to a small table in the corner each bearing another pint. Most workers would go off in the morning with a packed lunch, but a few better-off locals came in for a lunch-time pint, perhaps a sandwich from a limited range the public house had recently started to offer, or a pickled egg, and went back to work before the pub closed at half-past two. It was nearly closing-time when a voice caught Peter's attention.

'One more for the road then,' he called to the barman, searching deep for coins in his trouser pocket. 'I'm celebratin' today!'

The whiskery barman nodded. 'What's that then, Tommy?'

'My girl. Nicola. Left school and got 'erself a job. All grown up, she is.'

'That's good. Big step.'

'Left a few days earlier than the missus and I thought she would – thanks to that bloody arty-farty teacher at the Grammar!'

'Oh, yeah. I seen that in the Gazette.'

'Sent her home for summat she never done! Just like that! Blimey! These young teachers, still in nappies, wet behind the ears!' He sounded drunk, perhaps just bitter, possibly both.

Walter watched Peter get up, swaying slightly from the unusual quantity of alcohol now pulsing through his veins at some speed; he saw him put a hand on the man's shoulder and the man swing round to face him, beaming.

'Your dear daughter is not the only one to be leaving school early,' Peter yelled at the man, punching him like a Wild West outlaw in the Lone Ranger, smack on the jaw, with the full force that some adrenalin rush had uncannily bestowed upon him. For one surreal moment, Walter swore he could hear the William Tell Overture playing.

Things moved fast. Walter jumped up, unsure of what had just taken place, or why. The barman came round with a tweed-clad gentleman who appeared to be the proprietor and ordered Peter out or he'd call the police, muttering 'breach of the peace', 'respectable public house' and suchlike. The accosted man lay on the floorboards, dazed and unable to speak, with blood pouring bright scarlet from a cut lip.

Walter offered a handkerchief. 'I'm terribly sorry. My brother is under a lot of strain. Are you OK? Can I get you anything?' He stared earnestly into the man's eyes, really wanting to bring peace and calm to this sudden and unwarranted scene of violence. Was his younger brother having some kind of mental breakdown? Briefly raking through memories of childhood quarrels, he could not recall Peter ever striking another person. Peter was, if anything, the gentle, artistic one, whereas he, the possibly over-confident firstborn, was the more volatile son, prone to scrapes, fits of temper and what their parents would describe as 'outlandish behaviour'.

The rather pitiful victim, apparently Tommy, offered him a glassy stare, as if the assault had not quite registered in his brain and he was puzzled at his present predicament. He sat up slowly and raised the handkerchief to his mouth. Walter helped him to his feet and he stood, clutching a chair and wobbling like a baby taking its first steps.

'Can you … just go out and put a note on the windscreen of me taxi.'

'What – you have a taxi coming for you?'

He shook his head, '*My* taxi – Morris 10. Lady is due to go to her daughter's house in Guildford. Regular, every week. She'll be coming here any minute, but I don't feel so much like it now, bleeding as I am.' He rubbed his jaw.

'Do you feel faint?' asked Walter, somewhat torn, wondering where Peter was now. Should he stay or go after his brother? He tried to catch the attention of the barman, who was now taking a couple of quick last orders before closing-time. He came across once he'd rung up the till.

'Does your mate here need stitches?' he asked Walter.

'Er .. he's not my friend. I …' *I am the brother of the lunatic who did this*, he stopped himself from saying. 'I just happened to be here. I don't think so. From my childhood, I seem to remember lips leak blood like a pig's bladder … I mean … well, you know.'

'Tommy? You OK?'

Tommy nodded ruefully. 'That weasel twerp getting so aeriated was the teacher who sent our Nicola home. I seen a picture of him somewhere. Wait till I get word to the headmaster about this!'

7

The girls began by drawing up a list of friends they wanted to invite, first from school which was easy, then they began to consider others they vaguely knew and wanted to know better. This proved to be more of a challenge.

'Girls at the salon,' suggested Nicola who, Alison observed, had made herself very comfortable, curled up on a chintzy armchair in her parents' lounge. As hostess, she knew it was important to make her guests feel at ease, so she was pleased, both with herself and her friends.

Alison wondered what hairdressers would be like to talk to and did nothing to hide her doubts. 'But what are they like?' She had, after all, never been in a hairdressing salon.

'They're fun – and they've helped me settle in. I like them ...'

'Are they much older than us, though?'

'Mm. Well, Mrs Armitage is married ...'

'Obviously.' Alison rolled her eyes.

'She's the manager but still quite young. Rosemary is engaged but Barbara is just a year older than me.'

'Perhaps we could ask Barbara then – I think I remember her. She's a bit ...'

Nicola tilted her head, waiting for Alison to finish. 'A bit what? A bit common for the likes of you? You're such a snob, do you know that, Alison?'

Alison bit her lip; she just couldn't imagine hairdressers, as she imagined them with their hairspray and sloppy accents, coming into her parents' home for social reasons, but perhaps she should be open to new ideas. Would they mind, she wondered?

Molly interjected, 'I bet they're all really pretty and have lovely hair!'

Alison sighed at this pointless remark.

Nicola considered this. 'Yes, they are I suppose. Maybe …
well, who else?'

Alison gave Molly a sly smile. Well done, little Molly;
young hairdressers, with their glossy nails and high-heels,
would be fierce competition for the boys they were going to
invite.

'We must make sure we have an even number of boys and
girls – by the way,' said Alison, scanning the list she had made.
'Julian may have a few friends we don't know about.'

She thought about the Gazette reporter with his *lapis lazuli*
eyes and cheeky smile and was aware of a slight thump in her
chest, but he was too old, would have a girl already, probably
long since married … she felt herself blush and hoped the
others hadn't noticed her burning cheeks. How would she
explain that? She turned away from them, pretending to look
out of the window at a sparrow and blue-tit pecking on the
bird-table.

'This is quite hard … we don't want boys or girls who'd
make us look even younger than we are …' Nicola pointed
out.

'But it might make us seem older,' suggested Molly. 'As if
we regularly mix with these adults, older friends. People
probably don't think like that, anyway.'

They returned to the task, trying to think of neighbours,
old friends from Girl Guides, the Church and primary school
who had drifted out of touch, finally ending up with a motley
list of forty.

'You know, I think that's enough,' said Alison, looking
around the house a little doubtfully now, imagining these
rooms full of jazzy music, cigarette smoke, people jiving and
… whatever else might happen. She supposed her parents
wouldn't mind in the least; after all it was the kind of thing
they did often. They were great party-people; in fact on that
very evening they would be at the Devonish *soirée*, although
Julian and she were never included in such shenanigans.

'I could make some invitations if you like,' suggested
Molly. 'Perhaps do a little drawing on each one.'

'What sort of drawing?' asked Nicola, doubtfully. 'Kittens
and daisy-chains tied up in pink ribbon bows?' Alison was not

sure she liked the way Nicola took the mickey out of little Molly. It was decent of her to make the offer, after all.

'Well, if you like …'

Nicola snorted. 'I think maybe some bottles, glasses, cigarettes, sausages on sticks might be better …'

'Oh yes, I see. All right then. I'll do that. Thanks Nicola.'

The sun came out and they went out into the long garden that extended maybe a hundred yards, where it backed onto woodland and heath. The herbaceous borders, displaying a feast of colour, were initially and keenly planned by her father and now, with barely a square inch of soil showing, were maintained by a gardener, an ex-soldier who had been injured during the war and walked with a limp. The warm air had that summer smell, pollen-dusted bees buzzed in and out of the resplendent bright pink hollyhocks, lupins, foxgloves and delphiniums, while tortoiseshell butterflies fluttered around the spikes of a buddleia bush.

Lying like the three hands of a clock-face, on a tartan rug spread out on the mossy grass beneath a rowan tree, they were squinting up through the delicately splayed out foliage, dappled sunlight flickering across their faces. A distant ice-cream van was playing Greensleeves; they could faintly hear the rhythmic churn of a lawn-mower and a nearby blackbird trilling its heart out. Otherwise, it was peaceful. The house was tucked away along a driveway about half a mile from the village green with just one near neighbour.

Alison then fetched lemon barley drinks and the other two sat up as she handed round a tin of broken biscuits. 'You know what we said about not having any secrets?' Nicola and Molly nodded. 'I think we should get any secrets out now, don't you? It's part of the bonding process.'

The other two frowned at her as if she had spoken in a foreign language.

'Mmm. OK. You mean confessions,' agreed Nicola, with a wicked smile. 'Are you a virgin? Alison, you go first.' She was suppressing a giggle, Alison could see. *I didn't ask you here to be mocked,* she felt like saying. She wanted to tell them that was her business and retain an air of mystery, but realised she was *hoist by her own petard*, a metaphor she had recently come across and seemed pleasingly apt.

'It depends what you mean by virgin,' she stalled.

'I think we all know what 'virgin' means!' cried Nicola, laughing, and Alison wondered if Mrs Brown, who could now be heard clipping her lawn edges in the adjacent garden, had caught that.

'What about using a tampon? I mean …' I bet Molly hasn't cottoned on to Tampax yet, thought Alison.

'Don't be silly,' said Nicola.

Molly looked away, her cheeks turning a delicate, marshmallow pink, but she then turned and spoke, as if she genuinely wanted to answer the question posed by Alison. 'I think it means have we had 'sexual intercourse' and of course we haven't, have we? We're not married, or engaged and we don't even have boyfriends.'

'How come you're such a know-all?' said Nicola. Alison gave Nicola a black look as Nicola laughed at Molly's expense. 'Are you so sure we don't have boyfriends?'

Alison and Molly stared at Nicola.

'I've had loads of boyfriends – and a few times I did come close … er, well, you know, it can be … anyway, always remembered my Mum's warning words. She says we're all very fertile in our family – get in the family way just like that,' she snapped her fingers 'and I should keep my legs crossed. Not that I have any brothers or sisters …' Nicola stopped to consider this for a moment, as if it had not struck her before that this warning did not quite add up. How fertile was her Mum, if she'd only had one baby?

Molly was looking at her wide-eyed and open-mouthed.

Alison raised her eyebrows. 'She actually says that?'

'Course she does. What does *your* Mum say?'

'She once explained about what goes on in the bedroom and rubber johnnies and something else she says you can use when you're married and all that … and she read somewhere that, in America that is, there's a new pill you can take that stops you *ever* getting pregnant …'

Nicola's jaw dropped. 'She must be joking. How could that work? Sounds like witchcraft!' she scoffed.

'Mother does not joke like that. It was in a scientific journal. Anyway, she said it's best to wait if at all possible, I think that's what she said. So of course, I will. I mean there's no point in risking an unwanted baby is there?'

Nicola smirked. 'No. No point at all, Alison. Very sensible.'

'I mean, that would be just terrible! How could anyone be so stupid?' reinforced Alison.

'A sprog! That would be the end of life, as far as I'm concerned,' reflected Nicola. 'D'you remember that girl who was up the duff when she was only thirteen? She went to a home for unmarried mothers and I don't think she was ever heard of again.'

Alison nodded sagely. 'That was just frightful. My parents kept saying 'she's just a child', and 'how the parents could let that happen was beyond understanding' and that kind of thing. And her parents turned their back on her, turned her out, I mean, didn't they?'

'Yes, she had her kid adopted and she never saw it after that. Mind you, I'd think she'd be relieved. My Mum knows a nurse who works at the hospital ...' Nicola turned to Molly. 'You're quiet, little Miss ...'

'Please don't keep calling me that. I get enough teasing at home. I'm not really that quiet, you know, not really, if I'm given a chance to speak and someone actually listens. Anyway, I don't know this girl you're talking about. If you're *interested*, I am certainly a virgin, but I was kissed a couple of times.'

'Same boy?' asked Nicola, biting into two biscuits together, with a snap.

'No.'

'Proper kisses?'

Molly giggled. 'I suppose so. I was on holiday in Littlehampton with the family – it's quite good there for wheelchairs, nice and flat, and anyway, one evening I went out with my cousin Rose to the funfair, but I was only thirteen and the boy, well both of them, ... I mean, neither of them had a clue what they were doing. It just put me off. It was ... ugh! Disgusting, actually.' She paused as if she had just bitten into a lemon, as the other two hung on her words, waiting for more details, but none came. 'What about you, Alison?'

'I'll tell you when something happens. Maybe. If we're still friends, that is.'

Nicola gave her a playful thump. 'You can't just skate round it. We promised to stay friends through thick and thin for ever, and ... no secrets. Whatever we say, or confess to each other, we won't say a dicky-bird to anyone else.'

'It sounds like marriage vows! For better, for worse ...'

'Yes, it does and that's the deal. A kind of marriage between the three of us – with no secrets.'

'I wonder if our parents have secrets – from each other, I mean,' said Alison, pensively, thinking about her mother and how little she knew about her, or how she and her father met in the first place and what she did all day in London. So *many* secrets! These things just never came up in conversation, somehow; it must be because she never asked. She had heard somewhere that often people who had lived through the war, especially those who had fought, did not like to talk about their experiences. They preferred to draw a line, starve their memories of oxygen, and move on with their lives to a brighter future.

'Well some parents do, obviously,' said Nicola. 'They have affairs, cheat and what have you, don't they?'

'In films and stories, not in real life so much though, do they?' said Molly. 'Anyway, they don't go on having, well, you know, doing ... once they've finished with having babies ...'

Nicola hooted with laughter and hugged Molly. 'Oh Molly, you're so funny. Do you think that a man and a woman only kiss and canoodle just to have babies?'

'There is the passion and the heat of the moment thing, isn't there?' commented Alison. 'But I'm sure that all died out long ago with our parents ...'

Molly and Nicola nodded in agreement. There seemed to be no doubt on that score. After all, who could possibly imagine ... no it didn't even bear thinking about, thought Alison with a shudder.

'Anyway what is your secret wish?' asked Nicola, who seemed to want to move on. Alison wondered if she did not want to be quizzed on how far she had gone with her several boyfriends. Had she done more than kissing? She would certainly worm it out of her at some point, she decided, still feeling a little peeved for almost being made to look foolish by Nicola's direct line of questioning on the virginity issue.

A contemplative silence fell, each of them desperately wanting to come up with the best, funniest, most imaginative, the most enviable wish of all.

Nicola was the first to speak up; Alison suspected she probably already had her secret wish prepared; that was why she asked the question.

Alison said, 'Well, we already know about your dream ambition in hairdressing, so that doesn't count.'

'I know. I have a lot of secret wishes. Firstly, I hope to make enough money to buy my family a posh house, like this one,' and Nicola looked around the garden and house as she said this, an unusually solemn expression on her face. 'Do you realise how lucky you are, living here, Alison? It's beautiful. We'll have a smashin' party ...'

Alison had never really thought herself lucky; it was very quiet, dull and empty most of the time, at least when her parents weren't there. She shrugged.

Nicola continued. 'That's for the future. But I do want to marry a very rich, handsome man and have two boys and two girls.'

'That's not very original,' said Alison, absently squashing ants that had crept onto the rug, scurrying around for crumbs.

Molly considered this. 'But you would be looking after your four children, so how could you be running your successful salon at the same time?'

'Oh, I'd give that up by then, of course ...' Nicola had clearly not thought this thing through or done the maths. Alison imagined it could take many years to grow a hairdressing shop that could possibly buy her parents a house, but she could see there was no point today in shattering secret dreams so she kept mum. Mothers did not have to stay at home and be housewives, she certainly knew that, but this was not part of Nicola's plan. 'Your turn, Alison.'

Why me, thought Alison? Why not Molly? 'It's really no secret. My wish is to get a good degree and then see what the world can offer me. I'm not sure I want to have children, but if I find a man who … makes me … well, you know, want to have his babies …' She paused, feeling awkward trying to explain, having a somewhat soured view of marriage since overhearing her mother's memorable quote from Dylan Thomas; a character in *Portrait of the Artist as a Young Dog* referred to marriage as 'legalised monogamous prostitution' and her parents had laughed, admitting Mr Humphries, on his hobby horse, perhaps had a point! 'And if we get married then I suppose I would have to get a nanny or someone to take care of them. I do want a career, though, but something …' something, she thought, that has a touch of glamour that I can tell people about, that others will envy and admire me for, apart from her parents. 'Something that will make me happy and really excited every working day.'

Nicola and Molly were gawping in astonishment.

'Well,' said Nicola, 'that's certainly different. A nanny! I thought you had to have blue-blood in your veins to think like that. But you don't want to be a model or a film-star then? Or an air hostess? You're so good at languages, although … you'd have to spruce up a bit.' She said this with a straight face but Alison felt she was being made to look self-important and pompous and she regretted her high-flown confession. 'So what *will* you be? An exciting librarian who takes her spectacles off and dances around the bookshelves, singing *Volare* or *When Will I be Loved?*'

The all laughed. 'You could be a teacher or … work in retail?' suggested Molly.

Alison blinked in horror. 'What? Work in a shop?' Did she mean serving behind a shop counter?

'You can climb a proper career-ladder in retail, so I've read,' said Molly, and the other two looked at her with some respect; she sounded knowledgeable. 'Become a buyer, or manage a department. There's all kinds of openings. Actually,' and she paused as if she was about to reveal she had just won a million on the football pools, 'I've just got a holiday job in the baby-clothes and wool shop in the village. I'll get odd balls of wool free as well, although I just need the money at the moment. That's my main reason for doing it. My parents have stopped my pocket-money.'

'You're lucky to even get pocket-money!' scoffed Nicola, and Alison glared at her for such an insensitive comment.

'That must be hard. Anyway, good for you, but we're getting away from the subject, now, which is secret wishes,' Alison pointed out. 'Your go, Molly.'

'Make it a bit more interesting than we've heard so far,' urged Nicola, with a bored sigh.

'We seem to be just chuntering on about our ambitions in life after leaving school. I don't know what I want for a job, I have absolutely no sort of inkling as to that, but I do know that my secret wish is … to feel loved, really loved. Do you know what I mean?'

Nicola and Alison looked at her solemnly. The mood changed. Nicola reached out and squeezed her arm and Alison felt a strange prickle on the inside of her eyelids.

Early that evening, before their parents got home from work, Julian heard from Alison about the plan for a party. She showed him the list.

'Do you think Mum and Dad will approve of this?' asked Julian, thinking that he might get closer to some girls he had fancied since he was fourteen but had never had the courage to ask out to the pictures or something. There were so many of them, but they always seemed older than him somehow, even though he knew they were the same age; he felt his heart beat notch up slightly and was suddenly alert and open to ideas, as mind pictures of pretty girls floated and flashed across his eyes.

'They're always going to parties so how can they say no? They never say no, do they?'

'But we've never asked for anything quite like this …' he faltered. Why was he being so cautious? He didn't want to be the one to pour cold water on this idea.

Alison interrupted him anyway. 'I was thinking that, to play safe, we could hold it the evening when they are going to the big Devonish do. Brilliant, wizard idea, wouldn't you say?' Alison smiled broadly, a triumphant look on her face. She must have picked up the word 'wizard' from one of his friends; she was working hard to win him over.

'That does sound like quite a good wheeze,' he admitted reluctantly, wishing he had come up with it himself. He was thinking about that Nicola, the tarty blonde, but he knew full well his parents would not approve of her. They really would look down their noses at a girl from the council estate and, with her fluffed up peroxide hair, they would think she was a cloth-head, he knew that, and yet she was the girl he would most like to take out. The thought of it made things in his trousers slightly stir. 'Are you going to tell them, though?'

'What do you think?' Now she was passing the decision back to him.

He twisted his mouth and bit his lip as he weighed up the pros and cons. 'There's the risk they might say no, but if we do it and then they find out, they might be hopping mad and forbid any parties in the future ...'

'But at least we'll have had one good party. If they say we can't, then future parties might be off limits anyway.'

'Maybe. Or they might just think we're too young at the moment ...' He sighed, wanting this bash so much, wanting to eradicate any possible obstacles.

'Do you think, there's a chance we could do it, clear up before they get home ...?' Alison chuckled and Julian cast an amused glance at her. It was unlike his sister. 'Remove all traces ...?'

'You've been reading too much Agatha Christie,' teased Julian.

'I don't think they'd actually be angry, do you?' asked Alison.

'No. No I don't think they would.'

'Shall we go ahead then? Shall we?' Alison was shaking his arm, as if to gee him up.

Julian was excited now, but tried not to show it. 'All right then. Let me see that list again.'

Their parents were hardly ever there and, although they were interested in their activities up to a point, they rarely asked probing questions about what they got up to in their absence and, strangely, he and Alison had never really abused this privilege of being left to their own devices.

No question, they were a lovely family. Most evenings and weekends, the four of them would play games like Monopoly, cards or chess; in the summer, croquet, cricket, swimming, bike rides, drive to the south coast for picnics and strawberry ice-cream. Gordon had spent every spare minute one weekend about ten years ago, building a tree house for them; and on rainy Sundays they had a companionable time sorting out the family stamp collection whilst listening to the radio.

Harriet and Alison would talk about books more than anything; they had both recently read and discussed the new novel *To Kill a Mockingbird* written by an American writer, a woman by the odd name of Harper Lee. It made them both think a lot about people of different colour and how white people react to them; especially as a coloured family had moved into Appley Green and some villagers found it hard to accept them.

They would go to a concert or play violin duets, while Gordon and Julian might go fishing together, man and boy. Two weeks of the summer holiday were usually spent at a boarding house in Devon, but there was talk of them buying a caravan so they could all do some touring around Britain. Sometimes they might watch the television as a family, perhaps Brains' Trust or Panorama and lively debates always followed afterwards.

Julian and Alison often overheard their parents' discussing politics and current affairs, rather miserable events around the world and from such discussions they were excluded, thankfully. Overall, they were a close family, and it was true their parents had never refused them anything – like clothes, books or records. Perhaps, though, they had always known what would be an unreasonable request, such as frivolous games, fizzy drinks or a colour television. Like most children, Alison and Julian saw nothing very unusual in their upbringing; although now as teenagers they began to see that others were raised differently from them.

Aunts and uncles had been known to comment on how *sensible* the twins were for their age, whatever their age happened to be at the time, but for how much longer? This is what the sensible twins were both wondering.

8

As he tucked into a top-notch, full English breakfast, Walter observed the other clients at the Hunters' Lodge Hotel, now enjoying porridge or cereal, eggs, bacon, perhaps a kipper, and toast with pale farmhouse butter and English marmalade.

He had noticed in his room that the wardrobe, as well as the drawers, smelled of lavender; a little hand-sewn bag of it attached to each wooden hanger, thoughtfully done. It has a genteel, almost colonial, air about it, this particular hotel, thought Walter; and the mature gardens, with their eucalyptus and monkey puzzle trees, as well as common rhododendrons and silver birch, were really, really splendid. Of course, it was the most prestigious accommodation Appley Green could muster and staying there would seem freakishly extravagant to anyone not used to London prices. Yet, he thought, the shabby carpets were pre-war, the dark oak panelling was oppressive and the staff worked with as much enthusiasm as bored, work-weary clerks in a local council office. He felt like bursting into song just to see the shock on their faces.

He felt out of place. Tonight, he decided, he would go out alone and have a night to remember in Appley Green! He had no idea what it had to offer these days, but the locals must do something other than watch the confounded goggle-box, or 'idiot's lantern' as his father called it! He wouldn't expect a 'gentlemen's club' but there must be something of the old ways left, where you could have a sing-song or play darts. If this was successfully achieved, if he managed to blot out the less salubrious elements of his life, then he would seriously consider extending his stay. Last night Peter and he had chewed over the idea of buying a weekend cottage they could share and let friends use when they were away. They could probably get one for less than a couple of thousand quid, a sum that could be beyond the reach of most locals. Peter was just lodging at the moment over in Cowslip Lane and he was dilly-dallying now about what to do, where to go, how to earn his rent. Poor chap! He felt for him. Bit of rough justice done there, he suspected.

As boys, they were brought up in the small town of Rye in Sussex, where they acquired a love of painting; so picturesque, but it could be bleak and cut-off in winter. Walter had always liked this village, Appley Green, where their mother and father retired to years ago and kept pretty much to themselves. They used to have springer spaniels and a golden labrador, and he had heartbreakingly fond family memories of walking around the heath on Sunday mornings before tucking in to one of his mother's tasty roast dinners. Theresa had embraced its charm too and said she was always sad to leave such a welcoming place. Appley Green could not supply the salty, bracing ozone of the Sussex coast, but it did offer fresh, clean air that filled the lungs and your heart with life and hope; and London, where he made his living, was not so very far away.

He spent an uncomfortable morning on the residents' telephone, in a booth off the lounge. He ran up a considerable bill in a long conversation with his secretary, dictating letters and memos, speaking at such a slow place he thought he might fall asleep in the process. It might have been easier to write them up and send them by Royal Mail, but he wanted to get fresh ideas off his chest so they could be typed up within the day. Basically he imported cheap raw materials from the Far East, used cheap labour in certain quarters of London, or sometimes abroad, and sold goods at a vast profit to both upmarket retailers and the smaller up-and-coming boutiques; such a simple concept, yet his expanding profits never failed to surprise him.

Since he had faced the trial, some business liaisons had been stretched to the limit. People who did not know him well on a personal level, but believed themselves to be well informed through newspaper reports, tended to believe that there was no smoke without fire. After all, it was the woman's word against his, simple as that and insufficient evidence did not satisfy everyone as to his innocence.

Tonight he would paint Appley Green red! He chuckled to himself as he said this, needing badly to tell someone. He felt suddenly very lonely. Should he go alone or call for his brother? Peter was right when he said he was not the best of company; for a night on the tiles did he really want his needy face, his regrets, his worries for the future, all capable of dragging him down like a lead weight around his neck? Peter would use him as a sounding board for what he should do with the rest of his life; and whether he should keep fighting against some injustice that he, Walter, had not yet fully grasped. Then, just when the evening could not get more depressing if it tried, he would move onto their dying father and the fact that their own lives could be cut short by the same affliction.

After a pleasant enough luncheon at the hotel — a watery tomato soup, game pie with roast potatoes and broad beans, followed by a raspberry mousse that appeared to have pieces of real raspberries in it, unless the seeds had been added for effect — Walter was ready to plan the night of his life! He thought of times he had spent in the clubs of Soho, in Hong Kong, in the bars of Saigon; business trips spanning maybe fifteen years, even after he had married Theresa. He retreated to the hotel bar for a post-prandial double-whisky before setting off. Serving behind the hotel bar was a lovely looking girl with an intelligent look to her aquamarine eyes; yet innocent looking, perhaps working as a holiday job. Did she look about twelve because he was getting older? This kind of delusion can happen, so his mate Derek had told him. 'They're more likely than you think to be *older* than sixteen, you know.' Derek had winked at him.

'Now then,' he said, lighting up, 'What's a young beauty like you doing in a dreary place like this?' He liked the fine soft angora jumper she was wearing, with a matching cardigan loose around her shoulders; her small breasts stood out like two cones. The twinset was the pearly pink you would see on a baby girl.

'Serving you with whisky, sir,' she said with a gentle smile. 'Is there anything else you need now?'

He smiled at her sweetness; the tortoiseshell band she wore around her glossy chestnut brown hair reminded him a little of Theresa's style. Modern but tasteful. 'No thank you, my dear,' he said, 'unless ... there is something perhaps. Are you from Appley Green? Do you know it well?'

'My family moved here when I was eleven, so I know it quite well.'

'Ah, so how many years ...?'

'Lived here about six years ... yes, so I know it ... mm ... quite well, yes.'

Derek was right. She was older than she looked! 'What do people do here in the *evening*? Where can you recommend for a good time? Know what I mean?' She blushed; how beguiling! 'What's your name, by the way?'

'My name is Josephine.'

'Beautiful name. Are you partly French then, *Josephine*?'

'No – I don't think so. Please excuse me, sir, I have some customers to serve.' She moved away and he hoped she might come back. He also wondered for how long she would be working tonight.

He had finished his drink and was wondering whether to have another, when she suddenly reappeared, smiling. Perhaps he would have some delightful company this evening. He quietly congratulated himself on finding such a jewel and not yet left the premises! Still had that old magic.

'You were asking ... There's a small picture place in Bloomstock, but Appley Green just has the village hall where clubs and choirs meet up, rummage sales, that kind of thing. It's a converted old barn on the road that leads to Farnham, about a mile out, in fact. The noticeboard there will tell you what's on – square dancing, beetle drives, and oh, there's a bowling green close by.'

Walter groaned. This was not going so well now. 'Do you have a local paper?' Then he spotted a Gazette on a window-sill. 'Ah! I'll take a look.'

'I'm sorry there's ...'

'Please,' he said, turning, smoothly reaching to put a hand over one of hers. 'It's hardly your fault that the village doesn't throb with theatres or nightclubs.' She hadn't pulled away her hand. 'I was wondering what time you finished. Perhaps you could walk with me to the village hall.' Their eyes met.

'I could ask my parents.'

Walter swallowed. 'Ah. Are they staying here?'

She threw back her pretty little head, her laughter taking him by surprise. 'Well you could say that, I suppose. They own the hotel.'

'Oh, I see. How marvellous,' replied Walter, deciding not to order another drink, but rather to take his leave.

Still unsure where he and the evening were going, he emerged into welcome sunshine, its warmth caressing his cheeks. He strolled pensively down to the hub of the village where, every summer weekend could be heard the thwack of leather on willow, followed by cheers and claps of spectators carried on the heath-scented breeze. In early summer, Romany Gypsies stopped awhile on their way to strawberry, potato and hop picking in the fields of Kent, to graze their piebald horses and cook up some kind of delicious-smelling stew in a smoky haze outside their wagons. As the sun went down, they sometimes sang and step-danced and seemed very happy with life. Around mid-summer, a Mop or travelling fair turned up, suddenly packing the village green with bustle and colour; hurdy-gurdy music, sticky pink candy floss on sticks, coconut-shies seducing children with glittering prizes of teddy-bears and cheap ornaments, swing-boats filled with shrieking children, gilded horses bobbing and gliding endlessly round and round, and lads showing off on bumping, buzzing dodgems. Then, one morning, it would all be gone, with not a shred of evidence; children must have thought it had all been a bewitching dream.

A young couple were sitting on one of the benches, their baby in a smart cream and black coach built pram. He suspected most married couples stopped going out in the evening and having a good time once children came along. He did not know what it was like to be a father. He leaned against a tree, as he lit up a cigarette, and casually watched the man lift the baby out of the pram. It was a little boy, dressed in a Cambridge blue romper suit; just able to stand on his chubby, wobbly legs and wanting to chase after a plump white duck that had waddled over to them from the nearby pond, looking hopeful. His father held the child's reins tightly to keep him safe; he could hear the faintest tinkle of tiny bells. Walter felt his throat tighten, momentarily overcome by a great sadness that stabbed and ached like a physical pain. The memory flooded back of that darkest of days in the hospital when Theresa, just twenty three years old, had lost her fight for life in childbirth, along with their tiny baby boy. Ten years ago and still he felt the sorrow of that double loss and was very unsure of what kind of woman could ever fill the void. Since being hoodwinked by that floosy three years ago he had tried to keep out of trouble, but he craved the wonder, warmth and soft whisperings of a woman.

With great presence of mind, he calmed his grief, bringing himself back to the present. Now that Peter and he knew about the genes they were carrying, he must kiss a forlorn goodbye to any hopes of having a family now; it was too late, he thought, too damn late. Some months after Theresa had died, he thought that perhaps one day, when he had finished grieving for her and wanting her every minute of every day, he might find someone else who could be the mother of his children. He might have even found someone to love, who could love him back. But how would any of that now be fair on a woman? How could it be fair on any child, or its mother, if he may have only ten years or so left to live, perhaps less? The indications were unclear, but it seemed that his lifespan was likely to be cut short; their paternal grandfather had not lived to an old age. He and Peter were still coming to terms with the rawness of it, the injustice, the shock, whilst also facing the imminent loss of their father, who meant a great deal to them both – but meanwhile, he thought, stubbing out the fag end with the sole of his tooled leather brogue, he was going to make the most of every day he had left. But what did he want? It would take him a while to work this out.

He decided to avoid The Duke's Arms where Peter had had a moment of apparent insanity the other day; he feared he might be recognised, remembered, questioned, cautioned - and he could do without that. To be noticed was the last thing he wanted, for he knew he might spend the rest of his life looking over his shoulder for people who still held him to be guilty of rape.

As he swung his gaze around to the other side of the Green, he spotted the rather drab-looking inn, The Fox and Rabbit. It had always looked tumbledown, with its crumbling air of antiquity, beams and low ceilings; he did not remember his parents ever going there or mentioning it; he imagined it had a musty, spit-and sawdust taproom with a raggedy dartboard, maybe some bar billiards, and that would be about it. He knew from student days in Cambridge, though, that with the right company, such basics could provide surprisingly good fun.

He would see whether this was a fair judgement; perhaps it held hidden, more glamorous pleasures within. He pictured a bosomy barmaid, licking her wet, scarlet lips, a raven-haired beauty, who would flutter her eyelashes at him as she listened to his troubles; he imagined softly glowing lights, a selection of fine cigars; a tenor saxophone, smooth and low, carousers both seated and standing gently swaying to its pulsing rhythm. Friendly people with smiling faces would welcome him, 'Walter! How wonderful to see you! How are you, mate? Where have you been? We missed you!' He smiled at his own wilful imagination; but perhaps this, aside from the bodacious maiden behind the bar, could happen in time, if he settled here and became part of the community. For the remainder of his life, he wanted to belong, to feel at home, for without much family, he would need friends; yes, he would need trustworthy, genuine friends to support him through what lay ahead. Peter was talking about travelling so he would not be around; business partners could become pals, but just as likely to stab you in the back and, as their manager, he could not get too close to them. He did not believe in mixing business with pleasure; or someone would get hurt. It was hard to sack a chum.

He unlatched and pushed the door labelled Saloon, stood still a moment as his eyes adjusted to the gloom. It was about time for mid-day last orders, yet in here it seemed like the middle of the night. He looked around and walked slowly to the bar, all the while noting that there were about half a dozen people, all men apart from one girl. She was slender, too young to be in a pub, a bottle-blonde with thick eye make-up; but he knew he routinely underestimated the age of girls. This young woman was of slight build, but could be seventeen. She was in a public house with an older man for one thing; and for this reason, he did not really know why he was even pondering on this. She was taken, spoken for. He assumed she was a girl who 'was no better than she ought to be', as he recalled a favourite expression of a maiden aunt who lived far away, somewhere in Yorkshire.

He soon struck up a conversation of sorts with the landlord who consulted his watch and then swiftly served him, establishing that the weather had been wet, and surmising a possible improvement for folks going on their seaside summer holidays as, 'Gawd knows, we could all do with some sun.'

'So what do young people do for evening entertainment *here*?' Walter asked, sipping the foamy head of his real ale.

'What d'you mean by that, sir?' he replied, looking offended, as if Walter had criticised the entertainment value of his hostelry.

Walter sighed, feeling beaten. 'I mean the village. Sport, gaming, anything like that? Spot of dramatics? A band? I don't know, that's why I'm asking.' He shrugged, past caring.

The man was now looking insulted and Walter smiled politely as some kind of peace offering as he turned away to sit down. This was too much like hard work. In London, people serving usually made a little effort since their livelihood rather depended on a good *rapport* with their customers, but such a concept did not seem to have reached this particular barman. Walter began to think that if he were to live here he would want to go around changing things, people and their ways; it could be a very frustrating exercise. Is that how he wanted to spend the rest of his life? *The rest of his life …*

Suddenly, rather reminiscent of the other day in The Duke's Arms, there was a raised voice and a clattering sound; he swivelled to see what was going on. The man with the blonde had just slammed his chair into the table where she still sat and was storming out, leaving the young girl trembling and pink with embarrassment, staring down into her drink. She looked very vulnerable; he felt a compelling urge to save her from other men. Wipe that muck off her face and loosen that silly hairstyle, and there was a sweet little girl who needed help.

He ambled towards her, slightly unsteady on his feet. He imagined she might be in tears by now. As he came nearer, she looked up and stared at him, as if daring him to speak to her.

'Are you …?'

'Yes. Thank-you. I am.'

Walter wanted to laugh.

'I mean, are you all right? I wondered …'

'In what way 'all right'? Why would you want to know?' She narrowed her eyes and challenged him with a bold stare. 'What's it to you?'

Oh, this one had spirit! But she did not seem to want to talk, so perhaps he would leave her alone. Yet, he looked around; the other men were leering a little, as if waiting their chance.

'Do you need someone to take you home?'

The girl stood up, grabbed her drink, whatever it was, threw it over him and stormed out of the pub with strides as long as her slender legs could muster.

The men all laughed but beckoned him to go over, then were slapping him on the back. 'Worth a try, I suppose. If you knew her Dad you wouldn't have done that!'

Walter laughed, pleased to at least have triggered some sort of response, a sign of life. 'I was actually trying to see if she needed help.'

There were disbelieving looks all round. 'Pull the other one!' said one.

He good-naturedly put up a hand as if to fend off their teasing remarks. 'No. No, genuinely, she looked very young and her … friend … he seemed in a bit of a temper.'

9

Nicola chewed her bottom lip as she looked at the pathetic heap of clothes on her bed: an old plaid skirt, its pleats far from sharp; faded flowery cotton dresses that her mother had made and might easily wear herself; matching cardigans, all bobbly with matted armpits; and, frankly, not much else apart from the trews she had last Christmas; the yellow jumper she knitted herself and two blouses that her Mum had picked up from a jumble sale and altered.

She had been working now for a fortnight and each week had given her Mum a pound for her keep. She counted up what was left from her two wage packets and decided on her afternoon off she would go into Bloomstock and buy a pencil skirt and some bronze high-heels with pointed toes she'd had in her mind ever since she spotted them in the shoe shop window. Earning money was great.

She was meeting Martin from the little junk shop called *Antiques and Bric-a-Brac* next to the salon at eight o'clock; it had opened just recently and, with being neighbours, she had soon caught his eye. She felt very grown-up when he asked her if she would like to go with him to the Appley Green Theatre's production of *A Midsummer Night's Dream* on the common. 'It could be rather good,' he said, with a posh Surrey accent. 'Perfect setting for it and almost bang on midsummer. Or – it could be wet! I mean, if it rains …' He had this lovely smile and looked straight at her with trustworthy eyes. 'But it would be awfully nice if I had your company. You're so pretty, Nicola.' She had never had anyone speak like this to her. Think what Alison would say when she turned up at her party on the arm of this beautifully-turned out and well-spoken young man; imagine what her Mum and Dad would say! The nosy questions her Mum would have! He wasn't a boy – he was a man and a very handsome one at that. She was intrigued by him, too. Where had he come from and why was he selling dusty chests of drawers and moth-eaten squirrels like a barrow-boy?

But what should she wear tonight? Martin did seem a bit 'square' for his age; had a sort of classic look to him, black hair with a 'short back and sides' cut; always in a sports jacket, as if he might have modelled for a Littlewoods catalogue. What age was he, she wondered? He looked as if he could be over twenty; still not as old as that Steve, whom she never wanted to see again as long as she lived. When she said she didn't want to go out with him any more, she never expected a violent reaction like that. She felt stupid being left sitting there on her tod like a lemon in The Fox and Rabbit, and then in a couple of ticks, this perfect stranger waltzes up as bold as brass, trying to pick her up! The nerve! It made her furious just thinking about it. Would she ever tell her friends about that?

In fact, would she ever reveal the truth about boys she'd been out with? She couldn't believe how innocent Alison and Molly were! It was bordering on ignorant. They would be either shocked or very impressed with her experiences; perhaps a bit of both …

She rested on one heel, arms folded, regarding the dress with pink roses and a boat neckline. Although it was just too 'sweet', not her style at all, it could be the kind of frock he would like; at least it was mid-summery! Her white, plastic, really wide belt would cinch in her waist and make the skirt twirly and very girly. Checking her best pair of nylons for ladders, she hugged herself, feeling excited.

They had arranged to meet outside the shop where he worked and go from there. She didn't want him collecting her from home; she knew it was not an address to be proud of and didn't want to put a kibosh on this date first off.

Walter had decided to rid himself of Appley Green, thoroughly disheartened. He would drive to London, damn it, and find some bright lights, some life with a beating heart. With a look of thunder on his face, he strode out to his coupé and, as he put down the roof, heard a crunch of footsteps in the gravel behind him. He turned to see a grey-haired, distinguished-looking gent admiring his automobile, who most probably had just alighted from the sleek Rover parked a few yards behind him. It was, indeed, an object of some envy, an impressive piece of machinery by any standards and nobody knew that better than Walter himself.

'A handsome motor,' commented the well-groomed stranger, extending a hand in a forthright but friendly manner. Walter felt he should know who this person was, his face seemed familiar and he had an aristocratic bearing about him. 'Sir Matthew Phillips. Are you staying here long?'

They shook hands. 'Ah! Sir Matthew. I thought I recognised you but, forgive me, couldn't put a name to your face. How do you do. Walter Finchley.'

Just a fleeting frown appeared on the other man's face as he raised his chin and regarded him. Walter assumed he had made a *faux-pas* in not identifying such a local big shot at once.

'Of course, you are very well-known here in Appley Green and indeed ...' He tailed off, realising he was grovelling; it was not his usual style to be deferential.

'Not to worry at all. No, no.' There was a pregnant pause, as he stroked the gleaming chrome trim around a headlight. '*Finchley* you say?'

Walter swallowed. Had he read about the trial in the press?

'Yes, indeed. My parents used to live here. My father still does, but is now sadly in hospital, terminally ill. Mm. I'm here so I can offer some comfort and support in his last days.'

'So sorry to hear. Bad news, indeed. But d'you have other family here?' Walter could feel his stare now boring holes into his skull.

Walter considered this question. Did he mean at the hotel? 'I'm here alone – actually.'

Sir Matthew seemed more relaxed. 'So are you off to see your father now?' he enquired, his tone sympathetic.

'Actually, I've decided to take a spin back into London for a spot of night-life, which is a bit disappointing. I was hoping ...'

'But tonight! You can't miss the most wonderful thespian production of the year!'

Walter gave him a nonplussed look. 'Oh! What might that be?'

'Amateur dramatics! Don't get too excited, but every year, they always put on a damn good show. Midsummer Night's Dream. Never say Appley Green doesn't know how to give you a good time!'

Walter hesitated. He did love the theatre, but would this really cut the mustard? Village outdoor dramatics?

'If you want to get a feel of village life, you couldn't do better.'

'You're very persuasive, sir. What time and where is this amazing performance?'

'That's the spirit! Come with me! My wife's just coming. We can walk together.'

If he were aware of the scandal that clung to him like a family of leeches, he would not be so friendly, Walter assured himself as he felt his anxiety fade.

A string quartet was playing something a little like Mendelssohn, as Walter found himself sitting between Sir Matthew and his wife. Another couple they must have arranged to meet, now sitting to the left of his wife, were briefly introduced to him. He felt uncomfortable for apparently coming between man and wife, but they both seemed perfectly at ease with this.

'You can call me Victoria,' she said. 'It'll make a pleasant change from Lady Phillips, or Sir Matthew's wife. Sometimes this form of address ... you know it makes one feel somewhat of an accessory. Women have to suffer his kind of thing, as I'm sure you know. You look like a man of the world, Walter. Am I right?'

Unsure of the response she was seeking, he shrugged; embarrassment was an emotion he rarely encountered in any given situation but he suspected it may have caught up with him.

'It's so nice to meet someone new. You are new aren't you? To Appley Green? Tell me a bit about yourself.' Her oblique glance might have been seen as flirtatious, had Sir Matthew not been sitting on his right-hand side reminding him without a shadow of doubt that this lady was a well-bred, mature, married woman whose life in society was likely to appear in *The Tatler* or *The Lady*. She was of course just showing natural courtesy towards a stranger.

He cleared his dry throat, wishing he had a double whisky in his hand, then reached in his jacket pocket for the silver cigarette case loaded prior to his intended jaunt into London, and offered them to ... Lady Phillips. She smiled graciously and took one.

He explained his connection with the village; his brother, his father.

'We can help you find the perfect place! Word of mouth and so on. I'll make it my new mission in life. We ladies do like something to get our teeth into, now and then, rather than existing simply for domestic or ornamental purposes – and, of course, the other thing.' She smiled and he caught a whiff of what he recognised was Tweed perfume; it was a scent he associated with a not particularly favourite ex-lover, but somehow seemed better exuding from ... Victoria.

Walter was not sure how to respond to this without either contradicting or offending; so he threw her what he hoped was a charming, understanding smile and kept things simple.

'Thank you. What a generous offer,' he said.

'Now then, Walter, give me an idea of the kind of dwelling you have in mind. Describe to me what you *desire*.' She raised her eyebrows and he realised he had not imagined her suggestive manner; he had never met a mature married woman who was quite so ... so obvious, so bold. This was a novelty and he had no idea what to do with it.

The music petered out as an actor approached a Heath-Robinson stage, a platform sheltered beneath a spreading cedar tree, with dozens of glowing lanterns suspended from its deeply dark, mysterious branches. Theseus the Duke of Athens began, '*Now, fair Hippolyta, our nuptial hour Draws on apace. Four happy days bring in Another moon; but, O, methinks, how slow This old moon wanes! She lingers my desires ...*'

Walter turned to Sir Matthew who was still engaged in earnest whispers with a lady to his right. Then a respectful hush descended so that the troupe could be heard.

Walter's attention was caught over to the right of the stage by a stunning silhouette of black trees, mostly Scots pine, on the skyline against pearly orange-pink waves of sunset. He wanted to nudge Victoria to share its short-lived beauty with her, but when he more discreetly turned towards her, he saw that she was already dreamily gazing at it. She met his look and smiled; such a little thing, of no real consequence, yet it seemed like a private, almost intimate, moment between the two of them.

His glance then shifted a few degrees further to the right and he spotted the rather cheap-looking, but spirited, girl who had given him a dousing in The Fox and Rabbit. Even in the fast-fading dusky light, he recognised her profile, her hairstyle. How interesting! Surprising such a girl might be here; but there again, Sir Matthew had said this play was a chance to see the full gamut of villagers, or words to that effect. Appley Green … Hmm, its appeal was growing on him; these small, chance encounters were satisfying.

The girl was with another chap, who looked pretty clean-cut, well turned out, certainly not the lout who had walked out on her. Walter was genuinely pleased for her; they looked happy together, occasionally exchanging glances and little secret smiles. He envied them so much and felt that tightening in his throat again, but at that moment resolved that he would indeed find a second home in Appley Green and perhaps, in time, make it his first home. With perhaps only a few precious years left, priorities were fast shaking up in his head like the patterns in a kaleidoscope. Business was thriving, but did not represent the entirety of life itself. He would work to live, not live to work, and he would live life – to the full!

10

'Should we invite Edward Phillips?' asked Molly, and Nicola stared at her in disbelief, as if she had suggested asking the Pope.

Nicola and Alison had come round to her house; she decided that, if the trio were to hide nothing from each other, then they might as well meet her mother and see where she lived.

Alison's house, a relative mansion, had set the standard and Molly fretted over what the two of them would make of her parents' overlooked garden, small rooms, the trendy Fablon covered bookshelves – the ramps and odd alterations her father had made for a wheelchair indoors. She knew of housebound folk, confined to a bed or a chair, who had to make the best of it and stay put, but her father had done his best for his wife. Molly had swept and polished; made some fairy cakes, with a Viota mix to save time, and, as she decorated them with pink glacé icing topped with hundreds and thousands, her hands were shaking.

What she feared most was her mother asking them awkward questions or making remarks that were best left unsaid. She imagined the worst. Molly had no choice but to ask permission for them to come round one evening; after all she could scarcely let them in secretly via the tradesmen's entrance in the East wing! 'These are the girls who misbehaved at the school, like you?' her mother responded, predictably, in a 'let's get this quite clear' sort of tone. 'Hmm, the very same girls we told you not to talk to. They sound like trouble, but perhaps it's not a bad thing to meet them and …' Her voice petered out ominously. What? Give them a *piece of what for*? Advice? A good telling off? Hear their side of the story? What?

Once they arrived, together, she quickly introduced them to her parents and Susan who were mesmerised by *Double your Money* on the goggle-box, and took them upstairs to the bedroom she shared with Susan. Luckily David was out; so she didn't have to deal with his staring eyes and goofish remarks. It all seemed so pitiful compared with the lovely afternoon they had spent in Alison's garden; but it was drizzling outside and it would be pretty miserable sitting in deckchairs on their pocket-handkerchief sized back lawn.

'My sister will be coming to bed soon, so, I'm sorry but we won't have long.'

'We can always go in another room, though' replied Alison, who seemed genuinely puzzled as to what the problem was. Perhaps the kitchen, thought Molly, where they would be overheard and there was nowhere to sit? or David's room? She didn't think so, somehow.

Feeling the pressure of time, they got straight to the subject of the party, skipping whatever else might have been on their agenda.

So now they were considering Molly's audacious suggestion regarding Edward Phillips.

'We could ask him and make his evening a nightmare from hell,' suggested Nicola, with a wicked grin and a malicious gleam in her eyes.

Alison frowned. 'He … he's not so bad, really, you know.'

Molly looked at her, 'But surely you of all people must hate him? I mean, he never owned up to support you at all,' she said, indignantly. 'And we were all innocent.'

'He's so flippin' wet. You know what I mean? I do wonder if he's a nancy-boy,' said Nicola, as she fiddled with her kiss curls. 'Anyway, I gotta tell you about my new boyfriend – you are going to faint with envy when you see him …'

Molly was fascinated to see the colour drain from Alison's now pallid face; it was actually more interesting than listening to Nicola's flowery description of some man she must have cooked up from a magazine full of teenage love stories. How could she possibly be going out with someone like that? Over cocoa and cake in the kitchen, Nicola was still rabbiting on about this Martin who was so old – probably over twenty, she said! Surely not; he would expect a lot more than a goodnight kiss, even she knew that much.

Molly was working three mornings a week and all of Saturday and discovered a new side to her, meeting people that came into the shop, usually mothers and grandmothers, with their babies and toddlers. Sometimes the shop was bursting at the seams, especially on a wet day.

Not being reliant on her parents for pocket money sent warm ripples of pleasure through her. Its withdrawal was a punishment, but she had risen above it and proved her independence, which made her feel vibrant and happy; one of life's little triumphs and she had had few enough of them. She realised she was a different person at work from the child she was made to feel at home, despite her burden of household responsibilities.

But her prospects were very uncertain. Sometimes she thought she might skip sixth form and just make her way in life some other way, but it dawned on her that one day, supposing she had her own shop – like Nicola's pipe-dream of having her own salon – and then had a string of shops; one in Bloomstock, another in Guildford and Farnham, she would still be tied to home, virtually manacled to the kitchen table. With her mother's lameness getting worse, she stood little chance of breaking free however successful she was, unless she went to university. Somehow, they would allow that, get round the problems, because it would make them proud; there was no doubt about that, for they were constantly urging her to aim high, to try for the best university or at least teacher training college, but she had no ambition to teach.

Otherwise, she would have to live in Appley Green *for ever* and look after her mother, unless she got married, of course, but then, she would probably be expected to have her mother at home with her and her husband, and certainly that would be the case if her father died first. She had never had morbid thoughts like this before; they were frightening. There was talk now at school about careers, about choosing your subject with a view to becoming employable, for girls as well as boys, but how did a career fit in with an invalid mother and having babies?

Who could she turn to? She could never even broach this with her parents; they were too close to the problem.

This could discourage potential husbands! She *must* get to university; there was no other possible plan available. She needed to talk to someone about this. Was she being selfish? Should she stay and look after her mother until she died? Cook and clean for as long as twenty or thirty years? She could not foresee how her father would manage without her. He needs to earn a living, working six days a week to pay the bills and he can't cook for toffee; nor can he use an iron, which is odd seeing as he is so skilled with more complicated, powerful tools like that Black and Decker he got last month.

Molly felt desperate to see her friends; they would at least have some opinion that might help her see the wood for the trees and tell her she was just being beastly.

When they next met up in Jim's Snack Bar, Alison and Nicola listened to her plight but she could tell they soon grew a little bored and weary of her worries. As she noted how Nicola rested her chin in her hands, as if the weight of all her problems had been conveyed to Nicola's now heavy head, and Alison was twitching the curtain like some busybody looking for village scandal, there was a limit as to how much sympathy and support she could expect of her friends. After all, they were still quite new; a few weeks ago they had no special friendship at all, for throughout school life they had shared little common ground. Different personalities, outlooks and families; it was quite weird how close they had become. Her passion for university, driven by a need to escape a sad spinsterish future looking after her mother, was all-consuming as far as she was concerned, but would need to be faced pretty much alone.

Alison came alive again when she could get a word in about the upcoming party. 'So – we have the invitations. Done. Thanks Molly, they're beautiful. Can both of you help in buying and hiding party stuff – I don't want my parents to latch on.'

'They don't know?' asked Molly.

'Julian and I agreed, it's for the best. Then they can't forbid it and we can prove that we can do something like that and everything will be perfect afterwards. I can't see that any of our friends would deliberately make a mess, can you?'

Nicola and Molly could think of no-one. 'I could stash crisps and stuff in my wardrobe; my Mum and Dad never go in there. David said he would get some cider for us – he's old enough to get it from the off-licence.'

'Wizard! Thank him. He is invited, of course.'

'I never thought of you as being the secretive sort, Alison,' said Nicola, raising her chin and narrowing her heavily outlined eyes. 'Although, I think you're hiding something about … Edward. Do you fancy him?'

Alison choked on her fizzy drink, almost tipping the bottle over.

'Oh Gawd! Not another accident. It's like taking a toddler out,' teased Nicola. 'Well, that clinches it. Clearly you've got a thing going for Edward Phillips. But, Alison, he's so … wet and willowy …'

'Of *course* I don't fancy him!' Alison spat, clutching the bottle so tightly her knuckles turned white.

'Okay, Okay, hold your horses, keep your hat on. Only joking. My God, you're really cross, aren't you?'

'Are you protecting him, or something? We promised no secrets, remember,' put in Molly, now dying of curiosity.

'Look, I'll tell you because we made the pledge, but you, in turn must absolutely promise to tell no-one. This is serious, do you understand?' Molly and Alison were now hanging on her every word, nodding enough to make their heads fall off. 'Right, well we need to go somewhere quiet - and private. Let's go to the village green …'

11

George Bird met Sir Matthew's unswerving gaze from across his desk and felt distinctly uneasy, discreetly wiping his palms on his faded black robe. However, he was looking forward to passing on something interesting his dear wife had managed to overhear in the village.

'Well, the little matter of Peter Finchley has been dealt with now, as you know. Fortunately, memories are short when it comes to press reports.'

'Today's news, tomorrow's fish and chip wrapping, eh?'

'Quite, quite. Would you care for more coffee, or tea? Perhaps something a little stronger?'

Sir Matthew glanced up at the school clock on the wall above. 'A little early even for me, George.' He crossed his legs, folded his arms and sat up very straight indeed and George felt alarmed. 'The governors have met and taken my advice that you should … Hmm, well, consider your position.'

George was not sure what this meant. It was an expression not quite within his normal usage. He raised his eyebrows, tilted his head, inviting some elaboration.

'It was agreed unanimously that *you* should take the rap over the matter. There have been letters from parents, pointing out the complete breakdown in communication …'

'We had to establish the facts before we could …'

'No. Those girls were virtually turned out onto the streets …'

'With respect, Sir Matthew, you make it sound like some penny dreadful, as if they were about to … I mean, this is Appley Green, one of the safest corners of the earth. Children roam about freely all the time … and these are close to becoming adults. I am sure your own son is often out of your sight …'

'But legally, during school hours, we are responsible for our pupils. Had anything happened to them we could have

80

been prosecuted. Frankly, by making light of this, you are showing a deep lack of understanding and digging a hole for yourself. Can you not see that? The parents were then left to speculate, unable to make any sense of the situation. Quite rightly they were indignant, furious even, some more than others.'

'But, Mr Finchley was the cause of the whole ...'

'He, poor chap, has paid for his mistake, I think you'll agree. A mistake of inexperience, more than anything.'

'It was as well we got shot of him. He was clearly not fit to teach. I suppose you know what happened recently in a public house brawl?' He was beginning to feel pleasantly vindicated already.

Sir Matthew steepled his fingers. 'Enlighten me.'

'Our Mr Finchley, our ex-Mr Finchley, recently lost his rag and knocked out a man, a decent sort by all accounts, in this very village, the place where most of his pupils live. In broad daylight! I mean, this is the sort of character we are dealing with. Imagine if he'd become so enraged with one of the children as to ... to send one flying across the classroom! Thank God, this incident did not get into the papers, but village tongues always wag over such things.'

'Mm. I will have this investigated ...'

'I can only apologise for my error of judgement in ever selecting him in the recruitment process, for putting him forward to the governors in the first place.' Relief flooded through him as he saw Sir Matthew wavering.

'Shame. I wonder what happened there. I will get to the bottom of this – do you have any more information on the incident?'

George turned down the corners of his mouth. 'I don't pay too much heed to gossip as a rule, but of course this was pertinent. It took place at The Duke's Arms on the Bloomstock Road at around two-twenty, just before closing time. Not sure of the date.'

'And identity of the victim?' George shook his head. 'I am sure the staff there will remember. However, he has gone now, this really changes nothing. I am sorry to say that you have lost the general vote of confidence, with the parents and governors as well as within closed teacher circles. Bad discipline comes from poor leadership, George, and I would ask you to do the dignified thing and tender your resignation. Now would be timely, so that we can appoint a replacement for the autumn term. We cannot have parents so deeply dissatisfied with, and I am sorry to say this, but with *you.*'

George's head was swimming; he could not believe this was happening. He had not thought it would be necessary, but he would urgently need to raise the subject of Sir Matthew's son, Edward; after all, Alison Marshall, a reliable pupil, was adamant that he was the culprit and had been the one to spark off this whole sorry, absurd chain of events. Indeed, this was how the local newspaper had reported it, but to preserve the reputation of Sir Matthew, his precious son and the school, he had supported the confounded art teacher in blaming the two girls, Molly Watson and Nicola Bates, and his implication that the Marshall girl had lied! Now that his own career, his very survival, was at stake, everything had swapped placed; priorities had shifted, perspectives had slipped, and the truth must come out. What an unutterable mess!

To *hell* with Sir Matthew's public face and good name, his generosity to the school, the much vaunted gym, theatre and swimming pool! He had given the best years of his *life* to Appley Green Grammar School and there had never been a problem before. What was going on? Was Sir Matthew going to all these lengths to shield his own son and had he, George Bird, MA Oxon, suddenly become the chief *scapegoat?*

He would write to the chairman of the governors; pointing out that with Mr Finchley being such a poor role model in the community, it would be impossible for either them or him to give him a reference or testimonial of any kind. The matter of Edward and his homosexuality could be slipped in as something to make them sit up and reflect.

'I shall give this whole thing some serious thought, very serious thought indeed, Sir Matthew,' he said, mustering a smile as he saw Sir Matthew out of his study. Sir Matthew shrugged his shoulders, indicating perhaps that he could not see what further thought could be had on the matter. Decisions had been made.

12

Alison and her family were in Brighton for two weeks, staying in a hotel on the seafront. As a family they contended valiantly with alternating drizzle and drenching downpours that soaked their clothes but could not dampen their spirits. A blanket of sea mist and muggy weather was then finally broken late one hot evening by a dramatic, electrifying thunderstorm that the family watched from their hotel window. Harriet and Gordon declared this to be a good thing; it would 'clear the air'.

During their first four days, they had walked up and down the length of both West Pier and the Palace Pier and learned about when and why they were constructed. Alison looked longingly at the posters advertising shows and plays that were held in the Palace Pier concert hall; but whenever she hung back to read them, trying to decide if she had heard of any of the so-called stars, her parents and Julian would disappear ahead of her. She knew Frankie Vaughan was on at the Hippodrome summer show; there seemed to be a theatre in every street but such light entertainment did not prove to be a magnet for their parents.

They had braved walks along the pebbled beach in the bracing sea-air that at times seemed to go right through them and their mackintoshes; paid two visits to the grand Brighton Pavilion, with its heavy, lavish Chinese décor, again a very educational experience that reminded Alison of a school trip to a museum in Winchester. The Aquarium was more fun and Julian and Alison went there on their own while their parents were having a rest in their room ...

'I'd really like to just go off on my own, wouldn't you?' she asked her brother as they stared at some enormous black fish that gaped back at them through the glass.

'I should say so!' laughed Julian. 'Somehow being here makes me feel about nine years old – all the sticks of rock treats and 'be careful not to wipe your greasy fingers on your trousers' and 'there's a bus coming, now look both ways'.'

Alison nodded. 'I just can't stand it any longer, not all day every day. After all, at home we are as free as birds! But holidays? I feel so frustrated I could burst! Oh Julian, let's do something exciting! I mean, we could go off separately too …' After all, he wouldn't want to see Alma Cogan sing at the Astoria Theatre, would he?

That evening their parents were reading their library books in the hotel sitting-room – her father was locked into *Brighton Rock*, and her mother was glued to *From Russia with Love*. They had promised to play Canasta later before 'bedtime', but Alison and Julian had different plans.

Their evening meals were a kind of high tea, with perhaps poached eggs on toast or a tinned salmon salad, with bread and butter followed by cake. Tonight there were chips with slices of ham and a kind of chutney they had not had before, with mangoes in it. It looked rather like a kind of jam. After examining the jar, their parents reached for the small cruet dish of English mustard that they knew and trusted.

'We have a surprise for you both', announced Harriet, as she poured tea from a blue and white striped teapot into rose-patterned cups. Alison and Julian exchanged gleeful glances – at last, were they going to be let off the lead? Freedom! The irony of it was that their parents trusted them implicitly, they had often assured them of that, but they wanted to stick together as a family, to set the balance straight. They said that, with both working long hours, they missed their children hugely and felt somewhat guilty; so the family tradition always was for the four of them to spend holidays doing things as a team. As children this had worked; but now they were beginning to feel almost grown-up with friends who were out there in the workplace as independent young adults, it was less comfortable; they both felt hemmed in and desperate to find some other teenagers, especially of the opposite sex.

As if reading their minds, Harriet went on, 'You two are nearly adults. Of course, we, that is your father and I know that …' Alison knew something good was coming: perhaps some £sd in their hands to spend as they wanted in Brighton –

on a show, amusement arcades, the shops, the pictures. She felt quite fluttery with anticipation. Julian's eyes were gleaming like wet pebbles and very wide open. 'What is so extremely satisfying for us, as your parents, is that other people have also recognised that you are growing up. The most wonderful news! You know the Devonish party? You remember what we told you about that – it'll be the most amazing gathering of really bright, clever, wealthy, oh and witty people – some politicians too, businessmen, big shots from the armed forces, and of course all the Devonish circle of gentry and debutants and dowagers …' Her mother laughed gaily. 'Well, both of you have been invited to come too! Darlings, isn't that just too exciting for words?'

Alison and Julian looked at each other in abject horror. The party! It was happening the same evening, all organised, just two days after their return home.

Desperate whisperings took place after tea, when their parents popped up to their room to fetch cigarettes, precautionary woolly cardigans and pack-a-macs in preparation for an evening stroll along the front.

'Let's just go …' said Julian, thinking fast by the look on his face. 'We could … misbehave …'

'What!'

'Yes. Listen. If we show we're complete irresponsible nitwits, then they will think again about us being sensible enough to go to this Devonish thing. Our party can't happen without us being there!"

'Oh Julian! It would be a disaster, we'll never be able to let forty people know in time during school holidays, especially as we're here!'

'I know, I know.' He scratched his head. 'Impossibility.'

'So what shall we do? What can we say?' Alison could not grasp what on earth was going through her brother's head.

'We'll just say we are going in a different direction from them to look at … oh something … Tonight. Then, we'll see what happens … but try and cook up some … oh I don't know until it happens, some silly accident or something, that makes us look like children …'

'Whatever would that be …?'

'I said, I don't know,' said Julian, crossly, a note of panic in his voice. There was something not quite right about this whole line of thinking, but Alison could not come up with a better plan. She was now haunted by the vision of their friends and loose acquaintances coming to their house with bottles and, finding a note to say the party was cancelled, trying to find a way in or just making do with the garden. Someone would probably have a portable transistor radio or a wind-up gramophone that could work outdoors, then the neighbours would come along ... someone would complain to the police ... This could not happen.

Their smiling parents appeared. 'I've got the camera,' said Gordon. 'Apparently the forecast is fair for tomorrow, so should be a good sunset later tonight over ....'

'Sunsets are for the professionals,' teased his wife. 'Don't waste film darling ...'

'Just a couple. Good sunsets have scarcity value this summer,' he responded, good-naturedly. 'The point is this means a better day tomorrow – perhaps. Red sky at night, shepherd's ...'

'... pie tomorrow!' shouted Julian and Alison in unison, unable to resist what was expected.

'You children!' cautioned their father, pretending to chase or tickle them.

Alison suddenly stood still, risking a serious tickling, looking at Julian; with a mutual glance they exchanged the unspoken words: *no, we're not children any more, but let's be bad.*

It was clear that Gordon was chasing after sunsets and heading west, so getting away proved to be relatively easy with a quick, 'We want to look at the boats down there before it gets dark ... the other way.' Nobody asked what kind of boats, why or whereabouts.

'All right, you two. Do you have your Brownie with you, Julian?'

'No, it's in my room.' He shrugged. 'Never mind, you'd better go and catch your sun before it sets.' It would be a while yet, but he said it anyway.

Their parents were already walking away from them, arms linked and chatting, so they seemed to be worrying needlessly.

'I haven't got any money with me,' said Alison, her heart beating fast as she wondered what the evening would now bring. 'Did you bring some?'

Julian felt in his trouser pockets. 'Just a few coins. Here.' He poured some change into her hand, amounting to about five shillings.

'Thanks. That should be heaps.'

'We'd better find some boats ... so we can report back.'

Julian hurried away, probably heading for the magical Palace Pier, thought Alison, bright when fully illuminated but rather spooky when deserted, once its gates shut by mid-evening. Alison wanted to explore the back streets, just to gaze into shop windows, even if everything was closed now. She called out to him, as he strode ahead exactly like their father did, assuming his family was following in his wake.

'I'm crossing over. See you later, back at the hotel!'

He waved back at her. 'OK. Good luck!'

There were one or two gift shops, but everything was really quite drab and disappointing, not at all like London's Oxford Street or even the High Street in Guildford; little shops and a few pubs. She was too young to go into a pub and, anyway, on her own, that would look strange. Then she found a milk bar that was still open for milkshakes, teas and ice-creams, consumed standing up or propped on high stools. She stopped for a minute, fishing out the cash in the patch-pocket on the front of her peacock blue, sail-cloth skirt. There may be something else she would really need money for this evening, so she thoughtfully let the coins drop back in her pocket and walked on. So far, this was no fun; she needed friends and thought of Nicola and Molly. What would they do if they were here? Molly would be timid, heading back to the hotel before it got dark! Nicola would be in and out the back alleys, looking for adventure! But this was just a word – what did 'adventure' really mean? She couldn't go back and tell Julian she did nothing but wander around as aimlessly as a paper-bag blowing along the pavements. Perhaps she could get chatting to someone. She sat on a wall, looking out on the waves, the surf as it rhythmically pounded the pebbles in that relentless way the sea does. The whoosh and surge was soothing; there were few vehicles on the road and it was quite peaceful apart from wheeling seagulls shrieking like demented fishwives overhead. A girl with a skipping-rope came up to her.

'Hello! My name's Maureen,' she offered, pulling a half-licked round lollipop out of her cardigan pocket. Her ginger hair was in plaits and tied with pink and blue ribbon.

Alison thought she was about ten. She smiled at her. 'Hello then, Maureen. Are you on holiday?'

Surprisingly, she shook her head, sucking hard. 'No.' She pointed behind her. 'My Mum's got a guest house over there. We're not full though. She says it's the bloody British weather.'

'Goodness, where did you pick up such language? It's going to be nice tomorrow, my Dad says!' said Alison. 'Are you good at skipping?'

As Maureen skipped and skipped, counting, still with the lolly wedged in the corner of her mouth, Alison watched, appreciating the effort being expended for her benefit. Perhaps, she was thinking, she should just go to the pictures.

'Do you know what's on at the pictures?'

The girl shook her head. Alison knew of several cinemas and decided to explore and find out. She said goodbye to Maureen and headed off towards the Clock Tower. *The Last Days of Pompeii* was showing at the Regent, not something she felt keen enough to see, sitting in the dark on her own. She stared at the posters and looked around, now feeling embarrassed – and lonely. What should she do? Here she was, fancy-free, loose on Brighton streets and she could not think how to make the best of it. She noticed some couples and girls in groups, all dressed up smart, going in through another door and realised there was also a ballroom. People were going dancing! She had never really danced herself and wondered what it was like inside – bright lights and glittery, with band music and people laughing and having fun.

Suddenly a man was at her side, touching her arm. There was something about his eyes, twinkly and friendly, that reminded her a little of the journalist, the one whose good looks had distracted her so much she had not only blabbed to him but also allowed him to take her photograph. 'Hello, lovey. What're you thinking of doing? You look a bit lost!'

Yes – lost, that's just how she felt. 'I … I don't know. I was going to see a film, but don't fancy the one on the programme …'

'It's already started anyhow,' he pointed out. 'Although you could miss the trailers and *Pathé* news …'

'No. I really don't want to see that film,' she repeated.

'What about a dance, then?'

'I … can't really go in there on my own … you see, my brother is … with me … but he's popped off down the road …' An inner warning voice told her to say this.

'Ah! I see. But you don't want to be dancing with your brother, do you now?'

She shook her head, half of her wanting, wishing for what might not seem right, but then Julian had said, wasn't the purpose of this evening partly to show their parents they couldn't be trusted? She had forgotten about that, but now it seemed a good, if slightly mad, reason to be daring, to look trouble straight in the eye.

The clean-shaven young man, in his cheap suit and sharp shoes, crooked his arm invitingly. 'I'm Robert. Would you do me the honour of being my dance partner for a while?' His sidelong glance was cheeky and very, very alluring and he seemed awfully polite.

She paused for a split-second before putting her arm through his and, as she knowingly threw caution to the wind, Alison felt a swirl of adrenalin rush through her. The touch of his fingertips on her hand, so light it was no more than the brush of a feather, was like an electric current. He was older than her, of course, that was obvious, but somehow she felt more than fifteen, being paraded on his arm and swept off through a doorway like a princess on the way to something new, unknown and wonderful.

How she wished she had paid some attention to her appearance, but how was she to know the evening would turn out like this? Her skirt was new, bought for the holiday, the pink check blouse was last year's and a little tight around the bosom and her rubber-soled sandals were practical, not dancing shoes by any means. She excused herself to go to the Ladies' room for a moment, praying he would not evaporate while she was in there. She quickly released her pony tail, running fingers through her abundant glossy brown hair; then pinched her cheeks and bit her lips to give them some colour. There was little more she could do, other than beg, borrow or steal someone's lipstick ... She looked around; there were women of all ages preening themselves, smelling like a chemist's shop, ignoring her, some managing to titivate using a small powder-compact mirror. A redhead with a short bob that caught the light smiled at her and on an impulse Alison said,

'I couldn't borrow your lipstick, could I? I forgot mine.' It was a stunning flame-orange colour that she would never have thought to wear. She wasn't even sure what girls with brown eyes normally chose to go with their colouring; it was not something to which she had ever given a moment's thought. But tonight was different and no-one would ever know, or care.

The redhead, to her surprise, said, 'Course – can't have you looking dull and dreary when Mr Right could be in there waiting for you, now can we?'

'Thanks. I'm Alison.'

The girl, who spoke with a Cockney accent, did not volunteer her name but gladly handed over her Rimmel lipstick. Alison squeezed between two women to squint at the mirror, so she could, for the first time in her life, apply false colour to her lips. It was a little brighter than she had thought, but she smacked her lips together as she had seen women do and returned it to the girl.

'Suits you lovely! Good luck.'

What a nice girl, thought Alison, revising her opinion of girls who wore cheap make-up; her mother always used Helena Rubenstein cosmetics.

The man, Robert, was waiting for her, leaning against a billboard in the foyer looking very *louche*. In the looks department he reminded her of that marvellous Russian ballet dancer, Rudolf Nureyev, but with shorter hair than in pictures of him she had seen.

He ambled towards her, slinking like a leopard, in no hurry, but all the while studying her face in a way that made her feel special. He seemed to intimate his approval without uttering a word and she willingly believed all that his smile was saying. Her pulse racing, she wondered what Julian would say if he could see her now. Her parents would be astounded; it was only half an hour since she was with them, a child on holiday with her parents.

'You look – gorgeous,' he said, in his well-mannered way, sliding an arm around her waist. 'I don't know your name.' He was really rather well-spoken.

'Oh, yes. Pleased to meet you,' she returned awkwardly, unsure if they should shake hands. 'I'm Alison.' She could not think of what to say next.

The sound of band music told her there would be little chance for conversation anyway. As they entered the dance hall they were greeted by the general cacophony of laughter and people shouting in each other's ears. Instantly the rhythm made her want to sway; she had never heard anything like it and the floor seemed to bounce under their feet. Was this real rock and roll? It sounded a bit like Bill Haley and the Comets she had heard on Radio Luxembourg but here she could feel vibrations in the floor, into the soles of her feet, up through her legs!

Robert grabbed hold of her and pushed her round with both hands in a way that made her naturally twirl and she laughed, nervously. Without the faintest idea of what to do, she watched couples jiving around her and found herself following their moves and keeping up with what Robert was doing. He seemed an expert dancer to her, but what did she know?

The tempo changed and suddenly he was holding her close and she could feel a heat from him that was an awakening. She liked it. His hand lightly brushed against the back of her neck and she could sense what was coming. The dance slowed so that they gently swayed, bodies touching with his arms wrapped round her waist, and she had no choice but to put her arms around his neck, since they could have looked stupid hanging down at her side. He tilted back his head and gazed into her eyes and she felt herself gently melting. What was happening? She had no idea that a man could have this effect, not even with all her reading of books and watching of films.

She actually longed for him to be closer, to touch her skin. Some lights had been turned off and, glancing over his shoulder, her eyes opened wide at the sight of couples all around smooching. Imagine what Nicola and Molly would say when she told them about this! Perhaps this would be her secret, although she was not so brilliant at keeping secrets. Last time she saw her two friends, she spilled out to them the truth about Edward Phillips being a homosexual; and, for this betrayal of trust, she would probably pay dearly at some point in the future.

His mouth was wide and shapely, not too plump, not too thin and she felt those hot lips on hers and thought she would faint from the ecstasy she felt, feeling literally weak at the knees. She was unsure of what to do but it just didn't matter; her own lips moved in a kind of harmony with his, yet this was not how she imagined, not as it should be, not what she planned at all for her first moment of passion. They were perfect strangers! Feelings of shame fought briefly with a need for him to kiss her again. She could feel something hard pressing against her stomach and she knew what that was. After all, she had read about this and remembered well the biology lesson on human reproduction.

She felt his warm breath on her cheek and then he was murmuring in her ear, 'Shall we go out for some fresh air?'

Anything, she thought. She would do anything to stay with this wonderful human being.

13

He drifted off into a surprisingly pleasant sleep, bearing in mind his life might be cut short, any formula for future happiness was still undetermined, and levels of sexual frustration were sky-high.

The image of Victoria Phillips, her coral lips, dark green eyes, figured strongly in Walter's dreams, where he became drugged by 'love in idleness' or some other narcotic, and caused him to wake with an erection of which he felt proud. In the small hours, alone in his hotel bed, he laughed aloud then lay there on his back, sleepily reflecting on the extraordinary evening and what it could mean. As if he could possibly have an affair with the wife of Sir Matthew Phillips! What was her game? What was this she-devil playing at? Before turning over and plunging back into a peaceful state of slumber, he allowed the events to play over in his head.

Until the end of the evening when she took hold of his hand, he assumed that what he had experienced was simply her normal, airy, coquettish manner, but she touched his masculine hand with her own delicate, perfectly manicured fingertips in a way that told him this was no formal handshake. She had checked, with an obvious, showy kind of caution, that her husband was looking the other way and her gaze had locked into his in a way that made his manly parts tingle and go hot. 'I take it you love to go to the races? Walter? Am I right?' she said, huskily. She nodded to him, her pupils dilating darkly as if she had ordered them to, still holding his gaze. Of course, he nodded back; there seemed little alternative but to agree. 'Meet me ...' and she gave him the name of an Ascot hotel. There was no special mention of a race meeting, but the date and the time were precise.

What was he to think? This was tricky. My God, she was so sure of herself! For so many reasons, he should have withdrawn his hand, given her a puzzled frown as if he had not heard her properly, or perhaps misunderstood. He could have shaken his head, to indicate his indifference, if not positive abhorrence, towards horses. But of course he was only human, a man in need of a woman, rather desperately as it happened. Although he would never let himself be caught out again by a two-faced seductress, he was out to live life to the full; isn't that what he had promised himself? The memory of her full, shapely breasts sliding around in the claret silk gown she was wearing, such that by Act Three he was desperate to reach across and stroke them, cup their weight in his hands, slip his fingers gently down inside, this memory kept replaying in his head like a trailer, put out to tempt him into viewing the entire film.

It was so gratifying to think a woman like that was offering herself to him; it was this reassurance that he could attract any woman he wanted, that did indeed send him off into an unexpectedly deep and contented slumber. Good times lay ahead.

Realising his stay in Appley Green was becoming an extended one, Walter wondered if he should abandon the comforts of the Hunter's Lodge Hotel and avail himself of the more modest accommodation on offer in Peter's lodgings; apparently, his landlady had another room. This would be an interim measure, to tide him over until he found a permanent residence in Appley Green. A decision to settle in the village was almost firm in his mind; the attractions of the place seemed irresistible and, anyway, he could not spend his remaining years or months, dithering. Nowhere on earth was perfect and time was precious.

He tried to contact Peter several times, going round to his place, thrusting a scribbled note through his letter-box, phoning him, but so far had not found him. His landlady did not come to the door, nor did she answer the phone, which was altogether odd. He tried to call him before leaving for the Ascot hotel, but again, there was no reply. Later, he decided, he would make some enquiries with a neighbour or two; in a village this was often the best way to resolve such puzzles.

Since Walter was unable to track down his young brother, he made a couple of visits to their father alone. It was no use asking his father if he had seen Peter, for his memory was shaky, due to confusion possibly caused by new drugs, not to the condition itself, although the medical staff seemed uncertain about this, as opinion was also divided about which of three possible diseases he had. It was his medical history that had raised alarm bells, for his father and one of his father's three uncles had suffered something similar and died in their fifties; although Walter had never made the connection. The tablets were, however, keeping him alive, so he was told.

His father barely recognised him when he approached the hospital bed; the visits were becoming unbearably sad and it was unlikely he would last much longer. Walter had sought out the doctor on one occasion, for a candid opinion and was told that his father's appetite was so poor, he was declining fast. It was clear by looking at his wasted body and forlorn face, so very different from how he was just six months before, that the man, his face now pale and waxy, eyes deep in their sockets, had given up the will to live.

Walter was partly concerned for Peter – perhaps his younger brother was depressed. But Walter was also incensed, for his brother must realise the situation with regard to their father. Surely, even in a distressed mental state, he would think that he should be around for the possible demise of his only surviving parent. If this irresponsibility was typical of how he behaved as a professional, then no wonder … No, that was ungenerous, but none the less he did feel some bitterness towards this apparent selfishness of his brother.

With such bothersome matters weighing heavily on his mind, he went off to Ascot, hoping to find some solace in a dalliance he struggled to understand. The glorious Victoria Phillips was asking him to meet her. It occurred to him that this could be some almighty trap and he would find himself confronted by her husband, ready to denounce him as an 'utter cad' or whatever term Sir Matthew might use. But of course he was paranoid, he knew that.

Despite all these misgivings he found himself driving through the Surrey Heath landscape towards the place famous for its royal equestrian gatherings. He had checked beforehand; there was no race meeting scheduled for today; so unless Victoria had got the dates wrong, she must have something else in mind.

Of course, it is a lady's prerogative to keep a man waiting, thought Walter, as he sat in the heavily furnished hotel lounge lighting his second cigarette since arriving. He had skimmed through The Times and, from the French windows, studied the view of a lawn where some ladies were playing croquet. On the brink of turning round and driving straight back to Appley Green, he caught sight of her.

'Darling!' she cried, as she sashayed into the foyer, waving to the receptionist, making no secret of her arrival or their meeting. 'Walter! How *wonderful* to see you. I'm so very sorry to be so late; my chauffeur's wife gave birth today and it delayed him a little.' His eyes were drawn to her cleavage; it was so soft, velvety and inviting, causing recent erotic dreams to re-play in his mind in vivid Technicolor.

'I hope mother and child are both well,' he said, politely.

'Oh how sweet you are! Of course, of course they breed like rabbits,' she said, dismissively. 'Now then, how are *you*, dear man?' How did she make him feel so compliant, so subordinate, so ... what was the word? Emasculated?

'I am quite well, thank you. I trust you are well.'

'Oh my goodness, we sound like something out of Jane Austen, don't we now? Tiresome civilities. Now ...' she sat on a sofa and patted the cushion next to her, indicating he could, indeed he should sit next to her. She was doing it again. He did not like this. This lack of control was against his nature when it came to either business or his women. In a petty kind of way, this woman was controlling, manipulative, not what he needed, and he was suspicious of what her motives were. He felt tense, angry.

'You invited me here, Lady Phillips,' he said, flatly, sitting opposite her with crossed legs and folded arms. 'Charming idea, but ... Ah, will you have some tea?' He summoned a hovering waiter, taking charge, feeling better about himself.

'That would be divine, but ...' she hailed another waiter and instructed him of something out of Walter's earshot.

'Matthew and I have a suite here – we can take tea there. Mm?' she raised her eyebrows and threw him a mischievous smile. 'More private. I always entertain my guests there, such lovely views.'

'I see,' replied Walter, not responding to her suggestive nuances. 'How very ...'

She cut him off. 'I have found you the most desirable residence, Walter. I told you I would, didn't I?'

Walter actually found himself relaxing a little. Was this her reason for inviting him here? Was the rest simply cooked up by his fertile imagination?

She stood up. 'Come!' It was as if he were a pet spaniel. His eyes narrowed and his nostrils flared; the woman was irritating in the extreme, but it would be difficult to escape now. He had no alternative but to follow meekly behind; a sudden disappearance could cause offence and to offend Lady Phillips, could, ironically, also offend her powerful husband. Was *he* aware of this rendezvous? Of course not, he sighed, deciding to see this through as efficiently as possible and then make a hasty retreat.

The suite of rooms comprised a spacious sitting-room complete with an adjoining bedroom and bathroom, all furnished and fitted out in a contemporary style with clean lines and bright colours; she was meticulous in showing him around, flirtatiously asking him to test the double bed for its springiness. A tea trolley was wheeled in, with golden scones, clotted cream all the way from Devon, locally made jam and fresh strawberries, arranged on bone china lined with lacy doilies.

'But Walter, tell me, how did you enjoy the play?'

'It was well done. Being there also gave me a good taste of village life ...'

'People often think it's for children – because of the fairies, but it's really rather deep, don't you think?' Walter inclined his head, considering this deeply. 'I mean, it's a big debate about the meaning of love and sex, really. Don't you think so? Very erotic! At one point – I thought Oberon was going to … well never mind.'

Walter writhed with embarrassment. People he knew did not speak like this. Sex was something that went on, for sure, but behind closed doors, not talked about. He watched her remove the fine cashmere shawl draped around her shoulders and swallowed. She kicked off her shoes – not stylish stilettos – but rather soft leather that shouted quality and design with every step taken. 'So lovely to feel relaxed in here. A bit stuffy downstairs, I always think.'

'So, please tell me about the property you've found. How did you come across it? I've tried the local estate agent but they had little to offer.'

'Oh … oh yes,' she said, vaguely, reaching for her crocodile skin bag. She rummaged around in this for a few moments and then threw her hands up in dismay. 'Well, how annoying, would you believe it? I must've left it in our vestibule.' She did not sound too vexed or surprised.

Walter said nothing; hoping his silence might embarrass her.

She poured the tea, leaning over to display her strongest assets, then offered him a scone. 'Hungry?' Her eyes focused on his face intently, seriously; it was clear what she meant. Only an idiot would have thought she meant anything to do with the need to eat food.

On the drive home from Brighton, Alison and Julian sat sulkily in the back seat as their parents chatted on chirpily about the holiday and the forthcoming Devonish party.

'The thing is, Julian and I really don't *want* to go to the party, mother,' said Alison.

Her mother laughed. It occurred to Alison that nothing was more insulting than invoking laughter when you were actually trying to be serious. She looked out of the window and thought dreamily of Robert. Would she ever see him again? They exchanged phone numbers; at least, she gave him hers in case he ever came to their area. He said he might very well do; he said he would love to. He had never laughed at her, just given her those slow, gentle smiles of his. She realised her mother was talking.

'... you have no experience of these things, so you cannot possibly know what a missed opportunity this would be for you. As I said, you both have to think more like adults now. Bless you, my babies, you are growing up!'

'But, people there – we don't know them, and ...' Alison looked to Julian for support.

'They'll be so much older than us,' he put in.

Their plan had failed in deterring their parents. Alison did her utmost to ensure they saw that a strange man dropped her back at the hotel. She was brave enough to ask Robert to walk her back to the hotel and he was surprisingly willing to do this, considering everything ... She blushed to think of what had happened on the beach. Of course, he was a bit shy when he realised her parents were in the hotel lounge waiting for her to return and soon left, after politely shaking hands. To her surprise, Julian was still out, somewhere at large on the streets of Brighton. They seem surprisingly charmed by Robert, then somewhat distracted since they had assumed, until that moment, their twins had spent the evening together; once Alison had appeared without her brother, her parents were fretting.

Julian finally appeared at ten minutes past midnight, a little the worse for wear and smelling of beer and vomit. Perhaps her parents had not picked up the disgusting stench.

At this point, her mother began to blame herself. 'I should never have let you both go off on your own. Oh Gordon, we were so wrong to imagine they were quite ready for the big wide world,' she said. 'But there we are, no harm done. Safe and sound now. Did you have a lovely time? Lots of adventures?' It seemed incredible to Alison the way she made light of their bad behaviour, but this seemed to relieve her of the guilt she had fleetingly suffered. Basically, heaping the blame upon herself seemed preferable to feeling she had produced two badly behaved children, adolescents or young adults, or however she saw them; tantamount to a more serious failure as a parent.

Their evening of rebellion and the high-life, therefore, had caused their parents not to trust them with so much freedom in the future. Of course, it was obvious now that would be the consequence. Alison sighed at her brother's stupid plan; but there again, without it she would never have met Robert.

As far as the Devonish party was concerned, nothing had changed.

'Well, I'll go *happily* if I can take a friend,' suggested Alison, thinking madly of Robert.

Her mother frowned, as if reading her daughter's mind. She glanced sideways at Gordon, but his eyes were focused on the junction ahead. 'You mean, one of your school-friends?'

'Molly. I'd like Molly to come with me.' She had to think fast; it was too short notice for lovely Robert, and Nicola was away in Margate with her family.

'I'll find out if that'll be possible,' said her mother, at last. 'We should meet her first.'

Julian was giving her the blackest of looks, clearly wondering what on earth her plan was.

As Walter drove away from Ascot, he felt cheapened. He had almost allowed himself to be party to the oldest trick in the book. Again! Her motives were different, she would not go so far as to accuse him of raping her, but he had this unsavoury feeling she was a sexually frustrated woman, with an older husband who, for all his assets, was not providing everything she needed in the bedroom department.

His baser instincts to comply with her needs began to decline as their meeting went on. Mrs Phillip's dominant ways turned him off more and more; the house she had found happened to be coming on the market and also happened to be on their estate, and her bleating insistence on its desirability grated. He wanted to find his own place and Peter should play a part in this selection process too, if only he could find him. His thoughts kept wandering off to his possible whereabouts; he, and his landlady, really did seem to have disappeared without trace. He should perhaps report him officially as a 'missing person'. He broke out in a cold sweat thinking that his brother could have 'done something stupid' as they say – or eloped.

Victoria had then generously thrown out an invitation to a big party being thrown by the Devonishes – she said they could easily get him in.

'This will be an event the rest of Surrey will be gossiping about until the wedding. For Ted Devonish to become engaged is quite something; he is such a catch …' On and on she went about who would be there.

He decided there would be no harm in that. As a way of settling into a new community, what better than to slip into the upper echelons of society in the course of one evening? If the illustrious folk there were not to his taste, then he would simply have wasted a few dull hours. An introduction by someone like Sir Matthew would be perfectly respectable – oh, and his wife, of course.

He felt relieved. It had been a lucky escape, he suspected; the risk he had almost faced today, was of becoming the naïve victim of a 'kiss and tell' scenario. *You will continue to be my lover on demand, Walter Finchley, or I shall tell my husband that you tried to seduce me. If you deny me, you will not have the house I offered you, for a* **nominal** *sum and, in this community, your name will be dirt.* He may be wrong, but this was what her behaviour suggested to him – and thank God, he had got away, unscathed. Silly woman, as if he needed her, or her house.

14

Molly had just checked the top of her free-standing wardrobe, aware that if she perched on the front of its base, stretched and reached, the whole thing could topple over on top of her and possibly crush her to death. To avoid this, she piled up several books and magazines to act as a stool, as she had done before. Her main concern was to ensure the packets of crisps and peanuts were perfectly concealed by a spare blanket, for although she was certain her mother would be physically unable to look up there, and her father would have no reason to do so, she must take no chances.

Come the evening of the party, she would simply tell them she was spending it with friends at Alison's house. There was no need to actually lie; she could get away with simply not telling the whole truth. Even the people invited probably did not know the scale of this party, the likelihood that, if they all came, there could be around sixty people! There was another stash of savoury biscuits in the top of the airing cupboard, beneath clean sheets, somewhere neither parent used, since she was the one who put away the ironed linen and retrieved it when the beds needed changing.

As she stepped down, the books slipped beneath her and she fell awkwardly, her ankle bending over as she landed on the rag rug that further slid on the lino. Not wishing to attract attention, she managed to stifle a howl of pain. Her parents and David were in the room below watching TV comedy, so hopefully the sound of laughter drowned out any bump on the ceiling above them.

A few days ago Nicola had gone off with her family by train to Margate and Nicola was furious to miss the party, but the holiday at Cliftonville Butlins had been arranged for months. Nicola had not realised the exact dates, but her Mum and Dad saved all year round for this treat and of course she would go. Usually it was a modest B&B, but this year they were really pushing the boat out with aunts, uncles and cousins. Molly had already received a saucy seaside postcard from Nicola, who wrote in tiny writing: *Guess what? Dad had too much to drink; Mum got sunstroke; I came second in a beauty pageant!!! My 'itsy bitsy teeny weeny yellow polka dot bikini' must've done it. Not really!! old black bathing suit. Nicola'* and she had planted a lipstick kiss on the postcard. Unfortunately, her mother was the first to see this and, after reading it was so horrified, she told Molly to put it straight in the bin, for fear of germs.

Alison was in Brighton but of course, she would be back just in time for the party; after all, it was being held at her house and her parents were going to this big 'do' at the Manor House.

She envied them both for their holidays, but tried not to dwell on this too much. Her parents rarely attempted to travel; it was just too difficult managing the wheelchair. Everywhere presented narrow doorways, big steps and other obstacles that made trips out difficult; then her mother would tell the three of them to go on without her, but David and Molly never really wanted to do this with just their father. Leaving mother alone in a café, outside a shop, or stranded on a beach, just seemed mean, and on the few occasions they had tried this, she had worn a hurt, miserable look on her face for days afterwards. They had each tried taking turns to keep her company, but she could be a difficult woman to please, so that was not much fun either. Overall, it just never seemed worth it.

Molly enjoyed her time serving in the shop every morning and, in the evenings, she was working her way through a reading list from the school to prepare her for sixth form. She also knitted a green cable-stitch cardigan to put away as a surprise Christmas present for her mother, and taught herself to crochet from a library book.

In the shop, she adored the softness of the balls of nylon baby wools in pastel shades: lemon, sparkling white, pale blue, lavender and pink. It must be so lovely to dress up a little baby, she thought, knowing that one day she would have her own. She wished there was a baby in the family so she could make some little matinée jackets or bootees, but her cousins were all younger than she was and far away from having babies. Then she had an idea.

She borrowed some patterns and got to work; actually making tiny garments while she was in the shop, soon able to display a beautiful selection on the counter.

When the owner of the little shop, a lady with a tight grey perm, called Mrs Cooper, came in one morning, she said. 'Oh these are darling! Who made these?' She donned her spectacles, read the price tags and asked what the cost price was. Molly was not sure what she meant; she had bought the wool with her own money, then added on a little bit for the making of them to arrive at the selling price. She blushed, feeling guilty as she was planning to pocket the profit herself.

'Oh, I did. I wasn't sure ...' she said, biting her lip, 'of how to price them, Mrs Cooper.' She explained honestly what she had done.

'Well,' said her boss, smiling, and holding up a pearly white cardigan for a newborn, full of complicated lacy stitching. 'Not *all* mothers have time to do this ... Raise these prices a little, my dear, see how they sell, then we can come to some arrangement. Just use whatever wool you need and keep a written record, Molly. They're lovely. Well done!'

'Thank you. I love making them,' she said, glowing with pride. She did not often receive praise.

She set to and found she could make about three or four items a week, plus little bootees which could take as little as an hour. Her knitting needles and crochet hook were flying from dawn to dusk, for this seemed a great way to make extra pocket-money. She could do this, while being paid for serving in the shop. It could be very busy and was a profitable little business since housewives would always have babies, but there were often quiet spells, with few customers. Although most women could knit, a skill passed down from mother to daughter, it was good for customers to see the wools being used in the shop itself, and some of them realised they could not craft their own so perfectly or so quickly. Men began to come in, fathers-to-be Molly supposed, and gladly bought gifts that they saw as both practical and beautiful. In a little cash notebook, Molly kept a strict ledger of costs, profits and how many hours she spent working on the goods, ready to present to Mrs Cooper. She could also knit while watching TV, or reading, sometimes managing all three at once.

They had all been posted their exam results and Molly was pleased with hers. Her O' level grades were better than she had dared to hope, so the prospect of good A' levels opening the door to university seemed high. It was still her aim to go to university for all the reasons she had worked out before. What subject would she study? It was early days to consider this. Perhaps she should begin to think about what career she would want; and what would fit in with having a family of her own.

One evening she went to the pictures with a school-friend who was invited to the party and as she sat behind her shop-counter the following day with some relatively easy crochet work, she began to think about the party. What would happen? Who might she meet? It was the real highlight of her school holidays.

She had not seen Alison and Nicola since Alison had revealed the shocking truth about Edward Phillips. This was a huge secret that they promised to keep under their hats and Alison made it clear she had divulged it to no-one else. It was strange how all this sharing of secrets created such a burden of concealment from others.

Tomorrow Alison would be home and then party-day! She felt butterflies in her tummy, thinking about it, after the quiet time she'd had, pretty much working in the shop, reading alone in her bedroom, cooking meals, cleaning and running errands for her mother.

An unexpected visit from Alison, who came round to see her straight after arriving home from Brighton, really took her by surprise. It was nearly nine o'clock in the evening when there came a knock on the front-door. Their house wasn't like Nicola's, where people were always coming and going, neighbours popping in to borrow something, or pass the time of day with the latest gossip. Nobody else moved, apart from looking at each other, as if to say, *Who on earth?* so Molly put down her knitting and book.

Alison looked freckled, not exactly sunburnt, more weather-beaten and somehow different; the tops of her arms were blotchy where she had peeled and no, she had not developed a nice even tan. She was out of breath, seemed agitated, even a bit weird and, to cap it all, was wearing mascara.

'Molly! Oh heck, you'll never guess what's happened?'

Molly stepped outside and half-closed the door. 'What?'

'I have to go to the Devonish do with my parents. I can't be at home for the party.' She gave her a seemingly anguished look.

Molly had a hollow feeling in her stomach that comes with bitter disappointment. 'You mean the party is cancelled?' she asked, softly.

Alison gabbled in a whisper, 'Actually, no. There's no time for that. Julian is supposed to be going too and my mother is dead set on this, believe me, but he's going to pretend to be at death's door with the dreaded lurgy, at the last minute. We can't both do that or it'd immediately raise suspicion, so I *will* go, but you'll never guess what. Now the good news! Oh Molly, little Molly, you can come too!'

Molly tried to take all this in. 'You mean, I can go to the big society party? Me?'

'Yes, Cinders, you *shall* go to the Ball! So, is that all right? It means you'll miss the party at our house, but Nicola and I won't be there anyway; so we can do another one – perhaps for Christmas, maybe even tell my parents, I don't know, haven't really thought it through yet, I was in such a panic. It would make it just about bearable if you came with me. Say you will. Please.'

Molly was rather torn; it was difficult to know which would be the most enjoyable. Certainly she recognised that to go to the Manor House was a chance that would probably never be repeated in her entire lifetime; so her decision did not take long.

'I wonder who'll be there,' she said at first.

'Apparently anybody who is anybody, that's what my mother keeps saying, whatever that really means. It'll be quite a new experience anyway.'

Molly nodded. 'Yes. All right. I'll come,' she said. 'My parents will be … astonished.' It will impress them, too, she thought, never a bad thing. They would not forbid her a chance to mix with the upper crust, they wouldn't dare.

'Oh, goody-goody! I'm truly relieved.'

'How was Brighton?'

Alison's cheeks turned beetroot red; this was more than sunburn. 'I … I'll tell you later, I mean tomorrow …,' she replied, with a funny smile that she was failing to suppress, 'look I must go now, I have to unpack my case and sort out a frock to wear and everything.'

'Oh! That's a thought,' Molly groaned. 'Whatever shall I wear?' She had absolutely nothing vaguely suitable; in fact, she had no picture in her mind of what would be correct for such a social engagement.

'Look, I got you into this mess, I'll find you something.' Alison grinned, looking her up and down, as if she had never seen her before. 'Hmm. You are quite small. What bust?'

Molly gave her a shy smile. 'About thirty-two inches, I think .. although I shall soon need, you know … '

'Thirty-four with a bigger cup, I should think. That should be enough to go on. My Mum kept some lovely dresses from when she went to parties, before she met my father; I expect one of them will do,' said Alison, 'She was very slim in those days, maybe slightly bigger than you are now but nothing a nice belt or a silk scarf wrapped round the waist cannot fix.'

Molly was doubtful, but could see that Alison was really trying to help, and there seemed no other way of obtaining an evening gown good enough for this special occasion, even if she had weeks to plan it.

'Thank you, Alison.'

'Are you excited? I am now but at first I was in a state of utter shock, thinking of all those people turning up with no party going on. Julian will just have to manage the whole thing by himself. He's more than happy to do that; probably sees more ways of getting up to mischief without his sister looking on. Come round tomorrow evening. My parents want to meet you properly. Oh, and Julian will collect the crisps from you;

he'll have to find somewhere to hide them in his room for one night – before he falls ill. Bye now.'

Molly watched Alison frantically speed off down the road on her bicycle, loose hair flying in the wind, lights swallowed by the darkness. She did seem to have changed in some way, sort of carefree, fearless and more attractive. What had happened in Brighton, she wondered?

As she turned back to her family who were now blithely watching an episode of a new detective serial, she realised she and her friend hadn't even asked each other about their exam results.

15

The day before the party was cloudy and dismal but for the much vaunted evening, rain held off and the marquee erected in the Manor House grounds would be redundant as shelter from the elements; so was dismantled that afternoon. The hosts knew that guests would much prefer to stroll into the walled garden, examine the contents of the fish-pond; perch prettily on low walls or sink gracefully into rattan chairs and generally soak up the surroundings. These events were so much more relaxed and informal than they used to be. It was anticipated that later on, people might begin to shiver and reach for shawls and coats and, finally fill the drawing-room, hallway, library, an easterly-facing morning room and the dining-room, all adapted and modified for the purpose of entertaining approximately three hundred guests.

No-one could describe the gathering as select or intimate; the Devonish family declared they were delighted to share their celebrations with good people from the surrounding area. In other words, it did not really matter if you were from peasantry or palace and a few guests looked askance at their fellow men, 'just people from the village'.

Harriet tried not to let her disappointment show, as she used a little finger to decorously hook her long gown up from the gravel path. 'I'm no social snob,' she muttered to Gordon, as they swept past a group of Appley Green shopkeepers and tradesmen drinking beer by the rose-garden, 'but it's not quite what I expected.'

Gordon just laughed and squeezed her arm. 'Well, here's a damn good opportunity for you to put into practice all your left-wing principles, my dear, and rub along with the *hoi-polloi*. Never let it be said you are toffee-nosed!'

'Never!' she laughed. 'Anyway I must find Gloria and her mother. This is what I am so excited about.'

'You'd better not make that too obvious, or people will be asking questions.' He tapped his nose.

She nodded, slightly grimacing. 'I know, it's a shame, but there we are, we're used to it. Even so, when I see her just remind me, give me the nod and wink or something, as I shall be terribly thrilled, you know that, Gordon. I mean you of all people must understand that.' She stopped and said quietly, looking into his eyes. 'You, my darling man, are the only person who can possibly understand that.'

He looked at her sadly and nodded, patting her hand as they easily linked arms.

Molly and Alison had been timidly trailing in their wake since stepping out of their car, but on looking around felt waves of relief.

'Gosh!' said Alison. 'This all looks remarkably normal.'

'No gargoyles, midgets or Siamese twins you mean?' giggled Molly.

In some ways, this dusky gathering was not what they had imagined. They had both taken a glass of champagne offered from a tray and after a few sips, felt relaxed and mellow as any nervousness just melted away. For one thing, it was much less formal, not at all Jane Austen.

'Let's see if we can spot anyone at all that we actually recognise,' said Alison, casting her gaze around the terrace and lawns, everywhere lit with lanterns and candles. 'They must be frightfully rich you know. Imagine providing champagne and food for all these people and living in a place like this with staff …'

'It's inherited wealth, isn't it?'

Alison pulled a face. 'Rather. Not as if they've earned it the hard way. I'm a bit surprised at how obsequious my mother and father are – they're practically Commies, you know.'

Molly gasped. 'Communists? What? No, you're kidding.'

'Well, they're certainly socialists, not Conservatives like most people here will be that's for certain, but they're extremely secretive sometimes, you know … I'm only telling you this, Molly, as we have sworn to have no secrets and will never spill any beans we share …' she giggled, 'well, you know what I mean.'

'Obsequious,' muttered Molly. 'Hmm, that reminds me, brainbox, how were your results?'

She shrugged. 'Oh, ten grade ones. How about you?'

Molly suddenly felt inferior. 'Oh, I was pleased, not quite top grades all round, and only nine as I didn't sit the Latin exam, but better than I thought. Just one subject I'll have to re-take.' She groaned.

'Which one?'

'Science. Didn't fail but need a better grade. Physics and smelly chemistry just make me go to sleep, honestly. I can't get worked up about formulae and periodic tables and what happens when you pour sulphuric acid onto something else to make it fizz. I mean, I'm never going to be a chemist, so why should I care?'

'You could say that about any subject, though.'

'I use my maths,' said Molly, defensively,' and I spoke to a woman *en français* in the shop the other day.'

'She was French?'

'Of course she was, daft apeth,' she giggled, poking Alison in the ribs. 'Oops-a-daisy, better not make you spill your drink, like you always do …'

'By the way, you know you need Latin if you want to go to university, don't you?' Alison then went off into a dream, for she was staring silently over Molly's shoulder.

'Who or what on earth have you seen?' asked Molly, swivelling round to look.

Alison grabbed her shoulder. 'I can't believe it. The headmaster is here!'

'That isn't surprising. It would be strange for him *not* to be here'

'But … oh you don't know, probably, Molly. My parents learned that he was sacked!'

Molly looked at Alison, wide-eyed. 'What? What? Oh, tell me, tell me everything.'

'I can't tell you everything, dope, only everything I know.'

'Go on then.'

But then Alison was blushing like mad and pretending to fan herself with her hand. 'Oh, crumbs, alcohol has this effect on me.'

Molly looked over to her right where she had seen Alison staring again. A tall young man with a head of naturally tousled hair that looked as if it would refuse to be tamed, was strolling over to them. He had a camera round his neck, with an enormous lens.

'Hello. I remember you. You posed for me. Article about the school ...' he said.

Alison threw him a stern look. 'Yes! I had no idea you would print all the things I said ...'

He put up a hand and smiled. 'Well. You must realise I was just doing my job, reporting on things people say.'

'But I was only being friendly ...'

He raised his eyebrows. 'Oh, I see. Interesting.'

'And you took my photograph. I didn't know ...'

'But you were so keen to tell me the truth of what happened. It was the truth, wasn't it? I say, do you know the former school Head is here and ...' he was rubbing his hands together, 'so is Sir Matthew Phillips, bigwig governor, father of classroom prankster, Edward. Now *that* could be a fascinating conversation to accidentally overhear! Fancy a bit of eavesdropping? Any idea what happened to the teacher Mr Finchley? I heard on the breeze that he's completely disappeared off the face of the earth.'

Molly was listening agog, trying to take in so much news all at once, and Alison was apparently also lost for words.

Walter arrived a little late, parking his car in such a way that would block someone in, but this was hardly his fault as there were no available spaces left unless he encroached on the swathes of perfect lawn, which on balance, he felt would be an unwelcome liberty to take.

As soon as he had taken a glass of sparkling wine, which he knew was not champagne, and wandered onto the lawn, he caught sight immediately of the one person he had no wish to see. However, she was standing on the raised terrace close to the open French windows of the house, hanging on the arm of her husband, for display and respectability purposes he assumed, so perhaps the power of public scrutiny would keep her there.

This notion backfired somewhat when Sir Matthew's eagle-eye managed to catch sight of Walter above or through a throng of people. He hailed him at once like a long lost friend and the couple came towards him down the wide stone steps; there was no escape.

Sir Matthew seemed eager to speak to him and approached with a sense of purpose. 'Dear chap, how are you? Such a pleasant evening. Very good of the Devonishes to throw their house open like this, very good indeed.'

'Splendid party!' agreed Walter, raising his glass as if to toast their hosts.

'So how is your poor father?' asked Victoria, with a solicitous smile.

'He's not too good, thank you. We ... I fear he's failing fast. Very weak.' Walter addressed his reply to Sir Matthew, rather than his wife, refusing to meet her brazen, steady gaze.

'How very sad – relatively young, too, and, as you were telling me, this has all come on rather suddenly,' said Victoria.

Anyone might say it was 'nice' of her to ask. However, Walter had not come out this evening for this discussion, but rather to distract him away from melancholy thoughts about both his father and his brother. Then, to Walter's relief, Sir Matthew pulled him over to one side and, thankfully, Victoria disappeared, as if she were used to being dismissed by her husband, but the overall relief was short-lived; in fact, it swiftly turned to alarm as Sir Matthew said, 'Walter, I heard that your brother, Peter, has gone missing.'

Walter was taken aback. Did he know Peter? 'Well, perhaps you know more than I do! How did you ...? I mean, I haven't even reported him as a 'missing person' yet, although I was thinking of doing it tomorrow.'

'Well, I have,' he said, quite matter-of-fact. 'I knew from his neighbours that you hadn't seen him either.'

Walter's jaw tightened as his astonishment turned to outrage. What right did he have to interfere? Was he family or friend? No. Who did he think he was? He frowned and glared at Sir Matthew, refraining from saying what he felt, waiting for some explanation.

Sir Matthew took his elbow. 'Look, let's just get away from prying ears and – over there' and they walked together to a bench, away from the main party, that looked up to the house and backed onto a dark cluster of rhododendron and azalea bushes. Walter's whole body was tense as he was steered along. Sir Matthew continued, 'All that sorry business at the school. It was grossly unfair on Mr Finchley, I mean your brother, Peter, as far as I can gather. He was denied references due to a brawl that cast doubt on his character. Did you know that?'

Walter was shocked. 'No! No, I didn't know about the references – although I was with him when he gave one of the locals a punch on the nose!' Walter described what happened and Sir Matthew kept nodding, nodding, stroking his chin, thoughtfully. 'It was very unlike him – he seemed to momentarily lose his mind.'

'He informed me of the fact; thought I ought to know. That was all, nothing presumptuous, wasn't expecting my help, just informed me by letter. Yes, it concerns me that he may be a little ... unhinged. You know what I'm getting at? Hmm. Unfortunately, the man he assaulted was the father of one of the girls who ...'

'Yes, I did work that out,' said Walter, 'after the event.'

'I want to help find him, you know. His neighbours told me they were concerned. Whatever I can do, please let me know.' He put a hand on his arm and very gently squeezed it. It was a little unusual, man-to-man, a little .... effeminate, but he took it to be a rather private gesture of reassurance and comfort.

Would he be so anxious to support and assist him if he knew of his wife's recent attempt to get him into bed? He might be inclined to *blame* him for that. Now he must take every step to distance himself from Victoria; although he feared that if he offended her, she might cook up some lively, vengeful story that he was the one who had tried to entice *her*. If she did, he decided, he would flatly deny it. Without a flickering doubt, that is what he would do but, of course, he had gone along to the hotel at her bidding. How naïve that was, half-knowing what her intentions were! Who would Sir Matthew believe anyway, if push came to shove? His wife or a man whom he had known for just a few weeks?

As they walked back to join the party, each lost in his own thoughts, Walter noticed a young man with two young girls, watching them with interest. More gossip? Walter sighed. Is it always like this living in a village?

Mrs Devonish then approached out of nowhere and Walter felt he should perhaps stand to attention and salute, but he had the presence of mind to smile and shake her hand. To kiss her hand with a respectful bow would seem quaint and unnatural, and to kiss her cheek much too continental and familiar; after all, they had not met before, apart from a brief greeting on arrival.

'Good evening, Mr Finchley,' she said in an even tone. 'Sir Matthew has told me a little about you, but not that much. We are only too delighted to meet a newcomer. You are in business I believe?'

'Yes. I have my own company I run from an office in London. Importing and selling, on the whole!'

'You make it sound so simple and I'm sure it isn't. What kind of goods, may I ask?'

'At the moment, any merchandise that makes me a profit. Some clothing, furnishing, fashion accessories, basket-ware – many things,' he said, realising he made himself sound rather like a common holder of a Portobello Market stall. 'My enterprise is growing, I am pleased to say.'

'So you employ a few people?' He was right; she had no idea.

'Oh yes, six hundred and seventy-four in total, mostly here in Great Britain, manufacturing, wholesale and retail …' he paused to watch her face and yes, she gasped. 'That includes people working for me abroad as well, of course.'

'Fascinating. Frightfully modern and *avant-garde*! And you are thinking of living here, in Appley Green, yet working in London?' Walter considered how fast word gets round. 'It seems to be the way the world is going, with the growth of suburbia. Will it work for you?'

'Possibly,' he replied, non-committedly. He had begun to toy with the idea of setting up a small office in Appley Green; bring in a secretary and a couple of administrative people. Failing that, he would stay in his London house during the working week and treat Appley Green as his weekend retreat. He had read somewhere that in a few years' time it would be possible to send documents by phone line on a 'facsimile machine'; hard to comprehend but this was the future, apparently, and would revolutionise business communications …

Mrs Devonish's voice brought him back to earth. 'Do you have somewhere in mind – to buy, I mean?'

'No. Nowhere at all,' he stated plainly, wishing Victoria Phillips could hear him.

'Well – why don't you come and meet our local architect?' She peered around. 'Ah, there he is with his wife and daughter. Such a lovely man, with a delightful family so I understand. Apparently, he's really rather famous. Please.'

She indicated that he come with her, yet not in a patronising way, not like Victoria Phillips might expect him to follow. He wished he could forget her.

Gently interrupting a conversation, Mrs Devonish made the introductions and left them like the gracious ambassador she was.

'Mr Jeffrys, I have read of your work. Honoured to meet you. I really do admire …'

This was more like it. If he spoke to no-one else for the entire evening, this introduction would make it worthwhile. He was rather surprised the Devonish family and Jackson Jeffrys were not already better acquainted. What he had not told Mrs Devonish was that he had actually read about him in a glossy magazine while in Hong Kong but that would have sounded rather self-important. *Nouveau riche* was one thing, but jet-setter might be too much.

Alison and Molly were wondering if they might ever be introduced to the happy engaged couple, Ted Devonish and his fiancé, Geraldine Pyke, the banker's daughter. They caught sight of the tall young man and rather average-looking woman just once, but of course they were suffocated by an entourage.

Alison suggested they wander inside the house, as most people had done some while ago to attend the buffet, and *en route* met Alison's parents.

'Goodness!' cried her mother. 'Where have you been all evening?'

'Here, of course!'

'Yes, I suppose so.' Her mother giggled, as she did when cooking the Christmas dinner after a few glasses of sherry. 'I hope you've been behaving yourselves.'

Alison sighed. 'Yes mother. Impeccably.'

'We've been talking to so many people. It's just lovely … but I feel terribly guilty leaving Julian all alone and so ill at home and, oh, heavens above, I promised I would telephone him from here by nine o'clock.' She looked at her watch.

'You worry too much, my dear …' her father reassured his wife.

'You see, it's half-past ten – where has the evening gone? Oh Gordon!' She gave him a look as if it were all his fault, then hiccupped. 'Pardon me! Would you do this for me, Alison? I don't … ' Alison could see her mother was struggling to speak coherently, but was in command of rational thought just enough to realise it best not to set a bad example to her son. As far as her daughter was concerned, the damage was done.

'Make a telephone call to Julian from here?' Alison was delighted. She had been wondering how things were going back home. 'Oh, if you really *want* me to.'

'Oh, please. You're an angel. He'd like to hear from you, wouldn't he? If he's really ill – we'll drive straight back home and get Dr Miller. Tell him that. Now, run along – find someone in the house, a servant or some lackey and ask if you may use the telephone to make a cheap local call. Make sure they understand it's not long distance. We mustn't impose on their kindness. All right, darling?'

Alison tried not to look too keen, then turned and walked with Molly, speeding up once she knew her parents had turned their backs on them.

She laughed. 'What a bit of good luck! Come on Moll, let's find out what high jinks they're up to.'

Walter decided he should attach himself to a young lady. Firstly, this was a good opportunity to find one, and secondly he would not only ignore Victoria, but also demonstrate to her with some *panache* that his interests lay elsewhere, with someone essentially young and pretty. Did she not realise he was about ten years younger than she was? Yes, she most probably did, but it did not deter her, because she knew she had an exciting voluptuous figure, a sophisticated beauty and a great deal of money. She also had power and influence.

A waiter had just provided him with a glass with whisky, when he saw a young woman on the telephone. She looked *bien faite*, rather capable and confident, but she would almost certainly have a young man on the end of that phone. He undertook to eavesdrop, just a little, and heard mention of 'Oh Julian', which confirmed his suspicions. He turned slightly to see a fresh-faced girl, just leaning against the wall nearby, little more than her ankles showing below a dated, midnight-blue, velvet evening gown that seemed sadly loose and heavy on her slight figure. He guessed it belonged to her mother. There was quite a mixture of fashions and styles here this evening! He put down his glass and lit a cigarette to give him a minute more to watch her.

Then he inhaled deeply on his cigarette and breathed out thoughtfully. Weren't they the two girls who had been laughing with that young man with the serious looking camera?

He saw them both go off, heads together, giggling in some wonderful, girlish, conspiratorial fashion; the one on the phone clearly relaying the entire telephone conversation to the other. These two seemed so gay, he had a stupid urge to run after them, grab them both by the hand, to absorb some of their infectious, juvenile innocence and joy. Instead, he simply held back and watched them discreetly as they returned to a more mature group and allowed themselves to be introduced formally to what looked like a mother and her daughter. He had lost them.

16

Normally they would catch a bus from the railway station, loaded with suitcases and bags, but today Tommy decided not to wait but splash out and get a taxi for the short journey home. They sat in subdued silence; it was their last luxury for a long while.

'Back to the old grindstone soon,' said her father, with a prolonged sigh as he rolled himself a cigarette.

'That was the best holiday we've ever had, Dad,' said Nicola, thinking only of the boy she had met on her last day in Margate. It was tragic; she would never see him again, she knew that, but they had a rock 'n' roll time together. She felt her pulse race, just thinking about his kisses. He had insisted on her giving him her address, but she knew from magazine stories what 'holiday romances' were about. Out of sight, out of mind.

'Don't be such an old misery guts,' said her mother, giving her husband's leg an affectionate kick, 'it's always nice to get back home.'

Above all, Nicola was just dying to see Alison and Molly again. There was so much to talk about – like the party she had missed.

They arranged by a mix of phone-calls and word of mouth messages to meet up by the cricket pavilion as there was nowhere they could get so much as a cup of tea on a Sunday. Molly and Alison seemed thick as thieves, arms linked and giggling all the time, as they came towards Nicola waiting on a bench. Alison seemed to have changed; she was wearing a straight skirt, sling-backs - and bright orange lipstick!

They all shrieked and squealed at each other. 'Oh, we've got so much to tell you ...' said Molly, pulling her arm to make her hurry up and sit down. 'And Margate? How was it?'

Nicola rolled her eyes, 'It was smashing. All the aunties, uncles and cousins from the East End – we took up half the beach! Well, if I'm perfectly honest, it did rain a bit, but …'

'You won a beauty competition!' said Molly. Alison seemed unaware of this but looked amused, rather than impressed.

'Came second. Did you get my postcard, Alison?' It was a sober scene of the beach: *Lovely beach and fun in Dreamland. Went to Shell Grotto today. We are all well. See you soon. Luv Nicola.*

Alison nodded. 'I'm sorry I didn't send any cards from Brighton …'

'Oh yes! How was that?'

They were all over the place, bursting with excitement and unable to make much sense of each other. At last, once Nicola had finally grasped the concept that they'd had to forego the party at Alison's house, Molly began to describe the Devonish party.

'But, what happened? Did loads of people turn up? How …?'

'Yes, yes, Julian had a whale of a time. The only trouble was, it was still going on when my parents and I returned home. Mother decided to return earlier than planned, feeling guilty for leaving her poor, sick, diddums son at home all on his own.'

Nicola gasped. 'Your parents must have been bloody fumin'! Did he get a wigging? How did you explain?'

Alison giggled. 'Hats off to Julian, caught on the hop and fired up with a bit too much booze, he said quick as a flash that he'd called up a friend to say he was ill. 'Word was passed round', he said, as if it could in the time, but Ma and Pa fell for it. He told them a group of friends then rallied round like absolute troopers and came round to cheer him up!'

'But there must've been …'

'I know. A real crowd at the party, but word spread like wildfire that most of them must *vamoosh* pronto and they did!'

They left the recreation ground, deciding to wander along to the village Green and make the most of a rare sunny afternoon, knowing that tomorrow they would be back at school.

They sat down in the middle of the village green, where the grass had dried out in the sunny spell. Boys were playing football in the road; little girls were skipping with a length of washing-line, singing: *The farmer's in his den, the farmer's in his den, ee aye addy oh the farmers in his den ... the farmer wants a wife ... the wife wants a child ...'* just as they had done at their age. Mothers with prams were chatting on the wooden benches. Otherwise it was peaceful, with the very occasional car puttering round the green, splashing through puddles, honking at the boys who stood back to let it pass. One little lad whipped out a notepad and stubby pencil each time a car was spotted to jot down its registration number.

'How was Brighton?' asked Molly and Nicola noticed how Alison's eyes sparkled at the question.

She paused before replying, as if to compose herself and Nicola studied her carefully. She looked like somebody who was about to make something up, to snatch a story out of thin air, to lie.

'The weather was very on and off, we got such a soaking it was like a monsoon, but then some days we were as red as lobsters! Mother says the sun is very strong there.' Molly looked away and Nicola yawned. 'Brighton has some lovely architecture and ...'

'Did you meet any boys?' Nicola watched Alison's face twitch, taken off-guard.

A smile spread across Alison's face like sunshine across a field of wheat, a golden smile that had taken over, taken control. 'Might've done.' She blushed.

'Are you seeing him again?' asked Molly, eagerly leaning forward.

'Poof!' said Nicola. 'Holiday romances – I've been through that. They never last! Never!'

Alison looked as though she had been stabbed, her cheeks suddenly drained of colour.

'Oh don't listen to Nicola, Alison,' said Molly. 'What's he like?'

Alison perked up again. 'He is a *man* and really ... it's hard to describe, but he just felt so ... well ... oh, I can't put it into words ...'

Nicola laughed loudly. 'Oh! Alison's in love ...'

'Of course I'm not! Don't be so silly, Nicola. It does make you realise how young boys our age are when you meet someone mature like that though. You'll meet him one day.' Alison raised her chin defiantly.

'Anyway ... what happened at the Devonish bash?' asked Nicola, putting on a posh accent.

'Bash? Funny word,' giggled Molly. 'We had a smashing time. It was very grand, wasn't it, Ali?'

Ali? Nicola could see a closeness between the other two and felt painfully excluded. It brought home to her how important their three-way friendship was.

'Who did you meet there, then?'

'Oh, all sorts,' said Alison. 'Ted Devonish and his fiancé of course. A really strange old friend of my mother's ...'

'Why strange?'

'They were so entranced to see each other, apparently it's been years since they met and they used to work together but when I asked her daughter, Gloria, who's a bit older than us, what they did, they all just looked at each other and changed the subject. She said she had no idea but it was something to do with helping the war effort, hard to describe. Very odd indeed. They were so slow to say anything, I began to think they must've been, well, you know, something quite indecent, like can-can dancers or 'ladies of the night' ...'

'What?' asked Molly, frowning.

'Oh, never mind, only joking. Anyway, we met Gloria's mother who worked with my mother during the war and it all got more and more like the Mad Hatter's tea party. She seemed to be quite bonkers but my mother kept saying to shush-shush and giving me the most reproving glares. I thought she was seriously tipsy, but apparently, Gloria's mother is forgetful and a bit screwy, and rabbits on about spies and something called 'code-breaking'. Ma suddenly whisked us away but I heard enough to get the gist.'

'I'm not following this at all,' said Molly.

'Oh, it means they must have all been spies I suppose, my father as well probably because I know they met during the war. Perhaps they still are.' Alison shrugged. 'But then who

122

would they be spying for? Perhaps they were breaking the enemy codes – yes, that's more like it, surely?'

'So is Gloria nice? Did she go to our school? I don't know anyone called Gloria.'

'Oh no. She went to a terribly posh girls' boarding school in Gloucestershire and, anyway, she's over twenty. But we have agreed to be friends, even so. I somehow felt much older when I was there. Didn't you Moll?'

Molly nodded. 'It was like a dream. As soon as I got home I felt like a fifteen-year-old schoolgirl again, just as normal. I know just how Cinderella felt!'

'Parents don't seem to realise we're adults in children's clothing,' said Nicola and then they all laughed, looking at Nicola in her pencil skirt and stilettos, with her hair folded up in a neat French pleat. 'It's school. Once you leave you feel grown-up.'

'I just thought!' cried Alison suddenly. 'Of course you don't know. Oh, Nicola, there's so much to tell. The headmaster has been *sacked* and so we don't even know who will be there tomorrow yet but he's been quickly replaced. And Mr Finchley has *vanished* ... and we met a famous architect called Mr Jeffrys whose daughter Estebel is in the sixth form, but I never realised what her father did ... oh we had such a lot of fun, didn't we Moll?'

Nicola felt she was in danger of slipping out of this threesome. She had not shared this night of all nights, and now they would be at school and she would be left out, working in the hairdressers full-time, another world.

17

The first weekend after the start of the autumn term, Molly was behind the counter in the wool and baby-clothes shop. The owner was happy for her to continue on Saturday mornings, which was all the time she could possibly spare now, what with studying and the relentless toil of housework.

It was her little haven and she loved being there. On her own, she would work at her knitting and crochet and gaze out of the window at passers-by. It gave her a warm sense of belonging to Appley Green as she spotted people she knew and others she did not. When a customer came into the shop she loved to chat to them and found it a very easy way of earning a few bob. In fact, she enjoyed it so much she would have done it for nothing, but realised that made no sense and would be unfair on her Mum who needed her at home. The extra money came in useful and gave Molly a kind of independence. At least she didn't have to ask her Mum and Dad every time she wanted to go to the pictures, buy a new single or a pair of nylons – all regarded as luxuries by her mother who had 'lived through the war and knew what hard times were.'

Day-dreaming, bathing in the memory of the magical time she and Alison had at the party, she gazed onto the road outside and saw a man looking in at the window-display. Thinking he would probably be a father, or father-to-be, who were the best as they had no idea of what to buy and always appreciated her help and advice, she gave him a shy smile. Then, strangely, he walked on only to return seconds later; it was a classic 'double-take'.

The bell gave a ting-a-ling as he opened the shop door and came in.

'Hello!' he called, with a smile that lit up the whole shop. 'I was admiring the knitted jackets you have and those tiny crochet bootees and mittens sets with embroidered edging.

Tell me, are they produced abroad, do you know? I like the felt soles.' He was examining her goods displayed on the shop counter like an antiques expert might search a piece of silver for a hallmark.

Molly laughed softly and shook her head. 'No, sir. I make them - you see, right here on the premises, or at home.' She pointed to a rather bright pink matinee jacket she was making.

He gave his head a little shake as if to wake himself up from a dream. 'Really? But they are exquisite. Must take many hours of work. Do you make up the designs yourself?'

This man had a lot of questions. 'Now I do. I use a basic pattern for the number of stitches and take care to watch my tension, but then I add in all kinds of fancy stitches, lacy, bobbly and cable. And colour, ribbons or fine braids threaded through and lace here and there ... well, you see for yourself. I mix up knitting, crochet and sewing.'

'So they are totally original? Unique! Each item!' Rather than talking to her, he seemed to be speaking his thoughts aloud; in fact, he appeared to be thinking seriously, really thinking, stroking his chin, scratching his head, all the signs were there.

He turned to her. 'Are you under some contractual obligation to the owner of this shop? I take it you're not the owner? Forgive me but you look a little young for that!'

Molly blushed. 'I don't know ... I think I'm just ... er ... casual ... the owner takes a certain percentage of the profit, of course, on the garments I make.'

'Well, of course, of course, quite right.'

She felt very self-conscious at the way he was looking at her, very directly, scrutinising, his head on one side. 'I believe I have seen you ... somewhere ...' Then he slapped the side of his head. 'The Devonish evening. That's it. You were there, weren't you? With another young lady.' His broad smile told her that he was very pleased with himself, or pleased with something.

It made Molly laugh, which then made him smile even more. 'Yes, I was, by chance. Absolutely by chance.'

'Well, how lucky we are again! A chance encounter!'

'Appley Green is not that big. I imagine you're not from around here or you'd know how people bump into each other all the time, and we all recognise a stranger when we see one!'

He chuckled and held out a hand. 'Walter Finchley. How do you do.'

Molly blanched, her pulse racing. *Finchley?* The bell rang again as two young women came in, leaving their big prams outside; they could see their babies easily enough from inside the shop.

Walter Finchley. Not Mr Finchley. She felt suddenly adult in the way he introduced himself, and he was really interested in her baby garments, which had nothing to do with the fact he had seen her at the party.

'Are you here to buy something?' she asked, looking him in the eye, not shaking his hand. The two mothers would be wondering why he was holding them up and soon there would be gossip. Molly Watson talking on her own to a tall, good-looking, strange man and in no hurry to stop, if you please.

'I haven't decided yet,' he said, giving her a wink, apparently understanding the situation in a flash. 'I'll be back when I've consulted my wife. Thank you, miss, for your help. So hard to choose!'

As she served the two women who bought bibs, towelling nappies and plastic pants, her fingers were trembling. She almost gave them the wrong change, she felt so flustered; and just hoped they had not noticed.

The next hour or so passed hazily as she absent-mindedly served customers, waiting for Walter Finchley to return. So, was he a relative of Mr Finchley the art teacher, former art teacher? It was an unusual name. But the former art teacher had left Appley Green. Nobody knew where he was; so why was this person here? She was curious; of course, he would be here to try and help find him.

As promised, he returned, but was in a dash. 'I came back because I would very much like to discuss your skills with you … I have an idea. Please, I don't know your name.'

'Molly Watson.'

'Miss Watson. May I call you Molly? Would you mind very much meeting me at the Hunter's Lodge Hotel, perhaps for a cup of tea, on Friday next week? This is a business meeting, you understand?'

Molly looked away, embarrassed, unable to meet his gaze. Well, it wouldn't be any other kind of meeting, would it? He was a married man, much older than she was. It would have to be after school. How could she say that to him? She didn't want him to know she was a schoolgirl.

She mumbled that she would try and come along at about half-past four. That should give her time to go home and get changed. She could actually feel the blood rushing through her veins, her heart thumping with the excitement. Whatever did he have in mind?

He consulted his gold wrist-watch, the most expensive looking watch Molly had ever seen in her life. 'I am so sorry I must fly now. My father is very ill and I have to go to the hospital to catch visiting time ...'

Before she could offer him her sympathy, he was gone, like a dream. She wanted to twirl around the shop and sing the roof off. She wanted to tell Alison and Nicola! This was the most amazing thing that had ever happened to her! Not so much because of his plans, and nothing to do with his name; it was because he had noticed her, remembered her and smiled when she spoke.

18

The strange thing was that Edward Phillips did not show up at school and he was not on the register taken rather perfunctorily by the sixth form tutor on the first morning. Nobody had paid much attention as to who was present or absent, but Alison and Molly looked at each other.

'Perhaps his results weren't up to scratch,' whispered Molly to Alison, as the pupils split up to go to their subject teachers.

Alison shook her head. 'No, he's a pretty bright spark ...'

'Smart Alec, more like,' giggled Molly.

'He wouldn't dare fail anyway. Imagine! His father didn't send him to public school because he wanted to make a man of him and let him learn how to stick up for himself in the real world.'

'Where did you hear that?'

'What are you two plotting?' asked a teacher, breezing past them in the corridor. It was a rhetorical question as he did not stop for an answer.

'I didn't. I made it up,' said Alison, laughing. 'But whatever his reasons, he'd want Edward to do well, to prove something or the other; so that his son reflects well on him.'

'You're so wicked. I never know whether to believe you.'

'It was a little idea of mine I enjoyed and there may be some truth in it.'

'I suppose all parents are a bit like that though,' sighed Molly.

During break, Julian joined the debate when he saw them; he said he had been wondering where Edward was too. He had asked around boys who were friendly with him, but nobody knew anything. They hadn't seen him through the entire summer holiday, which made his apparent disappearance even more mysterious.

'Perhaps he flew away with The Finch!' said Julian, and while others laughed, Molly and Alison were horrified at the implication. Only the three of them knew about Edward's problem with other boys.

On his way out of school at lunch-time, Julian passed by the school secretary's office. She was no longer the 'headmaster's secretary'; it was said to be more modern to call her the 'school secretary'. She belonged to everyone, it seemed. She was pally with teachers, and pupils found her more approachable than when she had been kept on a short lead by Mr Bird.

He took his chance, on a whim, without thinking. 'Oh, Miss Collins, has Edward Phillips left – or is he ill, perhaps? No-one seems to have heard from him.' It seemed to him an entirely reasonable question.

'Oh yes. No, not ill. I think he's going to another school somewhere in London. A private, fee-paying school. Very expensive I believe, though none of my business. A place suddenly became available and his parents decided to take it.'

Julian was stunned by this news. It was a very unusual thing to happen, to remove someone from their school-friends and teachers who knew him. What bloody heartless parents! He imagined how he would feel if such a thing had befallen him. Then suddenly, voicing his thoughts, the words slipped out and he heard himself say, 'Well, it must be for the best I suppose, perhaps it's a special place for boys like him ...'

The secretary frowned and looked suddenly stern, clearly not happy with this sentiment. 'I'm not at all sure what you mean, Julian.' As if suddenly aware that she was being too chummy with these young people, she politely but firmly invited him into her office and told him to sit down.

'Now then, I think the headmaster would want to know what you mean by such a thing. 'Special place' for 'boys like him'. I beg your pardon?'

Julian fidgeted, 'Well, I meant ...' Whatever he said now would be wrong, so very wrong. Mentally deficient? Over-privileged upper class? A nancy boy?

'I want the truth. Because you cannot say that kind of thing without good reason and no good will come from making things up, Julian.'

He realised he was ringing his hands and felt sweaty. 'Can this be in confidence?'

Apart from being a responsible school secretary, she was now clearly burning with curiosity, her eyes sparkling, Julian could see that.

'Yes, of course.'

'I meant that I thought there might be some kind of treatment in a special place for boys ... well, who are ho-mo-sex-u-al.' He whispered the last word.

She closed her eyes as if relieved rather than shocked. 'I thought you meant he was some kind of idiot. I'll have to pass this information on to the headmaster, but I won't say it was you who told me. How do you know this, anyway? That Edward is ... what you say. Your source had better be good. Reliable.'

Now Julian felt really bad. This was a betrayal of the worst kind. 'I can't tell you that.'

'I think you had better or I shall tell the headmaster that you've simply been spreading malicious gossip.'

He kept tight-lipped. She began tapping her heels. 'Right well, I haven't got all day. You can go, but of course I will pass on your slanderous remarks to the headmaster. This will be his first introduction to a member of the Sixth Form. Lovely I'm sure. Enough to make him wish he'd never set foot in Appley Green Grammar School.'

No, no this was not fair. Julian stood up, looked her straight in the eye and cleared his throat. '*He* told me himself – and my sister. He was pretty upset at the time. Please don't pass this on, Miss Baker. He's not a pupil here anymore, and the new head doesn't know him, so ...'

'You seem to forget who his ... oh, never mind. Let me deal with this as I see fit.' Then she added, rather more sympathetically. 'Thank you, Julian, for being so responsible as to bring this matter to our attention.'

Our attention! *Their* attention! Cripes, thought Julian, this will get back to the board of Governors and ... then what?

Over lunch Julian said nothing to Alison as they ate their egg and cress sandwiches, a nice change from cold roast beef.

He had opened his big mouth without thinking and now he must think of a way to dig himself out of a self-made hole.

The new headmaster's name, Mr Savage, had caused some mirth in the lower forms *He looks a bit wild ... his bark is worse than his bite, so I heard ... wouldn't want to get caned by him! ...* and so on. Nobody yet knew if he lived up to his name and it was with some trepidation that Julian walked into his office and stood before him.

'Hmm. Julian Marshall. You'd better sit down,' he invited. 'My first day. Busy. So tell me, is this something I should know about, I wonder? Miss Baker tells me that you know first-hand that our governor's son, Edward Phillips, who has now left this school, has ...er ... unhealthy tendencies, as she puts it.'

Julian was relieved at how this man, whose exceptional height coupled with his surname did make him rather intimidating, had phrased things quite vaguely. He grasped his chance.

'That is for you to decide, sir, of course,' replied Julian, in as mature a voice as he could muster. 'He has left, as you say, and you have never met him ...'

'Actually, that's where you are wrong. I have actually met the boy.' He stroked his chin and shifted some papers on his desk, as if his mind were elsewhere. 'But .. mm, I need to speak to a few people about this before I can make an assessment as to whether to speak to Sir Matthew. Please keep this matter entirely confidential. You understand? Discuss this with no-one. I mean, *no-one.*'

Julian wondered if the secretary had mentioned that Alison was also party to this information. He assumed not, or he would have said so, would have told him to warn his sister to keep quiet. Did he think Sir Matthew was unaware? Julian racked his brains, but he was fairly sure that Edward had had some kind of spat with his father over it. At least no-one else knew.

'Certainly, sir.'

'Your foolish assumption was of course false. He has been moved to a private London school so that his father can see more of him – so I am given to understand. All right, that will be all. You may go. Get back to your studies and think no more about this. Is that quite clear?' He glared at him as if to warn him that there would be big trouble if he heard any further rumours.

Walter had come back to the Hunter's Lodge late in the evening, work-weary from four hectic days in London, when the hotel's receptionist handed him a scruffy envelope. It looked as if it had been used to clean the floor and stamped on a few times for good measure. He stared at the almost indecipherable date that seemed to be early August. Walter ripped it open, ran his fingers through his hair and flopped down in an armchair in the hotel lounge to read the letter. It was from Peter. Thank God!

I have decided to take a few weeks away from Appley Green to clear my head. I am of no use to father as I am, and feel sure he will hardly notice my absence now.

As he read on Walter noted there was no address at the top of the letter.

I will stay with our cousin Ned in Yorkshire for a while, then may go travelling. I cannot face all the idle chatter in Appley Green, what with the uncharitable way I have been treated and other things besides, of which you know nothing. Do not concern yourself. I am well. Please give my warmest regards to father, if he has any idea of who I am. Last time I saw him he called me Richard, so you see why he will not miss me. I am grieving for him already, because to me he left us a long time ago. I did visit him and said my own kind of Goodbye; he had no idea, it was for my own benefit. Please write to Ned if you need to contact me.

It was weeks since Peter wrote this. Walter imagined his brother's spirits must have hit rock-bottom, deducing that Walter had no interest in his sudden departure. Perhaps Ned had a telephone; he would need to check his address book. Peter did not realise when he wrote this letter that Walter was aware of the school's decision not to provide him with references, the 'other things besides' Peter referred to; but undoubtedly this had been the straw that broke the camel's back and had frightened him away. Poor devil, he must be feeling utterly demoralised, thought Walter, although he was still not sure if he could forgive him for deserting their father.

Walter contacted the police, using the hotel phone, and told them to hold off their enquiries. As soon as he had a chance he checked for a phone number for Ned, but there was none. He set to and wrote a letter to Peter at Ned's address and enclosed it in an envelope addressed to Ned to ensure it would be opened, in the event of Peter having already set off travelling. At last now he had done something and felt better for it.

He picked up his diary and as he flicked through, was reminded that he had afternoon tea planned tomorrow with that pretty little thing from the Appley Green shop. Whatever was he thinking? Despite himself, he found his mouth forming a smile, which had become a rare thing to happen over the past week or so.

19

It is strange how time can play tricks, sometimes passing so slowly when you want it to go fast and vice versa, mused Molly, as she ironed her mother's favourite flowery dress, her 'Coronation dress' she called it, made specially in 1953. It was kept for best and had lasted well. She looked down at the serviceable red, white and blue glazed cotton and realised she had singed it, she was so lost in thought. She went into a panic, scrunching it up into a ball and thinking where she could hide it, then rushed to open the kitchen window and door to get rid of the smell. There was no way this could be patched. Would the dark brown scorch mark wash out? She did not think there was the slightest chance of this.

She had been daydreaming, feeling that Friday would never arrive. She had not told anyone, not even Alison, about her *rendezvous*; somehow this was her special secret until such time as she knew what it was all about. She did not want to appear a complete ninny. What if it was all a hoax and she was stood up? Yet, a sixth sense told her he would be there. After all, she had given him no encouragement; he had simply steamed ahead with his ideas, whatever they were. He had something up his sleeve for sure, something to do with baby clothes? Just about the most unlikely thing to get a man excited! Her own excitement was mostly bound up in curiosity and also that other thing, the gossip she had overheard ...

Ironing the family's laundry always gave her time to think. Her thoughts strayed back to Sunday when her mother decided she must go to church. It did not happen very often; it seemed to Molly she was not seriously religious, but keeping up appearances was extremely important to her, that had always been obvious. All the nobs, toffs and pillars of the community seemed to attend church; so Mrs Watson felt she should join the congregation too, now and then. Molly had been hanging around while her mother ingratiated herself to the vicar in the churchyard after the Matins service, when over her left shoulder she overheard a conversation. Two women were speaking in hushed tones but she could make out what they were saying pretty well just from snatches.

'.. things that go on at the school ... Savage, new headmaster, George's replacement, well it's early days ...' 'it all happened very quickly ...' 'all those years George has given ...' '...he must be bitter...' 'well, of course, he chose to retire early, you know, he'd had enough ... but that art teacher ...' '...the one who disappeared?' '...quite so, George says he was defending and protecting Edward Phillips because he has homosexual tendencies ...' 'What! You mean the art teacher? Or the boy? ...' 'Both! Oh yes ... mm' 'Well!' 'I know.' 'The new head called on George to discuss whether he should divulge the truth about the son to his father, but it turns out Sir Matthew knows already ... Anyway ...'

Her mother was speaking. 'Molly! Can you hear me? Come on now. It's time we headed back; you need to get the Yorkshires on. That aitchbone will be cooked to a frazzle.'

'Coming.'

She would be meeting Walter Finchley, who surely must be something to do with The Finch – perhaps they were brothers, or cousins, and now she owned this massively shocking piece of information she wished she had never heard, but could not ignore.

Lost in thought after this momentous eavesdrop, she had pushed her mother's wheelchair back home through Appley Green where all was peaceful, typical of a Sunday morning with no shops open and most folks at home, apart from church-goers. David was by the back-door with his bike upturned, mending a puncture. Her father was sitting at the table in their living room reading the Sunday Express, listening to Two-way Family Favourites and smoking his pipe.

'American coloured boxer, Cassius Clay beat Tunny Hunsaker. 6 Rounds. Imagine that!' were his first words as he looked up. 'He's going places that boy ...'

Molly got to work in the kitchen, wondering if it ever occurred to him that Sunday dinner had to be actually cooked by someone, as well as the oven. Did he think all these newfangled gadgets did it all without human intervention? Did vegetables wash, peel, scrape and chop themselves?

He would carve the roast as if he were personally responsible for it and dole it out on the plates as the great family provider. Molly rarely got a thank-you for finding time to cook the daily meal. With a similar disregard for Molly's workload, her mother insisted they used linen table napkins rather than labour-saving paper serviettes.

As they passed round the horseradish sauce and gravy, her father made an announcement.

'Something you should all know. They've laid off my mate in the workshop; so there should be more repairs passed to me now. Bad news for him, but not for us, eh? Yes! I'll ask for a wage increase tomorrow.'

'That's good news, Dad, I suppose, if it means more pay for you. But I'm sorry for Bert. He's nice. Will he get another job?'

Her father shrugged. 'Course he will. He's young and strong. He can turn his hand to something else and there's no shortage of jobs.'

'So now we can afford to get some help in the house,' Molly threw in. It was worth a try but she knew at once what the reaction would be. Her father gaped at her, speechless.

'Now, we don't pay an outsider to do things we can do ourselves. Do we?' said her mother, as if spelling things out to a four year old. 'Look at how your father does all the make do and mend round the house. Always making, fixing. That's how our generation do things, Molly.'

Molly had held back. It was her parents' view of the 'work ethic'. There was so much she wanted to say, but it would only have ruined the Sunday lunch.

One day, she would speak her mind, but then was not the time. That evening, as she carried on ironing her father's and David's shirts, she wondered when that day would come.

Now, tomorrow was nearly here and she hugged this thought to herself, the most precious secret she had ever known. It was not for sharing.

20

During double-Latin that afternoon, Molly struggled to concentrate on Caesar's Gallic Wars. Surely someone had already translated this! Why did she need to learn Latin? Then she reminded herself how vital it was for her to go to university; it was her only escape route and she would do anything to make it happen, even disentangling this boring text that made her want to scream. Alison actually enjoyed this stuff, but then her father was some kind of historian or classics professor wasn't he? They probably had Latin conversations over cornflakes.

Once she had walked out of the school door, she took deep breaths to help steady her nerve. The biggest single hurdle of the next hour was judging what to wear, so that she looked her absolute best, but not so dolled up as to raise her mother's suspicion when she told them she was going to Alison's for tea. The clandestine deceit of it all thrilled her in a way she would never have expected of herself.

Having made a plate of sandwiches and checked there was some fruit cake in the tin for the family tea later on, she looked at her wardrobe. She had spent time in the middle of the night contemplating her outfit. If it was raining she would wear her rose-bud dress and pink cardigan with a mac and kitten heeled shoes; if it was fine, then the same but with light sandals and without the mac. It was cloudy but fine, so she decided to risk leaving the old mac behind and wear her strappy but comfortable sandals.

It would take about fifteen minutes to walk briskly across the Green, out the other side of the village to Hunter's Lodge Hotel, in a different direction to Alison's house, which made her anxious.

A flashy open top car drove past her as the gates came into view; she couldn't help but stare at it and was embarrassed to find that the car stopped just ahead of her, as if the driver had seen her looking. It reversed back and her heart nearly stopped as the driver was a man on his own. It's not as if she were hitchhiking.

Suddenly she was looking at the smiling face of Walter Finchley who reached across to open the passenger door and invited her to 'Hop in'.

'I'm so sorry, making you walk like this. And I expect you had to make your excuses at the shop. I really do apologise, but I was in a hurry last week and thinking very selfishly,' he said, one sentence flowing right on into the next one.

Molly sat up very straight, and smoothed down her full skirt. She was wearing a stiff, paper-nylon, waist slip underneath, to make her skirt stand out as she walked, but sitting down in the confines of a car, it became voluminous. Fortunately, Walter Finchley was focused on the road ahead and his continuing apologies.

She steadied her nerve and kept her composure. 'It's not far, and it was no trouble at all getting here. I've never been in the hotel before as a matter of fact. Locals don't use it much.'

'I seem to have taken up residence there! But not for much longer I hope.'

'Oh.' She nodded, not really understanding. It was none of her business.

'Did you knit the cardigan you're wearing now?' he asked, once he had parked the car and they were walking together to the imposing front entrance, its double doors flanked by pillars.

Molly laughed at his unusual question, for a man that is. 'Of course. I can't imagine who else would!'

'It's good,' he said, adding as he gave her another glance, 'and it really suits you.'

She blushed and looked away, pretending to study the heavy landscapes adorning the walls of the reception area. Walter quickly asked at the desk for tea to be arranged in the hotel lounge area and the staff seemed very keen to fulfil his request. She imagined he would be a good tipper.

He chose a table by a window that overlooked the grounds at the rear of the building. With great courtesy, he asked her which seat she would prefer, the one looking out, or facing inwards.

Unused to being given such options, she was tongue-tied. Then logic told her she should face away from prying eyes, so her choice was firm. 'I'd like to look out onto the gardens. Thank you.'

'Your wish is my command,' he said in a teasing voice that she liked. He had small dark hairs on the back of his wrist, she noticed, and though clean-shaven, his jaw had what she believed was called five o'clock shadow.

They sat down opposite each other. 'How's your father?' she asked, innocently.

He blinked and suppressed a smile. 'Er ... Oh! How did you know about my father?'

'I'm sorry I didn't mean to pry ... You said you were in a rush to go and see him in hospital.' She felt a sinking moment of doubt, wondering if he was a liar after all, just making things up to suit.

'Of course, of course. Sorry, Molly, I've had a ... difficult week. Well, to be honest, my poor father is not at all well.'

'I'm sorry.' She gave a little smile and looked down, unsure of whether to probe further. His father must live in Appley Green, but his son is not staying at his house.

A waiter appeared with tea, followed by a waitress bearing a cake stand filled with dainty sandwiches, cakes, scones and biscuits.

'Gosh!' she could not help but exclaim. Was this all for them?

'Please tuck in,' said Walter Finchley, as if such a feast were an everyday, normal thing, and after a pause, went on. 'He's not expected to live much longer.' He looked suddenly forlorn; she did not expect this. 'But we're not here to talk about such grey and melancholy things, are we?'

'No, I suppose not. You wanted to discuss my knitting?' It sounded absurd. A tall, dark, handsome stranger – married - had asked her to this quite palatial hotel to talk about plain and purl. Was she being terribly naïve?

'You have a very special talent – not just being able to knit, crochet and sew. It's your application of these skills. The ...

what's the word? Flair! Imagination! Creativity! All of those things. You could go far, Miss Molly Watson.'

Molly shook her head. 'Everyone can knit.'

'Believe me, you have a special way – I know places where you could sell your wares, but you need to see what's going on in London. Have you been to Chelsea? Or Carnaby Street?'

'I've never been to London.'

He sat back and regarded her as if she had lapsed into Arabic.

'I'm not suggesting you would sell baby garments – necessarily. You could design female fashion items and they would be snapped up. I know they would.'

'I'm not sure I understand ...' Molly was thinking of her A' Levels, housework, the limited amount of spare time she had. She had no real knowledge of fashion!

'The only way is for you to see what's going on in the big Metropolis! How about tomorrow? Saturday! It'll be buzzing.'

London! Molly quickly thought. It would be impossible. She worked in the shop in the morning and, even if she went in the afternoon, how could she make up another excuse to be out of the house so soon?

'I can't go tomorrow. I'm sorry ...'

'Never mind. I have some magazines, we can look at those first anyway. Vogue, Honey ...'

'But I would never have time to make all these things ...'

He reached across and gently squeezed her arm. 'No, no, no. Oh you sweet innocent thing! I would find you people to make up the garments. People! That's no problem at all. It's coming up with designs that young women your age are wanting so much now; this is where you could make it in this big brave new world of ours. Teenage girls don't want to dress like their mothers any more. I think you have the talent to invent new styles, to create original garments and accessories – that your mother would not wear! Bags – you could design fantastic casual bags in vivid colours! You see! There's a whole new bright world out there!' He flung his arms out wide and Molly laughed. 'Oh Molly, what stops you from coming to London tomorrow? Ah! A young man, of course.'

'No. I ...' Where should she begin? He thinks she works in a shop and has a boyfriend. In reality, she is still at school and lives with her parents. She needed time to think and decided to change the subject. 'Are you related to Mr Finchley, who taught at the Grammar School?'

He raised his eyebrows. 'Well, yes I am, as a matter of a fact. We're brothers. Clever girl. We don't look that much alike, but ... did you know him?'

She hesitated. 'I know one of the girls he accused of causing an accident in the classroom, before the riot.' She could not meet his gaze as she said this. 'She told me exactly what happened.'

'Oh. Oh dear.' He was digesting this piece of information. 'Would you mind telling me exactly what did happen?' At least he didn't ask if she was still at school. 'In a way it all seemed so trifling and, frankly, made me laugh at first, until I understood where it all led.'

'No, I don't mind. I can tell you.' She relayed everything faithfully, everything that happened that strange day at school, 'from her friend's point of view', and he listened attentively, his gaze wandering over her face. 'I heard he went missing.'

'I've had a letter from him now – it was delayed in the post. By about three weeks, I have to say.'

'Is he ... all right?' She asked, watching him closely.

'He is very upset to have lost his teaching post and the old headmaster refused to give him a reference.'

'Well I never quite understood why he stuck up for Edward Phillips.' She prompted him, but there was no flicker of embarrassment that she could discern. 'I hope you don't mind, but there is something I should tell you, as he's your brother.'

'Please, anything you know, tell me. I am relatively new to Appley Green so I don't get all the gossip.'

'How did you guess? This *is* gossip, but I overheard the old headmaster's wife, Mrs Bird, talking to her friend after church.'

'I see. Go on.'

'They seemed to be saying ... I mean, they did say Mr Bird was bitter at having been replaced, although his wife was insistent that he chose to retire early. I don't know about that …'

'No. Well perhaps this is all guesswork – it's how slanderous rumours start ..'

'That's true, but there was more. The thing you should know, even if it isn't so, because it's what is being said, Mrs Bird said that her husband says Mr Finchley, your brother, was defending and protecting Edward Phillips because he has homosexual tendencies and she made it clear to the other one that she meant they were *both* homosexual.'

Walter opened his mouth but seemed unable to speak. He ran his fingers through his hair. 'Molly,' he said, at last. 'Thank you for telling me this. You did absolutely the right thing, because I had no idea of this foul rumour. It is a disgusting lie, of course. I mean I have sympathies for homosexuals, but it is the fact that people make something of it and *turn* it into something shameful, for blackmail and all kinds of evil things. I've come across this kind of thing before.'

'Perhaps Mr Bird had this idea and passed it on to the new headmaster, as a kind of *revenge*. He probably blames your brother for the fact he got sacked. I bet you anything it wasn't his choice to leave. My friend's parents said it would've affected his pension and he would find it harder to find another teaching post at his age.'

'Now that, young lady, is speculation, but you're probably right, from what I can make out.' He sighed. 'I thought I had problems before, but now they seem to have grown! My brother said something in his letter about other matters that were weighing him down.'

'But he wouldn't have known about this, would he?' Molly pointed out.

'No, no. That's true. This is quite recent, presumably, blew up well after he left.' Molly nodded. 'Look, I didn't expect this kind of conversation when I asked you for tea. I am so sorry. Not your problem.'

'Even though I didn't quite understand Mr Finchley's stubborn refusal to listen to the three girls, I can see that he would find it difficult to swallow his words and what with Edward Phillips being the son of the school governor …'

'I've analysed the ins and outs of this so many times. It doesn't make a lot of sense, does it? He lost his job anyway.'

'As it turned out, but he didn't know it would turn out that way.'

'No.'

'Molly, please let me make amends for this. This was supposed to be all about *you* and now look where we are. Please say you'll at least have dinner with me tomorrow – we can go for a spin, out somewhere nice. Away from Appley Green. Please.'

'I'd like that,' said Molly, wondering how the devil she was going to pull this one off, but her whole being demanding that she must. At least there was no wedding ring on his finger; nor were there any signs of a Mrs Finchley in the hotel.

For the first time in her young life, she had spent over an hour feeling that she was important, intelligent, talented and – if his gaze was anything to go – not unattractive. She felt grown-up and there was no going back.

'Did you enjoy yourself at the Devonish party?' he asked suddenly.

'Oh yes, it was the most marvellous thing.'

'Then we shall have a good time – at least as good as that, I promise. Do you like to dance?'

'I've no idea – I've only jived a bit in my bedroom with my little sister … oh, that sounds silly. And we kept bumping into the wardrobe.'

'You like to jive. OK. So that's what we shall do. Jive and rock and roll and forget all our troubles and woe. Life's too short for all this worry.'

He took her hand and gently kissed it, in a very old-fashioned way. The touch of his lips was so soft, like a whisper's breath on her skin, that it tickled and she giggled.

'Do you really have a wife?' she said softly, looking up at him.

'You're very direct!'

'It's a fair question. You've asked me to go dancing and for dinner, not to discuss business I suppose?' She was amazed at how adult she was sounding. She didn't know where all these phrases were coming from. Probably from her mother's books and magazines she sometimes had to read to her aloud because she was too exhausted to read them to herself. What had her mother ever done to exhaust herself, she always wondered?

He smiled and his eyes were twinkling. 'My wife died a few years ago. No. Molly I would not be suggesting that I take you somewhere nice if I was married.'

'I'm sorry about your wife, but … I needed to know.'

'Quite right. We shall have some fun. After all, we have done nothing wrong, have we? And yet we have all these problems to sort out.'

'I know!'

He sighed theatrically. 'Life is *so* unfair!' With that, he walked her back to the car and offered to give her a lift back home. Molly tried to imagine the looks on her parents' faces if they caught sight of either him or his car. She said she really needed the walk but thanked him anyway. They agreed to meet at the hotel tomorrow evening at eight o'clock.

Now she could tell Alison and Nicola!

21

Alison had some news of her own when Molly next saw her briefly at the end of a school assembly.

'Something to tell you. Meet me after school, outside the main gate,' whispered Alison and then was gone like a puff of smoke. Their paths did not cross much at school now, as they were studying different subjects.

When they met up Alison said that, after much debate, she had persuaded her parents to let her do some work at The Hunter's Lodge Hotel. Just the mention of this embarrassed Molly, as if her guilty secret was out already. 'They didn't want me to at all. *Did I need more pocket money? Won't your studies suffer?* All this. But Molly, I just felt I need to *do* something. You know, outside of home.'

'I know exactly what you mean. You don't need to explain.' Molly gave a knowing little laugh.

'I'm waitressing in their main dining room, just on occasions when they need extra staff. So that'll be weddings and when rich people have parties and then there are business conferences as well. They said they have something or the other on most weeks. I can only do a few hours at the weekend.'

'Sounds really exciting.' Molly was thinking fast. Could it be a real nuisance when it came to meeting Walter, knowing she might be spied on by her best friend?

'By the way,' said Alison, 'something terrible has happened. You know all that secret stuff Edward told us?'

'Yes.'

'Somebody's blabbed. People know. I hear them in the village and at school. Nobody else knew, did they? Apart from you, me, Nicola and Julian?'

'No. Unless Edward has told other people.'

'He was desperate for us to keep it to ourselves, though.'

'His father knows doesn't he?' Molly felt herself blush, realising that she only knew that because she had overheard Mrs Bird.

'Does he? Sir Matthew Phillips?'

Molly nodded. 'I think you said so when you told me.'

'Oh. I'm not quite sure now. Well it's hardly likely *he* would be spreading the word, is it?'

'No, I suppose not.'

'Look, you haven't discussed it with anyone have you, Molly?'

Molly felt a rush of guilt. 'No, of course not.'

'Why are you blushing?' Alison was glaring at her.

'I'm not.'

'You are! You've told someone, haven't you?'

'No. Perhaps it was Julian. Or Nicola.'

Alison considered this for a moment. 'I'll ask him tonight. He doesn't usually keep things from me. Nicola? Haven't seen her for ages. Unlikely to be her, somehow.'

'Although people do chat in hairdressers.'

Molly did not want to repeat to her the gossip she had overheard, because this would include reference to Walter's brother. It would be a betrayal. She couldn't trust herself not to slip it in if they carried on with this chat; so she was determined not to be drawn into conversation any further.

'Did you hear from Robert?' asked Molly, changing the subject cleanly, knowing this would distract her.

'Oh. No. Not yet.'

'Think you will?'

Why was she not telling Alison about Walter? Something was holding her back. Was she ashamed of her own behaviour or did she still worry he might let her down and make her look naïve and gullible? She felt confused.

'Of course. He said so. But Brighton is a long way away. Unless he has a chance to come here, there's not much point.'

'So, no letter, or phone call?' She was being cruel and did not know why, twisting the knife. She must stop this.

Alison's eyes had filled with tears and her bottom lip was trembling, which was very unlike Alison. Now look what I've done, thought Molly! Upset a good friend for no good reason.

'Oh, I'm sure he will,' she assured Alison, but she could see it was too late to make amends and appease Alison with honeyed words.

Perhaps Walter will let me down, like Robert has let down Alison, thought Molly. That would be so hard to bear. But she felt sure Alison's one-night romance was not a patch on having tea with Walter Finchley, who for the time being would remain her delicious secret. It was only now and then, she wondered just how old he was.

Nicola carefully removed the rollers from a customer's head of silver hair. The lady touched the rolls of hair stiff with setting lotion to feel how firm they were and nodded in the mirror.

'That should last me the week, with a net at night.'

'You have lovely thick hair, Mrs B,' said Nicola, smiling at her reflection. 'I hope mine is as good when I'm ...' Nicola did not like to say *as old as you*, it sounded disrespectful, but her customer laughed and finished off for her.

'When you're past your prime, eh?'

Nicola smiled and carried on with brushing out the crisp coils, then got to work with her tail comb and began some gentle backcombing to give a little shape and extra body. Once she had shown the lady the results of her shampoo and set with a hand mirror to display the back, she reached for the can of hairspray.

The lady patted her arm. 'You're a good girl. Here now and don't say no, I won't have it.' She slipped a florin in Nicola's hand. Two shillings. Nicola did not like to take tips off old-age pensioners, but she knew it was no good refusing.

'That's very kind. Thank you, Mrs B.'

Nicola was about to gather up her next lady and settle her down at the washbasin, when she glimpsed Alison's face pressed up against the window. Nicola waved and beckoned to her to come in and, like lightning, Alison was at her side, pulling her arm and hissing in her ear.

'Did you tell anyone, anyone at all, about Edward Phillips, you know, what he told Julian and me?'

Taken aback, Nicola frowned and felt like shouting at Alison for her rudeness, but knew her boss was already

147

watching her to check she was not wasting time or neglecting her customers.

She glared angrily at Alison. 'No!'

'Are you sure? It's important.'

'Yes, I'm definitely sure. I can't talk now. Come round to my house tonight. After tea.'

Alison went off, looking just as worried as when she first appeared.

Nicola found herself washing the next head of hair rather more vigorously and longer than usual, distracted by this odd encounter. Already feeling left out of the threesome, she was shocked and hurt by this accusation and felt close to tears, desperate not to lose their friendship.

Alison came round after her dinner, and Nicola's tea, and was welcomed warmly by the family as Nicola introduced her to her Mum, Dad, Granny, Grandad and the dog, Boot, as well as a neighbour who had just slipped round to pay some catalogue money to her Mum. She had ordered some turquoise brushed nylon sheets that she said would brighten up her elderly mother's bedroom and save on ironing.

Nicola sensed that some privacy was needed so ushered Alison outside into the back yard and indicated that they should go for a stroll out of earshot.

'I'm sorry I barged in ...' began Alison.

Nicola shrugged. 'It was flippin' rude. What made you think ...?'

'Oh ... word's got out around the village. Somebody must've have spilled the beans.'

'Mm. Molly?'

'I don't know what to think. I asked her and she flatly denied it, of course, but she did look awfully guilty.'

'Well, it must've been her then. Have you heard from Robert?' Nicola linked her arm through Alison's.

'Not yet.'

'I'm sure you will. You can tell with blokes, can't you? You know deep inside when they're good 'uns.'

Alison's eyes dilated as she turned towards Nicola. 'Yes. You do, don't you?'

Nicola nodded eagerly. 'There'll be some perfectly good reason why he's not called. He might have lost your number or address.'

'There's directory enquiries though …'

'Did he know your surname?'

'I think so.'

'Well, maybe he's planning a surprise.'

'Mm. He might be. What about the boy in Margate?'

Nicola was about to enthuse about the letters she'd had and the flowers, but held back. That would not win her Alison's exclusive friendship which was what she badly needed at the moment. Clearly she must be suspecting that Molly, little innocent Molly, was the one who had betrayed her trust and if so, then how could they be sure of Molly's true friendship?

'No,' she lied and let it rest at that, watching a small smile creep across Alison's face.

22

Walter found Peter's landlady, Mrs Bannister, on her knees scrubbing the red doorstep tiles of her neat terraced house and he introduced himself. Her front border was as precise as a necklace, with autumn dwarf dahlias growing at regular intervals like beads on a chain. He was hoping she might be able to offer some clues as to his brother's intentions, future plans or whereabouts.

'First he told me he was going away for a week to see a friend … no, tell a lie, his cousin somewhere far away up North, so knowing he'd be away for a week at least I took a break myself and went over to my sister in Godalming – her place needed a bit of a going-over if you know what I mean.' She eased herself up stiffly, with a wince, but not pausing for breath. 'Anyhow, then I heard from him to say he'd *not* be coming back. Bit of a surprise. He did seem to take most of his belongings – apart from a few books and that; and there's a box of paintings and a big, flat bag kind of thing, what did he call it? His portfolio! Sounds so grand, don't it? Huge it is too, the box and bag had to go in the shed outside, his bedroom being quite limited for storage. Anyhow, perhaps you could take them off my hands now as you're his nearest and dearest.' It seemed to Walter as if she were speaking of someone who had died. 'He had the decency to send me two months' rent to give me time to find another tenant, so I have no quarrel with him, none at all. He was the model lodger was Mr Finchley. Kept himself tidy – and quiet.'

'Thank you. Do you have someone else for his room?' It half-crossed his mind that he could take up the vacancy himself, but the thought did not stay with him for long. He knew from Peter she was a good woman, who had lost her husband during the war and worked hard to make ends meet but such confinement would drive him insane, and just at a time of life when every day, every week was precious and to be enjoyed. 'Should I remove his things now, if they are in your way?'

'There's no urgency, but in due course …'

'Perhaps I could just take a look at the volume of stuff?'

'You mean, see how much there is?' She gave him an old-fashioned look.

Walter nodded. 'Indeed.' He was curious to see Peter's works of art for he was always shy and kept his paintings to himself, perhaps afraid of the honest criticism that family might offer.

Mrs Bannister led him through to her neatly tended back garden. Once inside the shed, she said, 'I'll leave you to take a look then; I'll be out the front if you need me, just need to do the brass.' Her down-to-earth dedication to lonely housework struck Walter as sad as it was admirable but he imagined it gave her satisfaction and pride.

'Your house and garden do you credit, Mrs Bannister,' he commented. 'I hope your new tenant appreciates you as they should.' He smiled and her round cheeks flushed with pleasure.

Peter was lucky that Mrs Bannister kept a clean shed, so his items were not full of cobwebs or damaged by mice. Walter sifted through the tea-chest of paintings, casting a look at some of them. An eclectic mix, derived from a period when perhaps the young Peter was trying to find his artistic self, included everything from abstract still-life to landscapes. One or two he did recognise. In the portfolio, however, were more recent works and Walter's jaw dropped when he saw originality of style, the way he had captured light, texture and form in a new way, somehow more intense than a photograph. They were entirely portraits or nudes and clearly the human face and body was now his *metier*, his *forte*. How strange, thought Walter that it seems an automatic thing to slip into French, as if the English language was unable to express artistic *nuances* …

He would give her a small payment for her inconvenience, he decided. 'I'll make the necessary arrangements to have them stored somewhere very soon,' he assured her.

Walter felt a tight, suffocating sense of closure, as if Peter had gone from his life, had disappeared for ever along with his undoubted talent.

As he took the walk back to the hotel, he thought about sweet, pretty, innocent, clever little Molly, who seemed to be the most cheerful aspect of his life at the moment. He did not want to rationalise it, or analyse his feelings or his motives but he felt quite ridiculously thrilled at the prospect of their evening out together and many more dates after that. With her, he could relax and, almost like having a small child, he could see the world and all that it had to offer through a fresh pair of eyes. The prospect of her company made him feel alive and happy.

He had found it hard to believe his luck when he passed by the shop that day and caught sight of her through the window. He remembered her instantly from the Devonish party, though she did not know that; he had played a little game with her. Perhaps their meeting again was fate, destiny, something that was meant to be; luck seemed too humble a concept.

He gave his head a little shake. A business man, used to spotting commercial opportunities; predicting profit and loss; extrapolating trends from account books; building a wide circle of associates and managing a workforce – this was his world, not a small village shop and a girl with freckles and wide blue eyes that made him feel seventeen again. But perhaps this was what he needed; it was certainly what he wanted.

He picked Molly up just before the phone box in the lane leading up the hotel, as she had stipulated and he did not question why he should not collect her from her home, but did assume that any girl in high-heels would rather not walk all the way to Hunter's Lodge. She probably still lived at home and the proper thing would be for him to meet her parents, since there was a wide age gap between him and Molly. This prospect presented a problem, for he could not bear the idea of anything standing in his way of seeing this precious girl.

She was standing at the roadside, quite demure as she clutched a white handbag with both hands, but she was also looking around furtively, as if worried someone might see her.

As soon as she saw him, she smiled and waved. He drew up alongside her, jumped out to open the passenger door and his eyes were drawn to her pale pink twinset with pearl buttons. The cardigan was hand-embroidered in silks with intense blue French knots, like forget-me-nots and cornflowers matching her eyes, drooping fuchsias in a medley of pinks and cherry-red matching her cheeks and lips, with delicate swirls of grass and stems weaving their way between the flowers. Almost William Morris-like yet somehow an original style and he knew it would be her own design.

He was unable to suppress a genuinely warm, but mischievous smile as she stepped neatly into his car. 'You look good enough to eat.'

She did not blush but just laughed that way she had, not a giggle, not forced, just a genuine, little laugh that he loved. She was so unspoiled, so innocent, so sweetly malleable, so … virginal. He tried to dismiss thoughts of *Lolita* he read last year; sub-consciously trying to convince himself she was at least seventeen. He would find out in due course.

'Where are we going?' she asked as he drove off.

The car seemed a more intimate space with the roof on.

'Oh, a little place I discovered recently. Not too far. I guess you don't want to get home to your parents too late.' He watched her obliquely as he drove.

'Huh! They are unlikely to wait up for *me*.' Her face looked glum and pinched.

'I see.' Then he grasped the steering wheel firmly, as if it were her shoulders he was holding. 'No. Actually I *don't* see …' It was the look on her face, not the words she spat out, that he did not understand.

'My mother is usually in bed by about nine o'clock, with the help of my father when I'm not there. She's wheelchair-bound and sleeps downstairs. My father and brother will not be concerned that I am late at my friend's house …'

'Now Molly, I don't want you telling lies to your parents. You'll land me in all kinds of trouble.'

'My parents must know *nothing* of you. That is, if you intend taking me to London and … They would spoil everything. *Everything.*'

Walter frowned. He felt a little uncomfortable about this. 'I thought perhaps it might be an idea if you introduced me to them …'

Molly looked horrified. 'No! Please. Just trust me about this. My parents are … difficult. All I want to do is …'

'All you want to do is …'

Molly looked away out of the window into the dusky evening light as the car motored smoothly onto a wider road and Walter put his foot on the throttle.

'… escape,' she whispered.

Walter swallowed. What happened to the sweet, compliant Molly, the girl who was so innocent, so sweet she could be trusted never to deceive him in any way? He had not bargained for this. Romance was just burgeoning for he had not even kissed her yet, but now, although highly unlikely, if he decided to end their friendship, she could punish him by telling her parents that an older man was seducing her and he had the distinct impression that they could be … well, difficult, to use her word. No. That was just his imagination running away with itself because of his past experience.

'OK!' he said, wanting to bring a smile back to her worried face. 'Let's escape!'

There were few decent cafés outside of London and a hotel seemed a trifle seedy in the circumstances, so he had planned something else. He had persuaded a new friend of his to vacate his country home for an evening, so that he could use it and arrange for a cook to come in and provide an outstanding meal. His friend had an excellent collection of LPs and singles, plus the newest model of television and Hi-fi.

He saw the sign to the village and turned off the road into a gravel driveway.

Molly put her hand to her mouth and gasped. 'Where are we?' He watched her wonderment and felt delighted by it.

'It's a friend's house, but this evening, it's all ours.'

'Oh, really. Well, it looks very beautiful, but …'

'Don't worry little thing. We shall be looked after by servants! There we are, see the cook, she's come to the door to welcome us.'

Molly looked bewildered and he loved that she was. He wanted to give, to give and to give to this enchanting child and make her love him. How had this happened so fast, he wondered, his entire body pounding with desire?

'Do you think we've made Molly suffer enough?' said Alison to Nicola as they walked arm in arm across the green on their way to the village hop.

A few months' back she would never have imagined it possible that she would be out on a Saturday night with a school-friend who lived on the council estate, going to a dance! And why? To meet some boys, an even more unbelievable idea.

'Have you seen her this week at school?' asked Nicola.

'I've deliberately avoided her. Not exchanged a single word. She must've noticed and yet she doesn't seem that bothered, as a matter of fact.'

'She's tougher than she makes out, is Molly.'

'A brazen liar, maybe.'

'I don't want to fall out with her, though. Not really. Do you? I mean, maybe someone else did spread the Edward story around.'

'OK. Let's go round to her house and confront her. Well, let's see if she wants to come dancing with us first.'

Nicola nodded and off they strode together, ignoring the wolf whistles from a group of young men outside The Fox and Rabbit.

A glass of sherry, to the tune of Mantovani's strings, was followed by grilled grapefruit with a glacé cherry on top. She was duly impressed by the deft manner in which Walter opened a bottle of wine with a corkscrew. They never had wine at home; it was much too expensive. Molly wondered what would follow, and although she could detect the aroma of chicken which reminded her of Christmas, she guessed it would be done in some kind of special sauce. There were other savoury smells coming from the kitchen she could not identify and Walter refused to spoil the surprise, watching her intently but kindly. She felt a little as if she were some kind of prize, or treasure, he would never wish to hurt, only to please. Far from minding this attention, she felt as if she had accidentally wandered into paradise.

She wondered if he would kiss her goodnight later and could not stop this thought, wishing and hoping that he would. She had never really felt drawn to a boy before, let alone a man, and certainly not a man like this, rich, handsome, polite and kind who admired her! She blinked and pinched herself now and then to check she was not dreaming. He poured her a glass of red wine and she sipped it. At home, alcoholic drinks were strictly for Christmas or if someone was in a state of shock, for medicinal purposes, like when her father found a woman who had fainted in their road and he found, surprisingly quickly, a tot of brandy and rushed to her rescue. The woman seemed to know him but they never saw her again.

The heat of it flooded through her body and she knew if she took too much too fast she would probably be sick and she wanted to enjoy this meal, certainly not let it go to waste, which would be a crime. She looked around the room that did not belong to Walter, but to his friend. It was different from anything she had seen before, very artistic and simple in its plain, modern furnishings. She guessed a wall had been knocked down to open up two rooms into one. It reminded her of pictures she had seen of a home in Scandinavia, that boasted a lot of knotty pine and big windows. Yet the house was a traditional kind of building, which made her curious.

'Who does this house belong to?'

'A chap called Mr Jackson Jeffrys. He's an up and coming architect. Met him at the Devonish party. He's built a brand new place – quite spectacular – tucked away in the woods near Appley Green village, but he's not got round to selling this house yet.' He must be terribly rich, thought Molly. 'The building work has been going on for years, but few of the locals have seen it. It'll cause a stir when they do!'

'Why? Is it ugly?'

'No. Far from it. But some might see it as shockingly modern and what they call minimalist, gleaming white with a great deal of glass and a flat roof.'

'Sounds very space-age, but I like that kind of thing.'

'That's because you have a naturally artistic nature. It makes sense that you can embrace change.'

'Really?' She took another sip of wine and met his gaze, feeling increasingly grown-up and all of her sixteen years, more so than at any other single moment since her birthday that had passed by unremarkably.

After what Walter told her was *coq au vin*, followed by a dessert that was apparently a cheesecake that she had never tasted before, not quite a cake, or custard tart, or blancmange but something creamy, with a hint of lemon, that made her lick her lips over and over, with her eyes closed. She sensed Walter was watching her again, but nothing would stop her from enjoying every mouthful to its fullest extent. It was topped with a bramble jelly.

'Normally I like it with raspberries or blackcurrants, something sharp, but Mrs Beeton out there had to use what she could find – blackberries from the woods. I gave her the cheesecake recipe I got from an American friend, and she's done a good job.'

'It is the most gorgeous thing I've ever tasted.'

'Nothing less than you deserve.'

Molly gave him a slightly cynical look. 'Sorry,' he said, seeming to understand at once. 'Was that a bit much?'

'A bit, but,' she sighed, 'how could I possibly mind?'

Molly felt limp and warm and utterly happy as Walter left the table for a moment, returning quickly.

'She has cleared up out there already, so I've told her to get home. She came on her pushbike and lives quite close by.'

Molly did wonder, very hazily, who the cook was. She did not recognise her when she arrived, and hopefully they were far enough away from Appley Green for 'Mrs Beeton' to be anyone who would have recognised her.

Their conversation over dinner had covered many surprising things and flowed naturally. As she got up from the table, Walter was beside her; the music playing was a gentle ballad sung by the unmistakable Elvis Presley. This was not the rock and roll he had promised but why should she care? He held her hand, then gently kissed her cheek and Molly felt herself melt away inside. In a Eureka moment, she realised what all the fuss was about, in an epiphany of understanding, she knew why people did stupid things sometimes and allowed their feelings to run away with them, out of control. Now she knew what those feelings were.

She instinctively raised her chin and his lips sensuously brushed her mouth. A little wobbly, she allowed herself to be guided by him. His arms were around her waist and they both swayed to the music, as if the rest of the universe did not exist. She could feel the full length of his body and felt suddenly hot.

'Molly,' he whispered, his voice soft and husky. 'What are you thinking at the moment? Where are your thoughts?'

'My brain has turned to marshmallow, I can only feel that I am the happiest girl because I am with you. Is that too much?'

'Oh Lord, Molly! No, you sweet thing. Never too much.' Trembling, he kissed her tenderly on the lips, then fiercely, over and over and she kissed him back, learning fast.

'What about the knitting?' she asked, her voice slurred and now giggling.

He pushed a stray strand of wavy hair off her face and gazed into her eyes. 'Yes, do not fear, we shall get to that, but not … just at the moment.'

23

'Molly, what were you up to last night?' Her father was shouting in her ear, and she woke up with a start and a groan, blinking just enough to bring him into focus.

After a pause, she replied. 'I was at Alison's. I ... told you.'

He stood towering over her bed, a murderous look on his grim face, fuming as though he might hit her if he unfolded his arms for a single moment.

'Then how come your friend, Alison, and that other tarty blonde one, came round here looking for you? Eh?' He then put his hand on the bedclothes and shook her. 'You're a little liar!'

She sat up, frightened, rubbing her eyes, unable to think clearly, but realising she must say something fast. The chances of such a thing happening were so remote, she could scarcely believe her ears.

'Oh, no, it was another friend. Alice. I must've said Alison by mistake, slip of the tongue ... another girl, someone you don't know.' Yes, I am a liar, she thought, but what alternative is there now but lies, lies and more lies? 'She lives a little way out of Appley Green and ... her father brought me home.' He looked uncertain. 'Did you see his car?'

'Er .. no. I was sound asleep in my bed at the unearthly hour you got home, but I heard you all right, creeping up the stairs. It must've been close on midnight.'

'Well there were two other girls there who stayed overnight, but I said I must go home because of getting Mum up in the morning ...'

'Huh! Well, you're too late for that, aren't you? She's downstairs having breakfast, no thanks to you. Do you realise what time it is? Half-past nine!!' He tut-tutted. 'Young people these days.'

'Well, you managed without me, then.' She looked at her father and smiled.

He narrowed his eyes. 'You, young lady, had better watch your step. You're not allowed out now until we're sure you can be trusted. Is that understood?'

He strode out and slammed the bedroom door. Molly said, under her breath, 'That's what you think.' Next weekend Walter was taking her to London and nothing, no-one, would stop her going. Meanwhile she would go round to Alison's for a chat. Why did Alison and Nicola come round for her last night? They'd never done that before and, moreover, they weren't exactly on good speaking terms at the moment.

After clearing up the Sunday lunch dishes and settling her mother down in an armchair for a nap, she took a walk round to Alison's house, despite her father's ruling. How could he stop her? He depended on her too much; and she was beginning to realise that she was the one who actually held sway in the household, for how could he manage without her?

She knocked on the front door and Mrs Marshall opened it.

'Hello. Molly, how lovely to see you. We haven't seen you since the big party.'

'No, that's right,' Molly smiled; she liked Alison's mother.

'I'm sorry, Alison's not here. She went off to meet someone in the village. I'm not entirely sure when she'll be back. You may find her on the green, I think that's where she was going.'

Molly thanked her and headed towards the village green, lost in her thoughts, wrapped up snugly with memories of the evening with Walter and excited about the London trip next weekend. Would telling Alison and Nicola about Walter spoil things? Would they make derisory comments, tell her she was being foolish and naïve? They had both been quite horrible to her lately and she was not enjoying their friendship at all. Unable to bear the idea of spoiling her dreamy state of mind, she decided to retreat into her own private paradise and go home. She could do some jobs and homework to make sure that going missing next Saturday, for a whole day, would cause less outrage from her Mum and Dad. She must work hard to get into their good books!

Walter had suggested they set off early, in case the drive there took longer than usual for any unforeseeable reason. After pretending to eat breakfast, for excitement had killed her appetite, she was waiting for him at the same place as before. There was a nip in the air, and fallen leaves swirled and skittered around the lane; he was late, which made her so anxious her heart was racing and she felt sick. The notion of him letting her down now was just unbearable, for today, not only was she spending time with a man she adored with all her heart, but also she may learn something that could change her entire life. He was going to open her eyes to 'something that would inspire her and make her realise what she could do with her talents'. Those were his words, etched on her brain.

As she stood there, she looked up in the direction of where the hotel lay, and saw with horror that Alison was walking towards her. There was no escape; she must have seen her too. What should she say?

Then Walter's car appeared. She crossed the road with haste, to get into the passenger seat, not even giving him time to get out and do the gallant thing of opening the door for her. There was only one option; to pretend she had not seen Alison, carry on regardless and keep calm. Walter leaned across and kissed her on the lips; although the autumn day was cool, the sun was shining in a clear sky, so the car had its roof down. Alison must have seen everything.

There was a woollen tartan rug on the seat for her use, but she had no need for it as she was aglow, her pulse racing with anticipation and the sheer bliss of being with Walter. They drove along merrily, Walter turning to look at her often, his hand reaching across to clasp hers. She wondered if it was possible to die of happiness, she felt such a thrill and an ache inside her, all at the same time. Was this really happening?

They talked almost all the time, of everything from the safe return of two Russian dogs in Sputnik to Princess Margaret's wedding, above the hum of the engine and the whoosh of occasional cars passing them by from the opposite direction. How they were both feeling was not something either of them voiced; but glances and smiles between them said it all.

Just beyond Fulham, in Chelsea which Molly had heard of, Walter parked the car in King's Road to show her a shop called Bazaar run by someone called Mary Quant. Molly stared at the clothes modelled by display mannequins in the window. She had not seen anything like it before; they gave her a curious feeling of being alive. She wanted to wear these clothes; they were garments her mother would not understand in a million years; there was nothing sweet or flowery to be seen and she looked down at her own clothes, feeling like a quaint country bumpkin. Even girls striding along the pavements looked different from any she had ever seen in Appley Green, wearing thick patterned stockings, short skirts and dresses with hemlines above the knee. One girl returned her admiring gaze with eyes heavily made-up; her white lips pouting at her.

But most people in general seemed very scruffy to Molly and she commented on this.

Walter laughed. 'Ah yes! Bohemian! Big music scene here.' He steered her gently by the elbow towards a café called Fantasie. 'Jazz, skiffle and all kinds of clever arty sods live and work around here.' He sounded a little contemptuous, thought Molly, and she was both shocked and thrilled by his bad language. The people here seemed a far cry from his artistic brother, whose appearance was relatively groomed and conservative.

It was crowded inside, smoky, noisy, full of life. Intelligent looking, talkative people drinking freshly brewed coffee, and Molly breathed its intense aroma in with her eyes closed. Some smart girls were smoking cigraillos, cigarette-shaped cigars, she had seen advertised. Molly thought of the café in Appley Green – it had the same kind of thick atmosphere but this was far more sophisticated and contemporary.

Like a stab in her chest, she was reminded of Alison seeing her that morning. Tomorrow she would go and see her and, hopefully, Nicola since she would be forced tell them about Walter now. They would be curious, insistent, demanding and perhaps she should be ready to face a barrage of accusations of secrecy and deceit that flew in the face of their special relationship. She sighed, knowing deep down that she really needed friends, and could feel Walter's gaze even without looking up at him.

'Don't look so worried! Are you all right?' Walter was looking at his watch and telling her to drink up. 'We've a lot to get through today.'

'Where are we going?' she asked.

'I'm not entirely sure,' he said, laughing. 'London is big! There's so much. I'd like to take you to a market, Camden or Portobello, but there's only so much we can fit in to a day.'

'Oh, and the waxworks! I've always wanted to see them.'

'Madame Tussauds? We could spend many years of Saturdays here and still not do it all. Let's just be content today with as much as we can cram in. It's Walter's wonderful mystery tour!' he answered, wrapping his arms around her and kissing her affectionately on the forehead. If he were leading her to the North Pole, she would have followed. 'I hope this is the first of many. I mean there will be many more trips, Molly, won't there?'

Did he mean what she thought he meant? He was serious about their future together. They had not known each other for more than a few weeks; he had not met her parents; he was the first man who had ever really courted her and she was still at school, although he did not know that. It was a lot to take in, but her heart told her that he was the one. She could not imagine any boy or man ever making her happier than Walter did.

As they drove deeper into the thick of the city, she reflected on the mess and building works everywhere along their route, slum terraces alongside what Walter had explained were offices and blocks of flats being constructed. She commented on the number of black faces in the crowds, African or Caribbean she thought, such people rarely seen in Appley Green.

'Immigrants find it hard to get decent housing and work — because on the whole people do not like them, for no good reason, unless there is a fear of them taking their jobs. Most of those I've met are better educated and more pleasing than many Anglo-Saxons I know, but they end up in the shabby neighbourhoods where rents are cheaper. Do you know that many of the Sikh postmen in Walthamstow have university degrees?'

Molly loved how Walter was so caring of other people; she had never met anyone who spoke like this. 'I had no idea ...'

'Other people tend to think their presence turns parts of the city into slums, but they have it the wrong way round. It's the rest of the population that keeps them there! They tend then to stick together with families and people they know of the same culture so you get the ghettos ... it may take a few generations for them to integrate properly ... sorry this is getting a bit too solemn for our jolly day out!'

'No. I like to know about these things. It's all so new to me and complicated. Is it safe in London?'

Walter began telling her scary stories about gangland crime in the East End, then as they passed by some bare gaps between buildings that he explained were old bombsites, he moved on to his memories of the war. He could remember four days of shelling in the docks when he was about fourteen or fifteen years old.

'Peter was evacuated to the country, to a village beyond Appley Green, well away from the Aldershot barracks and Farnborough airfield. That was our first connection with the area, as a family. But I stayed with my parents in Hackney.'

'What did your parents do?'

'They ... they were in the rag trade where most businesses are run by Jews, as I expect you know. My parents worked every hour God sent to make a living. But ...' he broke off with a broad smile, 'we don't want to talk about times gone by. Good times lie ahead, Molly! *Good* times.'

She watched as he then looked away, a light frown on his forehead as if he had just remembered something.

After a drive through Kensington, with Molly gasping at the grand, beautiful architecture of the Natural History Museum, Walter parked the car again.

'There are some *boutiques* here you must see,' he said. 'The little shops.'

'Why do you call them *boutiques*? It's French.'

'It's the cool word for small.'

'Oh, cool! They are different, so full of new things ...' He held her hand as they walked along, his warm fingers spreading comfort through her entire body, then paused briefly to throw a few bob into the hat of a filthy, bearded, down-and-out who was sitting hunched on the pavement, looking like little more than a heap of rags. Walter even doffed his hat to the poor soul and his kind gesture towards a tramp filled her with pride. Her mother would not understand that one bit.

Walter had stopped outside a shop called Biba and they both went inside. It was like an Aladdin's cave and she thought how Nicola would love this. When he insisted on buying something for her, Molly wondered how she would explain new clothes to her mother. Her parents thought she was with a 'friend', Alice, in a nearby village, though she knew they were already deeply suspicious. It was almost as if they knew she was lying but had come to realise there was nothing they could do about it. She had promised to be back to cook Sunday dinner.

'Choose something!' Walter was pressing her. 'If you don't, I'll choose something for you.' He made it sound more like a threat than a promise.

In for a penny, in for a pound. She was drawn to a dress with a geometric design, but wondered if it would be terribly expensive. 'Perhaps a scarf or something a bit like this.'

He smiled broadly, in a way that showed his perfect teeth and made his eyes crinkle in the corners. 'You like the dress?' She nodded shyly. 'Try it on.'

The magical transformation that occurred was like a bud of new life unfurling within her. She stepped out of the changing room to show Walter and smiled confidently, head held high. He was her new world and she loved it.

He paid for it quickly and they left.

'Could we ... I mean, is it too much trouble ...?'

'Sweetheart, what?' He squeezed her hand. 'Are you all right?'

'Yes, yes. Never been more all right, and more than all right, but where is Buckingham Palace? Could we drive past it? I don't know where places are in London ...'

'Of course we can! Come on, let's go.' He broke into a run and she held on to his strong, warm hand, terrified of losing him on the crowded pavement.

Once back by the car, both breathless, he held her tightly in both arms, swirled her round and kissed her very firmly on the lips.

'You are a very special girl, Molly, I want ... I want so much to make you happy!'

Tears filled her eyes. 'Then – you've succeeded, but I'll be even happier when I've seen Buckingham Palace!'

Not only did she see the palace, but also Westminster, Big Ben, the dark waters of the River Thames and then on to Piccadilly Circus all from the comfort of his car that sailed along through the busy streets like an ocean cruiser. He had put up the roof 'to protect them from the smoky air,' he said, referring vaguely to 'that killer smog I remember so well.'

'I'm not stopping here, but we can have something to eat in Soho. It's a bit seedy but so cosmopolitan. Swing and jazz clubs, delicatessens with Italian and French food that'll make you drool with pleasure!' Molly laughed, loving him so much, thinking of her parents' unmovable distrust of all things foreign especially when it came to food. *I feel I am in a dream.* 'You *must* see Carnaby Street ... Are you hungry?' His eyes were twinkling as he spoke.

'I'd give anything for one of those hamburgers from a Wimpy!' she said shyly, meaning it with all her heart.

He shrugged and mocked her with a stern look. 'But next time, the Ritz.'

24

There was a massive international event at the hotel and the conference manager asked if Alison could come in for six o'clock on Saturday morning to help lay the breakfast tables. It would only take an hour or so, but because there was a big dance on the Friday evening, setting it out the night before, as they normally did, would be unfeasible with the staff they had. For double pay, Alison agreed. Her parents were pretty liberal about the whole thing and rather admired her efforts to make a few bob. 'Financial independence is never a bad thing for a woman,' her mother had said, rather mysteriously.

She came away from her shift, emerging into the day's dawn, and glimpsed a grocer delivering goods around the side door leading to the kitchens. Then, as she walked along the hotel drive-way, she saw a milkman driving his float up to the hotel, looking smart in his peaked cap and uniform. He waved to her and she waved back and she could hear the stacked bottles chinking and him whistling as he softly motored past. The world seemed surprisingly busy at this time of day, when she was usually still in bed. She felt pleased with herself; her little wage certainly put pocket-money into the shade!

As she reached the lane, a large open-top car went by her. The driver did not seem to notice her; there was no sign of a wave from him, no doubt he had bigger fish to fry. She had seen the car before in Appley Green; it was the sort that stood out as opulent, as not belonging. She watched it drive on, squinted, then opened her eyes wide. A young woman was standing at the side of the road and gave the driver a little wave. She gasped. Molly! Molly? She was about to call out but the shock of what followed silenced her. Molly nipped across the road, got in the car and was quite thoroughly embraced – kissed – by the driver! She stood stock still, her mouth hanging open, and the car disappeared as if it had all been a dream.

The little minx! Molly had a secret life! She ruled out all explanations for the encounter she had witnessed, such as an uncle or someone giving her a lift for some outlandish reason at this hour of the day. The man in the car had *kissed* her, *on the mouth*! It was unmistakable; she had seen it with her own eyes.

Deeply injured and furious that her friend should be so secretive, so sly, she was unsure of what to do with this piece of information. She had shared Robert with Nicola and Molly, even though the memory of him now was fading round the edges. They had agreed to always keep no secrets from each other. How could she keep this from them? If she was capable of such deceit, then it seemed more likely she was the one who had betrayed their trust over Edward Phillips.

She must tell Nicola and they could decide together what to do.

Walter dropped Molly off at the green, before returning to the hotel that had thankfully reverted to a state of relative calm on Sunday morning. The influx of guests had now almost gone. Friday night had been seething with hordes of people, some speaking various European languages, some of them in uniform and wearing medals. Upon enquiry, he was told it was some kind of reunion of ex-armed forces and their families and he began to notice tearful faces.

As he spread hotel marmalade on hotel toast to go with his mid-morning coffee, he began to think of how his life could be with Molly at his side in a home of his own. He had no affection for his house in Hampstead, substantial though it was. His business success came a few years after the death of Theresa and they had lived a modest married life in a much smaller house in Notting Hill, all he could afford at that time. The Hampstead house held no special personal, emotional memories, apart from last night with Molly; generally speaking, it was a place he returned to alone after an all-consuming day, or time spent abroad, working to grow his empire.

His future life did not somehow belong to Hampstead; it lay in the village of Appley Green with Molly, despite the fact that other connections with the place were now being painfully severed. The family home was now sold, as instructed by his father before he went into hospital, knowing he would not be going back there. It was not a particularly attractive house, deep in the woods and shrouded by tall pine trees that Walter found oppressive. It was not a house he yearned to inherit and his father must have known this. It had a family of tenants who were now moving out; another chapter of life closing down.

As he walked to the hotel lounge to see if there was a Sunday newspaper available, he became lost in thought about Peter. He must accept whatever his brother was doing, whatever path he was following, and stay in Appley Green for his father who today was moving from hospital into a nursing home to be cared for. The doctors had done all they could.

He thought of how different dear Molly was from anyone or anything else in his life at the moment and the joy she brought him. Her naïvety and sweet but spirited nature made him see everything through fresh eyes as if she were a small child who knew nothing of the vices and real badness in the world. He silently vowed to himself that, if he did nothing else he would make sure he helped to change her life as she deserved. She had a special talent and from what he could glean, her home life was unhappy. He planned to take her to one of his factories to meet some of his designers.

Would it be right to ask her to marry him? He could not promise to be the husband she needs, there at her side until they become old together. How old was she? His first sighting of her at the Devonish party suggested she was probably no more than eighteen, trying to look older; but behind the counter of the little shop, she seemed very capable and in charge. Perhaps she *was* a little older. He had tried to draw this out of her, but she always skilfully skirted around the subject. He would never understand women, but it might seem churlish to press the matter! But he sensed there was a considerable age gap maybe as much as sixteen years, which would be considered totally scandalous, but he might be dead in, say, fifteen years' time, or even sooner, and she could be left a relatively young widow. How could he offer her what she undoubtedly would want? How could he leave her with fatherless children?

But if he did not make love to her again soon, he might as well be dead.

Nicola was astounded and angry in equal measure. With shaking fingers, she lit up a cigarette in the salon during a break between customers and stared blankly at Alison, obviously thinking hard.

'What do you think?' asked Alison.

Nicola exhaled away from Alison's face, her bottom lip jutting out sideways. 'It's like a betrayal. I think we should send her to Coventry for a bit. Our special pledge can't work if one of us slides off as sneaky as you like and has secret boyfriends.'

'Much more than a boy, I can tell you!'

'Even worse, then.'

'Have you always been honest with us?' asked Alison. 'I have.'

Nicola paused. 'I've kept nothing from you like that! *Old* boyfriends, I haven't told you all that, but I mean, this! This is truly shocking!'

Mrs Armitage, her manager was coming over and Nicola began fussing about with spiky plastic rollers in a box.

'You'd better go. I say we just avoid her for a bit.'

Alison nodded and left.

25

Molly and Alison were both signed up to do Christmas post deliveries in the run up to the big day. It was something of a tradition for sixth formers in the school holiday and they all enjoyed the camaraderie of meeting up at the Post Office well before sunrise. The small shops in Appley Green were displaying glittery gifts, doorways bedecked with holly and tinsel, cotton wool stuck onto windows and wide-eyed, bucolic Father Christmas models beaming like ventriloquists' dummies. The chemist had branched out into dressing table sets and bath cubes; the butchers were suggesting whole hams big enough to feed the entire village, although most families would settle for a few slices off the bone.

As she set off from her house, Molly, did not feel as excited as she had last year. Last night, she overheard her parents having a barney that began in bickering whispers but grew into a shouting match. It would seem her father had damaged his back and could barely move and for some strange reason, her mother was showing no sympathy at all, but rather blaming him for bringing it all upon himself. It was unsettling to hear her parents going for each other, hammer and tongs.

Now the weather was foggy, damp cold creeping through her duffel coat, making her shiver, and her gloves had a hole in the right index fingertip that she'd only just noticed. She had tried to eat some cereal before leaving, but this barely eased the nausea she was feeling.

She avoided walking with anyone to the depot and put on a cheerful face when she saw her school-friends, all wrapped up in knitted scarves and bright bobble hats. There was a buzz as they each collected their haversack of Christmas cards and adjusted the shoulder strap, ready to pace around the neighbourhood, posting goodwill and cheer into letterboxes.

'Hello Alison!' Alison had been a little cool with her over the past few weeks, probably since the day she had caught sight of her and Walter in the car, kissing each other like seasoned lovers. Attempts to meet up with Alison and Nicola had failed for a while; then when they did meet up, it was clear they were hurt for being kept out of the romance in her life. She had lost their trust. This hadn't seemed that important to her as she carried on day-to-day, floating around as light as a cloud in a bubble of happiness. Life with Walter had become her reality, and the rest was just something to get through.

Two days ago, he had said, 'I feel that with Christmas on the horizon, I must make an effort to find Peter.' It felt like the proverbial rug being pulled from under her feet.

She tried so hard to understand in a logical way. His father had died and Walter seemed to have no other close family. He must find his brother, check that he was all right, wherever he was, whatever he might be doing. Her brain was telling her this, but her heart was breaking. Would he be back for Christmas? He gave no such reassurances and the thought of being completely without him for more than a few days filled her with a sense of loss, almost as if he had died.

Her parents knew she had a boyfriend, but strangely had stopped plaguing her with questions. She knew they needed her and *they* knew they needed her; perhaps that was enough to explain their quiet capitulation.

After the post-round, the group of Christmas 'posties' were huddled together outside the Post Office and she could overhear them planning to go to the café.

'Coming, Molly?' asked one of the girls.

Her stomach rumbled and heaved. She looked away. 'Sorry, I have to get back home – my mother needs help with the washing today.' There was a bitter taste in her mouth.

'Just ten minutes. Go on!' The girl was someone she often shared a desk with for French lessons.

She realised that she needed food; all that walking in the fresh-air had made her ravenous. She had earned money this morning; surely she could treat herself to a bacon sandwich or beans on toast, made by someone else for a treat? A far cry from the more sophisticated meals she had shared with Walter, but at this moment of extreme hunger, worth more.

Molly smiled, hoping the food would extinguish the pangs and strange hollow feeling she had in her stomach.

'Oh all right.' She looked at her watch. She could be home in about half an hour.

The café was crowded, stuffy, filled with cigarette smoke and smells of burned toast, fried food and coffee, which was becoming just as popular as tea. She felt herself retch and a boy in the crowd noticed, as she put a hand to her mouth.

'Are you OK?' he asked, seeming genuinely concerned. 'You look done in.'

'Yes. I'm fine. Just a bit empty I think.'

'Me too, I'm starving.'

He was nice enough, and they chatted about Christmas and what their families would be doing. He was the kind of lad her parents would like her to be courting. Soon she sank her teeth into the soft white bread of an egg and bacon sandwich, like a starving dingo. She chewed and felt the food going down in lumps, feeling the nausea fade away with every swallowed mouthful. What a strange kind of sickness this was. Then, as she looked down at the plate, now empty save for a few crumbs and smears of brown sauce, a realisation dawned and she gasped aloud.

She had refused to take any notice of the fact that her 'monthly visitor' as her Mum primly called it, was nearly ten days late; it would come soon, for sure. But then, the scene flashed embarrassingly before her eyes, of when Walter had a mishap with a French letter – what he called his Durex. He spared her the details, but there was clearly something amiss. He was desperately sorry and kept apologising, and she laughed at the fuss he was making and thought how worldly she had become in just a few weeks. She had learned fast. 'Just one little accident is not the end of the world,' she had said to him, yet with all his sighs and curses you would think it might be.

As she left the crowd and made her way back home alone, insisting she must hurry back now, her emotions were in turmoil. Her heart was thudding with fear of what might possibly be happening. Her parents! Imagine what they would say! It did not bear thinking about.

Then, in an emotional U-turn out of her control, feelings of elation swept through her at the exquisite thought of making a baby with Walter. If anybody would look after her, he would! He would marry her for sure, take her away from the misery and solve all her problems. If only she could tell him now, right now this minute!

For the rest of the morning, her spirits dipped and soared, but this thought began to keep her riding high on a glorious wave of anticipation, fed by the delights of wicked subterfuge that had become the norm. By the end of the day she was picturing herself at Walter's side, with a gold ring on her finger and was mentally choosing a layette for their baby from the wondrous stock of tiny garments in the shop. Surely, once he had recovered from the shock, he would be amazed, proud and delighted!

After four days, she had heard nothing from Walter, for he could not write a letter to her home. She had told him firmly not to, before he left, but now a reckless part of her rather hoped he would. Her mother would seize it and demand answers to questions until she extracted everything; she knew just how it would be.

The big secret she was nursing was now growing into something explosive. No letter; no phone call - for they had no phone; no monthly 'curse'; and no Walter.

She decided that she must renew her pledge with Alison and Nicola and confide in them; to share such a massive secret would surely win back their friendship and if ever she needed a friend, it was now.

26

The funeral had been the saddest of days. His father, who finally gave up his fragile hold on life, was now buried in the Appley Green churchyard next to his wife and there had been few to mourn him whom Walter actually knew. As far as he was concerned, the church was more or less filled with strangers, whose names he found in his father's leather-bound address book. He had, after all, been living away from his parents since he did his National Service.

He did not burden Molly with his loss, the tragedy of it, for she was his escape, his way of making life enjoyable and sweet. It was not up for discussion, as far as he was concerned. 'How long had he been ill? How old was he? He was in hospital – what was his illness?' Molly asked these questions candidly when he told her of his passing away, but he evaded them. The disease that had shortened his father's life could do the same to him, and to Peter. This had been confirmed as a possibility, unless there was some medical breakthrough.

He clung tightly to Molly, physically and emotionally and she was probably unaware of just how much he really adored her. One afternoon, as they lay scandalously naked beneath the counterpane on his bed in the Hunter's Lodge hotel, his feelings for her rose to another level; yet the stronger and deeper his love for her grew, the more he inwardly debated how he could offer her what she needed and deserved.

One evening, he impulsively pulled the car over so they could amble up to a viewpoint in the woods to watch the sunset. It was chilly and they wore light sweaters but no coats. He put an arm round her as they stood gazing at the rippling pink-orange sky. He remembered his father taking him there one afternoon, when a murder of crows the size of ravens were cawing raucously in the tall Scots pines to the left of where he now stood with the woman who should, in reality, be his wife.

He broke the news to her softly, not really knowing what he meant as he said it. 'Molly, I feel I ...' he paused as the words did not come easily, 'I must find out what is happening with Peter. He is, after all, my little brother and went off deeply unhappy.'

Molly nodded. 'Of course. Yes, you should,' she said, seeming to understand that they would be parted for a while. The search could take days, weeks, even months to trace him and he was not sure if she realised that.

'Can you just leave your business?'

He was astounded and deeply touched at her practical response to the notion that he might be missing for a while. She constantly surprised him.

He kissed her forehead with great affection. 'Do not worry your pretty little head about that. I have excellent managers. A few things will assuredly go wrong, but nothing that will stop the earth revolving as normal. This is ... this is more important.' Again, she nodded, rather more gravely now. 'I'm so very sorry I won't be here in Appley Green for Christmas.'

At that she merely shrugged – bravely, it seemed to Walter. 'Perhaps that's just as well, really. I shall be with my family and it would be ... well, we couldn't ...' She stumbled over her words.

'I'll write to you,' Walter assured her. He was unsure of whether to give her the diamond ring he had in his pocket now, or when he returned home. The uncertainties about their future were looming large in his head.

She looked away, saying nothing. 'May I remind you, I still haven't met them,' he commented, more as a question. 'Your parents?'

'No.' She paused for a moment, frowning. 'You see, with you being so much older, I just know they would be horrified ...I mean, appalled!'

He threw back his head and laughed. 'Am I really that bad? So horrific? So appalling?'

'Oh no! No, of course not. You are the best thing that has ever happened to me.'

'As you are to me, my darling girl.'

She then turned to Walter, a look of despair in her eyes. 'You mustn't write to me at home. My mother would spot a strange letter immediately, especially if it was by Air Mail. It would stand out like a Belisha beacon!'

'If you told them about me and why I was going travelling for a while, then what harm could that do? I really would like to meet them. I'll have to one day.'

In the twilight, Walter could see she was confused, as if reality had suddenly kicked in and her bubble of happiness had burst. 'But ... they want me to go to university and make something of myself, even though they need me at home. I can't see how they'll manage, but ... Anyway, a boyfriend is not really part of their plan for me at the moment, although they would probably go easier on a boy my own age.'

She seemed terribly honour-bound to her parents. 'So, it really is the *age* thing, isn't it? And university? How would you do that now?' She clammed up, looking utterly distraught. 'Well, come on, cards on the table! I'm thirty-six, you know that. You've never told me just how old you are, hard as that is to believe. When I first saw you at the Devonish party, I assumed you were one of the fillies of marriageable age, clearly looking for a husband, though quite young. Then I saw you again, a young woman at work, but worthy of something more ...'

'Walter, I am still at school,' she confessed, sheepishly.

Walter felt as if he had been punched in the stomach. No! A schoolgirl! His mind went blank for a moment, as he absorbed this information, the blood apparently being drained from his brain.

Their relationship suddenly seemed so very wrong. How could he have been so blind? So stupid? He put a hand to his forehead for moment or two, collecting his thoughts. He turned to walk back to the car as the light had almost gone and their interest in the sunset had passed. Molly walked quietly at his side.

He turned to look at her sternly. Please let her *not* now tell me she is a fifteen year-old. He glanced at her sweet face, so naïve, and thought with horror that she could be much, much younger than he had assumed. He shivered.

177

'Tell me straight now, Molly' he urged her, his voice husky, 'how old are you?'

'Sixteen, just a few weeks ago. I'm in the sixth form. I was one of the girls in your brother's class.'

Now this nymph was smiling impishly, as though pleased at her devilish trick. He felt angry at having been duped, something that was not new to him, and he did not like it. Before it was an older woman who had caught him out, cast blame and finally dragged him through the courts where the final verdict did not really give him his freedom back because his name was tainted. He withdrew his arm from Molly's shoulder, thrust his hands in his trouser pockets, kicking stones in his path as events of the past few weeks played over in his mind. Whilst not illegal, suddenly their love affair was … he searched for the right word … improper. Plenty of older men went out with younger girls, exploited them, took advantage, but he was not one of them. Yes, it was improper and he felt he had, albeit unwittingly, taken advantage of her naivety.

He stopped, turned, grasped both her hands and pulled her to him roughly. His feelings for her were the same, but the damage was done. 'Molly! You should have told me. You do realise that, don't you?'

She gave him a penetrating gaze that nearly stopped his heart. 'I'm sorry, Walter. But in a way, I'm not sorry at all, because if I had, would we be … where we are today? Happy and in love?'

He shook his head slowly, stroking her hair with great tenderness. 'No.' Tears rushed to his eyes, knowing that he regretted nothing, if he was absolutely honest. He hugged her tightly against his chest, feeling her heartbeat, cherishing the softness of her breasts, and trying desperately to commit to memory her particular scent that even then he knew would haunt him for the rest of his life.

Once back in his hotel room, after a few whiskies, he lay on his bed sad and alone, letting matters settle in his head. He must release her, let her go, however painful this would be for both of them. His search for Peter would give them both a cooling off period and she was young enough to forget. Once out of reach, another man, younger than he, would come along and the golden memories of their time together would fade.

He slept badly that night and next morning was gone by ten o'clock with a light bag and a passport, before his warring emotions could stop him.

PART TWO

27
1962

The train pulled out of Oxford station with a solid *choo-choo-choo-choo*, gathering pace, building up louder, faster, into a rattling rumble, accompanied by whooshes of steam, then pierced by a shrill whistle. As the sound dropped back, like brushes on a drum, *dudda-dudda,* in 4/4 time Alison noted, she gently patted the seat in time to the soothing rhythm. The wheels now clunked and rolled along as she sat back, wondering whether to use the time reading *Plato's Republic* - or *Lady Chatterley's Lover.* She decided the dapper gentleman who had kindly raised her small case onto the luggage rack for her, might be shocked to see her engrossed in such notorious literature. Her parents claimed the book was just challenging the Obscene Publications Act and what it stands for, but Alison decided that D H Lawrence may have twigged that most people were secretly drawn to reading about sex, simple as that. Plus, the power of sex could not be excluded in any real and meaningful portrayal of real life in fiction.

As *Plato's Republic* lay unopened on her lap, her thoughts naturally turned to what lay ahead. *I have a grand idea!* her mother had written in a letter and Alison's heart had plummeted. It turned out she had sent virtually the same note to Julian, also studying at Oxford, reading Psychology, Philosophy and Physiology, known as PPP. When they got together they agreed that their parents had actually come up with a more than passably acceptable plan. In fact, they had never come across such extravagance! *It is also to celebrate the year of our 20th wedding anniversary,* she wrote, but Alison thought this sounded like a good excuse to justify a few days of gratuitous hedonism, perhaps to distance themselves from the possibility of the world ending with a nuclear war.

This was the end of their first term and, although most students had already gone home, she and Julian had stayed on at Oxford until now, since they knew their home would be unbearably empty, and as cheerful as a tomb. Her mother and father moved to the outskirts of Windsor to be within easier reach of Oxford and still able to travel into London for work. They felt Windsor had a superior ring to it, preferable to some suburban areas, the 'subtopia' they secretly despised, despite their left-wing principles. Not quite socially settled into their new place, however, they decided to spend Christmas in Appley Green!

They were booked into the Hunters' Lodge Hotel from the 23rd of December until New Year's Day. What strange memories that place held! She would never forget that early morning when she had spotted Molly and her secret *paramour* kissing!

Her first thought was that she might have a chance to meet up with both Nicola and Molly. How odd and wonderful that would be! Now they were worlds apart, but after the turmoil they had been through together, she had never forgotten them. They kept in touch with letters, but these had become less frequent as time went by, putting their initial schoolgirl pledge at some risk; their promise, that is, to always share their innermost secrets. The whole business with Molly and the baby had given an unexpected twist to their friendship, for sure.

Now they would all have some catching up to do! The finger on her left hand that just last month bore an engagement ring could tell a story, for a start.

It was a treat to be on a train, draughty and smoky though it was. For a mid-term, weekend visit to their home near Windsor she had hitch-hiked with Julian but for this special occasion, her brother was following on tomorrow, Christmas Eve, also by train. They decided hitching lifts would have been none too easy with a suitcase and bags of gifts in tow, besides which their parents had irresistibly offered to pay the fare, probably feeling guilty for not driving to Oxford to fetch them due to work commitments.

She hoped for a chance to see Gloria, too. Their firm friendship, that blossomed after meeting at the Devonish party, was cut short by the distance now between them. Gloria was studying Mathematics in London and Alison relished the idea of a girl-friend from home doing something out of the ordinary. The big gossip, moreover, was that she had recently caught the attention of Ted Devonish, now securely married to Geraldine *née* Pyke. Alison pulled out from her briefcase a letter from Gloria, written in her quaint style, received a few months ago where she had confided in Alison. *I had a chance encounter with the couple in Kensington … He listens to me and looks at me in a certain way? Do you know what I mean? Or, am I just imagining things, do you think? Of course I have no intention of flirting with him, you must understand that. I want a career and have absolutely no wish to cause trouble of that kind. But Mrs Devonish, Ted's wife, that is Geraldine, cast a beady, jealous eye on me and seems to want to cultivate a sisterly friendship, as if this somehow will ease the situation … I am sure I do not understand her motives fully, but I try and avoid both of them when I come back to Appley Green.*

Her style of writing reminded Alison of Jane Austen; Gloria seemed to belong to another social planet from her and she sometimes wondered if they would ever meet again. The last leg of the journey brought Alison slowly trundling into Appley Green station and as the train pulled to a halt, she donned her scarf and woollen gloves. She could see that, even though the winter sun was as high as it goes, there was still a hint of ground-frost in shady places.

Her father was waiting on the station platform dressed warmly in his worsted overcoat, red muffler and trilby hat. 'Hello!' she cried, as they gave each other a gentle peck, the bristles of his beard against her cheek a familiar comfort. As a family they did not go in for public or even private hugging but Gordon's beaming smile was all she needed. 'You look very Christmassy!'

Every year since she could remember, the red scarf came out a week before Christmas, then was put away with the Christmas baubles on twelfth night. At any other time of the year it was impossibly bright. With this in mind, she hoped he would like the present she had for him!

As her father drove to the hotel, she felt a wave of happiness flood through her. A Christmas tree stood tall on the village green and the windows of the Fox and Rabbit were glowing from within like a lantern.

In the lobby of The Hunter's Lodge gaily decked with swags of red ribbon, holly and fir, her mother rushed forward and, uncharacteristically, wrapped her arms around her. Then she grabbed Alison by the shoulders, leaning back a little as if to examine her general condition.

'Darling, are you eating enough? Isn't this wonderful? No cooking to do, and such a lovely log fire! Julian called to say he's coming tomorrow. Just the four of us! We can play games and gorge ourselves, oh darling, I can't tell you how much we miss you both.' Alison smiled, her mother sounding like an actress in a radio play.

Climbing the wide staircase to her room, Alison bit her lip, wondering doubtfully if she would be able to escape at all during the few days they would be here, before returning to stay in their Windsor home until the start of the academic term. Although she was now old enough to have a mind of her own and do as she pleased, her parents had made it clear that she should have nothing more to do with Molly and Nicola. But she badly wanted to see them, to see how they were and she could not stop imagining what Molly's little boy might look like, although she knew there was no point.

Nicola was rushed off her feet at *Nouveau Salon* where she was assistant manager. Fully booked up until after the New Year, it seemed everyone was having their hair done for a party or just to look their best on Christmas Day and New Year's Eve. Beehives, bouffants, bobs, waves, flicks, velvet bows, to say nothing of colour and peroxide; all manner of creations were in high demand, some specifying the Jackie Kennedy style or to come away looking like Brigitte Bardot. Business was booming, Christmas tips were coming in too, and things were looking good for Nicola.

'Thought you'd like to know before we close for Christmas, Nicola,' said her boss, Mrs Armitage, catching her when she was on her own in the little back kitchen, 'that we're planning to open another salon in Bloomstock. I'll be moving there to oversee the whole thing, and, although I haven't spoken to her yet, I plan to take Rosemary with me. Barbara can stay here and we'll get a trainee in, and you, m'dear, can run this salon. Do you think you could do that, Nicola?'

Nicola tried to answer calmly, hiding her excitement. 'I could do it. Yes,' she replied, nodding, feeling awkward. 'Thank you, Mrs Armitage.' She had to stop herself from curtseying, she just felt so unspeakably *grateful*! How would Barbara take that, she wondered?

Mrs Armitage frowned. 'Are you sure? You don't look very happy about it.'

Then, without knowing what was happening to herself, Nicola burst into tears, laughing and sobbing at the same time. 'Oh, oh, I am, really. Very happy. Thank you.'

'It'll mean a decent pay rise for you, dear …'

She felt her life was falling into place. Her dreams just might come true after all. She may not be the owner, but she was a 'manager' and she was on her way!

Once released at the end of the working day, she positively skipped home, swinging her handbag, until she suddenly slipped on the dimly-lit, icy path crossing the village green and felt a sharp pain in her ankle. She gasped with the shock. Wincing and squealing a little in an agony she had never known, she sat on the frosty grass verge, rubbing her leg and looking around for help. It was nearly six o'clock, everyone was at home having their tea and she was very much afraid she was about to faint …

'Molly! Molly! MOLLY!' There was a sharp ringing of a small brass hand bell that intruded on the haunting melody of Acker Bilk's *Stranger on the Shore*, her mother's current favourite record. Three rings. It meant her mother needed the commode.

'Come on Susan,' said Molly, 'clear that table, it's smothered in books. You need to lay it ready for tea. David'll be here soon with Janice, and he'll be expecting everything to be ready.'

Susan groaned, but did as she was told, piling the mess onto a tray ready to take up to the bedroom they still shared. 'You don't realise how you need to work undisturbed when you're a genius!' Susan gave her a wicked grin as she pulled out a white tablecloth from the sideboard drawer.

'Even geniuses need to eat,' said Molly giving her sister a tickle in the ribs. 'And you can put something a bit more cheery on the record-player ... *Let's Dance* or *The Loco-motion*, maybe ...'

Before going to see her mother, Molly quickly checked on the array of food ready for the big day. Neighbours were coming round in the morning for a glass of sherry and a few things on sticks: cheese and pineapple, cocktail sausages and stuffed green olives. The capon was in the fridge, stuffed for roasting, and a Christmas pudding was ready to be re-steamed. Susan was going to help decorate the iced Christmas cake with some coloured marzipan holly leaves, berries and, behold, a robin! Her brother David had provided some Scottish shortbread and his fiancé, Janice, had made a Yuletide log from a recipe in a magazine. She still needed to make custard for the apple pie tonight and start off a trifle for Christmas Day tea-time ... bread sauce and chipolatas she could sort out tomorrow ...

She removed her apron and slipped away.

'It's almost too late,' said her mother. '*You* are too late - almost.'

She heard David arrive, clapping and rubbing his hands together, exclaiming how the weather was enough to freeze something or the other she would rather not hear. This was tame compared with jokes and language he picked up from work that their mother described as 'coarse', but of course it had the desired effect and Susan was laughing. It confirmed what she already knew, that she was needed here not just for the sake of her mother, but for her sister. She had a mind of her own though, thank God. Susan Maughan was belting out *Bobby's Girl*, Susan's favourite single ...

'Come on, baby sis!' Her brother was ordering Susan about and this irked her far more than his fruity vocabulary. 'Where's the beer and crisps?'

'I think we have to wait for Molly – she'll tell you what we can have.'

'Listen here. I still live here and pay most of the bills. I'm entitled ...'

Molly came back in. 'Hello David, hello Janice, how are you? You're quite right of course. And once you're in a house of your own, I am sure you'll both enjoy cooking meals every day ...' She could've bitten off her own tongue with the sour comments that poured out of her mouth these days. 'Only joking!' she said, lightly, regretting her words. 'I think you'll find some bottles in the back porch, keeping cold, possibly frozen, but dinner is nearly ready.'

'Great,' said David, waiting for someone to fetch it for him, adept at switching to the role of guest when it suited. He and Janice were monopolising the hearth like fire-guards, shivering, with sound effects. 'Bunking off early and no work for two whole days, eh, Janice?' Molly heard her future sister-in-law giggle.

'Those bottles, David. They won't walk to you of their own accord, I'm afraid ...' said Molly as she went into the kitchen to dish up the steak and kidney. 'Susan! Can you please help Mum get to the table?' Damn! Now *she* was giving Susan orders, but how else could she get everything done?

28

Alison thought she might catch Nicola on her way home from the salon.

'I need to go to the chemist,' she whispered to her mother, who looked up from her book and nodded discreetly. Secrets and little lies – they had started already, but once the shops closed down for Christmas it would be more difficult to escape.

She dressed in all the warmest garments she had brought with her. People coming into the hotel lobby were blowing on their fingers, stamping their feet and hugging themselves to indicate the severe cold outside. 'Must be blowing from the Arctic,' said one. 'Too cold to snow, I reckon,' said another.

Alison walked briskly down the road into Appley Green, then took the path circling the green to keep near the streetlights. Everything was sprinkled with glitter, the frost lending a sparkle to every blade of grass, little twig or roof tile, hanging in the air as silver, frozen mist. She reached the small chemist's shop just before they were closing and purchased some Vaseline for her chapped lips, 'to pay lip service' to her excuse for nipping out, she thought, with a chuckle. The salon was on the other side of the green so she decided to cut across, although it was quiet and dark by now. Maybe she was too late; Nicola would probably be home already, unless they worked later today.

Then she heard a shout and saw someone sitting in the shadows by the path. 'Help!' came the female cry. Without hesitation Alison called out, 'Hello! What's happened?' and rushed forward, taking care not to slide on the treacherous path.

It was a surreal moment as they recognised each other in the dusky light, with squeaks of excitement; it took a few minutes for them to calm down and make sense of the situation.

'Does it hurt a lot? Can you walk?'

'It's flippin' agony. Do you think I'd be lying here half frozen to death in the dark if I could *walk*, you daft apeth?'

'Sorry. Let's see if I can help get you up ...'

'Ouch! Ow! No ...'

'Try and hop, look I've got you. Try, Nicola, try! Oh Lord!'

Frantic efforts got them nowhere and Nicola was now in tears. Alison, thrown into a panic, ran for help. Everywhere was closed and the village was deserted, so she knocked on the door of the nearest cottage. The couple there were most sympathetic and luckily owned a telephone, so quickly called for an ambulance, probably secretly wishing to be shot of this untimely problem, but they did not show it.

Whilst in no way would Alison ever have wished such pain and sorrow for Nicola, the silver lining was that at least she could return to her parents, much later than planned, armed with an honest story instead of a pack of lies.

'Well, how frightful! Poor Nicola,' said her mother, now mellow with sherry and festive goodwill to all mankind, once explanations for her daughter's late return to the hotel had been digested. 'Was it broken?'

'Nicola was sure it was, but they said it was just a really bad sprain. Her ankle swelled up like a fat marrow, but they put ice on it ... I guess it would've been even worse if she wasn't already lying in Arctic temperatures.'

'Darling that's almost black humour, but I suppose it's your optimistic streak coming through. You've inherited that from me.'

'Anyway, I shall have to visit her tomorrow, poor thing.'

'Of course, even though it'll be Christmas Day, or perhaps *because* it's Christmas ... yes, you must be a good friend. Take them something.'

'You'll have to take us as you find, my love,' said Mrs Bates, as she tugged open the front-door. 'Sorry, it's stickin' a bit, we don't use this door much.' Alison followed her down the small hallway. The house was chilly and smelled of paraffin and damp clothes. 'We got a bit of a leak in the loft – it's as cold as a graveyard up there. Cracked pipe, no chance of getting it fixed today. We'll just have to hope it don't bump into the electric … and how are you now then? Enjoyin' yourself up there in Oxford, are you?'

'Yes, thank you. I'm so sorry about the frozen pipe. How awful for you. Are you managing to keep warm?'

Lily Bates shrugged. 'Daren't heat the water in case … you know, the tank may be empty, I dunno, it's just what you need on Christmas Day, isn't it? Dad's been getting the paraffin heater goin', and we may need to have a couple of bars on the electric one out here. Flippin' 'eck, this is like 1947. Never known it so cold.'

'I thought we might have a white Christmas,' said Alison, cheerfully.

'Let's hope not. That's all we need.'

There were no tempting aromas of roast dinner, Alison realised. Compared with their former house in Appley Green, the new home in Windsor and the luxury of the Hunters' Lodge, this seemed like entering another world, rather hellish, almost like stepping into a Dickens novel. Her student halls at St Hilda's offered much greater comfort and style than this old council house. Water was trickling down the mouldy wall in one corner, a damp patch spreading insidiously across the new wallpaper. It made her actually want to cry. Nobody should be like this, especially at Christmas.

She could scarcely believe how easily she had slipped away from the fairy lights, mince pies and strewn wrapping paper in her parent's cosy hotel bedroom. She was not entirely sure the hotel Christmas idea was going to work out; it all seemed a little strange in practice, but at least her mother did not have to cook, as she kept reminding the family. Alison felt a rush of gratitude for spending Christmas there and not here in this dismal house.

Nicola was lounging on the sofa in her parents' small living-room, wrapped in a gold satin eiderdown, listening to her transistor radio; her Grandad was sitting in a chair, flicking through the Daily Mail. Such a kind, caring family, as had been proved over the business with Molly and her baby, Alison knew that and yet she could not help pitying them.

Nicola sat up and grinned. 'Hello! I hope you come with glad tidings!' she said.

Alison handed her a package and what was obviously a book wrapped in holly paper. 'Some mince pies and sausage rolls from the hotel. How's the foot?'

'Ooh! Smashing. Thanks. I'm taking aspirin and I gotta rest it.'

Her Mum was coming in and out, fetching, tidying, brushing, dusting. 'So she's no use to me – ah, bless her! Now, I must see if the gas is OK, or we'll be having no more than a sandwich for dinner today ...' She went off.

'My Dad's doing a few taxi runs today. There's quite a call for it, folks getting round to family, people who don't have a car. Probably getting a few tipples too!'

Alison nodded. 'Have you seen anything of Molly?'

Nicola waved to her Grandad to see if he wanted a sausage roll and he rose stiffly from his chair and staggered across. Alison realised, too late, she could have helped him out, but nobody seemed to hold it against her. He nodded and smiled, seemingly very contented.

'Molly?'

'Yes. When did you last see her?'

Nicola frowned and chewed thoughtfully. 'Mm. A few weeks ago, I think.'

'Where? How was she?' Why was Nicola making such hard work of this?

'Crotchety.'

'Is she working? In her last letter, ages ago, she told me the early hours at the baker's shop were no good. Didn't fit in with looking after her mother ...'

'Her father doesn't work at all now, you know. She got a job at a ... what d'you call 'em ... vending machine factory. Clerical, and they let her come in late and go home early, provided she doesn't take a dinner-break. I think that's how it works.'

Alison sighed. 'Sounds dire,' she muttered.

'Better than working on the factory floor, she said. She ... she's a different person, you know, from how she used to be. By the way, I got promoted. Nicola Bates is now Manager of the Appley Green branch of *Nouveau Salon*!'

Alison squeezed her arm and, again tears welled up, which was very unlike her. The memory flashed back of the afternoon the three of them had spent in the garden, sharing secrets and dreams, when Nicola said her abiding wish was to earn enough money to be able to buy her parents a nice house.

'I'm so ... pleased. You deserve it, oh Lord ...'

'You're crying!'

'No, no I'm not,' she sniffed. 'Well, it's because I'm happy for you. Such great news.'

Nicola nodded and picked up the wrapped book. 'The family are opening presents later, when we can all be together. Oh, I got you a little present.' Nicola tried to get up but yelped with the pain of moving. 'Flippin' heck! D'you know I'm sure it's fractured, must be more'n a sprain or a twist,' she mumbled.

Alison felt humbled. 'Don't try and walk – can I get it for you?'

'I didn't have time to wrap it last night, but it's in a brown paper bag – over there.' She pointed to an old sideboard that her mother had covered in red and white Fablon, sticky-backed plastic that was all the rage.

'You shouldn't have,' said Alison, as she stepped across the room.

The bag was open so she could see what was inside - some large rollers and a can of hair spray.

'Oh thank you, just what I need. That's really kind.' There was a pause. 'Nicola, how on earth are we going to get anywhere near Molly? We must find a way to see her. We *must*.'

191

29

Replete from a late Christmas lunch, Alison, Julian, Harriet and Gordon sank onto the leather sofas and chintzy armchairs in the hotel lounge and wondered what to do next, conversation suddenly a little strained. With a previous agreement to avoid any thoughts or discussions of Cuban missiles, the threat of nuclear war and possible annihilation of mankind, keeping genuinely cheerful was not easy.

The hotel Christmas tree was not theirs, the other guests were strangers and Alison began to wish they were at home, not in the small Windsor house that as yet had no place in her heart whatsoever, but back in Appley Green. Her new bedroom had her old Teddy and books in it, but no real memories of its own; the garden, planted and tended by others, painted no homely pictures in her head of childhood games and her parents trundling around with shears, rakes and wheelbarrows doing chores to help the gardener keep the borders in tip-top order. The kitchen was newly fitted with the latest gadgets: a neat fridge, a twin-tub washing-machine and spin drier; cabinets on the wall that kept everything dust-free and out of sight, and a fancy tin-opener screwed onto the wall.

During the meal she and Julian had been grilled on their Oxford lives. Were their bicycles in good order? What new friends had they made and had they been punting on the river? Isn't Blackwell's just the most amazing bookshop and what was their favourite section of the Bodleian? Did they get on with their tutors and how many cigarettes a week do they smoke? Did they keep their rooms tidy? As usual, her parents said nothing of their work and she knew it was a waste of breath to enquire.

She wondered what sort of a Christmas Molly was having since she was almost bound to be thinking about Christmas last year and two years ago - two different kinds of hell on Earth. Molly's parents would never let their daughter see either

her or Nicola, and yet, what right did they have to turn them away? They were adults now.

'Anyone for Monopoly?' said Gordon and they all fell in, glad to have an activity. The smell of Manikin cigar smoke hanging above his head like a cloud took her back to all Christmases past.

Her mother caught the eye of a waiter as he breezed through, looking rather harassed. 'Could you get me a Babycham please? Anyone else?' Imagine having to work on a Christmas Day! Alison hoped the young man was getting double-pay. From the time she had waited on tables, she knew what it was like back-stage in the hotel kitchen. Her father ordered a malt whisky, Julian a pint of mild and bitter, Alison a vodka and lime.

'How grown-up you both are now,' commented her mother.

'I shall be going to see Nicola again tomorrow,' said Alison. 'They have so many problems in their house. Christmas is completely spoiled for them. A burst pipe, no hot water. I'm not even sure if they managed to have a hot meal today.'

Brother and parents all looked aghast. 'But that's *frightful*,' said her mother.

Gordon shook his head sorrowfully. 'Hmm. Shouldn't happen in these days of rising prosperity. I hope the council will fulfil its obligations *pronto*, once the Bank Holiday is over ...'

'Couldn't we invite them here?' suggested Julian, brightly.

There was an awkward silence. Her parents' socialist principles were being sorely tested.

'I ... I think they might be embarrassed at that, dear, you know people have their pride. They wouldn't want charity ...'

Alison stared at her mother, sitting at ease, sipping her drink, letting the bubbles tickle the end of her nose. What a paradox she was! What an enigma!

'Would you excuse me?' Alison asked, taking great care to be polite, not wishing to rock the family boat in any way. 'I'm going for a little walk.' Before anyone offered to join her, she added. 'I just fancy a stroll round the village. See you later.' She made a hasty exit.

Once she had called to see Nicola, who was still languishing on the sofa, she decided to walk round to Molly's house. People were never mean to each other on Christmas Day! Were they?

Molly and Susan were still in the kitchen clearing up. The air was rich with gravy aroma, cinnamon, sprouts and cigar smoke, a blend unique to Christmas.

'You could finish making the trifle now if you like, Susan, just put that cold custard on the top and then we can add a layer of whipped cream just before tea-time ...'

'Did you get almonds, glacé cherries and angelica?'

'Yes.'

Susan clapped her hands. 'Good-oh! I'll make a noughts and crosses pattern. It'll be wizard!'

Molly half smiled. 'Lovely.' The doorbell rang. 'Who on earth can that be?'

'We've had enough of neighbours ...' groaned Susan, over her shoulder, as she went to see.

David was the first to get to the front-door. 'Oh! Oh, hello. Er ... Merry Christmas ...' she heard him say.

Molly could hear a female voice and was instantly curious. Christmas Day, when everyone was with their families ...

'Thank you David! How are you? Could I have a word with Molly? I guessed she'd be here today!' Molly's eyes opened wide and she held her breath. She left the kitchen in a hurry. Alison! This made no sense. Was it possible? With everything that happened, Alison's name, along with Nicola's, was banned in this household.

Her father was ahead of her and put out an arm to bar Molly's path. 'Not so fast. So! Alison. Well, Merry Christmas to you! Here's a surprise. You've got a nerve young lady, if I may say so, coming round here ...' He was rude, but Molly could sense real anger in his relatively restrained manner.

'Mr Bates. I apologise for intruding on such a day, but I would just like a quick word with Molly, then I'll be gone.'

Alison sounded unusually polite, presumably not wishing to upset any festive apple-carts.

He gave her a sour look. 'Oh yes. And then you'll be plotting your next move. Some other deceitful act. You can't blame me for not trusting you, Alison.'

'Dad! Let me get past. Of course I can speak to my friend,' shouted Molly, pushing him with all her might to get past. His elbow very nearly caught her on the chin and she ducked to avoid it.

'Mr Bates!' cried Alison. 'There's no need for that! Goodwill to all men. Surely. It's Christmas Day.'

A call came from within. Dorothy could emit an amazingly ear-piercing cry when moved to do so. 'Bill! Is it that girl? The posh one? Don't you let her in, don't you dare!'

'Don't worry mother. *I'm* going *out* to *her*!' cried Molly and suddenly she was there, the cold biting her nose, giving Alison the most unexpected and thorough hug. Her face crumpled as tears spilled silently down her cheeks. The front door had slammed behind her and she wondered if she would be able to get back in. How wonderful if they had shut her out for good!

'Oh Alison, I can't begin to tell you, you've no idea how pleased I am to see you,' she said sniffing, trying not to sob aloud. Alison handed her a neatly folded clean hanky with lacy corners. It was an act of kindness that Molly was not used to at all, prompting more tears.

'Molly, Molly …' Alison cradled her and swayed a little and Molly felt such warmth and comfort she thought she might pass out. 'What are they doing to you in there? Are you a prisoner?'

Molly broke away from Alison. 'It's just you and Nicola. You two are forever forbidden, you know that. They're terrified you'll lure me away again. They couldn't cope …'

'They do well to be terrified because that's just what I bloody feel like doing … They would've somehow coped if you'd gone to university …'

'How can we meet again? Properly?' Molly looked earnestly into Alison's face. 'I'll have to go back in soon or there'll be the most terrible scene.'

'Molly, this is not right. You're grown-up. You can't let them keep you under house arrest! Your father looked quite violent!'

Molly gave a wry grin. 'Oh, they let me out for good behaviour – to do shopping and go to work.'

'How and when can you escape? Just tell me and I'll fit in with whatever you say. Anything.'

'The day after Boxing Day I'll need to go to the bakers and butchers, and the day after that, on Friday, I'll be back at work.'

'What time will you be going shopping on Thursday?'

'Hard to say, but I'll try and do it around ten o'clock.'

Alison nodded. 'I'll find you. How are you though? You look as thin as a sparrow and utterly worn out?' Molly shrugged. It was no good lying. 'Nicola is in a state too. She's laid up with a badly sprained ankle and they have a burst pipe ...'

Molly gasped. 'You've seen her already? Why are you here anyway? Your parents moved away. I never thought I'd see you again.' Alison outlined the situation briefly. 'I see.' Molly was now shivering. 'God, it's cold. I'll see you on Thursday, Alison. I can't tell you how good it is to clap eyes on you. Best Christmas present ever!' She squeezed Alison's hand tight and then walked down the covered alleyway round to the unlocked back-door.

By the time Alison got back to the bosom of her family it was afternoon tea-time, but her mother had moved on to gin and tonic and her father was clasping a large glass of whisky. They seemed to have found the decadence they were seeking in a gathering of what she assumed to be other residents. British reserve appeared to have been put on hold in the hotel lounge.

She approached them and eventually caught their attention, as they sat contentedly chatting in armchairs. It would have been nice if she had been missed, just a little! 'Where's Julian?'

Her mother's eyelids drooped and her gaze moved lazily. 'Julian?'

'Yes, your son. My brother. Where is he? Has he gone out?'

'Don't be silly, darling. He made a phone call and then said he was meeting some friends and would be back soon.'

'Did he say who? Or where?'

'I think there's a 'lock-in' at the Fox and Rabbit. Or an old school chum's house if he found himself locked out ...' Her mother chortled. 'Not entirely sure, to be perfectly honest with you, sweetheart.'

'I'll take a wander and see if I can find him.'

A strange kind of family Christmas this was turning out to be, thought Alison, as she trudged off back out into the dusky cold of Appley Green. A bitter north wind was stirring the treetops, but other than that all was peace and calm. She wondered fleetingly where all the birds went to keep warm and liked to think of them with heads tucked cosily under their wings, buried in downy nests 'as snug as a bug in a rug', as her father used to say at bedtime when she was little.

Nicola was housebound, Molly was captive, and she had arranged nothing with her other old friends from school. They would all be with their families, playing charades and tiddlywinks, watching TV, hugging a fire and eating too much Turkish Delight and dates, cracking nuts ... She swore under her breath. This was a bad idea, mother!

Moreover, Julian had managed to sneak off without her! This was something she had not anticipated but she did begin to figure out how she could work his bid for freedom to her advantage. If only she could find him!

Then she thought about Gloria and saw a phone-box. She fished out her pocket diary and purse from her shoulder-bag and, standing under a streetlight, flicked through until she found her list of phone numbers. Bloomstock 328 – Gloria Spackman. Would she be at home this Christmas with her family? Would she even want to see to her now they had drifted apart?

'Bloomstock 328.'

'Mrs Spackman?'

'Yes.'

'So sorry to disturb you. Merry Christmas! This is Alison Marshall. Is Gloria there? I wondered if I could speak to her please.' She recalled Mrs Spackman's rather strange behaviour at the Devonish's party and wondered if she was quite the full shilling.

'Of course, my dear. Hold on just a sec.' There was a clunk as the receiver was put down to rest and the fading sound of footsteps.

Then, 'Alison? Hello, what a lovely surprise! Where are you? In Windsor? Or Oxford?'

'No, I'm in the Appley Green phone box! How are you? Could we meet up?' She didn't want to sound as desperate as she felt. 'I mean, we … the family … we're staying here over Christmas, for a few days and I thought it might be nice to seize the chance to see you.'

'Smashing! What would you like to do?' Alison breathed a sigh of relief, hearing her friendly voice. 'We have a bit of a houseful here but you're more than welcome. There's a group going huntin' and shootin' tomorrow, but I'm not for that so perhaps … you know where we live?'

Arrangements were made and Alison's spirits rose. Good things might happen after all. She would find a way to get to Bloomstock on Boxing Day. It wouldn't be that hard, surely? Who had a car?

30

'Gloria – you're a miracle-worker!' said Alison, as she stepped out of the vast Armstrong Siddeley saloon onto a gravel driveway. 'Thank you so much for fixing this.' Mr and Mrs Spackman had arranged for their chauffeur, Arthur, to pick her up from Appley Green, and drive her to their home. Alison and Gloria had been chattering nineteen to the dozen in the back seat and now Gloria, and Arthur, understood the plight of both Nicola and Molly. They stepped into the hallway of what could be fairly described as a small stately home as Gloria spoke in hushed tones.

'You know, my dear mother is going through a fearfully philanthropic phase just at the moment. I think it's what they call 'the mid-life change' – one of the side-effects, you know. She loves to help people – says that it's to balance out her working life where she has to deal with a mountain of bureaucracy and paperwork.'

'What does she do?'

'Something administrative in Whitehall, but so dull it doesn't bear discussing, so never is. It's a family house rule! Although I sometimes think that keeping it all to herself drives her a little mad.' Gloria giggled nervously, as if unsure if this were funny or sad. 'During the war, she did something similar to what your mother did, so I believe, whatever that was, terribly secretive. Helping the war effort in some way ...'

Alison nodded. Yes, that did sound about right. How wonderful they had this common ground. She giggled too, feeling light-headed with joy to be with a young, intelligent woman in whom she could confide anything. After all, Gloria had confided in *her* the massive secret about Ted Devonish, top-drawer married man, giving her the eye.

'It's so good to see you, Gloria. Really. I think I might have gone insane stuck in that hotel, lovely though it is in many ways. I should be grateful, really, but ...'

'Look! Stop wittering, Alison. I have a corker of an idea. Why don't we gather up Nicola and Molly for a grand reunion just for a couple of hours. We could get Arthur to fetch them. I'm certain that mother would approve of this, as it's Christmas and everything.'

'Who's Arthur?'

'Silly! The man who drove you here of course.'

'Did he fight in the war?' asked Alison. 'We had a gardener before who walked with a limp just like Arthur.'

Gloria nodded. 'Yes, he's so lovely and would do anything for us. He can drive perfectly well but knows he's lucky to have a job, being lame and handicapped ...'

'But we should feel lucky and grateful he fought for us ...'

'Absolutely, of course. My parents would do anything for him, by the same token. Anyway, don't worry, I'll arrange all this right now. They'll be here by lunchtime!'

'He'll never get Molly away from her parents! And Nicola might be needed at home, although she's not much use. Perhaps she's up and about by now, I don't know.' She shrugged.

'Well, we'll send him off with an invitation and assurances to have them back by tea-time. He can be very charming ...'

'When Molly's parents see that amazing car, they'll be so squirmingly ingratiating and deferential. It's the kind of thing they love ... I can imagine her mother telling her church friends all about it.'

Gloria gave her a hug. 'It'll work out. Trust me.'

'Is Arthur married?' asked Alison, *à propos* of nothing.

Gloria gave her a sideways glance, smiling as she shook her head. 'He's a bit old for *you*, dear!' No, Gloria, it was Molly who had a *penchant* for older men ...

It was decided that Arthur would go off alone on his mission, armed with two invitations, hand-written quickly by Mrs Spackman but in the neatest of handwriting. If Alison had been with him, then both sets of parents would have smelled a rat. She knew that Molly and Nicola would work out what was going on and now all she could do was keep everything crossed and wish hard, maybe even pray a little.

Gloria and Alison were drinking mulled wine and dipping into a box of glorious liqueur chocolates when they heard the Armstrong Siddeley return. It was a matter of minutes before Nicola stumbled out of the car, followed by Molly who looked wan and dazed but then could not stop smiling as she looked around.

Alison thanked Arthur profusely. 'Did you have any problems?'

He seemed tickled by the whole plot. 'A few stony glares and funny looks from the Watson family. They all came out to clock a view of the car, and me I suppose. I do look mighty impressive in my uniform, you'll have to agree!'

Alison laughed and nodded. 'But any … resistance? You know, trouble?' She pulled a face.

'Not once they'd read the invitation. No.'

'Brilliant. How are the Bates family?'

'They were more concerned about me and my gammy leg! Nice, ordinary folk. They asked if I'd had a sprain too. But they were pleased for their daughter to have a little treat, I think.'

Alison decided she could get the ins and outs from Nicola and Molly and she just thanked him again, reaching up to give him a kiss on the cheek. It was very unlike her, but she felt a wealth of gratitude towards this man and Mrs Spackman – and Gloria. Oh, the goodwill this Christmas was flowing in abundance.

The three young women, standing with arms around each other, watched him drive off to the garage where the car would be put under cover, scarcely noticing snowflakes settle on their hair and faces. Gloria tacked on to make a foursome, linking arms with Alison.

'Oh! An almost white Christmas. How lovely!' said Molly.

'It'll be all gone by tomorrow morning, always turns to slush doesn't it though?' commented Nicola, as they tried to move together, 'But soon I think everything'll be looking like a Bambi wonderland!'

Gloria's young man then arrived and took her off to the garden room, on Mrs Spackman's insistence. 'Well, we've heated it specially, so please use it,' she urged them. 'You can watch the snowflakes and soon, the moon and stars. Can we do anything more romantic for you than that?'

In a happy and warm atmosphere, Alison, Nicola and Molly sat by a log fire, as if transported by a miracle, and looked at each other, each with their own thoughts. So many questions were lurking behind the pensive looks they were giving one other, Alison wondered how they would begin to deal with so much emotion.

'How long is it since we three were together?'

Molly answered in a split second. 'Nineteen months, when our plot was discovered …'

Nicola reached out to Molly and squeezed her arm. 'You know so exact? But, course it was, how could we forget?'

Molly blushed in her old way and looked down, wringing her hands. All the self-confidence she once regained seemed to have gone.

31

When Molly first saw the big car draw up she thought it was Walter. At last! At last he had come back for her! She knew she would first be angry with him, beyond belief, and the questions piled up in her head. *Why did you abandon me so heartlessly? Did you not realise I thought you must have died, for what else could have possibly kept you away all this time? Oh Walter, Walter, did you ever love me at all?*

But she knew, once he had calmed her down and comforted her, she would forgive him and the joy of seeing him again had already overwhelmed her fury. Never had she stopped loving him, despite the anguish he caused. Her heart began to race.

Then, from the front window, as she pulled back the net curtain she saw a man step out of the car. He was smart and tall and walked with a limp. He wore a peaked hat. It was not Walter.

As he spoke to her on the doorstep, his words blurred and faded, her heart sank, all strength draining out of her. Something about Mrs Spackman inviting her to a Boxing Day party at her house and he handed her an envelope addressed to just her. She was light-headed, though aware of her father behind her, reading it over her shoulder, then going off to tell Dorothy. Molly could not tell what he made of it and she did not care. The middle-aged, uniformed man with kind eyes said very softly, 'I'm Arthur. You have some friends who want to see you,' and he winked. 'Young old school friends.'

It dawned on Molly what was going on. Gloria, that posh girl she met a long time ago … her surname was Spackman, and then she put two and two together. She barely heard the question her mother was asking, just wondering if the dress she was wearing was smart enough and decided that she really had nothing better.

After a firm goodbye and promises not to be long, she sank gratefully onto the back seat of the beautiful black car that smelled of leather and polish, discreetly wiping away tears with the back of her trembling fingers as Arthur drove smoothly in the direction of Nicola's house. What a lovely floating motion; this is what a baby must feel like in a proper Silver Cross carriage pram, a thought that made her wince.

Inside Molly's head, the startling thought of seeing Nicola and Alison fetched up painful memories. Can I cope with the wonder and sorrow of it, she wondered? The last time she sat in a car as opulent as this was with the love of her life and where was he now? She stared hard out of the car window at the Surrey heathland of bleak winter. Where?

The only people who knew what happened were Alison and her parents; Molly's parents and David; Nicola and her parents. As far as the rest of the village was concerned, Molly went away 'to do a residential catering course but didn't like it and gave up after four months'. Her mother and father were insistent that this charade must be played out and played down, so that questions would not be asked and her absence would attract as little attention as possible.

'You see,' her mother would assure her, 'it's all for the best, for everyone, isn't it Molly?' Molly would nod, for what else could she do? Better than the whole of Appley Green crying, *For shame! Shame on you, Molly Watson!* Was it best for her, though, or for her baby who was wrenched from her arms at six weeks old to be adopted by well-meaning strangers, just when the bond between them had grown as strong as forged steel, as unbreakable as a ship's rope? The dearest little boy knew his mother, recognised her voice, face and smell and would look up adoringly into her eyes as he nursed from the breast. She had never loved or been loved so and this was a child that was half her and half Walter, who, despite what he had done, she still needed and wanted so much it made her ache with loss and longing.

Then her parents drew a clean, sharp line under the whole shameful and unfortunate 'incident' as if it had never happened. They assumed the worst of the baby's father, for who and where was he? Clearly, he was no more than a philanderer who had fled his responsibilities and not stood by her. Molly, on top of being held guilty of immoral behaviour, became their object of pity, so young, so gullible, so naïve and this was a humiliation she had to bear every single day, perhaps until her parents died.

Now she would have the chance to open up and talk, but it was Christmas and nobody would want tears and misery today. She must put on a brave face.

As the three young women sat snugly by the fire, each of them in a separate state of wonder that this miraculous reunion had transpired, Nicola and Alison seemed to be waiting for Molly to speak, as if unsure of what to say, afraid of saying the wrong thing.

'So, how are you two then? Lovely place, very good of Gloria and her parents. Whose idea was this? I mean, who came up with such a devious plan?' She gave a nervous laugh.

'We sort of cooked it all up between us, but Gloria's trump card was the lovely Arthur, their chauffeur!' said Alison, passing her a small, wrapped package.

'Oh thank you! I'm sorry I don't have anything, I had no idea …'

'Don't worry – to be honest neither did we, and this is just something I was given by an aunt.'

Molly smiled.

'I don't have anything for you either,' confessed Nicola, 'I never expected us to meet up, your parents are such ferocious guardians. I tried you know, several times …'

Molly closed her eyes momentarily and nodded. 'I know, I know and I am sorry, but I just …' she shrugged, '… gave up the fight. Anything for a quiet life.' Nicola and Alison exchanged glances. 'Compared with you two, I feel such a failure.'

'You made one little mistake …'

'But it wasn't a *mistake*!' retorted Molly, her calm demeanour suddenly broken. 'I had the most wonderful … love affair and all with my eyes open. Yes, there was an accident – obviously, but you must understand. Please, you are the only two people on this planet who might believe me, Walter was going to marry me, but when he found out I was still at school, maybe he had to think hard. He went off to find his brother but I always believed he would come back, that we would marry and he would love his little boy ...' She held back the tide of emotion that raged through her, raising her chin. 'He never even knew about the baby, you know that ... Something must've gone wrong ...' Her voice trailed off and she stared away wistfully.

'Maybe he had second thoughts ...' said Alison, gently.

Molly shook her head. 'No. He loved me.'

Nicola said, 'You still think he's gonna come back?' Molly nodded. 'You must ... long for the life that might've been ...' Nicola reached out to squeeze her arm.

The tears would not be denied now and flowed hotly down her cheeks.

'Yes. Yes, of course I do, every single minute of every hour of every day. I can't seem to break the habit.' Nobody would ever understand that Walter held the key to open up the rest of her life into a sunny wonderland, filled with love, career, marriage and babies and every comfort she might have wished for. She was not just an object of reckless passion that meant nothing.

'You are young. I mean *we* are young, with the rest of our lives ahead of us. You will love again, Molly. You will!'

Molly looked at Alison sternly, yet trying to smile with all her might. 'Do you think so? Nothing can bring back my baby.'

'I was engaged to a man I thought would be, well obviously, my husband till death us do part, but then it all went wrong.'

'Oh! Oh, Alison, how awful. I think too much of my own problems, you see. My mother tells me I'm selfish and sometimes I am. I mean, when I was in the home for unmarried mothers, I had time to really think about what life has been like for my mother. Because she's always been rather cold ... and demanding, sympathy for her suffering deserted me over the years, but then I realise what a bad hand she had been dealt. I added to her troubles and now I must make amends ... especially as my Dad has very little work now on account of his back. Some days he can barely move. They need every kind of support … sorry I am going on a bit too much. You see? You see what I'm like? And you were telling me about your ex fiancé? Who is he and what happened, Alison?'

'Oh, never mind. We just realised that we wanted different things in life. He expected me to have no career and become wife and mother, full stop.'

Molly swallowed hard. 'I see. Not for you. It was brave to stop it before you entered into marriage.'

Alison nodded. 'Divorce must be awful. People judge you and see you as some kind of wicked person if your marriage fails. A broken engagement is bad enough.' Someone came by to throw some more logs on the fire and asked if there was anything he could get for them. Tea and cake?

Their eyes lit up. 'It would be rude to decline, wouldn't it?' said Alison with great charm. 'Thank you so much.'

'I wonder if we'll see Gloria again? She looked very dizzy eyed and wrapped up in her young man, didn't she?' commented Nicola.

'Well he only has another day on leave and then he's back to Germany. He's an officer with the armed forces …'

'Oh that must be hard,' said Molly. 'To have a husband who is posted abroad and may even be called into active service at any time. I hear them on Two-Way Family Favourites on Sundays.'

'They are very happy together though, that's the main thing.' Alison then looked around, obviously about to huddle for whispers. Molly had seen that gesture before. 'Apparently, Ted Devonish has been making unseemly advances towards Gloria!'

'But he's well and truly married and spoken for!' exclaimed Molly.

'I know. She only told me in confidence, but it seems it's a marriage that may struggle to stay the course, if he's got the roving eye already!'

'The family couldn't take the scandal. Not a family like that, with them being gentry,' said Nicola.

'Quite. Anyway, she's not interested and is giving him short shrift, as far as I can gather. Ted is such a lovely gentleman, though, I can't help but think his wife must be the one at fault.'

'How can you possibly tell? Nobody really knows what goes on in other people's relationships,' said Molly.

'You, Miss Molly, are very wise and I should shut-up. Oh, look here comes tea. My word, this is like being at the Ritz!'

Then they realised, as if waking from a trance, their conversation had been so absorbing, people around them had all gone to the various windows in the room to stare.

'That is serious snow!' they heard a man say. Alison was the first to jump up and take a look.

'My goodness,' she cried, as the other two followed behind her. 'It looks about four inches deep!'

Huge snowflakes like goose feathers, were shoaling down thickly, smothering the gravel-drive with a magical white carpet, draping trees and statues with white blankets and shawls. Someone had tried to drive off, but the car skidded on the underlying ice and he abandoned his vehicle, laughing as he cautiously staggered back to the front entrance of the house, his breath like a cloud in the frosty air.

The noisy hunting party arrived in the driveway, some on foot, others on horses that were guided round to stables beyond a small paddock on the east side of the house.

Mrs Spackman appeared before the girls, sipping a hot toddy. 'Arthur, good man, is going to try and get people who've travelled from afar to the station, although there is a rumour that some trains are not running today. But don't worry, girls, make yourselves at home, please stay for dinner and he can give you a lift back to Appley Green later. Do feel free to use our phone ...' and off she went, graciously spreading reassurances to other people who, once they had allowed themselves to become a little entranced, were now confronting the reality of a difficult journey home in time for work tomorrow.

32

Two days later the brilliant snow lay stubborn, crisp and deep, refusing to turn to grey slush in the time-honoured fashion. More snow was forecast, roads were impassable and Molly, Nicola and Alison were beginning to enjoy an unplanned break in Gloria's country home. Each night, thinking it would be their last night away from their families, they took turns to sleep on camp beds and studio couches that Mr and Mrs Spackman kindly provided. Luckily this was a family used to large house parties and if they were to be stranded anywhere, this was probably one of the best places to be. Yesterday, there was rabbit pie for dinner and plenty of Christmas leftovers! Today the menu was offering trout with almonds followed by a spiced plum crumble and the girls began to feel guilty.

Gloria's boyfriend, Michael, had gone back to his posting in Germany but she was in good spirits, as ever, thinking about her return to work once she could get into London. He had a large army lorry, with chains around its huge tyres, fetch him. Michael's friend, Giles, was scheduled to spend some time in Aldershot and future postings were uncertain; so he stayed on and helped amuse the girls.

He seemed particularly struck by Molly; they found they had a common interest and it was obvious to Molly that Nicola and Alison were conspiring to leave them alone together at every opportunity, making excuses to be elsewhere in the house whenever he appeared. Molly was not seeking or expecting romance, but she clearly enjoyed his attention and companionship.

Sometimes his interest in her and the questions he inevitably asked were awkward. 'Are you going to art college, then Molly?'

She shook her head. 'No, this won't be possible. I … I'm needed at home. My parents have a few problems, my mother is housebound and my father is not in the best of health now.'

She stopped, realising she was sounding pitiful, like a victim of circumstances when her situation was to some extent, of her own making. The fact she had no A' levels was because her education had been cut short, nobody's fault but her own, but she saw with surprising clarity that she would never reveal any details about this to Giles.

In any case, Giles did not dwell on this scenario. 'But you have a talent you enjoy.' He had a gentle manner and kind, smiley eyes that seemed utterly trustworthy. There are people in this world, mused Molly as she discreetly watched him, who are not exciting, and may not make your pulse race, but whom you could never imagine would deliberately harm anyone or speak ill of another person. He was looking at the sketches she had done while at the house, her attempts to capture the warm conviviality of the indoors as well as the Christmas card scenes of the great outdoors. 'Do you realise how good these drawings are?'

Molly smiled and shrugged modestly. 'I've always enjoyed making things, usually clothes, you know, like most girls and their mothers do, but in the last year I started to look at other art forms and found I loved to draw, adding a little colour here and there, just with colouring pencils. I hope to move onto painting at some time, but am not sure how to handle watercolours properly. Maybe I'll work my way to using oils. I love the French impressionists and grand masters like Turner, how they get such effects of light, I mean I can't begin to think how ...' She stopped and blushed, realising she was gabbling; but it felt so good to talk to someone attentive.

He gently squeezed her arm in a simple gesture of understanding. 'Once this snow shifts I would love you to come to my home − I live in the barracks of course, but I inherited a little studio in Appley Green; well I call it that, it's more of a ramshackle lean-to on the back of my bungalow, but it does have a lovely aspect that captures the light in the morning. I paint there and it takes me away to another world ...'

'A world where you can forget some of the horrors you must see in active service.'

'Hmm. Well, so far I've been lucky, though you never know what the future might hold. I'm just a clerk, really in more of a backroom, administrative role. I've never been a ... well, a man of action.'

She handed him a sheet of the drawing paper that Gloria had so kindly found for her. 'Please, show me something of your style.'

Giles's eyes crinkled and he smiled broadly. 'Now you're embarrassing me ...'

'Oh. I'm sorry.'

'No, no. I meant you're flattering me into believing that I can show you something you don't already know.'

'I want to learn. I think I have a passion for art, but somehow cannot find my way.' She wanted to say that once there was a man who knew more about her capabilities than she did herself, but she had no idea where he was or if she would ever see him again. Her eyes filled with tears and Giles was looking at her, a little mystified and certainly concerned.

'Please,' and he reached across to touch her arm again, 'Don't upset yourself.' He paused to give her time. 'I cannot bear to see someone so young and pretty in tears for reasons I cannot imagine.'

She looked away, willing herself to stop those tears. 'I'm sorry.'

'Nothing to be sorry about. Now,' he said, in a common-sense way that she needed, 'let's both draw the same thing and then compare our styles. How's that for a plan?'

'What shall we draw?'

'Hmm. Something that stays still? People are unreliable, and dogs even worse. How about the hearth? There's a variety of textures there, a coal scuttle, a log basket, flames – well, they flicker, but never mind!'

Molly looked at the large inglenook, with horse brasses tacked onto the blackened beam above, and various pokers, cast-iron tongs and toasting forks leaning against the wall. Hammered copper bowls filled with fir cones gleamed in the firelight. Yes, she could do something with this. She stared at it with new eyes, aware of the glints and shadows she wanted now to commit to paper.

Thus began a relationship that perhaps saved Molly from falling into a downward spiral. She could feel that sense of being rescued and soon found her heart beating fast when Giles sought her out. By the weekend he was gone, military vehicles finding the means to carve a route through the drifts and ice that local councils struggled to break and disperse. Trucks filled with grit and rock salt and many men with shovels were doing their best but there were reports that it was impossible to tell where roads were and some drifts were twelve feet high after the northerly blizzard of fine snow on Saturday.

'How can we get home?' asked Alison, when the four of them were gathered together in the big country kitchen, the warmest room in the house, sipping hot Bovril. 'Without an army rescue, I mean!'

Gloria replied, 'Well trains are not running, neither is the bus and Arthur tried to take out the car today and slid into a ditch – quite gently but very thoroughly! He had to abandon the car and walk back here; Daddy says the local garage doesn't have the kind of recovery vehicles needed for this sort of thing.'

'Nobody round here has ever seen anything like this,' said Alison. 'I heard on the radio that the river Thames is starting to freeze in parts and that somewhere even the sea could freeze over! It's that cold!'

'Perhaps we could walk!' put in Nicola, who was now fully recovered from her sprained ankle. 'It's only ten miles.'

Molly and Alison looked at her. 'Do you think?'

'So long as we have boots, and take food and drink with us. We may be able to wave down some heavy duty type lorry or something that could give us a lift on the way.'

'It's worth a try!'

A rosy-cheeked Mrs Spackman, dressed in many layers of thick tweed, emerged through a door at the back of the house, walking briskly and purposefully towards them. 'Girls! We need you. We're getting a working party together to clear the drive. All hands to the pump.'

Glad to have something positive to do that might help, they all drained their mugs and donned the warmest clothes they had, Gloria lending them extra jumpers and gloves. They had not come here equipped for Arctic conditions. Shovels, brooms, pickaxes, rakes and spades were distributed and they all worked like navvies to scrape, dig and heave piles of snow to the side of the driveway. The snow was still coming down, covering the frozen driveway with another mantle. It was almost a hundred yards down to the country lane and the hope was that local authority lorries with rock-salt and maybe even snow-ploughs would make some headway today with clearing local highways and byways.

'We're sure to get some more grit and salt soon!' a man, unidentifiable in a navy-blue balaclava, called out cheerfully.

There was much laughter and throwing of snowballs, as the girls put their backs into the task. It was the least they could do to repay their kind hosts and might enable them to eventually return home.

'I keep wondering how they're gettin' on at home,' said Nicola, breathless and red in the face. 'It was bad enough, without all this.' She stopped still for a moment and looked serious.

'Everyone will be pulling together!' said Alison. 'It's the bulldog war-spirit. Nobody can go far and neighbours will help each other, for sure.'

Nicola nodded. 'S'pose so.'

'My family have had to stay on at the Hunter's Lodge. Lucky them! I expect a hotel like that will have ways and means to keep guests fed and warm.'

'I can't imagine how mine are coping – just basic things like cooking a meal without me, and what if they can't get to the shops?' said Molly.

'It might do 'em good!' snorted Nicola. 'Your Dad, David and Susan can manage between them, I'm bloomin' well sure.'

'It's Susan I worry about. She'll be put upon.'

'She's a plucky, bright spark though, isn't she? She won't stand for it I bet!' Alison reassured her.

'She is the main reason why I realised I must stay at home, you know. I couldn't bear for my parents to wear out her confidence and use her like a drudge.'

Accompanied by an assortment of excited, wagging dogs, Mrs Spackman appeared cautiously bearing a tray of steaming mugs of hot chocolate and a tartan tin of shortbread. Her nose had turned a not so healthy-looking shade of lavender and they rushed to help her as she stumbled across the treacherous, uneven ice. 'Just to keep you going for a while, although it's probably cooled already. What a marvellous job you're doing! There'll be bacon sandwiches for lunch and I should think you'll be done by then. We're going to see how the horses can cope with this amount of snow. They may prove to be better than wheels, but they've never tried skating on an ice-rink before!'

Then she was gone to her next mission.

So the day and another night passed. That evening the phone lines were down and there was a power cut and, whilst oil-lamps and candle-light were magical and could have been romantic had there been male company, the girls' spirits sank as the temperature plummeted in the house. Huge baskets of logs were brought in, with the fires and Aga range the only sources of heat now. Not many houses had central heating, certainly Nicola's and Molly's did not have radiators, although Alison's parents' new house in Windsor did have that luxury. None of them could remember ever feeling so numb with cold but they could hardly blame the Spackman family for not sharing their own hot water bottles. They pushed their beds together in a huddle and tried to hatch a plan in the dark.

'Should we try and walk home tomorrow then?' said Nicola.

'We could! There's no harm in trying, is there?'

'It'll be fun!' said Molly, surprising even herself.

'OK. We'll ask Gloria if she can help with getting us kitted out in suitable apparel …' said Alison.

33

They set off early and the Spackman family waved them off, wishing them all the best and giving them well-meaning but rather obvious advice.

'Don't be shy. Knock on people's doors. In these special conditions, they'll be happy to help.'

'Make sure you stick to the roads, don't go astray or get lost in the fields and woods, or on the heath, whatever you do.'

'Hopefully we can hitch a lift from someone,' put in Alison cheerfully.

Mr and Mrs Spackman looked at them. 'I think that's unlikely,' said Mr Spackman, 'from what I hear. If the roads were passable I would drive you myself, but ...' he shrugged and sucked on his pipe, 'you never know! You may be lucky!'

By noon they had covered about three miles and knew they must hurry up to get home by nightfall. Dusk would fall by about four o'clock.

They had managed to beg a mid-morning hot drink from a family in a hamlet they passed through; everywhere people were kind and sympathised with their plight, even though they had problems of their own. Folk were unable to get to work; farmers were struggling to help their livestock survive; and everywhere power was intermittent and burst pipes meant many households had no water. They ate their sandwiches as they walked along, as stopping just meant feeling cold. Abandoned vehicles littered the side of the roads and, despite the beguiling azure sky and brilliant, sparkling landscape, at times it seemed like the end of the world, an apocalyptic scene from a science fiction novel.

One thing it did was give the three of them a fine chance to talk; it helped to pass the time and they all found it therapeutic.

'You were saying before, Molly, that what decided you to live at home with your Mum and Dad was 'cause of your sister…' Nicola probed. Molly nodded. 'But were there other reasons, too? I mean, you could've just left home, found a job and lived somewhere else. People do that these days!'

'When I was in that dreadful home for unmarried mothers, I had some time to think. Having a baby makes you realise what your own mother went through to bring you into this world, then I started thinking about what a terrible life my Mum has had. She had polio as a child. Imagine that! She was a little cripple, although she never ever talks about that, but I know what polio was like. And then, after a few years of young married life, she got the arthritis and became less and less able to walk. Yet with all the pain she managed to have three babies – well four actually, because there was another one between David and me that was stillborn. To give birth to a baby that had no life in it – ah! You two haven't felt the pain of childbirth, the only thing that keeps you going is knowing there will be a beautiful baby at the end. I lay awake at night, just thinking about how she must've suffered and no wonder she can be crabby at times, and she has few enough visitors …'

'Maybe if she was a bit more friendly, she would have more friends …' put in Alison, but Molly flared up at this.

'You can't imagine what she's gone through. You with your family, all healthy, wealthy and well cared for! I'm sorry, but you have no idea.'

It went quiet for a moment. 'I'm so sorry,' said Alison. 'You're right. I have no idea.' She cautiously put an arm round Molly's shoulders and Molly reached a hand up to clasp hers.

'I don't mean to take it out on you. It's just, well, that's the other reason why I had to return home.'

'My Mum was so excited when she had this idea that she and my Dad could adopt your baby …' recalled Nicola, slipping her arm through Molly's. 'She thought it would be easy enough …'

Molly's eyes then filled with hot tears that rolled freely down her ice-cold cheeks. 'I know. I haven't been able to talk about all that to anyone, you know! It's been torture keeping it all bottled up inside.'

'It was hard enough for us to keep quiet, it must've been a thousand times worse for you.'

Nicola's parents' offer was one of the kindest things Molly had ever came across. 'It could've worked, too. I could've seen him grow up and he might've realised one day I was his true mother even if I was more like an auntie. Somehow it could've worked.'

'But your parents wouldn't even listen. I remember.'

'They were afraid of the shame it would bring. They wanted me and my mistake to just be pushed under the carpet, removed from their lives. It was the only way they could deal with it.'

'That must be hard to forgive ...'

Molly's jaw tightened. 'Yes. That was *impossible* to forgive, actually. And they wouldn't even listen to anything. I couldn't tell them he was an older man – they'd have just said he was a rogue and had deserted me. I couldn't discuss it with them, it was pointless.'

'My Mum couldn't have any more babies after me,' said Nicola. 'She told me that her innards were damaged when I was born and then she had her womb taken away. She'd always wanted a houseful of children, she said and I'm the most ... the most precious thing she has.' Her bottom lip wobbled and she bit it to steady her emotions.

'Gosh we are getting sad and tearful, aren't we?' asked Molly, forcing herself to smile. 'I'm sorry, I've brought this on.'

'Don't be silly, Molly. It actually helps all of us to be able to talk about these things.'

Alison brought them back to earth. 'Do you know we are coming close to Aldershot now and it may be only another four miles to home. We might just do it, if we stick to the roads. I wonder if the streetlights are working?' The Spackmans had spared them a torch and Alison checked it worked. 'We may have to walk the last stretch in the dark, but we can manage that, can't we?'

It was silent all around, apart from their own voices and breathing and the crunching of their wellington boots. They had seen no traffic, apart from one tractor pulling a trailer piled perilously high with fodder that ground its way down a track and disappeared into a frozen wilderness.

'You know, my parents have always been good to me and Julian, although my mother would never have been able to give up her career, whatever it is she does. She would've been just miserable at home with two babies the same age. But, we survived didn't we? And, on the whole we are a very close and happy family. But, and this is a big but, I will never forgive them for how they reacted to you and your pregnancy, Molly. My mother as good as said that you had been a 'silly girl' and must 'make amends' for what you had done. She even referred to you as a 'fallen woman' – perhaps it was their way of warning me that if I made such a mistake I may not get any support from them. I don't know. I thought she was a more forgiving kind of person. But they were unbelievably harsh and then tried to forbid me from seeing you again.'

'I reckon both of your parents would look down on mine, any rate,' said Nicola.

'Your parents, Nicola, are the only kind, open-minded, warm-hearted people in this whole sad, sorry story, though,' Alison pointed out.

'Nice of you, but actually don't forget my Mum was *wanting* a baby to look after, even after all the years since I was born. The adoption would've satisfied her own needs, more than anything …'

'Anyhow, it was rules and regulations that scotched it in the end,' said Molly. 'I was willing to defy my parents, actually, but was told, instructed, that once the baby went for adoption, no contact between the baby and its natural mother was *allowed*! It would just cause more pain and confusion in later life. That's what they said, and I wanted the best for my little boy.'

Alison chuckled. 'When my parents packed me off to the Cotswolds to Auntie Doris to make sure I kept away from you, they never expected me to take you and Nicola with me! Oh boy, that was a little crazy, wasn't it? A bit much to hope Auntie Doris could take you in!'

'Crackers! My parents will never get over me disappearing like that but their way of coping was to just bury the memory of it along with my baby. But it showed me what true and good friends you were and still are! You actually put me before your parents! The fact you did that for me, even if the plan didn't work, it helped lift my spirits later when I was in that horrible place with those horrible people.'

'Whatever was it like, when the day came for you to ... you know, to hand over the baby?' asked Nicola, softly.

'I was told to give up the breast feeding after just a few days, so as not to form a strong attachment ... so I gave him his bottle and ... held him very close to me ... talking to him softly about his father and how he would love him so much if he knew him. He was six weeks old. I was trying to decide what to give him to take away so one day someone could tell him his real mother loved him with all her heart. I wrote a little letter on a scrap of paper ... Of course, from what they said, there was no way it would ever be given to him, but I thought maybe one day those terrible rules might change. Then a woman, whose name I can't even remember, came in, asked if his nappy had been changed and said his new parents were ready to take him, to take him *home*, they said. She said what a lucky little boy he was to go to *such a loving home, such a caring couple*.' Molly drew a deep breath, 'The sadness, like a physical pain, of Mark being taken from me was the worst kind of ... agony ... you can possibly imagine. I felt as if all the life had been sucked out of me.' No tears came as she said this, for she had long ago wept for hours through many nights, feeling that she would never recover from such anguish.

Molly's tale had thrown them into a somewhat sombre, reflective mood. The last mile made talking difficult in any case, so they kept in single file on a narrow pavement that had been partially cleared for pedestrians. A wind got up and soon a blizzard was cutting into their faces as they trudged onwards. Alison led them using the torch to light up the way forward and the other two tagged on behind. Appley Green was in darkness apart from a few dimly lit windows indicating candles and Tilley lamps here and there. Mingled with relief, a heavy sadness fell over them as they realised their journey was over, but one thing they knew for sure was that they would meet again very soon, although all they wanted now was to eat and sleep for a long time. The three of them were joined in hope that their families would allow them the use of what tonight was the most coveted prize, a hot water bottle.

34

The freezing winter seemed never-ending but, like a bright light shining ahead, Gloria's wedding was set for mid-summer and Molly looked forward to this, especially as it would offer another chance to see Nicola and Alison. She swept the pavement in front of the Watson's house, wondering at how mounds of gritty snow could persist in shady places as late as March. This marriage was going to be a significant Surrey event, since her parents were well-heeled, with ancestors both of the landed gentry class, and other scions accorded with military honours in battles past and blessed with money accrued through trading with India. The girls had learned all this during their stay there. It was no surprise her fiancé was an officer in the army and would be posted abroad. For the time being, Gloria had explained, she would continue to live with her parents, but she and Michael were looking to buy a house of their own in Appley Green so they had a base for when he came home on leave. Both their parents were happy to contribute financially to help keep them within reach. Molly was pleased for her and did not begrudge her the privileges she enjoyed.

Apparently Michael had warned Gloria that for someone of his rank, it would be expected for her to join him in Germany, but said Gloria, 'They can't make me!' Always feisty, there were some heated exchanges, as she made it clear to him that she intended to combine married life with a career at least until she had a baby. He said that she would have an essential role in military life, in welfare and helping wives of lower ranking husbands. For him to not have her support, would look extremely strange and could even be to the detriment of his career. She was sure their love would see them through and told the girls she secretly hoped that she could have some other career of her own once they were out there.

Giles told Molly that he and Michael met on a training exercise at Sandhurst many years ago and, despite the differences in social standing and rank, they became friends, especially as they both regarded Appley Green as home. They discovered they were born in the same maternity hospital in the same year but having gone to very different schools, they did not meet up again until they were young men.

Molly, Nicola and Alison all secretly confessed to each other that they hoped to be bridesmaids, but of course this was never going to happen. There were classier candidates and, indeed, the subject was never even broached. Gloria had insisted, however, that her three friends from the village would be invited to the big day and they were brimming with excitement.

Giles now regularly collected Molly from her parents' house on his time off for many a visit to his modest but cosy home and despite his gentle manner, asserted that he had every right to do this, which of course was true. They were officially courting and Molly had learned to smile again. They spent hours painting and listening to music and getting to know each other rather well, although she always successfully avoided any mention of the biggest event of her life. He was affectionate but not sexually demanding and, for the moment, this suited her just fine. It was love and friendship she craved, not passion that she would one day have to feign.

It fascinated Molly to see what undeniable lust could make even the best of men do. At Gloria's engagement party that she held just for a few friends of hers and Michael's, it was startlingly clear to Molly where others missed the signs, that Ted Devonish still adored Gloria. The way he tilted his head and smiled at her as she spoke to him, his gaze travelling around her face, now and then falling below to admire her figure – it was the same as she remembered Walter's tender way of feasting his eyes on her, even before he ever told her he loved her. Ted Devonish was a married man, of course, and she could barely restrain herself from following this *risquée* cameo that unfolded before her eyes. Gloria seemed oblivious and not in the least interested, but Ted Devonish openly worked Gloria into conversations with other people, enthusing about her modern ways, her spirit, independence and intelligence.

Molly also watched, as the weeks went by and she saw and heard things in the village; Geraldine Devonish became vindictive for she too had noticed what was going on with her husband.

'Gloria, I think you should be wary of Ted Devonish's wife, Geraldine,' cautioned Molly one day when they met by chance late one afternoon on the village green.

Gloria blinked, obviously taken aback. 'Whatever are you talking about, Molly?' It was as if she had conveniently forgotten what she had confided to Alison in her letter a while back. Perhaps there was some guilt she was trying to hide and Molly was careful not to reveal that Alison has passed her secret on to them.

'Jealousy can make people behave oddly ...'

'I really don't know what ...'

'Gloria, it's obvious Ted is obsessed with you. Can you not see that?'

'Oh what absolute rot! For goodness sake, Molly, what the devil is going on inside that woolly head of yours?'

Molly felt a surge of resentment rising within her, not to be taken seriously when she simply had her friend's best interests at heart. How could Gloria now deny what she had more or less told Alison in the first place?

'Never mind who said what, but you know what gossip is like and I've heard that she has been saying bad things about you and it's obvious why.'

'Are you suggesting I've encouraged Ted in some way?' Now it was Gloria's turn to become angry and defensive and she glared at Molly. Ah! So this is what she was afraid of.

'No! I'm not, but just be aware – he has a thing for you. He really does.'

'It's not like that. We've known each other since childhood ...'

Molly did not want to quarrel. She smiled. 'I hope I'm wrong, I really do.'

Now feeling insecure about her own convictions, Molly left her to hurry home with the shopping. Perhaps she had an overactive imagination; maybe she was mistaken, and *maybe she was wrong about Walter too.* Perhaps all along she was hoodwinked and led astray by nothing more than the charm and attention of a scoundrel; and yet she would always love him.

She could have done without the domestic scene that confronted her when she arrived home laden with bags of groceries, vegetables and fresh bread. It was the end of her working day and she just wanted to turn on the wireless, have a cup of tea and maybe read the Daily Mail to catch up with what was going on in the wider world. Her father, now at home most days, unable to work due to his sciatica and suspected slipped disk, was bullying Susan.

'Never mind your homework, Susan,' Molly overheard as she came in via the back door, 'just you make sure your mother's comfortable first, that's all I'm saying. You can do your homework after tea ...'

Then Susan was shouting back. 'But I'm meeting my friend after tea. It's all arranged. I need to do this now – I've got an important maths test tomorrow and a history essay to finish ...'

Then there was a slap. 'Don't you argue with me, young lady. You do as you're told.'

There was an ominous pause and Molly held back, listening the other side of the living-room door, clutching the bags, waiting to see what would happen next.

Susan's voice was calm. 'You do that again and I will report you to the Welfare people,' she said, cool as a cucumber. Molly wanted to cheer! Her little sister's spirit would not be broken easily, plucky girl.

Molly then swept in as if she had heard nothing, but winked secretly at Susan. Their father had sheepishly retreated, tail between his legs.

'His temper gets the better of him sometimes, Susan, and then he knows he's done wrong afterwards!' So used to being the peacemaker, she could hear herself almost defending her bully of a father when this was far from her intention.

'Huh! He'd better not do that again. I shall report him! I will, Molly, truly. I'm not afraid to and I'm not afraid of *him*.'

Molly cradled her arms around her sister who was actually trembling and hugged her close, welling up as memories of similar incidents came flooding back. She stroked her hair and kissed the top of her head. Children did not report their own parents, but it was heartening to hear her sister's unquenchable strength of character; it would carry her far.

'Well done, my little spitfire ...' she whispered.

Giles and she went to the pictures that evening and somehow Susan's great show of courage and determination cheered her greatly. It gave her hope that she would not have to bear the burden of her sister's safety and happiness for ever and a day. Susan was still young but was showing healthy signs that she could fight her own corner and would not be used as a doormat. Teenagers seemed a lot more rebellious these days.

When Giles asked her if they could meet on Saturday at the Hunter's Lodge for afternoon tea, her heart skipped a beat. She could see a glimmer of hope burning brightly. There was something in his twinkling eyes and soft smile that told her he had a plan, something special to ask her.

At the vending machine factory she stared at the columns of sales figures she was copying by hand into a ledger. Someone came along and unceremoniously plonked a typewriter on her desk.

'You can learn to type now – you have to copy type. All right?' With that, the clerk who had deposited the machine was gone.

She stared at the Olympia model before her; then walked over to a typist called Marjorie, whose fingers were flying, clattering across the keys, thrusting the carriage return to the left with a dramatic zing every few seconds. How would she ever do this?

'Marjorie,' she said, interrupting her gently with a tap on her shoulder that nonetheless made her jump. 'How do I teach myself to type?'

'Just have a go, first. I never went to secretarial or college or nothing, just learned on the job really. I don't touch type, nor nothing. You know, I have to somehow look at what I'm copying and at my fingers at the same time. You'll get used to it. Stare at the keys and remember where all the letters are. You know how to start a new line ... like this!' And she gave the carriage return a theatrical thwack. 'If you make a mistake, you can use a typing rubber or some white stuff to paint it out.' She got up from her seat and came over to Molly's desk to see what she had been given. 'Oh, this is numbers mostly, you'll soon get the hang and it's not like it's important business letters where you can't make a mistake. Good luck! Just give me a shout if you get into a pickle!'

'Thanks, I will. I mean, I expect I will!'

Tentative at first, Molly fed some paper in and began to type as she had seen many others do in the office. She felt quite excited as this was something new for her and made a change from the endless copying by hand. Soon she was filing the new typed list in the folder following on in sequence from her previous entries and checked with her supervisor that she had done the thing correctly and received assurances that she had.

By afternoon the moves already became more mechanical, automatic, her fingers reaching out for the number keys as if with a life of their own. Her thoughts began to stray. What if Walter comes back and she is married to Giles? Even if she never sees him again, can she pretend he never existed? This was a new conundrum with which to wrestle, whereas before most of her concerns had been with her mother and more often with Susan.

35

Summer 1961

Catching sight of Peter in an art gallery in Vienna had a dreamlike feel. Walter froze stock-still, unable to take it in. His long search of Europe, following vague signs and threads of hope, had finally come to fruition and now he had to pinch himself. His brother was alive and within sight. He paused to cast a watchful eye over him before announcing his arrival, this anticipated surprise making his heart pound with excitement and apprehension.

Did Peter actually want to be found? This was unlikely since it almost seemed he had deliberately covered his tracks to hide his whereabouts. Whether this was true or not, Walter felt that he must know the reasons for his brother's disappearance; he felt a burning need to understand his motives. Did he not realise the worry he had caused and was he aware that their father had indeed died? In his letter he felt he had said his goodbyes and that the father he once knew and loved had already departed.

Walter re-read Peter's letter just that morning before setting off from the small hotel where he was lodging for the night. He had said *Please write to Ned if you need to contact me.* But of course because the letter had gone on some adventure of its own before eventually arriving battered and bruised at the Hunters' Lodge Hotel months ago, Peter had heard nothing back and probably presumed that Walter had washed his hands of him.

Peter was looking somewhat unkempt, for all the world like a bohemian artist, in need of a shave and a haircut, but his face was tanned and his manner imparted a kind of serenity as he softly padded around studying the massive paintings hung on the walls of this great gallery.

Walter decided the time was right and made his move. He simply sidled up to his left, the direction in which he was proceeding, and stood alongside Peter, stroking his chin as he contemplated the landscape before them. He heard the sharp intake of breath before he turned to face Peter's astonished face.

'Walter! Walter? What the ….?' Peter grabbed his shoulder as if testing that he was real.

'So how are you?'

His eyes were wide with disbelief. 'This must be a dream! How the devil did you find me? I take it this is not a chance encounter?'

'Hah! Hardly, old bean. This morning was a stroke of luck. I had the name of your hostel or hotel, whatever it is, and you had asked a porter there for directions this very morning. So. At last! For nearly twelve weeks, with the help of this,' and he pulled a small photograph of Peter from his wallet, 'I have worn the various cloaks of spy, special investigator, sightseer, pilgrim, mad brother crazed with obsession …'

'Are you trying to make me feel guilty?' Peter's tone sounded defensive.

Walter's jaw tightened. '*Why*, Peter? What the hell were you thinking? I got your letter, but all too late – it arrived weeks after you posted it …'

'I had no message from Ned …'

'I can see how that might have looked, but, you know, things happen! And you had no faith in me whatever, that's clear. You thought I didn't care where you were – whether you were alive or *dead*? I mean a few weeks, all right, but to let months roll by without word.' Walter spoke with some anger despite wanting nothing more than brotherly reconciliation. 'How could you? Dad died you know …' His voice was echoing in the cathedral-like space so they made their way in silence to the exit. The atmosphere in the vaulted hall was as peaceful as a library where such an emotionally charged discussion was out of place and frowned upon by the austere officials seated to guard the room and its contents. Now emerging like coiled springs into hot sunshine they found a place where they could relax with a beer and snack.

'How did you find me?' asked Peter, as if wanting to clear the air and start afresh.

'Ned told me you planned on doing some kind of Grand Tour on the cheap, taking in the European capitals, wanting to find the pulse of the art world ...'

Peter laughed and Walter was pleased to see how amusement softened his brother's features. Perhaps he had found what he was looking for.

'Did Ned actually say that? In his broad Yorkshire accent?'

'He quoted you verbatim as if it were taken from a foreign phrase book! But, Peter, without the clues he gave me as to the rough route you had in mind and list of hostels, I would never – *never* – have found you, so I owe him a lot. I wouldn't have known where to begin. As it is, I have enjoyed myself immensely once I could detach myself from the purpose of my trip. Paris, Brussels, Rome ... wonderful! I have to thank you for giving me this opportunity.'

The irony, perhaps sarcasm, of his comment was not lost on Peter. 'Walter, I'm ... sorry. What about the business? Who's looking after that?"

'Sold it! I flew back to London to oversee the final stages of what has proved to be a very good deal, a larger company that has more or less taken over. Decided to use the money to make the most of the rest of my life. So this tour of Europe's capitals would have been on my itinerary anyway.'

'Did you get to Madrid? Or Barcelona?'

Walter shook his head. 'There's a limit how many miles I could drive – so headed east ...'

'Athens?'

'You mean you've been to all these cities? Peter, are you all right for money?"

'Yes, I have and yes, I'm surviving. A restless soul, me. All that bitterness ... in Appley Green, and then seeing the poverty in northern England. Have you any idea of how some people live there? I know there are grim conditions in parts of London but it's a far cry from Surrey – the dark, dirt, crowded terraced slums and tenements. It spurred me on to run, to escape and find sunshine and life!' He threw his arms out, as if embracing his new chapter with great passion. 'I gave Ned as much as I could spare and have picked up a few commissions already. So I'm hopeful.'

'How did you get the commissions? I mean how would you begin without anything to show of your work?'

'Oh, well I took photographs of my paintings from home and displayed them.'

'They are startlingly good. Your newer stuff, that is. I had to remove them to storage for you.'

'Oh! Wonderful. What a relief! What a brother I have in you, Walter. Thank you. Without knowing how long I would be away, I didn't make arrangements. I wrote to Mrs B to ask her to keep them somewhere safe if she could, but heard nothing back so this has been a constant, nagging worry in the back of my mind.'

'I can imagine.' His paintings were of more concern than the people he had deserted, it seemed.

'I made friends quickly in the Paris art world, despite the Parisian reserve, and was able to share a small gallery space to show my portfolio in this way, with the photos, and then, well, an English Duke – can you believe it, heard me speaking in English, maybe his French was not so good, and said he liked my portraits and would I be interested in painting his eighteen-year-old daughter who was staying in Paris with him and his wife for a few weeks.'

'Did it go well?'

'Yes, they were pleased and recommended me to the owner of a French château in the Dordogne.'

'So what are your conclusions?'

'I shall return to Paris – the artists' quarter there is where I felt most comfortable ... and I can speak the language, which helps. Vienna does nothing for me.'

'So you are a proper artist now?'

'That is my intention. Even if I die young, at least I have found my *niche* in life!"

Walter admired his brother's new-found confidence and raised his glass to him. 'Good for you, little brother. I am proud of you.'

Peter looked embarrassed, and cleared his throat. 'Hmm ... so what are your plans, then, if you've sold up the firm. I find it hard to believe that you would do that when it meant so much to you. Wasn't that a bit rash?'

Walter considered this, realising how his life was in a state of some disarray, in need of direction and fresh purpose.

'I lost business since the trial, which was bloody demoralising, you know Peter. People who did not know me personally believed what they read in the papers, and then read more into it.'

Peter said nothing reassuring and Walter wondered if, even now, his own brother still held doubts about his innocence.

After a pause, Walter continued. 'Anyway, in view of our father's illness I decided to make every day count and not be hidebound with work, but now ... to be honest, I'm not sure what I want. Unlike you.'

'Work does give purpose, but needs to be something you enjoy, not just the old treadmill. Hmm. Anyone ... special in your life?' Peter gave him a sideways look, narrowing his eyes, as if wary of treading onto dangerous ground.

Walter paused. 'Yes, there was someone ...'

'Was?'

'It couldn't work out. Little minx led me up the garden path. She's still at school ... in Appley Green. I thought she was older.'

Peter shook his head as if condemning him. 'Oh lord! Who? Someone I know, presumably.'

'Maybe, she might not want you to know. We ... we made mistakes.'

'So it's over?'

'I'm not sure if we can retrieve what we had.' He felt unmanly tears threaten to well up and turned away, thinking of the happiness Molly had brought him with her innocence and love. 'When I returned to London, I did go back to Appley Green to find her, but her parents were impenetrable! She had gone away to college apparently to learn cookery ... and had a whole new life ahead of her, so they said. It all sounded so wrong. They were lying, I was convinced. They refused to tell me how I could find her.' Walter scratched his head. 'Her talents lay elsewhere. I mean she was a born designer, creative;

231

cooking was more of a chore she had to do for her parents …not out of choice.'

Peter was studying him, drumming his fingers on the table, clearly trying to pick up on clues as to the girl's identity.

'So what do you think they were hiding?'

'Oh, I have no idea. Maybe it's all true.' He sighed. 'I suppose they were guiding her into something that they thought would be useful for her and for them, with no thought of what she might want for herself. I know they were difficult and demanding parents, Molly always said they would never accept me, for example! The age gap.'

'Well, I can see that, actually. And if they'd found out your past history … Oh, Walter.'

Walter was silenced and felt utterly forlorn.

He quietly reflected on the letter he had left for her on that visit to Appley Green. She never got back to him. Had her parents even bothered to send it on to her? He doubted this, feeling he had reached something of an *impasse*. Clearly she could not forgive him for abandoning her, for that is what it probably felt like to her, but maybe that was for the best. Tough love was, after all, an act of kindness.

But he knew now that he would always love Molly and the idea of letting her go did not rest easily with him. The very thought of her finding another lover who could be a husband for life and give her children made him ache with want and jealousy. The uncertainty of his own health posed doubts, and he could not deny the overwhelmingly anxious moments he had that his time on Earth could be cut short, but he was no longer convinced that this possibility should rule over his remaining years.

36

1963

'You see, Gloria was brought up by a nanny as her mother always had a career during and after the war where she had to work away from home, so she says, so she's not so keen to be a stay-at-home mother either. She's very bright and clever and loves her work, though I don't understand what it is she does,' said Molly, chattily. Giles was busy tidying up paints as Molly poured tea into flowery, bone china cups.

'Mmm. Tricky. I don't think it'll work, for her to stay behind. Now they're married, she'll be his army wife and that's an end of it. Michael told me.'

Molly was worried for Gloria and for herself. She pensively stroked the sapphire engagement ring on her finger, nervously wondering about her unknown future as an 'army wife' and having babies with Giles. Butterflies were running amok in her stomach.

She had gently encouraged him to make love to her, desperate to find that ecstasy she had known, though he was strangely shy in that department. Tremblingly she had seduced him, leading him to his own bed, feeling wanton, a voice inside her head saying *Look what happened last time! Will you never learn?* But Giles was careful to take precautions, they were soon to be married and it all felt so different from Walter. Safe, secure, it was not a reckless moment of passion for either of them. He passed no comment on the fact she was not a virgin; perhaps he had not even noticed. If he had, ever the young gentleman, he would not feel it right to enquire.

How she longed to be a mother again, once she had a wedding ring on her finger! Would painful memories of love and loss be forgotten by holding and loving another baby, hopefully many babies? Would seeing them grow and prosper bring her and Giles joy and contentment in the years ahead? There was not a single day when she did not think of Mark, her lost child, the one she would never know.

'I … I can't imagine living abroad,' she said softly, masking the extreme emotions surging inside her. Despite all her longing to break free from her parents, this would be a step too far. Her parents' health was worse than ever, money a problem for them, David and his wife were living in Guildford. To abandon them completely would make her uneasy.

'Well, my postings will be different from that of an officer and I shall be in Aldershot frequently. I'll never be sent to a war zone, as I'm more of a back-room boy, you know that. We can work round it. Is it your family you worry about, my darling?'

As Giles put an arm round her shoulders, Molly was aware of his understanding, of how he was always tuned in to her thoughts and needs. He would be a perfect husband, no doubt about it. He was a good man and she knew he failed the medical examination needed for fighting on the front-line as a 'real soldier'. This had once slipped out accidentally in conversation and he was embarrassed; so from thereon would never refer to it or supply details.

Molly nodded and squeezed his hand affectionately, holding in her own guilty secret. There was some niggling, undeniable doubt in her head that imagined Walter suddenly turning up like a bad, shiny penny to find her, when she might be in Germany. She was strangely relieved to know that she could stay in Appley Green; those old feelings of needing to escape seemed to have fled.

'What about if they had paid help?'

Molly frowned. 'What do you mean?'

'We could provide …'

'No. Nobody can expect us …'

'Better than you working all hours for them as well as running … our home, don't you think?'

Soon a plan built on compromise was drawn up as a happy solution and Molly began to see her life as it would be very soon. A small wedding was booked for the autumn and in no time at all she was busy designing and making her wedding gown and a dress for Susan, one very thrilled bridesmaid.

Nicola shrieked with joy when Molly called in the salon to tell her the news and luckily caught her between customers, sitting at the reception desk doing paperwork. An engagement ring was one thing, but to have a date booked for your wedding in the church and a reception in the village hall was another.

'Have you and Martin set a date yet?' whispered Molly. 'You've been engaged for nearly two years, haven't you?'

'He wants to do the thing properly and wait until he can afford to rent somewhere really decent to live.'

'Very sensible.' It occurred to Molly that Nicola probably earned more than Martin, who ran a quiet *bric-à-brac* shop in the village, but of course she would want to have babies. She wondered if they were sleeping together but did not dare ask.

Nicola groaned. 'Mm. I'd be happy sharing a shack with him, but he's ...'

'You'll be all right for bits of furniture and knick-knacks,' said Molly, laughing.

'I know – wherever we live he'd want to fill it with old stuff. I want contemporary really, but ...'

'Marriage is always going to be a compromise, Nicola.'

'You're so wise Molly. Dead right though.'

The night before her wedding Molly lay tossing and turning, unable to sleep. The reality of her future life with Giles was weighing her down as if she were facing a life sentence. Did she really love him? How many times had she asked herself the same question over the past few weeks and never come up with a convincing answer?

She could *never* feel what she still felt for Walter. The two men's personalities were poles apart, but Walter was clearly not coming back and no other man, not even Giles, could ever recapture the thrill and wonder he had brought her. *Never.* Giles adored her, not with all-consuming fervour but with a gentle kindness that was the best she could hope for. Of course, she would marry him! Anyway, how on earth could she *not* marry him now? Tomorrow was her big day, with friends and relations travelling to see her tie the knot. She wished she could feel the excitement that this warranted, instead of a dull ache in the pit of her stomach; she wished, deep down that Walter would turn up in the church, as people often did in films and novels, and call the wedding to a halt, plucking her from Giles's side, grasping her by the hand and rushing her off to that life of wonderment she so craved.

Even her own mother seemed to have noticed her lack of enthusiasm for the wedding, future plans, or any mention of her fiancé.

'He's a good man, Molly,' she would say, giving her a funny look, almost as if she could read Molly's mind that was filled with indecent pictures of another lover. 'You could do worse.'

You could do worse! These words rang in her head for days after her mother had uttered them. This marriage was as good an offer as she was ever likely to get. If she never married, then life would be tough - childless, too; so she should be grateful. She should, perhaps, even see this less than perfect arrangement as a kind of punishment for her earlier immoral behaviour.

After a night of disturbing, dizzying dreams, with Giles and Walter constantly swapping roles in hideous confusion; her mother commenting on her every move over her shoulder; a small boy squinting at her, reproving her for deserting him … she woke in a sweat but glad to be awake, away from a nightmare world that was infinitely worse than her reality.

It was out of the question that Nicola and Alison could be bridesmaids, so it was just herself and Susan getting ready in a flurry of hair-rollers, the cheap scent of hairspray, mascara and lipstick, a wedding veil that Susan helped clip into position upon Molly's bouffant bob, white satin shoes and finally zips, buttons and bows. Two hired cars were due to arrive for Susan, her mother and some relatives, and both bride and bridesmaid were ready. Bouquets and buttonholes arrived just in time and, at last, Molly felt flutters of excitement, looking forward to seeing Giles at the altar, to feeling his calming influence.

She drew in some deep breaths as she went downstairs. Just her father and Molly remained in the house that half an hour before was filled with noisy relations she barely knew trying to find a mirror or somewhere to get changed. Now it was so quiet she could hear the soft tick of the mantelpiece clock. As she entered their living-room, she saw her father's eyes fill with tears, which astonished her in so many ways.

'Will I do?' she asked with an awkward smile.

He nodded. 'You look beautiful, our Molly.' Perhaps, thought Molly, these were the first sincerely kind words he had ever given her. She must be doing something right.

That she was at least bringing joy to her parents filled her with a kind of happiness as they made the short distance to the church in a gleaming silver car, a V of wide white ribbons tied on the bonnet gently flapping, villagers waving and blowing kisses.

Nicola and Alison sat on a round table of eight people, with some of Molly's cousins from Surrey and Hampshire, varying in age from around seven to eighteen. They felt as if they had been relegated to the children's corner.

It occurred to Alison how few people knew that Molly had given birth to a baby boy, not even her brand new husband, and only she and Nicola knew who the father was. This painful secret had been so closely guarded that, on Molly's strictest instructions, Molly's parents were left with the notion that some untraceable, travelling Gypsy had seduced their daughter and vanished along with his family group to some unknown destination. Their parents had a poor view of Gypsies and Molly thought that, in her parents' minds, the blame would more easily attach to this unnamed vagabond than it would to a man of thirty-six years who had abandoned her, uncaring that she was bearing his child.

It was all soon conveniently 'forgotten'; Alison knew that the Watson family never discussed, or even mentioned, what was seen as an appalling mishap.

Dorothy Watson was helped by an usher she struggled to recognise, deciding it must be a nephew she had not seen since he was about twelve. She slid from her wheelchair into her seat at the top table and he discreetly wheeled it away to the back of the village hall.

Giles' father, sitting next to her, seemed painfully quiet as if doubtful of what to say to a disabled person, for fear of causing offence. They had met twice before and he had made no attempt or progress in overcoming his awkwardness. Dorothy was used to this; people would either stare or ignore. *How different my life could have been, if only* ... was a notion that clouded her outlook every single day, however hard she tried to appreciate the sunny aspects of her life.

She could scarcely voice her thoughts to her daughter's father-in-law; so she sat quietly mirroring his mood rather than pushing him into a forced conversation. She was not entirely sure if Molly's marriage would be beneficial to her, but overall it seemed a good thing that the family now had the support of Giles, who appeared to be quite the gentleman. She could not help but wonder, as she leaned forward to watch the pair out of the corner of her eyes, looking calm and content but not holding hands, not gazing at each other. She could not help but wonder about the striking looking man who had once come looking for Molly; it was fairly obvious to her from his earnest manner that he was the father of Molly's baby. He seemed almost old enough to be her father! He had fled soon enough, she supposed, panicking once he had realised there was a baby involved – and yet, having deserted her, he had the cheek to come back looking for her. Too late, mister! It must have been a moment of passion and Molly had been taken in hook, line and sinker; so she could not help but think she was well shot of him.

She was secretly proud that Molly had kept this huge secret to herself all this time. There was absolutely no point in prying, in opening up old wounds; it was best left alone. She would forget this stranger in time, even though it was clear from the frequent faraway look in Molly's eyes that he was in her thoughts, even as she now sat next to her husband on her wedding day.

Weeks, then months rolled by, Molly devoting all her time to making curtains, cushions, patchwork quilts and rag rugs, providing splashes of colour to make Giles's bungalow into a real home. Once these were in place, she turned her attention to inessential, decorative accessories – canvas-work, tapestries and embroidery, meanwhile knitting herself cardigans and Giles cabled sweaters, crocheting table mats and bags, often used as gifts. He loved and approved of everything she made but Molly could not stop herself from imagining what Walter's comments would have been. 'Lovely' and 'nice; would not have been in his vocabulary, but rather, 'Molly this is wonderful, you are the most talented, clever girl,' picking her up and swirling her round as if she were sixteen. He would have noticed and questioned details. 'Is this design original? How did you come by the idea for this extraordinary *motif*?'

She held back from making baby clothes she once so enjoyed creating, especially with Walter's encouragement; tiny, pastel-shade, garments so soft to touch, that could be completed quickly, giving instant pleasure. Matinee jackets and bootees would always have special associations, but perhaps it was bad luck to collect a layette before there was any sign of a baby.

37

1965

Walter wondered what to do for Christmas, even though this was still two months away. It was family time; an occasion when loved ones coalesce, which posed a problem for him, a feeling of not belonging, his identity in tatters.

As he sat smoking a Gauloise cigarette outside a small Parisian café, watching the world go by, he considered his options. Should he pursue his burgeoning relationship with Monique, a young sophisticated woman who seemed to be hungry for an English husband? She was a little younger than him, widowed, with two delightful children. He enjoyed her company, partly because her English was excellent so he did not have to struggle with French syntax and vocabulary; and he was forming a bond with her ten year old son and eight year old daughter that was heart-warming. With Monique he could enjoy true family life, but there was the old chestnut of how long he would be around to be a stepfather to them. Also, although for some reason an Englishman appealed to her, she was pretty much determined to live in Paris where her friends and family kept her rooted. He must make a decision soon, as Christophe and Mireille were becoming attached; to sever connections would become more painful as time went by.

He sighed as he watched a young family pass him by. We all have to die sometime, and few people, including himself, can predict when. His anxious mood was bringing with it disjointed, fleeting thoughts and he then found himself wondering if there would be a repeat of the big freeze that had made history last winter. He thought of Appley Green, the cosy village community, the girl he still loved and feelings of guilt swamped him. Thinking of how he had felt when Peter disappeared, he wondered what Molly must have thought of him, vanishing so heartlessly? No surprise that she never responded to the letter he left – too late – for her parents to give her.

He had consorted with a number of attractive women since leaving but always, even at the most intimate moments, he was haunted by Molly's face, her laugh, her innocence that none of them seemed to offer. The delights of her company, the rapture of their lovemaking, the bliss that a shared future offered them, were overwhelming his rational thoughts. He wondered what she was doing right now and whether she ever thought of him.

Feeling a sudden urgent need to connect with Appley Green, Walter decided to send money to Mrs Bannister, Peter's landlady in the village with a note asking her to post him a local newspaper or two. Hearing about the local news might help him to make a decision. Would village life be too parochial and suffocating now he had broadened his horizons and experienced life on another level in the capital cities of Europe. Would he be bored? If he returned, what and who would greet him? As he lit another cigarette and ordered a *croque monsieur*, he speculated again on what Molly might be doing with her life. Was she now engaged in the catering trade – perhaps working in a hotel or one of the new restaurants and cafés that were springing up in England? Or had she followed her natural talent, her artistic bent after all? How he would love to know. The idea of her being with another man was too agonising to even contemplate, so his thoughts did not take him there.

Analysis was one thing; feelings were another. Even before receiving a local newspaper, as he chose a postcard of the Eiffel Tower for Mrs Bannister, he sensed with great clarity what his heart was dictating.

As he walked away from the souvenir stall on the pavement of Boulevard St Michel, he spotted Monique, Christophe and Mireille just before they saw him. He was filled with confusion, their sudden presence intruding on his thoughts of Appley Green and Molly, and as they rushed towards him he could tell instantly that something was wrong, very wrong indeed. He had never before seen Monique look so distraught, nor her cheeks shining with tears.

241

At first Monique poured out long, emotional sentences in French that Walter could not make out. She seemed to have forgotten that he struggled with the language - even though he regularly read *Paris Match* - especially with understanding the spoken word, and she appeared to be hysterical.

All he could do was embrace her kindly but firmly until she calmed down, gently speaking in English, hoping she would realise that he had no idea what calamity had befallen her.

'My sister and my mother – killed! A car accident,' she said at last, between sobs but in clearly intelligible English. '*Les gendarmes sont arrivés ...et les médecins, les ambulances ...*' she went on lapsing again into her native tongue that Walter's schoolboy French could just about follow, with many recognisable words that shook him – '*horrifique*' et '*désastre*' ....

The shock caused Walter to freeze; momentarily unable to move, speak or think straight. He had been introduced to both these ladies and could not take in the tragedy of what Monique was saying as she went on to describe what had happened the previous evening. Her sister's baby boy had, by some miracle, survived and was being cared for by nurses at the hospital.

Mireille and Christophe were both now in tears, frowning, not able to take in everything their mother was saying but aware of her anguish and its cause. The news was clearly still fresh to them, their distress raw, and Walter, whilst holding Monique's hand, squatted down to their level to draw them to him in a comforting embrace.

They moved away from the crowded pavement to find somewhere more private, finally settling inside a quiet, smoky café where most customers were choosing to be outside in the sunshine. He ordered *cafés au lait et deux tasses de chocolat chaud* and they sat huddled in a dark corner, talking through their emotions and what this meant.

'I am – how do you say? *Marraine ... parent spiritual,*' she hesitated, unable to find the English word.

Walter offered, 'Spiritual parent – ah, godmother? I see, you are the one who cares for the spiritual wellbeing of your sister's child.'

She nodded and smiled gratefully. 'Yes, and the father of Sophie's baby never stayed around. She was an .. unmarried mother? Single.' She had not divulged this before and, much as she loved her sister and now grieved for her, she sounded ashamed. 'I adopt him, of course, it is my duty ... and my great wish.'

As the full implications of the situation sank in to Walter's brain, she heard this woman, who had lost her own husband to cancer, and bravely brought up their two children alone, and had now so cruelly lost her mother and her only sister, say, 'Oh Walter, *Dieu merci*! Thank God, I have you! Please, will you come with me to ... *la salle mortuaire d'hôpital* ... Would you stay with the children while I ... you know, say my last farewells.'

'Of course, of course ... whenever you are ready.' He reached across the table to squeeze her hand reassuringly and she clutched his arm like a person drowning.

It was obvious to Walter that Monique already thought of them as a couple, as a man and wife who were heading for commitment, for marriage, and she had naturally assumed that this life-shattering accident might accelerate things. It was equally obvious to Walter that he must not make promises he would not keep; he was startled by the realisation that he did not love her – enough.

A week went by and Monique had become increasingly needy, emotional and dependent upon Walter. She had finished with work, in the perfumery department of the Galeries Lafayette, to enable her to care for her baby nephew, Jean-Paul.

'Perhaps in time we can find an *au pair*, a nanny, *peut-être* ...' The word *'we'* rang alarm bells and Walter knew, there and then, that he must come clean. The two children were back at school and now was as good a moment as any.

They were sitting on a park-bench taking a rest on their way back to Monique's apartment.

'Monique, I have something to tell you,' he began. She understood the tone of his voice and regarded him intently.

'We have a good relationship. How long is it now? We have been seeing each other for over a year and ... of course, I am very ... fond of you and the children.' Already Monique's expression had changed to one of concern, even with the slight language barrier, painfully aware of his careful choice of words, of every *nuance*. 'You are having a terrible time and, of course, I will stand by you ... and *support* you in any way I can. Really. I will. But ...' Tears were now visible, about to spill down Monique's cheeks.

'I love you Walter. We make love. No?'

Guilt coursed through Walter, beads of sweat on his brow. He fully appreciated his grave mistake with Monique, in some ways similar to the one he had made with Molly just a few years ago. He was already full of regrets for leaving Molly, suspecting the anguish he may have caused her. Now he was about to stir up more emotional havoc and he did not feel proud of himself. He wanted to make reparations, not add to his list of shameful misdeeds. With Monique, an easy, casual romance had slipped imperceptibly into something more serious and one-sided.

'I'm sorry if I've given a false impression. It was wrong of me, not intentional, but the truth is I cannot marry you, Monique.'

'You don't love me?'

How could he inflict the most hurtful blow to this desperate, decent, good woman, when she was already down?

'There is more to it. You see, I may not have long to live ...' Now her lips trembled and she looked at him in absolute horror, hands fluttering nervously to her mouth. 'My father died of a hereditary illness and it could be that I shall die young too. It would be wrong of me to say I will be a father to your children and for them to later suffer another loss.'

She frowned, absorbing and reflecting on his sentiments and, although based on truth, he was not sure how credible it all sounded.

'But I shall be here for you, to help. I am not going anywhere in a hurry. I am your friend.' He was equally unsure of how she would interpret this. Would they still be lovers? Would she expect financial help? Expectations were fuzzy, unclear, but his confession was at least the first step to a seismic shift in their relationship. He would not suddenly leave, but neither would he be her future husband. She was free to find another man to fulfil this role; it was as honourable a solution as he could come up with, without telling a web of lies, or making promises he could not keep.

38

1968

Walter picked up the pile of the Appley Green editions of the *Bloomstock Gazette* that Mrs Bannister had posted to him some time ago. When they first arrived, it was too painful for him to sift through their pages, as they dredged up memories he found difficult to face. She had said in a note that she normally kept them for 'household purposes such as when I clean the brass' so she had quite a few and in light of his generosity – the two £5 notes he had sent her – she was more than happy for him to have the lot.

Gazettes arrived at irregular intervals and, some months later, over coffee and croissants, Walter browsed through a batch that was new to him only to find a startling headline *Post Mortem of Sir Matthew and Lady Phillips' Son and Heir.* Sparking his curiosity, he read on urgently to find that Edward's death was undoubtedly suicide; the body of the twenty-three-year-old had been found in a hotel in Brighton and it was now confirmed he had deliberately taken an overdose of amphetamines. Probably Purple Hearts thought Walter. Appalled by this tragic news, Walter remembered so clearly the time when Molly had confided in him the rumours in Appley Green, the preposterous implications that Edward and Peter were homosexual lovers! How vicious wagging tongues can be! He had never raised this alleged coupling with Peter, deeming it unworthy of serious consideration. However, now Edward had taken his own life it was a very grave situation indeed – and the reasons for his suicide seemed obvious, putting two and two together. He could not withstand the pressure, the stigma, the unkindness of people and the shameful shadow he must have cast on to his family name. What an unnecessary loss! What a crying shame! How many more times would he wish he could just turn back the clock?

Should he write a letter to Sir Matthew and Lady Phillips? Should he offer them his sympathy, his condolences? He was not sure if they would even remember him and after the unseemly behaviour of Victoria, he had been glad to be shot of all connections with the couple, but this ... somehow he felt too close to ignore it. He read the article again. There was no mention of any scandal, or his sexual preferences; but he, Walter, knew.

He spent some time perfecting the wording and finally posted what he hoped was an appropriate letter.

Molly left the drapers in Bloomstock with a spring in her step. It was half-day closing and she had plans to meet up with Nicola who was putting on a birthday party for her second child, little Louise. She was three years old, a gorgeous little bundle of chubbiness and fair curls; quite different from her older brother, who took after his father, Martin.

Molly said she would help with games and do a craft session with the children, making big flowers out of tissue paper. The colours were psychedelic bursts of orange, shocking pink, lime green, purple and the raft of bright rainbow colours tucked under her arm seemed to reflect how she felt. She had given up all hope of ever conceiving, but now Giles had reluctantly agreed to explore the possibility of adopting. At last there might be a way for her to have a baby, even if not hers biologically.

He refused to see a doctor, but Molly suspected their infertility was his problem, not hers. He was very sensitive and refused to discuss it as a problem, probably not wanting to upset her, assuming it was she who could not have children, not him, but Molly remembered him once referring to having mumps in the year before they met. He laughed as he described how he looked like a fat hamster with swollen glands in his neck, apparently unaware of the possible side effects.

The irony was not lost on Molly, and the bitterness that rose up in her at times could not be denied. She had given away her beautiful baby boy, Mark, perfect product of love. Her love child had gone to a strange couple who could give him a better life, and now ... now she would be the one to

247

adopt a baby that really belonged to someone else, or perhaps an orphan. An orphan would be better, yes, she would stipulate to the agency that it must be a baby who had no living natural mother, for how could she look such a baby in the eye and feel that she had the right to bring him or her up as her own?

Nicola opened the front door of their little terraced house, the rasping sound of *Born to be Wild* blaring from her Dansette record-player. 'Oh, am I glad to see you! It's merry bedlam in here! I'm trying to get the tea ready and they keep nicking sausage rolls off the table ... Oh I like your hair! What've you had done? A shade blonder?'

Molly nodded. 'And light home-perm just to give it a bit more body. Susan did it for me. I put it in rollers each night though, or it goes frizzy ...'

'Mmm. You could just blow dry it with a styling brush – I'll show you later, it'll give you a softer look .. Oh, you don't mind me saying do you?'

Molly laughed. 'Course not, you're the expert, good to have advice. Look, where shall I put all this stuff and what do you need help with now?'

Nicola turned the sound down. 'Please, can you help get Louise ready? Lovey, come here now, away from those fairy cakes and let Auntie Molly get you into your new frock and put those special ribbons in your hair.'

The little girl needed no encouragement and came running towards Molly, grabbing her knees in a big hug. Molly swooped her up in her arms and twirled her round.

'So, who's the big birthday girl?'

Always, such moments of happiness were overshadowed by the stinging reminder of occasions she had missed. Every single birthday of Mark's would send her into a pit of depression; she felt so alone in a mire of what she could only describe as grief.

'Me! Me!' she shrieked.

A few days later she and Giles had a meeting with an adoption society that worked in tandem with the local authority's welfare department. They were assessed and said they would be informed when a suitable child became available. When the social worker said the child might be black and not necessarily a babe-in-arms, Molly felt hope shrink back into disappointment. No! It must be a baby, a tiny baby she could fool herself into believing was her own, nothing else would do.

'I'm not sure about the adoption route, Giles,' she said softly, as they lay in bed that night, with the light turned out.

He squeezed her hand. Always so accommodating, his response was understanding and undemanding. 'Darling, give yourself a bit more time to think about it. We don't want to get ourselves into something we might later regret, do we?'

His relief was obvious. He had allowed himself to be persuaded that adoption would give them the family Molly so craved, but he really was not that keen himself. Oh, if only he would be open with her and admit what he was thinking!

Now a qualified barrister, Alison was practising law in London. Her work was her life and, as she sat down at lunchtime on a seat in the beautiful, secluded gardens around the Inns of Court, to pen some quick notelets to friends, she wondered what she could say to Molly. Last time she saw her, she seemed downcast. With no family of her own – and what a *crying shame* that was, in view of her past – and no real career, since she had put her heart and soul into being the model wife, always with the hope of becoming pregnant so she could then be the doting mother, she said she felt she had no purpose in life. Her mother, with deteriorating health, had to go into a nursing home and her lonely father of course missed her, and was depressed because he had nobody else to clean and cook for him, now Susan was at university miles away in Leicester.

'Giles is planning on setting up a nursery when he leaves the army in a few years' time,' she had told her.

'What! For small children?' The wide-eyed look Alison had given her made them laugh afterwards.

Molly grinned. 'No, you clot. Flowers, shrubs, seeds, garden tools as well. All that. He's got it all planned out in his head.'

It was always about her husband, never about what *she* might want to do; sometimes she felt like giving her a shake, a good talking to. *Molly, for goodness sake, follow a dream or two, decide what your passion is and do it! Life is not a dress rehearsal.*

However, she thought carefully about what she would actually say in her letter. It would be tactless to relate the stimulating, fulfilling life she led; maybe it would be better to dwell on the negatives. After all, she had no husband, no children, albeit she enjoyed many relationships and that suited her just fine; and she could not see herself in a motherly role. No woman could have everything … yes, that would be her theme.

She wondered whether to mention a secret that was burning inside her. Even after such a lapse of time, the subject of Edward Phillips always made her feel extremely uneasy. Would its revelation rock the boat? Would it cause Molly too much anguish? An odd friendship had grown between Geraldine Devonish and Gloria Whittaker, as if Ted's wife felt she could better monitor the possibility of an affair by keeping close to Gloria. Geraldine Devonish had told Gloria, who had told Alison, 'Victoria, Lady Phillips that is, has received a wonderfully sensitive letter – rather a belated one – from Walter Finchley, the dashing brother of the disgraced schoolteacher, Peter. Well, and you'll never guess - it was from Paris.'

Molly would be relieved to know that Walter was alive and well enough to write a decent letter – but pretty peeved to know that he was living another life in France. The father of her baby had never contacted her, not once. He was the bastard, not the baby.

Another selection of Gazettes arrived and Walter flicked through page after page of the rather old issues, picking up various headlines. Mrs Bannister must have been having a bit of a rummage.

The Devonish family figured a lot and he felt a connection with them, having at least met Mrs Devonish the elder, as well as Ted and his wife – what was her name? He read quickly through an article about some proposed changes they were making to their estate, and then some on-going saga about their public support for a group of Romany Gypsies who worked seasonally in their fields … eventually he found a reference to some fundraising event where, ah yes, Geraldine was presiding and doing good work. Well, so she should, thought Walter, since she had married into a softly cushioned, privileged life. In another issue of the paper, there was a photo of a society wedding attended by Ted and Geraldine Devonish where they did not look happy. It occurred to Walter that they never did, not when they were together. True love is a *rare and many splendored thing*, once found to be treasured, but to be trapped in a loveless marriage must be hell.

He found an entertaining piece about the famous architect he had met at the Devonish party. Jackson Jeffrys, whose house had played such a part in his wooing Molly, a really charming and successful man, full of vision, a thoroughly fulfilled individual. His spacious, white, minimalist house in the woods had certainly made waves in Appley Green. He envied him, as his gaze swept over the family photograph – him, his lovely wife and three splendid children. Walter sighed.

Peter's old landlady was good enough to send him the newspapers now and then; he never knew when to expect them. He opened up another copy from a few years ago, dated 1965, and scanned the weddings section; it was a chance in a million that he spotted it, but somehow the name *Molly Watson* and the photograph of her and her husband, Giles Perriman, stood out and smacked him in the face. Of course, logically, it was no surprise that she married, but the reality of it was such a shock, he felt physically sick, as if someone had suddenly punched him in the *solar plexus*. For a long time, unable to move, think or speak, he carried on staring at the two of them with linked arms, facing the camera not each other. Did she look happy? Radiant? Was her face alight with joy as he remembered it when they were together?

Oh Molly, my love, my true love.

Monique, her children and adopted nephew were waiting for him to join them for lunch. Their relationship was cool; the hurt Monique had felt by Walter's lack of commitment towards her had made her cold, but resigned to accepting his help. He put on something of an act, pinned on a smile, whenever they all met up for the sake of the children, as if they were his own and he and Monique were a divorced couple.

They would meet for a civilised lunch and then, he decided as he strode down the Parisian boulevard, he would allow a couple of weeks to ease himself away from Monique - and then, he would head for Surrey.

39

The postman came early. Molly poured herself a cup of tea and settled down eagerly to read Alison's letter, over a bowl of cornflakes liberally drowned in creamy, gold-top milk and sprinkled with sugar. It was always good to have news from another world and she admired her friend for her achievements, almost incapable of imagining what it was like for her in her lofty career, where men prevailed. But Alison had always been different; so bright and clever, destined for great things. Molly felt quite honoured, flattered that she found time to write to her. They really had kept their schoolgirl pledge to keep in touch through thick and thin.

Then her stomach lurched. Walter Finchley! She gasped and felt the blood drain from her cheeks as she read on. Just the mention of his name was enough to make her feel weak. The shocking news of Edward Phillips had rocked Surrey when it appeared in all the newspapers. Sir Matthew was even on the television looking pale and ghastly in his grief, but nothing could compare with the effect of this extra news – that Walter was in Paris. What did this mean? Her mind raced along with her heartbeat. He had found his brother presumably and decided to just stay there, never *once* thinking to somehow let her know. What had she done to deserve this treatment? All these years, why had he just abandoned her? Did he really imagine that she would just forget him? It had all seemed so incredible that she had long since concluded the worst, that he must have had some fatal accident or illness and now, her eyes filled with tears of joy for he was alive, mingled with heart-wrenching misery in that he cared nothing for her.

'Darling, whatever is the matter? Bad news?' Lost in emotional turmoil, she was suddenly aware that Giles was staring at her across the breakfast table, his face etched with worry. How long had he been there? He had popped out to get a newspaper and she had not even heard him come back into the room.

She briskly put the letter back in its envelope and smiled at him, unable to stop her chin trembling. 'From Alison. Just … her latest boyfriend has finished with her. So sad. And she mentioned about the Edward Phillips tragedy. You know. Brought it all back.' She sniffed and blew her nose. 'I'll make some fresh tea, I think this pot's gone a bit stewed.'

'Of course he was in your class at school. Remind me, what did they say was the reason for his … taking his own life?'

'They couldn't be sure. He never left a note, did he?'

'No explanation then?'

She shrugged. 'Apparently not,' she said, leaving for the kitchen to make fresh tea and, clutching the edge of the sink to take slow, deep breaths.

Giles was opening his post and when Molly calmly returned to the table he looked at her, holding up a typed letter. The corners of his mouth were turned down.

'Bah! I shall be away for a month, I'm afraid. Posting in Cyprus. Leave after the weekend, back by the end of November.'

'Oh. Oh dear, well if you must, you must! It's your work, your duty, it pays the bills and I'm lucky to have you here as much as I do.'

'And I am a luckiest man in the world to have such an understanding wife.' He rose from his chair to come round and kiss her very firmly on the cheek. 'My darling Molly. I do love you.'

Alison was taking a few days off work, planning to go on an off-season package holiday to Majorca, when the weather would not be unbearably hot. For one who had been brought up on wet English seaside holidays, early October in the Mediterranean would be heavenly. Moreover, it seemed terribly good value compared with staying anywhere half-decent in Great Britain but the greatest attraction was that it was all organised, as she had little enough time to worry about booking flights and hotels herself. She would drive first to her parents in Windsor, then to see her friends in Appley Green. It was a long time since she had been back to her roots.

Both Molly and Nicola had jumped at the chance of putting her up in a spare room and, not wishing to offend either of them, she decided to stay at the Hunter's Lodge.

I don't want to put either of you to any trouble, she said, in a letter. *We could have dinner there – just the three of us, wouldn't that be splendid? My treat.*

Once they had ordered from the menu, they sat looking at each other, as if assessing how much each of them had changed. Alison wished she had dressed down a little for the occasion; she was so used to wearing tailored, expensive suits in dark colours with a crisp white blouse, that her wardrobe was sadly lacking in casual clothes. Both her friends had made an effort, respecting the rather posh ambience of the hotel's new dining-room, and they did look wonderfully modern. They also looked slightly uncomfortable, probably not used to eating out without their husbands.

Nicola's hair was a creation to behold, with a heavy fringe and voluminous bouffant; she clearly still supported a style that needed the skills of a hairdresser, a lot of rollers and back-combing. Her mini-skirt was very short and her eyes loaded with make-up. It was a look that had been common in London for a while but was now changing to something more subtle, that Molly had captured. Her elfin, Mia Farrow haircut and plain shift that might have been designed by Coco Chanel, suited her so well she could have been a model. She looked simply slim and beautiful. If only she could smile more.

'So what are you both up to? Tell me everything,' invited Alison, as the prawn cocktails were served. 'How are your little ones, Nicola?'

She noticed a sadness in Molly's face as she asked this and realised her *gaffe*. Then Nicola made it even worse.

'They are the best thing ever. I mean, I know you must find your career very fulfilling and exciting, but honestly, having a baby is the most miraculous thing that can happen to any woman …'

Aware of Molly's tense look, Alison cut her short. 'Well, not for me! We're all different, you know. But I'm glad you've found maternal bliss, Nicola, I really am. Would you like a Babycham, Bloody Mary or something?' She hailed a hovering waiter in a worldly, business-like manner and sure enough, he came running.

'Still no patter of little feet for you, then Moll?' asked Nicola, and Alison gave her a warning glare. 'Sorry ...'

'No, no, it's all right. It's not quite worked out how I ... how we, Giles and me, planned family life together. If I'd known I'd have probably put more effort into a career, done a college course, but then I'd never get a grant now and anyway it wouldn't be fair on Giles ...'

Alison reached across to squeeze her hand. 'Oh Molly, you always worry so much about other people ...'

Molly shrugged. 'I went to London a few weeks' back, looking for ideas. You know if things had been different, I might have gone into fashion design, but well that's all pie in the sky really. I see that now.'

'This was what ... Walter had in mind for you, wasn't it? He had faith in your talents,' said Nicola.

'Huh! Leading me into a false paradise, we all know that now, don't we?'

'Do you ... still have feelings for him?' asked Alison.

'That's a shocking thing to say! I'm a married woman. Of course not. Now, please let's talk about something else.'

It was obvious to Alison judging by the colour of Molly's cheeks that she was lying, perhaps not even realising she was lying.

'Remember we always promised to tell each other our secrets, Molly. Has that stopped now, for some reason?'

'No.' Molly looked awkward. 'Giles and I considered adoption, but I decided it's not for me. I mean, we decided – it's not for us.'

How very sad it is, thought Alison, that somewhere out there is Molly's little boy living with his adoptive parents. The law is indeed, an ass. It was generally held that no single woman could support herself and a child, and that adoption gives a baby the best start in life, but some day these restrictions stopping natural parents and their offspring being known to each other would be repealed. Human nature and the strength of blood-ties would prevail, she was sure of it.

'I can't criticise you for not confiding in us completely unless I do the same thing.' Alison sipped her vodka and lime, checking she had their full attention. 'I have a big secret that not even my parents know about – and they never will. You must understand that. Never.'

She had them both on the edge of their seats, literally agog.

'No, I'll tell you after dessert.'

Alison could not help but bring up Edward Phillips' suicide, which pretty much kept them earnestly talking for most of meal. This led inevitably to the revelation of Walter's whereabouts but, again, Molly refused to be drawn on the subject of how she felt.

'So?' The remains of a pear-upside-down pudding had just been cleared. Nicola gave Alison a quizzical look. 'We are *burning* with curiosity. Aren't we, Molly?'

'Well, I don't think Alison should feel forced to tell us something so massive. It must be something quite bad if she hasn't even confessed to her parents! Will we then be forced to report you to a policeman?'

Alison chuckled. 'I think you should know that you're not the only one who made a mistake, Molly.'

'What? You mean ..?'

'Yes, I was pregnant. These things can happen, even though I am on the pill ...'

'What, that new contraceptive pill?'

'Of course. But it doesn't work if you have a gastric bug that ... well, you get the idea.'

'But you don't look pregnant ...'

'Oh no, of course not. I had an abortion, but to tell you the truth I think that would upset my parents more than my being pregnant ...'

Molly was staring at her, pupils pinpricks, face ashen, jaw so tense she might have had lockjaw. She stood up, pushing her chair behind her, grating on the tiled floor. She dipped a hand into her bag to retrieve her purse, pulled out some notes, flung them onto the table and stormed off without another word.

'Alison, how could you? How cruel and mean are you? Don't you realise how desperate Molly is for a baby, even now? How could you make life seem so cheap?'

40

Walter allowed himself the luxury of the night-ferry train from Paris to London and arrived reasonably refreshed from his journey. In the taxi from Bloomstock station, since the Appley Green station had been closed down, he felt an excitement coursing through his body, head buzzing, fuelled by a rush of what he supposed was adrenalin. Did this stem from the prospect of being in Appley Green? Or, was it from the idea that he stood a very good chance of seeing Molly? Since villages, however charming, however alluring, were not well known for raising the pulse, he knew in his heart the cause of his emotional state.

He had no plan of action yet he knew he must take control of the situation. A chance meeting would need to be contrived, for the last thing he wanted was for Molly to spot him first, especially if she was with her husband! Or she might hear of his arrival on the grapevine and then hide away from him. He could hardly blame her if she did.

'Can you drop me here please?' he asked the taxi driver as they approached the village. He would walk the last stretch of a mile or so to get some fresh air and clear his head.

A sharp wind brushing his cheeks like cold fingers told him that the air was several degrees cooler than in France and he realised that, in his hasty departure, he had left without an overcoat. A linen jacket had been quite adequate for Paris in autumn. In his bag was a fine cashmere sweater that might look a little odd worn beneath the jacket, but he decided to stop by the side of the road to retrieve it from his hold-all. There was no point in shivering beneath a cloudy sky and it was unlikely anybody here would challenge his sense of style. *How French had he become? Oh, Lord.*

As he strode out, it became obvious that he would need to make enquiries and do some snooping, both done with the utmost discretion. He must not mess this up. What would come of seeing Molly he had no idea; all he did know was that he could not live, could not die, without seeing her again. The more focused he became the more it became clear to him that it was vital he catch the expression, the first instinctive reaction, on Molly's face when he appeared before her. This might tell him what he really needed to know.

There would be risk at every turn. He decided to stop off at *The Fox and Rabbit* where he could ask a few questions perhaps, find out the latest village gossip. At least he came already armed with some of the news gleaned from the local rag.

It felt good to clasp a tankard of good old English ale, much as he liked fine wines and the occasional tipple of *pernod*. He stayed at the bar.

'How's life treating you then? Been away for a few years. What's the latest?' he asked in a cheery, convivial manner. *Ça va?* would have covered it.

The barman grunted. 'Quiet. Hmm. Still, can't complain.'

'Ah ha. So, do you cater for weddings here at all?' Walter was not sure of his line of questioning, only that it might lead on to recent, village weddings.

The barman's eyes lit up at the prospect of potential business. 'Well, we'd never say no but can't take more'n say about fifty guests. You planning on one then?'

Walter smiled and shook his head. 'No, no, not me. I was just wondering … just curious, y'know.' This was no good. 'Where do most people have their wedding parties in the village?'

'Well course there's the Hunter's Lodge for the county set …'

'But an average sort of couple?'

'Some use the village hall …' This conversation required a lucky break; he needed to push harder, be more specific.

'Well, an old mate of mine, Giles Perriman, I think he may have had a reception there.'

'Ah, probably. I know of him. Army chap, comes in here, with his wife …'

Walter closed his eyes and held his breath, heart pounding. It was ridiculous, he silently told himself, that a few words could have this dramatic, visceral effect on him - a middle aged man! The barman had left to serve someone further down the bar. He had lost him. Quickly downing his pint so he could ask for another, he knew what he must find out. Where did they live now, Giles Perriman and his wife?

But as the pub filled up with lunchtime customers, he could not engage him in further chit-chat. Walter began to feel anxious, wary of being too open with any local people in there. The village was not huge, people knew each other; they could start asking him awkward, leading questions. Someone might remember Peter and he could so easily say the wrong thing.

He came away feeling deeply dissatisfied with his feeble enquiries, then suddenly punched the air. What was he thinking? What were telephone directories for? Telephone numbers of course, but did they not hold addresses and did not many more people now have a telephone at home?

He spotted a telephone kiosk across the village green and headed straight there. Someone was inside making a call and he lit a cigarette to pass the time, keeping a cautious eye all around him, pacing round restlessly.

Soon he was flicking through grubby, dog-eared pages for *Perriman* and found what he was looking for; now he must locate Copse Lane. The name implied a quiet spot which would make him more noticeable, so he would need to amble past as inconspicuously as possible in the first instance. Running his fingers through his hair, he seemed to remember there was a map of sorts on the Parish noticeboard; so he headed towards the church.

But there was no such map; either he was mistaken or it had been removed. He decided to ask a young mother who was passing by with a pushchair and she gave him directions to a part of the Appley Green woodland he did not know. It took him twenty minutes to reach it on foot, but at last he found himself in *a cul-de-sac* outside the very house where he knew Molly lived with her husband. It was a freshly-painted bungalow, small with a neatly kept garden and colourful curtains in every window. There was no sign of a car.

He could feel the pounding of his heart, was aware of clammy palms, and wondered anew at the effect she had on him, the very prospect of seeing her making him feel energised. Perhaps, he mused, the excitement was compounded by the fact that he was spying and must not be caught at the wrong moment.

Would it require a vigil to work out the comings and goings of the couple? This lane was awkward for it led nowhere except to the woods via a footpath. He could see nowhere to hide, so walked past a little way, then turned round and strolled past again, taking a sidelong glance. Giles Perriman might be in there; or Molly on her own, or both of them, or neither! There was no way of knowing.

He decided to go back to where the lane branched off the Farnham road from Appley Green. If Molly was at home, she would perhaps need to go into the village at some point. He espied a bus shelter so snuck in there, took a seat and lit another cigarette, feeling slightly ridiculous.

Nothing happened so by mid-afternoon he made his way back to the village, wondering where he would lay his head that night. He needed to lie low. Would it be wise to stay at The Hunters' Lodge? Walking pensively, he decided he would … and then a fresh thought struck him. Tomorrow, he could try calling their telephone. If her husband answered, unlikely on a weekday, he would ask for a common name, say, Susan, thus appearing to have called the wrong number. If it was Molly, he would ask for, say, David, but would then at least know she was at home. Yes! He had a plan of sorts.

He asked for sandwiches to be sent to his room, managing to avoid human contact in the hotel before finally subsiding into a fitful sleep.

41

After his substantial breakfast was served, but only partially eaten, Walter made his way to the hotel telephone, furtively glancing around, fervently hoping nobody recognised and remembered him, unlikely though this was, even in a close-knit village.

The phone was ringing at the other end, reverberating in his ear. Five times it rang and nobody answered, his heart pounding beneath his shirt as if trying to get out. Then, as he was about to replace the receiver, there was a voice.

'Hello, this is Mrs Perriman,' the female voice said. Was this Molly? He could not be sure from its tone, yet it must be. He was flummoxed, momentarily forgetting what his plan was; he had 'dialled the wrong number'.

He spoke quietly in an assumed northern accent, feeling like a very poor actor in a shamefully amateur production. 'Oh aye. Is Susan there?' he asked, longing to hear the voice again. 'Can I 'ave a word wi' Susan?'

'Oh, no, my sister's away at university. Why do you think she'd be here? May I ask who's calling?' Understandably, her voice rose in volume and pitch; although polite, it smacked of mistrust.

Panic gripped him. Of course! *Susan is the name of Molly's sister!* And the other name he had in mind was, of all names, David! *Her brother's name.* His mind was sharp now. Both chosen randomly by virtue of the fact there were hundreds of Susans and Davids, maybe there was some unconscious process going on in his head. How could he have been such a dunderhead?

He floundered, his mouth dry, palms sweaty. Was she there on her own? He couldn't call back again, it would arouse suspicion and he couldn't ask for Giles, for that would make no sense at all.

He gathered his thoughts quickly. 'I think I must have the wrong number, I'm so sorry to have bothered you ... Mrs

Perriman.' His guard had dropped, the feigned Yorkshire accent had vanished. *What was he doing?* He slapped his leg as a reprimand for being such a fool and clumsily dumped the receiver with a clatter.

That, he thought, really did not go well. In fact, it was farcical. He scratched his head thoughtfully, then with some speed returned to his hotel bedroom before setting off to Copse Lane. He would have to assume that Molly was there alone until he discovered otherwise …

Breathless and hot from half-running, Walter lurked about twenty yards from the Perriman residence. He didn't know what to do other than wait for something to happen. Perhaps he would see Giles emerge and make his way towards him, in which case he would march straight past him, avoiding his gaze. Perhaps Molly ….

As he was thinking, imagining what it would be like to see her, his eyes widened. A smart, young woman with short hair carrying a bulky, soft bag was closing the gate of the house upon which his gaze was fixed. Molly. She looked different, but yes, it was Molly. This was it.

He remembered that he wanted to catch her reaction, to see her eyes light up, to know how she felt about seeing him.

As she approached he turned away as if looking out for a car coming from the other direction, or a person he had arranged to meet. He paced around a little and checked his watch. Then he turned and she was there, no more than two yards away.

Her unsmiling face turned pale and she stepped back. *She silently stepped back two paces.*

Giles was still in Cyprus; he would probably write a letter soon so Molly waited until the postman had been, but there was no blue Air Mail delivery for her today, just a gas bill and postcard from Alison on holiday in Majorca. She said a few words by way of an apology but this changed nothing for Molly. It was not just the fact she had *told* her and Nicola about the abortion, but the fact that she had *done* it. Her spirits had been rather down since walking out on her friends; Alison seemed to have no thought for her, perhaps no knowledge of what she was going through these days, coming to terms with being forever childless. She had really wanted to enthuse to her friends about the orders she was getting, but felt it best to wait until her friends asked; her new venture was exciting for her, but would probably come across to them as a very modest way to earn a bit of 'pin-money'.

After taking a strange phone call from a man who said he must have the wrong number, she tidied up pieces of fabric, fragments of Kapok and shredded nylons used for stuffing cushions, and tiny bits of thread that drifted willy-nilly around the bungalow when she was busy sewing. She took a deep-pile hearth-rug outside to beat in the old-fashioned way and then swept and hoovered to get all the floors looking spick and span. She was making soft furnishing items for other people now; word had got round of her natty craftwork and she had a list of orders for curtains, cushions, table runners and many smaller items like bespoke table mats, upholstered foot-stools, everything designed to co-ordinate with the customer's colour scheme and style. Patch-worked, quilted, tasselled or plain – whatever they wanted, she would do. If they had no idea what they wanted, she was never short of suggestions that always seemed to please. Window blinds were her latest venture, using the tie-dye process of colouring.

She hoped the stranger who called was not some kind of pervert, or a burglar checking to see if the house was empty … someone on drugs perhaps. She had read about such people.

When Giles was away it was easy to get into bad habits and not put things away at the end of each day; so fine dust and fluff would hang in the air and then settle on everything. She whisked round with a duster and a can of spray polish.

She must deliver some linen hand-towels she had embroidered for Mrs Wilson, the solicitor's wife, who lived in a house overlooking the green. It was a sunny, dry day and would only take half an hour to walk there. Then she would pick up a few things from Appley Green village shops and maybe look in on the new, very popular boutique that had opened up there. It felt good to be earning money again, doing something she loved. Maybe the boutique would take some of her crocheted bags.

She was deep in thought as she strode away in comfortable flat shoes. She espied a man ahead she did not recognise ... her heart fluttered. There was a time when she kept imagining she saw Walter, a kind of wishful-thinking that always led to heart-sinking disappointment. Surely she was over him by now; yet the unequivocal beating of her heart eloquently told her otherwise. Of course it was not Walter, that would be ridiculous ... he lived in France, she knew that now.

She swapped over her bag from her right hand to the left, and began thinking about whether she might suggest to Mrs Wilson a cover for her bathroom ottoman to go with the towels. The wrong number phone call came back to her as she looked up and came face to face with the man, who suddenly turned to face her, as if to deliberately take her by surprise. An instinct made her step back away from him. His manner was unnerving ... but ... My God! Was it Walter? He looked older, grey-haired, but then he would be. Could it be him?

Yes. It was Walter, come from nowhere, intruding on her life, her thoughts and emotions. Paralysed with shock, she felt disorientated, light-headed, as if she were hallucinating.

'Molly,' said Walter.

'Walter,' she responded, her voice hoarse as her throat tensed and tightened.

'What am I doing here?' he asked, smiling, speaking her thoughts for her. 'I had to see you, to find out how you are.' He shrugged. 'It's that simple.'

Simple! Oh, it's that simple, is it? She was unable to speak, deeply unsure of how she felt on seeing him. Did she hate him with a vengeance, or adore him still with a passion? She was drowning in a deeply enmeshed blend of conflicting emotions.

She breathed deeply. 'What do you want of me?' A light-headedness had turned to anger. 'I'm happily married, you know.' She wanted to hurt him.

He took her elbow, as if he must touch her, but in an uncompromising way. She flinched at the thrill. Walter was asking, 'Can we talk? Is there somewhere we can spend a little time together? Please, Molly.'

She wondered if her neighbours might notice she was walking back to her bungalow with a strange man, while her husband was away. It was the kind of thing upon which village tittle-tattle thrived.

With a kind of inevitability, she turned around and he walked alongside. She could feel the heat of his gaze, the beat of her heart. With a chaos of questions burning inside her, she could not begin to put them in order. He must know where she lived, or why would he be waiting for her so close by? It made her shiver with pleasure, with horror.

As she led him up to the front door, she heard the sound of a car slowing down and turned to see if it was someone she knew. Alison! Of all the unlucky timing, she thought, this takes the biscuit! One of the very few people in her life who might know who Walter was and the part he had played in her misery … She pushed past Walter to stop her in her tracks and send her on her way. Now was not a good time! She felt gripped by a panic that these two could start up a conversation with catastrophic consequences. Alison had always made no secret of the fact that she felt bitter towards Walter for leaving her pregnant friend in the lurch, refusing to accept the fact that he had no knowledge of his baby.

Alison was already out of her car, staring at Walter. She would recognise him, thought Molly, from a photograph she had once shared with her friends.

Molly spoke first. 'Alison, please. Can I call you later?'

'I'm on my way back to London, stayed with parents last night in Windsor and did a detour – quite a long detour to come and see you. To make amends, you know.' Her gaze shifted back and forth between Molly and the arrestingly handsome man who looked shifty, apparently waiting for Molly to let him in.

Molly felt bad now, as it was quite a long drive Alison had made specially to see her.

'Just a minute, I'll put him in the dining-room for a moment and we can at least sit down with a cup of coffee and …'

'Is that … Walter?'

Molly's profound shock prompted a knee-jerk reaction. 'Walter? Walter! Pull the other one! No, he's an insurance man. Just hang on till I settle him down and then come in. OK?' She left Alison quickly to rush back to Walter, unlocking the front door with trembling fingers.

'Walter, sit here for a few minutes would you? I need to see my friend, she travelled a long way, I can't just send her away.'

Walter stared at her, unbelieving perhaps that he was not being given precedence. Molly supposed that he, too, had come from afar. However, he was in no position to argue, so following her suggestion, he took a seat.

'I'll bring you a cup of coffee,' said Molly, closing the door on him.

Alison knocked gently on the front-door Molly had left ajar and Molly beckoned her to come in, straight into the lounge.

Molly knew she must feign calm, keep composed, act normally. 'Now, I'll just put the kettle on.'

'Molly, I just wanted to say to you in person that I regret very much what happened the other evening. I am a thoughtless cow, sometimes.'

'Mmm, well, I probably over-reacted, but I'm just picking up my life, looking forward to good times, after spending too long fretting over children I am clearly never going to have.'

'I am *so* sorry. By the way, the meal was on me, and in any case you left far too much money. Here …and no arguments.' Alison put some pound notes on the coffee table but Molly did not take them. 'The good thing is that I've decided to specialise in family law, you know … it seems an area that needs professional help and …'

Molly nodded her approval. 'Oh, that sounds a very … worthwhile … thing to do …'

'You deserve better. It's not as if you can't have babies … we know that.'

'Shhh. I mean, keep your voice down. Walls have ears.'

There was a long pause and Alison met her gaze, with chin raised. 'The insurance broker? Do you think he's the least bit interested?'

There was a knock on the door, then Walter's voice but she could not make out what he said.

Molly jumped up like a startled rabbit. 'Hold on a moment, Alison, I'll just deal with …' She did not want these two to see each other at close quarters. It was remotely possible that Walter might recognise Alison, as well as *vice versa*. All those years ago at the Devonish's party when Walter had first spotted the two of them together …

Molly quickly and firmly indicated to him that he should stay put for a few more minutes, out of sight. Everything seemed detached from reality, bordering on a Brian Rix farce and, despite this interruption, the fact that Walter was in her home would not sink in properly.

Alison had disappeared when she returned to the lounge, to make coffee in the kitchen.

'Hope you don't mind, thought I'd make myself useful.'

'That's fine. Thanks. There are some biscuits in the orange tin there. I should take him a cup perhaps … the insurance man … he has another appointment so I'm really sorry but I don't have long. It's nice of you to call, though,' said Molly, feeling guilty for both lying and cutting the visit short. 'I could come and see you in London some time. On the train.'

'That would be fab. I can show you round a few places … yes, we must do that.' Her smile was oddly unreal, perhaps false.

They had a stilted conversation for a few minutes about Majorca. Molly breathed a sigh of relief as Alison drained her cup, put on her gloves and stood up.

'Well, you've had your chance to open up. It's none of my business, despite the fact we always shared our secrets with each other, perhaps ill-advisedly in my case, but don't imagine that I am fooled, Molly. I saw how you blushed at the very mention of Walter's name when we had our meal, and no wonder. Now it's obvious you're trying to hide him from me. It's him, isn't it? You're seeing him? Deceiving Giles! I can't believe it, Molly. I'd never have thought it of you.' Outraged, her voice had grown loud, unrestrained and really rather intimidating. She could not seem to help herself.

Walter opened the door and Molly's heart thumped. Had he been eavesdropping?

'Please, do *not* blame Molly,' he said. Oh my Lord, thought Molly, he thinks he's doing the decent thing. 'I sprung a complete surprise on her this morning, no more than ten minutes ago … we are old friends …'

Alison nearly exploded. 'Don't stand there and tell me you are 'old friends'! I know who you are. The man who seduced and deserted a young, vulnerable, single mother, who had to give up her baby because she had no support from her parents. You are the worst kind of man, who neglects responsibility, and I can't think how, after so long, you have the brass nerve to just turn up out of the blue …'

Molly felt faint and sat down, struggling to take in what was happening. Now Walter knew! She had been determined to keep this a secret from him as his knowledge of Mark could only lead to massive trouble. What if Giles found out?

Perhaps aware of what she had just done, the *maelstrom* of feelings she had just churned up, Alison went suddenly mute, regarding the forlorn spectacle of Molly with her head in her hands.

Molly did not look up. 'Alison, please can you go. You must leave us now.'

42

For a while, perhaps a never-ending two minutes, Molly and Walter sat contemplating each other, absorbing the situation, as if the ability to speak had been ripped from them.

Walter was the first to break the frosty silence. 'Molly, I am so sorry. I had no idea. Am I really that heartless cad your friend just described?'

There was a pause as Molly still wrestled with a tangle of emotions, thoughts and unanswered questions. 'I didn't want a baby to be the only reason for you to *want* to come back to me … but in any case, I had no idea where you were. There was no way of finding out. Have you any idea how …?' Molly's face crumpled. *How much I ached to hear from you? How it felt to give away our baby boy to another couple?*

Walter's eyes filled up and he put his hands over his face. 'If only I could turn the clock back,' he muttered, as if to himself. 'You have a child, *our child?*'

She tried to stem her own tears. 'He was adopted. I have no children.'

Walter looked stunned, unable to speak, just regarding her blankly, uncomprehendingly. 'Please, if you can, tell me what happened, Molly. If you can bear it.' He moved across to the sofa where she sat and took her hand comfortingly in his. The warmth of his touch was as she remembered it. 'I have never forgotten you, never stopped loving you, despite the years that have passed by.'

How could he say that, thought Molly? She tried to keep cool and collected. 'I will,' she said. Yes, he should know how she suffered! 'But you must promise me one thing first.'

'Yes, of course … anything.'

'It cost me dearly to give him away, and keep away, so the least you can do is respect this. You must swear that you will never try to find him.' Hiding the fact that her heart was pounding and her mouth had gone dry with nerves, her tone sounded formal, business-like, she knew that.

He frowned fleetingly, looking puzzled. 'Of course. I swear.' It surprised Molly at how lightly the words seemed to trip off his lips. Barely ten minutes had passed for him to take in the momentous truths that he had a son and must vow never to see him. Perhaps he was desperate to please her …

'Also, I don't need to know everything you have done since you left, your life in Paris … yes, I discovered this much, but only recently.' She explained about his rumoured letter sent to Sir Matthew Phillips and his wife. 'But … but I really do need to learn from you, if I am ever to find peace in my head, why and how you could leave me. Did it never occur to you that I might be pregnant? You remember that time …' She turned away from him, ashamed and embarrassed. 'And your … declarations of undying love.' There was a hint of sarcasm in her voice and she rolled her eyes. 'Did you stop caring for me? Did you just forget me?'

He was shaking his head. 'My darling Molly, I failed you so badly. To be perfectly honest, it never even occurred to me that you might have a baby by me. You see, in my marriage to Theresa we never 'took precautions', as they say, because we wanted to conceive, but we never did. With other women I was always careful, you know. One mistake happened with us and I just didn't think it likely or even possible…'

'No, you didn't. You did not think at all,' said Molly, bitterly, not enjoying what she was hearing. Of course, a red-blooded, attractive man would have sex even if not married, but it was unbearably painful to hear. She felt herself stiffen against the softer yearning for his touch he had begun to arouse in her. 'So, you went in search of Peter? You see I know little more than that!'

Walter gave her a summary of how long it took to find Peter, how he worried about him and whether he would indeed ever track him down. His explanations in the cold light of day of why he cut himself off from her were harder to understand for there now seemed to be many reasons. Firstly there was her young age and the age gap between them, then the fact that he might contract the same disease as his father and leave her a young widow with children. He had hoped that she would forget him and find happiness with another man, and there was his mission to find Peter. As he spoke, Molly felt as if he were trying to rationalise his careless approach to their affair; a lack of responsibility just as Alison had said.

'I am here because I had to see you. I could not rest easy until I did. I still have very deep feelings for you, Molly.'

'Well, I'm married now. To a man, who is ... steadfast, reliable, loving. Too little, too late, I am afraid, Walter.' She amazed herself at how solid and unwavering her voice was. 'What is the point? Of us, I mean.'

Walter looked utterly crestfallen. She stood up like someone wishing to end a meeting but he came up to her, and searched her eyes longingly with his gaze.

'May I have one kiss?' he asked.

It seemed a modest request and although feelings of betrayal and disloyalty tore through her, she nodded, feeling shamefully weak. She needed to feel his lips on hers, there was no denying it and maybe this was her only chance. Perhaps the time for her to rekindle the passion she had felt for him had now passed and was unattainable. A kiss would tell her something ...

She closed her eyes and felt his arms wrap around her. Oh my God! Why did it never feel like this when Giles held her? His breath was warm, with faint nicotine tones just as she remembered it, not unpleasant as it was inextricably bound up with erotic memories that now rose up in her mind. She found herself kissing him back, despite urgent warning voices whispering inside her head.

She pushed him away. 'No,' she said. 'This is wrong. You must go.'

Travelling back to Paris to make arrangements to move back permanently to England, to Appley Green, Walter reflected on how his life had changed, and how the future might shape up. He would never give up on Molly, certain now more than ever that life was scarcely worth living without her. She had consented to see him 'now and then' but there could be nothing more between them, nothing that would upset her marriage.

He had no choice but to agree to her conditions; it was little more than keeping in touch, with no secret dates, letters, phone-calls or Christmas cards, nothing that would arouse suspicion with Giles. He must resign himself to keeping his distance, but cheered himself in the knowledge that he would 'now and then' see her in the village. Their paths would doubtless cross in a perfectly natural way.

The fact he had a son, somewhere out there, now old enough to go to school, play football, laugh and joke, to do those rough-and-tumble fights little boys have with their fathers, was an addictive concept. Pictures in his head filled him with joy, yet pained him beyond endurance. He must see him. He must.

And yet, this was the very thing he had promised Molly, to never seek him out. He had forfeited the right to track him down, and if he broke his promise, then any remote chance of reconciliation with Molly was reduced to nil. She was married, he could not come between her and her husband. Discretion was of the essence.

He began to conjure plans of how he could possibly find out where his son was, without anybody else knowing.

43

1975

Molly looked through her birthday cards, after Giles had left for a month's duty in Germany, still in high spirits from the celebration party they had held the day before he left, about twenty friends in all. She was thirty. Saying goodbye to her twenties seemed a momentous milestone.

What would the next decade bring? Giles was planning to leave the armed forces within a year or two, with plans to start up a new business and he very much wanted her to be a part of this. It seemed like a rosy future for them both; they did get on so well together and had grown closer and closer over the years. Yet, still she looked enviously upon women her age with several children, and at times even reconsidered the idea of adoption, but had heard that she might even have to look abroad, perhaps to Vietnam or somewhere equally foreign. It was not an easy, straightforward process, apparently, and the longer they delayed the harder it would be, with age being against them – already!

Then a daring idea popped up in her head, when she was really half-asleep, in the middle of the night when mad ideas have a habit of being seeded. Acknowledging this, she nonetheless lay there thinking it through until daylight crept in between the curtains and she heard the post landing on the doormat. Her head was in a whirl. Perhaps she was going mad.

Walter knew Molly's birthday, when it was and how old she was. Any birthday with a nought at the end was a special occasion and he wished he could somehow let her to know that he had remembered. He had even jotted it in his diary and it was this note he looked at now …

The last time he saw Molly was on the village green about six weeks ago. He had adopted a habit of ambling around the village whenever he had reason to go to the shops or Post Office at times when he might catch sight of her and have a brief word. He was still able to live comfortably off the proceeds of selling his business years ago, which he invested wisely to give him a profitable return. His health was good and he often wondered how different his life might have been if he had never set eyes on Molly, never left to seek out Peter and had kept running his firm, living in Hampstead.

To keep himself occupied he had set up a small soft-furnishing shop in Appley Green, knowing that the fabrics, wallpapers, table lamps and haberdashery would keep Molly as a regular customer. This was not the sole reason for his choice of commerce; it fitted in with what he knew and indeed a network of suppliers, including the company that was once his. He was soon making money without even trying and had become a known figure in the pulse of village life and not a day went by without him considering how lucky he was not be hounded any more by his past, not to be constantly looking over his shoulder for accusing fingers.

It was mid-morning and he was glancing through his diary to check on his schedule for the month of June. The day was a gloriously sunny Saturday and the village was quiet – he suspected that families had headed off to the coast to get a tan.

He looked up and caught sight of Molly across the other side of the green, pulling one of those new wheeled shopping bags. Wearing a yellow summery dress, a straw hat and big square sunglasses, she looked so stylish and pretty he wanted to rush out and grab her round the waist and whisk her off to a flower-filled meadow … he closed his eyes and sighed.

When he opened them again, she was entering the shop and instead of heading for Sylko, buttons or braid, she came straight to him.

'Beautiful day!' she said, smiling. 'Walter, can you shut up shop for half a day? I thought, just for once, to celebrate my birthday we could do something together … something memorable, perhaps.'

Walter thought he must be dreaming. Could he imagine anything more surreal or wonderful than this moment?

Within seconds he had turned over the sign in the door to 'CLOSED'. They arranged to meet discreetly by a certain large oak tree on the road to Guildford in an hour's time and she was gone! Like a phantom, a fairy ... He blinked.

He almost suspected she was playing a trick on him, but how could she possibly do anything so cruel? It was not her nature. She would be there, he was certain.

Molly's heart was beating so hard, so fast, she felt sick, as she made her way to her assignation with Walter, still in awe at her own temerity. A sensual, vital part of her was excited beyond measure, the other half berated her guile and deceit. How could she do this to Giles? But he would never know, the voice of sanity assured her, as she strode on carrying a loaded picnic basket and rug, although that still did not make it at all acceptable.

Her intention was to arrive a few minutes late, like a bride keeping her groom waiting. She knew he wanted her, he had made it so plainly obvious many times, but she wanted to build up his desire such that recklessness would be inevitable! Her friends had always told her off for not putting herself first more often.

He was there waiting for her, just as she expected, sitting on a mossy log. He gave her a cool, languorous wave, as if feigning a relaxed state of mind, and she wondered what was going on in his head. He must be totally mystified, as ever since he moved back to Appley Green she had taken care to keep him at arm's length, never giving him an ounce of encouragement. But it was her special birthday and the sun was shining, enough to make anyone have a spontaneous outburst of irregular behaviour, surely!

As she came close, he stood up, lightly touched her arm, planting a decorous peck on the cheek, perhaps weighing up what she would feel was appropriate. A warm feeling of control, of having him in the palm of her hand, flooded through her.

He took the basket from her in a gentlemanly way, pretending to groan at its weight. 'Oh you've brought a feast. Thoughtful – as ever.'

She smiled, tilting her head on one side, slightly flirting with him and led the way to where she knew was a bank of grass, kept short by rabbits, secluded yet with a quite breath-taking view across the heath.

'They say you can see St Paul's from here!' she said, lightly, as she spread out the tartan rug.

'Really?'

She laughed. 'No, not really, I'm joking.'

He shook his head, bemused. 'Anyway, happy birthday.' He brought out a small box from his pocket that quite took her breath away. It was the kind of thing that could only contain a small item of jewellery – possibly earrings, but more likely ... 'This may seem out of place now, I don't know ... well, of course it is, but this, my dear girl...' *my dear girl* – how dare he? '... is the ring I had ready to give you that evening ... you know, the last time I saw you before I left for Europe.'

She was unable to speak. Had he really intended to marry her? Even before the pregnancy, which he'd known nothing about anyway? Was it her age she had concealed from him that really had turned him away? *Was it all her fault?*

'I ... can't take this. You must realise that,' she faltered, staring at the cluster of diamonds.

'If you don't then I shall throw it away.' He made as if to jettison it into a cluster of brambles, there and then.

Instinctively, she grabbed his arm. 'Don't do that. But, you see, I would have to hide it, it would be ...' *like permanent reminder of what is going to happen today, she thought, but could not say.*

He slipped it back into his pocket, wordlessly. It seemed he would do anything rather than offend her.

She reached out to hold his hand. 'Walter, the fact that you had a ring does change things a little. I mean, you were serious about us having a future together, until ...'

'Yes, I was, but it seemed very wrong to be proposing to a schoolgirl.' His short laugh was mirthless, mocking, as if he did, indeed, blame her for everything going wrong.

Against all her best plans for this afternoon, she felt weak with emotion, with regret, with guilt at all the vengeful thoughts she had had about him. She silently squeezed his hand and he turned to kiss her forehead with affection.

'If only … if only things had been just that bit different, we could have been so very happy,' he said. 'We could have brought up our son together, we could've run a business and been utterly fulfilled …' He seemed unaware of how much his wounding words were tearing her apart.

Tears now threatened but she blinked them back, momentarily holding her breath at the same time. Her hand reached to the back of his neck, she pulled him towards her and they kissed with such visceral passion, with such anguish and bliss that she knew anything could happen now. She wanted him and he wanted her; there was nothing and no-one to stop them.

On Sunday, Walter took a long walk in the woods to try and clear his head. He had not slept well, as throughout the night he tried to make sense of what had happened yesterday.

Molly had made it clear that her marriage to Giles was rock solid and that nothing would break them apart. She was a girl of principle, deep down and yet … yesterday, if anything it was she who had seduced him. He had not anticipated for a moment that their somewhat clandestine meeting would lead to lovemaking, although admittedly they had both been swept away by their emotions … and he had not come 'prepared'. She assured him afterwards that there was no possibility of her getting pregnant for she was 'on the pill'.

'I have no children, as you know. Since giving away Mark, I couldn't face childbirth,' she had told him. 'It would bring back all the sorrow of losing him.'

It seemed a rather strange logic, but brought home to him just how much she still suffered from parting with their baby. His resolve was strengthened by this thought. He must find him! If he did nothing else, he would find their son!

He had already set a few things in motion, treading carefully through a legal minefield, and keeping anonymous. An old, dear friend who had been his business lawyer, with whom he went to school, was the only person in whom he had confided. Basil Rafferty was already working discreetly on the case, contacting local agencies and authorities to find someone who was willing to delve into the archives and, possibly breach certain confidentiality laws that protected personal information.

'I'll wait to hear from you,' he told Basil. 'Let me know if you find out something – anything. I have to keep my distance. Remember I promised the mother that I would not do this, but sometimes … well, I feel it is for her own good that I do.' *Who am I kidding, he thought?* When he said this, it was for purely selfish reasons; he had a burning need to see his one and only child, to look him in the eye even if this was as far as he could take it.

But now! Her rationale for not having children … it did not quite make sense. You would think that parting with a baby would make her want to somehow replace … no, not replace, that was crude, the wrong word … he struggled to understand. He would have thought she would want to create another child who could give her the fulfilment she had tasted, that was snatched from her so cruelly. Perhaps a reunion with Mark would help; it could hardly make matters any worse.

44

1976

'You have a little girl, Mr Perriman,' said the midwife, looking up from where she had been busy for so long, while the new father had focused manfully on mopping Molly's brow and murmuring words of encouragement. 'A beautiful, perfect baby …'

His eyes were brimming. 'Wonderful!' he choked. 'We have a little Molly, sweetheart. It's like a miracle.'

Molly smiled at him, blissfully happy. 'After all this time, who would have thought? The most wanted baby in the world …'.

They had already discussed names in the preceding months. 'So it's Stephanie. Hello Stephanie Perriman!' he said, stroking the baby's cheek as she lay swaddled in Molly's arms. Giles had a favourite cousin with the name so it had pleasant associations for him. Molly chose it first because she wanted a strong name, not too girly. She had read somewhere that it meant 'crowned in victory' and that a person with this name 'would have a deep desire for love and companionship and would want to work with others to achieve peace and harmony.' She liked this. It was precisely what she wanted for her little girl.

The unspoken sentiment that a baby boy would have overwhelmed her with conflicting emotions, reminding her of Mark, faded now in her newfound happiness. Giles still knew nothing of Mark and must never know. He would find it painful and perplexing to come to terms with his wife being a one-time pregnant schoolgirl; it would change his perception of her for ever, she felt sure of this. It was deception of a sort, but also a kindness.

What happened to Walter was tragic, but, she reasoned, he had brought it upon himself. She had kept her distance from him, since their dalliance in the woods, hiding her pregnancy, and on the one occasion she did come face to face with him, she made it clear that he must forget what had happened between them that day. He looked crestfallen, begging her to stay and talk for he had something to tell her, but she would not be drawn. She kept her resolve and strode away with closed ears and sealed lips; somehow she had found the strength.

A few weeks later, it was talk of the village that a haggard looking Walter Finchley had been found loitering around school playgrounds in the county and was arrested under suspicion of stalking. Molly closed her eyes after reading an account in the local newspaper, confirming to her that he had broken his promise. Thank goodness the full truth had not come out, but she could deduce from this that he had gone searching for Mark, probably thinking he knew best, and all without even telling, let alone consulting, her. Having done no actual harm, he was released, with insufficient evidence to hold up in court. His shop now lay empty; he had gone who knows where?

'Here, have a hold ... she's yours too!'

Molly could see Giles was in a state of awe and wonder, gazing adoringly first at Stephanie and then at Molly.

Molly cast her eyes lovingly over the face of her new-born, her final everlasting secret, wondering who she would look like as she grew to be a strong and lovely woman.

Afterword by Author

In 1960, when the book starts, the Sixties were not yet swinging but lodged quite firmly in the 1950s. I was thirteen, in Gloucestershire, so the story in *Secrets of Appley Green* is flavoured with memories of that decade. It has been a wonderful project, a reason for me to read books of the Sixties, both fact and fiction, and I hope that the blend of living my teenage years and stimulating research has resulted in an enjoyable and credible story.

I would like to stress earnestly, however, that all the characters and storylines are entirely fictional. Old school-friends may be looking for traits they recognize, but no – please don't!

The link with *Shades of Appley Green*, published and set in 2012, is a strong one but to say too much about that might spoil things. It is perfectly possible to read one without the other – but I would recommend that, if you read this one first, which is fine, you follow up with *Shades of Appley Green*.

Happy reading!

If you enjoy reading any of Miriam Wakerly's books please let others know by leaving a review on Amazon

Thank you.

About the Author

Miriam Wakerly's first novel, **Gypsies Stop tHere** was launched the day after she retired in 2008; **No Gypsies Served** followed two years later and in 2012 **Shades of Appley Green**. All are credited with many 5* reviews. Following a year battling cancer with surgery and treatment, she finished this her fourth novel, which has a strong link with **Shades of Appley Green** set in 2012. All her novels so far take place in Appley Green and were launched in Waterstones.

Her career history includes teaching, public relations and marketing in the IT industry; and community work. Now retired from work other than writing, she lives in Surrey, England with her husband. Her two daughters live and work in Margate and her son in London.

Miriam Wakerly has a BA Degree in Combined Studies (English, French, Sociology, Politics) from Leicester University. She is a member of the Society of Authors and one of the first Independent Author Members of the Romantic Novelists Association.

Find her on Twitter and her blog, Miriam's Ramblings.

Gypsies Stop tHere

No Gypsies Served

Shades of Appley Green